Sign up for our newsletter to hear
about new and upcoming releases.

www.ylva-publishing.com

OTHER BOOKS BY JD GLASS

Drawn Together

PUNK SERIES:

First Blood
Glass Lions
Punk Like Me–A Tale of an Authentic Rebel
Red Light

punk and zen

PaRt 1: tHe ReMiX
(Extended DJ Cut)

JD GLASS

I know that it's easier fought than won
Everything that's good? Already done
Every one of us has got to try
It's the only answer to the why

When everything just falls away
You learn that nothing gold can stay
Love Calls Again

When the world comes crashing in
And the good guy never wins
Love Calls Again

I know what it's like to push too far
Perception makes it all seem so hard
Please don't stop—don't throw yourself away
You can make it to another day

When everything just falls away
You learn that nothing gold can stay
Love Calls Again

When the world comes crashing in
And the good guy never wins
Love Calls Again

"Love Calls"—JD Glass

LOVE BITES
MY FACE IS GREEN NOW IT'S TURNING BLUE
I THINK I GOT IT FROM FUCKING YOU
MAKE IT GO AWAY

"Make It Go Away"—Adam's Rib

I KNOW WHAT YOU'RE THINKING.

You think you've seen this before, heard it before, felt it before.

But it's not true—not for any of us.

Especially when it comes to that crazy, crazy, little four letter word.

Yeah.

Love.

As in L.O.V.E.

That thing everyone wants, and searches and reaches for, and a few, a very rare and lucky few, even get to experience: could be from a friend, could be from a parent, could be from a partner.

Maybe.

The lucky ones.

Because honestly, otherwise?

It *sucks*.

See now, here's the deal about love, such as it is.

First, there they are, the boy/girl/alien of your dreams, and they are bee-yoo-tee-fool, with an emphasis on *fool*, and of course, they have a tragic story—what else could make them so alluring, if they weren't just so strong and vulnerable, so needing to be rescued and loved, and of course, you and me, the idiots with the good hearts, do just that—rescue and love—hoping, because we're so darn noble, and worthy, and deserving, and darn it, just so *nice*, that when the pain is over, the boy/girl/alien will see that love was here with them all along, inhabiting our bodies.

Second, of course, there are challenges, obstacles along the way: you have to prove your love, prove that the object of your affections is worthy of love, because of course, being so damaged, they're not very trusting, and we'll just have to understand that, be patient. It's not us, it's them, and after all, they knew they were never very lovable to begin with—they just somehow seem to push everyone who loves them away.

We, of course, swallow this hook, line and sinker, and vow to ourselves that WE, YOU, I, will be the one, *the very one*, because of our goodness and purity of love, to prove to the damaged basket case of a boy/girl/alien once and for all that yes, love is real, life is good, and sex, well, okay, it would be nice (oh so very, very nice) but not necessary, because, after all, this is true love—and there are no conditions on true love, especially for those (read: *us*, the suckers) who are noble of heart. Besides, that's not what we're all about, since we're so noble and good and all, and we don't want the poor wounded boy/girl/alien to think we're just in this to get laid.

Really.

Third, and it never fails, comes the come-here-no-go-away sequence. Conversations tend to run along these lines: "This is never going to work, it's not you, it's me—get out!"

This is generally always followed by tears and groveling, vehement statements as to why we, the hero of this epic aren't really good enough, the tragic departure scene and then, a call on the cell phone when halfway home on a five hour or more drive: "Baby, I'm sorry, I miss you, I need you, come back."

Whereupon, the knight turns the steel horse around (or gets on the bus, the plane, pulls out a bicycle or walks) back to the scene of the original bloodletting, all forgiveness and understanding, because after all, they're hurting, they've had a damaging past, and we're here to heal that—*all* of that.

At about this point, casual friends and distant cousins have started to make comments, like, "Hmmm, why don't you hang out with *us* tonight? We have a few friends coming over, remember [insert name of puppy love crush]? Yeah, we just ran into each other, and wouldn't it be great? If we all hung out like?" or other such things like, "Geez, are you okay? Wanna talk about it?"

Our most intimate of friends and family are just telling us directly, "Lose the crazy boy/girl/alien, because seriously, you're getting, no wait— you *are* brain damaged. C'mon, we'll get you drunk, we'll get you laid, and you'll feel much better."

And the really sad thing is, how did they know we weren't getting laid? Seriously.

All this suffering, and no loving to make up for it. Oh yeah, maybe, a couple of times, maybe even a lot—the first few weeks—but then, all that *baggage* shows up (damage, remember?) and, well…it just ain't happening anymore.

After a long time of this (and we, the noble rescuers, put up with this for a while, sometimes years, because the boy/girl/alien never really breaks it clean, so we have hope) we finally realize that we've been had, taken for a ride, to the cleaners and back, tire tracks on our backs, nobility wasted, heart sore and certainly not nearly as trusting or as nice as before. Sometimes the rescuer becomes the boy/girl/alien to some other undeserving good sort, and the cycle continues: hallelujah and pass the ammunition.

It's true: how someone hurt you, you'll hurt someone else and on and on it goes. Because Love leaves no innocents behind and everyone's got blood on their hands.

Everyone.

Even you and me, the "good guys." There aren't any innocents, not in the end—not with this.

This is one type of love, and I'm sad to say, I've not only witnessed this happen to beloved family members and friends, but I myself have followed this sad, sad pattern.

There's another reason why love *sucks* like the center of the black hole our Universe revolves around, though, and I'm not talking about the reasons already listed above. I'm talking about real love, true love, where you love and you fight, and you laugh and you cry, you never ever get to make love as much as you'd like too, and when you do, it's like Chinese food because you come and you want more, even if you're too tired to do it again, and all the time you spend together isn't enough—you may have friends and family and share each other's, spend time in and out together, but time together and alone is precious, and almost jealously hoarded, and the absolute *best* part of your day is when you finally get to hold each other and fall asleep together, the *most* beautiful thing is waking up and they're right there, right next to you, and the absolute worst—just simply the *worst*—part is saying goodbye for the work day.

So, now what happens? No one really ever wants to do the dishes and occasionally you flip a coin to see who gets to walk the dog or clean the cat litter, and when is money never an issue, but the truth, the absolute truth is, you deal with separation anxiety every single moment you aren't together, and while you enjoy doing things and have healthy relationships outside your duo-ism, your couple-hood, your togetherness, the simple fact remains that nothing ain't nearly as much fun as when your love is there.

This…does not go away. *Ever.*

You deal with the day-to-day crap of living, you deal with the missing of one another, and you ache, your heart sore and sick, arms and skin empty, until you're together again—even if you do end up rolling your eyes at the damn spoon in the sink and laughing about who forgot to pick up toilet paper.

Oh, sure, time passes, two, five, maybe even almost a dozen years go by, and you learn, because you have to, because the damned world is way too busy to let lovers be, to shove the emptiness down, and maybe, sometimes…

You even let it go for a moment or two.

But still, like a shovel to the back of the head, it slams you then buries you in burning coal, because you miss, you really and truly miss your boy/girl/alien, your *soulmate*, for cryin' out loud!

So you get in touch, just to connect for a moment, even if it's just to talk about that damned spoon again, because it doesn't matter to either one of you whether you're fucking or fighting, as long as you're doing it together.

STUDIO B

I'VE BEEN DREAMING AGAIN AND SOMETHING TELLS ME
I'M STANDING ON THE WALL—IF I DON'T JUMP, I'LL FALL
I'VE BEEN FEELING AGAIN AND I REMEMBER
THERE'S NOTHING LEFT TO GAIN DRINKING FROM THE PAIN
I SAY GOODBYE FOR THE MOMENT—I SAY GOODBYE AND I'M FROZEN
I SAY GOODBYE FOR THE MOMENT—I SAY GOODBYE AND I'M GOLDEN

...

DON'T CRY FOR ME

"I Say Goodbye"—JD Glass

I SAT ALONE OUTSIDE THE control room, because with the exception of the bassist who was doing some back-up vocal takes, everyone else had found somewhere else in the building to be for the moment; grabbing food or cigarettes or some other stuff. No such luck for me, though. I was sucking down a cup of tea that was probably too cold to do any good, as well as missing milk and sugar to boot—which is the way I like it, but unfortunately, milk was out if I wanted to sing—and trying to collect myself.

Through the soundproof glass doors, I could see the hands of Mr. JJ "Bear" Jenns, the engineer, flying over the hundred thousand points of light, buttons, sliders, and whatchamacallits, eyes closed and grooving along to the sound that wasn't merely enough for him to have flowing through his head set, but also had to be pumped through the studio monitors.

As for myself, I couldn't tell if my teeth were rattling and my hands bouncing because I was nervous or because I could hear the tracks for myself, and they were making circular waves in my cup.

So much for soundproof, I thought wryly and grimaced. I sighed with acceptance of this moment, then quickly downed the rest of the tepid, brown, sweet water.

The cup crunched loudly to my ears as I crumpled it in my hands out of sheer nerves, then tossed it in the can. I knew it was time I got my ass up and off the sofa I'd parked myself on to walk back into the studio, because it sounded like the backup vocal had been nailed to me. This meant it would any-second-now be my turn to do a final lead vocal take.

"All right then baby, let's give it a listen." Bear spoke into the microphone hooked through the soundboard.

"I think I'd like to try that again." An alto female voice floated back into the room through the monitors.

"Well, I think it sounded pretty damn good," Bear commented mildly. "Wasn't pitchy or anything. Come on, take a break, hear it for yourself, and then see what you think." He waved "come here" through the window into the studio. "We'll roll it under Nina's take."

Now, a word about Bear: Bear was, well, big. His chair was custom made, large enough to hold three people comfortably and still it bent under him, and though his military style beard was neatly trimmed, his hair was wild, totally curly and long, sticking out at crazy angles. He used that mane as a holder for this foot-long, inch-wide pencil he manipulated the knobs and faders he couldn't reach by himself across that tremendous soundboard/mixing console/mother ship/communication center.

In a word, he was huge: larger than life itself, and more real than stereo color. Of course, my mind may have over reacted to the situation by painting things in hyper-realism, but then again, I'd never been in my own recording studio before, or worked with my own hand-picked engineer.

I heard the pop of electric disconnect, the head set was put down, and Bear slid his chair along the huge board to open the door to the right of it.

The foam-padded door opened, revealing dark long hair pulled back into a ponytail parked over a pair of usually clear but now stony blue eyes and lips that weren't smiling. A shirt that had been pulled off due to the threat of heat exhaustion hung from the waist band, leaving only a black tank top over black jeans, and a bass guitar slung over a strong bare shoulder to complete the picture.

Words floated in with the body.

"Dude, I think there's one section—a measure towards the end of the break—that I'm going to need to redo," she said, voice slightly hoarse from effort. "Ya know baby, you're just a perfectionist," I said and smiled, walking towards her. "Because from what I heard? I think you nailed it."

Samantha's eyes lit up when she heard my voice, realizing I was there.

"Hey, you're back!" Samantha answered with obvious delighted surprise.

A smile that's just for me graced her lips, and her arms reached out as I neared. I was completely caught up in the pull I always feel between us and it was less than a heartbeat before I was where I wanted to be and her lips were where I really needed them: on mine.

No kidding, no shit and I'm sure to some, no surprise, either, I live, and I mean *live*, for those kisses: soft and sensual, filled with tenderness and love, or hard, demanding, and speaking in the most direct way of good ole' fashioned primal lust.

All of them inflamed desire, but this wasn't the time or place—there was a job to do, and we were paying by the hour, here. A greedy moment or two, okay, well maybe it was more, of that sweet fullness, a line of fire running from the tip of her tongue through me, and we broke off, both of us breathless and my face flush and warm, just in time to hear Bear speak under his breath.

"Okay, if I balance the highs here and pan through the mids—"

"I'm ready to give it a shot, Bear," I interrupted, and he whirled in his chair to face us, pushing that mutant pencil back into his tangled curls. "This is one hell of a hot track." He grinned. "You sure you inspired her enough there?" He nodded his chin at Samantha. "I mean, don't let me interrupt, do what you need to do to get her, uh—" he flushed into his beard "—get it, down, er, done."

I glanced back over towards her.

Either Samantha was blushing or she was feeling the after effects of our friendly little greeting, because her face was as red as mine felt. I squeezed her hip gently and let go.

"Time to get this show on the road," I murmured in apology and moved towards the sound room door, but Samantha tightened her grip a moment and pulled me gently back to her.

Her lips brushed against my ear. "We'll finish this later," she softly growled, sending warm chills along my neck. "And Frankie should be home."

"Definitely—and awesome!" I enthused in just as heated a tone, and I turned my head for a quick kiss, which was exactly when a flash went off in my face, blinding me momentarily.

I heard a laugh I recognized.

"Oh, that was perfect love, just keep going," the laughing voice said. "Don't let me stop you."

I blinked away the white and green clouds in my eyes. "I'm blind. Candace must be here," I stated loudly.

The light clouds faded and shifted from green to purple, and a slight figure approached and resolved itself in my view.

"Hey, you know I couldn't miss this," the animated young woman said in the slight Brit accent that was distinctly hers, while she gave us each a hug. "You didn't do your takes yet, did you?"

Ah…Candace.

How to describe her?

She was perhaps a few inches taller than me and currently, she'd been coloring her wavy hair black and keeping it short so that it never came past her chin. She had incredibly beautiful green eyes, deep and dark forest green, and Candace made up in sheer energy for at least two people. Her presence was so vibrant, you actually had to stop to count how many people in the room. Truth be told, most of them were usually her—her and her whatchamacallit, her aura.

Well, that and her camera, too.

Outside of being one of the most dynamic people I'd ever met, Candace was a class-A, number one photographer, who just happened to specialize in rock 'n' roll. I, for one, was glad she'd gotten sick of doing A&R—Artists and Repertoire—assignments for the label we'd all worked for and took up the flash.

Her photography was so fantastic; I actually liked the way she made me look in photos, and that's saying something because I generally *hate* my pictures. Besides, in addition to the wonderful eye she had for composition, Candace was actually a friend, and when it came to the band's link to the public, I trusted her either to take our pictures or guide us in the right direction professionally; she knew her shit, she knew it cold, and she knew she knew it, too.

The light flare finally faded from my eyes and I could see clearly again. "I'm just about to go in, actually."

"Glad you could make it."

"Hey, just wanted you to have that 'live' feel." Candace smiled and flashed her camera at me again. "And I wouldn't miss this, anyway."

I kissed Samantha's cheek, my eyes still light-blind from the second flare. "Let's do this thing," I told her, my nerves shaky in my throat.

I turned again for the door.

"Sit and listen with me," Samantha said to Candace as I pushed through the foam baffling to the doorknob, twisting it firmly. I could see the bounce of the camera flash through the room as Candace took some shots of Bear and the soundboard.

"You know, love, when these girls get down, they rock it all night," I heard her tell Bear, and I couldn't help but smile.

I closed the door behind me, and made my way to the microphone that had been suspended from the ceiling for me. That was done because a mounted one would have picked up sound from my feet as I danced and grooved. A set of headphones hung from an otherwise empty mic stand, just waiting for me.

I slipped them on.

I glanced around at the drum set behind me. It sat on a riser that was filled with sand to dampen vibration, and my gaze quickly swept across the various amps and guitars next to them in stands. I'd been in a vocal booth in the corner of this room before doing "scratch" vocals—a guide track for the band so that the recording would feel "live"—but that had been with the whole band, together.

Now, though, I was standing in the center of the studio.

Alone.

I reached up to the microphone and made a few minute adjustments for my height and comfort.

"Okay, Nina baby, you hear me?" Bear asked in my ears, his voice loud and clear.

"Yeah, you're fine," I answered back into my own microphone.

Through the glass I could see what might have been one or two people coming into the sound booth to sit behind Bear. *Probably the rest of the band*, I figured.

Samantha's voice cut into the silence of my headphones. "Kitt's here, love."

"Hey Kitt," I greeted enthusiastically through the mic, because it was Kitt when we were in public, and "Frankie" when it was just us.

Oh, but I was happy and seriously relieved she was there as I waved "hello" to the glass. One of those shadows might have waved back.

Suddenly, I felt strange, and a huge lump formed itself in my throat. This was completely different from either the rehearsal studio or a stage performance, and it was so very weird, singing in front of the band, having them watch instead of actually playing with me.

An idea struck me.

"Do me a favor, Bear?" I asked. "Lower the lights out there, and give me a dim spot, okay?"

"You want the smoky nightclub effect?" he asked, his voice perfectly stereo-balanced in the center of my head.

"No, I want the 'it's so dark in here we can barely see our instruments, never mind the audience' effect," I explained. "Where the light is so weird it makes the space very intimate and everyone's hanging on to the sound and just feeling everything going on—like a low-burning fire."

"Uh-huh, uh-huh." Bear nodded, and the lights dimmed.

I could barely make out Bear's figure behind the board and Samantha, Candace, and whoever else was there dissolved into vaguely humanoid shadows. The sound stage blackened around me for a moment, then a small, warm, light resolved above my head, directly in front and over the microphone. The overall effect was similar to candlelight, but without the fitfulness that wax and air display.

"That good?" Bear's voice asked, almost hushed in the environment we'd created.

I forced the air in and out of my lungs slowly. *Focus, determination*, I thought to myself, and drew up in my mind the song and its structure.

"That's perfect," I answered in a steady voice, letting my breath out gradually.

I breathed again, still slow, still focused on muscle and air. I tried to ignore the sounds through my headphones of Bear readying the console and chairs scraping behind him.

Chairs? I asked myself. *Now who's watching this?* But I shoved both the question and the curiosity away. It had no place here, in this now.

"In a moment, Nina," Bear's voice came again, strong, sure, and confident in the semi-darkness.

This was what he did, and did best: capture musicians, music and emotion blended and expressed, phrase followed by phrase, note replaced by note, building and shaping the ephemeral—for all time.

No pressure, no, none at all, I told myself, *this is just going down on permanent record.*

I swallowed as I nodded, reaching deep within to draw into my gut all the emotions that I needed to do the music justice, and the events that had created them into my mind, because before this studio, before the music for this recording ever existed, this was my life—before all of it, even Frankie and Samantha, though I suppose you could say that in some way, they'd always been there, all along.

Suddenly, it all clicked.

I was there, I was in the moment.

I was ready.

My headphones came to life again when drumsticks clicked the opening time into my ears, cuing my entrance.

"One, two, three, four…"

GIRLS JUST WANNA HAVE FUN/DOMINION
I REMEMBER INNOCENCE AROUND ME
I REMEMBER LOOKING AT THE SKY
I REMEMBER HEAVEN USED TO GROUND ME
I REMEMBER KNOWING HOW TO CRY

"I Fall"—JD Glass

I WAS AT THE IN place, the hot spot, the place to see, be seen, and be cool. Welcome to the Redspot, located on ever-so-friendly Bay Street on Staten Island, New York, home of antiques and "junque" by day, and the, I mean *the*, coolest place in the counterculture by night.

My second year of college was over for the summer, my apartment was only a few blocks away, and I didn't have to be anywhere but school in September and work on Friday. But since it was only July, and this Thursday, there were no obligations for at least another day yet, and that wasn't until ten at night, baby.

"Mas tequila!" Van roared, slamming his shot glass down on the bar in front of him, hair falling over his chin. He stared through the strands at his glass, as if fluid would magically appear in it.

"What are you talking about, 'more tequila?'" Trace teased from behind him and shoving his shot glass to the side, she slid into his lap, beer in hand. She held her green bottle to his lips, and he gulped at it desperately.

"That's your fourth Flaming Sambuca, and the third time you've almost set yourself on fire," she reminded him in her honeyed whiskey voice and withdrawing the bottle from him, she replaced it with her lips.

Her wavy, long black hair fell down in a curtain over them both.

Well, that was more than enough of a show for me, I thought, and turning my eyes from what had evolved from a make out into a mauling, I decided to check out the scene.

The bar was built on top of a long-ass, old, bright red, Cadillac convertible with the chrome sticking out just far enough to make a comfortable foot rest. In the long narrow corridor the front bar created (because there was a back room, too), a couple of TVs hung from the walls, showing cartoons and underground videos. Sound bins hung alternately from the ceiling throughout the room, pumping up the music from the juke box and the light was just enough to make out faces, sit in a corner and write pretentious poetry, or read your beer label, but not enough to show the tiredness, sorrow, or just the effects of too much partying—which was probably a good thing, if you really think about it.

I put my own drink down on the bar, just an orange juice mixed with cranberry. I'd already done a pitcher (or was it two?) of Red Death shots with Trace, so I was slowing down a bit. Oh, and by the way, Red Death is an Alabama Slammer mixed with Kamikazes—that's the best I can explain them. You'll just have to go ask your bartender for a few of 'em, okay?

I had all night to play, I didn't want to get too messed up, you know, so I made my decision. I was going to the back room to dance. The scene up here in the front was lame, and no way was I going to play appreciative audience for Trace, who loved to perform for whoever was available, or just watch the damn TV. I could do that back at my apartment if I really wanted to, and I didn't want to.

As I wove through the press of bodies to the back corridor, then took the sharp right to the couple of steps into the dance room, I nodded "hellos" to people who greeted me as I passed. I loved those steps: they were painted to look like a giant, triple-level piano keyboard.

The guitar riff from the Cult's "She Sells Sanctuary" gave way to the opening harmonics of the New York Choral Society and the start of "This Corrosion," by the Sisters of Mercy. At ten minutes long, this is an incredible song lyrically as well as awesome to dance to, and my feet were already moving towards the center of the dance floor.

I waved up to Darrel up in the DJ booth, his blue Mohawk proud and high on his head and bobbing in time to the rhythm. He waved in return and continued his mixing. I lost myself in the throb of the music.

Spinning and twisting to the beat, dancers mixed and mingled as people admired each other's style, of dancing, clothes or body, and I ended up dancing with a girl I didn't really know but had seen there before. Darrel and I referred to her between ourselves as "Blue," because that's the color she always wore.

Tonight was no exception. Her latest variation was a body hugging electric blue mini dress with a skirt that ended a scant two, maybe three inches below her definition, leaving several inches of bare leg above her spider web patterned thigh-high stockings and dark hair teased up into a tousled bunch. It was too dark to tell what color it really was, but I'd seen her in that dress before. We didn't say a word, but just smiled and played moves off of each other.

For the record, she danced very well.

"Thanks for the dance," I smiled to her as the song changed into the next.

"No, thank you," she responded with a smile of her own and we said nothing for a moment or two. Awkwardness crept into the silence.

"Well, I'll see you around the dance floor." I grinned to end the silent discomfort, neatly ending this interchange. My line was polite and just a touch charming, and that was always my preferred ticket out of an awkward situation. Remember this for future situations (and there's always one).

"Hey yeah, see you 'round," she returned.

Grin still in place, I waved and turned to make my way to the bathroom—might as well check on my hair, I figured.

I nudged my way back through the body press, up three little stairs that took me out of the backroom, and turned through a narrow corridor towards the female-designated plumbing facilities.

Odd, I observed. When that place was empty, it was literally as cold as a meat locker, but add people, then turn up the music, and you could barely tell the place was air conditioned it was so steamy, unless you were in the small corridor, or in the bathroom, like me.

I waited patiently for a spot to open in front of the mirror-wall opposite the toilet stalls and once there, I gave myself the once-over, starting with my hair—the most important part. Amazingly, it still looked good.

Shaved to the skin right to the top of my ear, buzzed to fuzz another half inch, and an inch long layer to the temple level with my brow, the rest of it flowed straight and long across my head and down to the center of my back in a modified Mohawk that spread to the width of my temples as opposed to a simple narrow stripe down the middle of my head. I'd brushed it over to the right, and it arched across perfectly, leaving a curtain I could hide behind I wanted, or to be pushed back if I didn't.

Right now?

I didn't.

My main mission accomplished, I checked the rest out. There was no need to worry about makeup. I rarely wore it, with the exception of a little eyeliner and mascara every now and then—hey, that stuff will ruin your skin, ya know. And I inspected my clothes, making sure everything was where it was supposed to be.

Skin tight black cotton and Lycra covered my body from throat to not quite mid-thigh, with sleeves that came to my wrists. I twisted to see my back: yup, everything was in place, or not, depending on your point of view. I was covered in the front, but the back was open to my waist, and the sleeve-tops were cut out in such a way that my shoulders, shaped from years of swimming and a few other sports, were bare to the top of the tricep. Sheer black stockings, calf-high black riding boots and a simple, silver ankh on a black velvet choker around my neck completed the outfit.

I like the look, it's working for me, I thought. It was definitely a female look, no mistaking that, but not, you know, girly. Strong, yes; maybe even a little dangerous. I liked it. *Woman with an edge,* I thought to myself, and nodded slightly with satisfaction.

It was my night off. I was buzzed just enough to feel good but not out of it, and filled with restless energy that dancing with a pretty girl only stoked hotter and higher, making my skin tingle. I was definitely ready for anything, and I wasn't going to merely wait for it to come my way.

A face reflected next to mine in the mirror. "Hey—fancy meeting you here." It smiled at me.

"Small world, it is." I smiled in return at the reflection of my dance partner, and ran my fingers through my hair quickly, just to make sure nothing was out of place.

I faced her head on, leaning my back against the little ledge that ran the length of the mirror, and crossed one booted leg over the other. Of course I had a "cool" attitude—bathroom or no, this was my place to work, to hang out: my world, my territory.

I couldn't help the amused grin I wore as I watched her check her makeup, decide it was okay, then make a quick inspection of her hair. In the bright light of the ladies room, it turned out to be light brown with a few blonde streaks in it and whether that was from the sun or chemistry, was up to the eye and mind of the beholder.

However it got that way didn't matter, though. In my beholding eye, she was definitely, no doubt about it, very pretty and she had great legs, too.

"I don't mean to sound trite, " she said, "but have we met? Before, I mean? You seem so very familiar."

There was a musical lilt to her voice, a very slight accent to her words, as she spoke to me, a little half smile in place. The quirk of her lips told me she wanted to play that old game.

Ah, but I was feeling just too good, and there are some games I don't like to play, especially old ones. But…if she wanted to play…

We'd do it *my* way.

I merely arched an eyebrow at her and re-crossed my legs.

"Funny you should say that," I answered, glancing casually down at my nails before looking back up at her. "Because I know exactly where I've seen *you* before." I straightened and put my hand out. "I'm—"

"Nina!" Trace came calling into the bathroom, "Richie asked if you could take over for Darrel—he's sick or something." She barely glanced at Blue as she walked right past her and slid next to me by the mirror. "He said he'll pay you double your shift, just remind him at the end of the night."

Trace stopped herself a moment and her gazed raked me up and down appraisingly, as if she hadn't just seen me ten minutes before.

I returned her perusal with a bland look; her inspection bothered me.

"Very good look for you, by the way," she said and smiled, then lifted slender fingers to tweak the forelock that fell over my cheek. "God, you're so fucking cute," she added, cupping my chin.

Her steel grey eyes locked with mine a moment, and the longer the moment held, the more my discomfort grew. It was just a little too close for comfort.

Her intensity pulled at me, began to cut through my shell and even as I felt the muscles grow tight in my neck, I tried to talk myself down, away, and just somehow out from the feeling that swelled within me.

She always does this, she doesn't mean anything by it, I reminded myself by fixing the image of her draped over Van's lap firmly in my head.

She'd approach that edge between flirting and more, although she'd never outright proposition me, then pull something like, well, making out with Van. Honestly, it always made me feel pretty darn rotten, like if I'd just done this, that, or the other thing, she'd be with me instead of whoever.

Tonight though, instead of making me feel bad, it was just pissing me off.

"Thanks," I answered shortly and twisted my head away from her hand.

I scowled at the mirror, checking my hair. I hated my hair being messed up, I hated my head being messed with, and I hated being called "cute."

Teddy bears were cute. Puppies and ducklings? *They* were "cute."

My mother thought I was cute, but then again, my mother also wanted me to be straight—we were working on that: my mom understanding, that is, not my being straight.

Fuck that, and fuck cute.

I didn't want to be cute, I wanted to be hot. Woman with an edge, dammit, not Li'l Bo fuckin' Peep. And besides, she was making me lose points in front of this girl.

Cute.

Damn.

You know, points are all about the respect of your peers and your chances of getting laid.

That's it.

Period.

On the imaginary scoreboard, "cute" was dismissible, not desirable. Cute and horny did not, do not, and will never go together.

Hot, though…

That's something else altogether. Hot gets some, cute gets a pat on the head. Did I mention that I hate that? I felt like Trace was trying to say, or rather imply, that I was a teddy bear with teeth, and how ridiculous is that?

But, I didn't let any of that show. My boss needed an answer, and Trace was waiting to deliver it. *What the hell,* I thought to myself, *I could lose myself in the music.* This was always a good thing as far as I was concerned, plus I could earn a few extra bucks towards a guitar I wanted.

Work was work, I decided, and besides, I was only a little buzzed, just enough to feel the edge. As long as I didn't drink anything fermented for the rest of the night, I'd be fine. It's not as if I was operating heavy machinery or driving, anyway.

"Tell Richie I said yeah, and see if he can have Darrel cue up the next one, I'll be there in half a minute," I directed.

I decided to not to theorize out loud exactly why Darrel was suddenly so ill he couldn't spin tunes anymore. Just between you and me, though, my suspicion was one too many Jell-O shots mixed with some pharmacology up in the booth.

"I just want to—" I indicated my hair to her.

"Oh my God, you're Nina, the DJ!" Blue interrupted excitedly from behind Trace's shoulder. "I'm here every Friday and Saturday you spin the Elemental Experience, and for your Experience-the-Experiment Wednesdays!"

Her eyes were wide with recognition (or admiration or something that at that time I didn't recognize), and those eyes looking over Trace's shoulder were green, like a pine forest at dusk—and I've always been a sucker for dark green eyes.

But sure, right, like she didn't know who I was before, I thought to myself a little cynically with an inward smile. I remembered what nights Darrel and I had both seen her—and debated which of us she'd rather date.

I told Darrel I didn't fucking care one way or another, but I didn't tell him I'd have put the money on me.

Outwardly, I grinned at her anyway over Trace's shoulder, and Trace spun so quickly to face her, I'm surprised she didn't hurt the floor.

"Oh, I'm sorry," she apologized. "Didn't mean to interrupt."

Trace didn't seem the least bit repentant in my opinion as I watched her check the girl out for herself. "Okay well, " she addressed me, her inspection complete. "I'm gonna drop off your message and grab everyone. See you in a few," and she strode off to the door. "Oh, one last thing?" she poked her head back in. "Don't do anything I wouldn't do." She smiled evilly at me as she nodded her chin toward Blue.

I cocked an eyebrow back at her. "That leaves me with a lot of options, you know." I shook my head in mock confusion.

Trace just kept smiling her wise-ass smile at me and disappeared from the door.

I took a step in that direction myself, then stopped. I glanced over my shoulder at Blue and that incendiary dress. I didn't want to just leave her hanging. She seemed nice enough and the lines she used *could* have just been a casual, sincere attempt at conversation.

Besides, that would have been rude. Right?

Right.

"Hey, I'm sorry, but I've gotta go," I excused myself and gave her a smile. "Work calls. It was very nice meeting you. See you out on the dance floor." I returned through the corridor to the back room.

Darrel had left a slow ambient track flowing through the sound system and the dance floor lit by a dim orange-red glow. The last tune had left the room filled with a dark and throbbing energy, a low and restless feeling that was not so much sexual as sensual, but lacking joy.

Darrel's brought these people down, where am I going to bring them? I asked myself as I made my way to the booth in the very back corner of the room. I opened the door and went up three steps to my little world...

This little square in the sky, the "sky box" as we sometimes called the DJ booth, was surrounded by walls on three sides, and the front that faced the dance floor had a sturdy bench that held the soundboard, microphone and headset, two turntables, a disc player going from the middle to the right, all the way to the wall, and a space for discs, drinks, or sometimes, dates, all the way to the left.

A Plexiglass wall separated the DJ from the crowd, so that whoever was spinning could observe and be observed, but still have that illusion of separation. Except for the empty space all the way to the left—there was no Plexi there, because that's where people could call up requests or attempt to talk with the DJ, and the waitress could drop off water or whatever other substance that was requested.

The back wall was filled with bins of records and discs, as was the space under the turntables. I flipped through the discs Darrel had set aside. *No, no, no,* I thought as I quickly discarded each selection, *not where I'm going.*

What the hell had he been thinking? Sure, the music he had picked was decent, but there was no direction, no theme, not even a unifying mood, except for the bleakness his ambient tune was setting.

I had a few more minutes to pull out the next few tunes that would create the mood I wanted, but there was no way I could just abruptly alter the environment Darrel had created, even if it was confused. That would have been terribly uncomfortable for the people out there, and would leave them feeling disoriented.

No, I was going to evolve it, bring them down, all the way down, then raise them to where I wanted them to be, the fall and the redemption, all in one night; and I'd provide the soundtrack that would guide them all the way through.

I ran my fingers lightly through the racks, pulling this disc out, discarding the next, setting it up and in order: the songs, the occasional patter, the lighting.

I was set.

I took my selections and instead of placing them on the prep area, I placed them on the stool before the turn table so I could make faster changes that way. Besides, since all I had to move were my hands, I wouldn't have to break my groove.

It's always a good sign if the DJ's dancing too. But this arrangement had another benefit: it made me less accessible to the crowd, since I almost never had to step directly in front of that open space.

Under the counter itself was a small shelf (and under that was a waste basket) with paper towels, electrical odds and ends, and baby wipes, you know, pre-moistened and soaped towelettes, but without the lotion, and I grabbed one of those, quickly wiping my hands free of any detritus they may have picked up. Hey, have to keep those discs clean, you know.

My hands now lemony-fresh, I placed the headset around my neck so that I could reach the phones up to my ears without messing up my hair and set up the first disc, listening for the groove I wanted to slide myself into. Oh yeah, that low dark throb I was going to take down, all the way low down through, then twist it up. *Take that moment and dance, baby,* I thought as I brought the faders up for the first piece I'd selected.

I raised my eyes from the board to scan through the room and feel the vibe, and I watched as Trace and Van ambled through the crowd and into the dance area, settling in a spot about fifteen feet away from the booth.

Trace waved to me then pointed. I followed the line of sight she drew out for me and saw Blue dancing her way over to the booth. I looked back at Trace and shrugged my shoulders.

"So...what?" I mouthed back at her.

Trace just smiled back at me and, maintaining eye contact, she slowly and deliberately snaked out her tongue to lick Van's neck.

Why did I keep looking as his eyes fluttered shut?

Though I couldn't hear it, I could feel the groan that came from his lips. Still watching me watch her, Trace proceeded to trail up into his ear. At that point, his arms came up and around her, and they were mauling each other again.

I shook my head and broke the eye contact. I didn't have time for this shit, I had work to do. I snapped my headset firmly around my neck and slid it over my ears, careful not to mess my hair—which is why it went around my neck and up as opposed to on my head and down in the first place. I smoothly set my mix, letting the heavy opening cadence of that first tune fill my head and the room.

I took a breath and let it out slowly. It was time. I reached for the microphone, and keyed it open. "Darrel and the Daze have left the building for the night," I intoned solemnly. "You are now..." I let the first riff swell through and I watched with a small smile of satisfaction as the music started to take effect.

"In..." I let the chords build through and conquer the older tune as it faded out of hearing.

"Dominion," I breathed, letting the song of the same name sweep at volume through the room.

This was another Sisters of Mercy tune, and by the by, Sisters of Mercy are a very cool band, sort of, well, dark and moody and dance-able all at the same time, which I definitely recommend you check out—try the *Floodland* album.

But still, what a tune to pick for first choice, I reflected. Boy, I was in some mood.

I set the lights to give off a bit of a flicker, since there's nothing like the "dungeon-disco" effect, and checking my mix for the next tune, I closed my eyes and sank into the groove myself, at peace and at home in my little musical world, feeling fine, just fine, thank you. Of course that moment of peace couldn't last. What is it they say, "when you least expect it, expect it?"

I felt a gentle touch on the bare skin of my back and as I opened my eyes, a hand holding plastic cup of water appeared before me. That was nice. Wow, sometimes Trace could really set me off, and sometimes she could be just so damn sweet, so considerate, it drove me fuckin' crazy.

It was like she'd been raised in my home—nobody ever said they were sorry—okay, well, my parents would force us to say it if we got caught doing something, but otherwise, nobody ever said those words; they "did" it instead.

For example, say my brother Nico and I had an argument and it was his fault? Later on, he'd come over to me and say something like, "Hey um, wanna go play some video games? My treat," or if it was me, I'd catch up with him and hand him a cup of hot chocolate or something. Our parents did it too, I mean, if they were "wrong" (which, of course, never happened), they'd pick up a book one of us wanted or take that person out for a Saturday afternoon, something along those lines.

We "did" it—we didn't just say it.

Well, okay, I was known to say it on occasions, but I always backed it up with an action because "actions speak louder than words."

Trace "did" it, too, although she might every now and then say it, but usually not. I took the cup and gratefully tossed back and swallowed more than half of it before I realized it was a tequila pop (tequila and 7 Up in case you were wondering) and not merely plain water.

As the combination of sourness and soda fizzled against the back of my throat, my eyes opened wider and I automatically gulped down what was left in my mouth before handing the cup back.

"Hey, thanks, Trace, but I'm not drink—" I stopped cold.

It wasn't Trace—it was Blue.

I was momentarily speechless as I pushed my headset off from my ears. No one, ever, and I mean *ever*, had entered that booth before that I either didn't know or didn't personally invite. This was unheard of. This was—

"Your friend let me in," she told me, neatly plucking the cup from my fingers with a smile. "She figured you wouldn't mind."

A set-up. That's what this was. I looked back out into the room and didn't have to scan far. Trace was right by the "request" window, smirking at me, and I leveled my eyes at hers as I leaned over to catch her ear.

"Trace, what the fuck?" I asked her in a loud whisper. Invading my domain and all—sheesh, you know?

Trace tweaked my hair again. "You're so fucking cute when you're mad," she laughed, then reached up and kissed me, full on the lips. Her lips were soft and full, and they pressed oh-so-hard against mine. When she finally let go, she bit my lip.

I tasted blood.

"If you did some of the things I would" —she stroked my cheek— "you'd have more fun." Trace drew a finger across my lip, taking the red stain she'd left with it, and I watched, angry, stirred, and mesmerized, as she slid it between her lips.

What was wrong with me, that I let her get to me like that? I couldn't stop her if I wanted to, and I wasn't sure I did.

Trace smiled as she brought her hand down. "Mmm…delicious," she commented, then smirked at me. "Now go have fun—I absolutely fuckin' dare you."

Her smile turned wicked: a flash of teeth, eyes sparking her challenge. She held my eyes a moment, then gave me her back, dismissing me.

My mind swirled as I straightened up and turned around to face my "guest," and as the carbonation burned through my stomach, I felt the tequila send a flush through my body, warming my skin, and thrumming in my chest.

Blue simply observed me, cup in hand and eyes narrowed in consideration. "I told your friend I wanted to speak with you, and she said she'd help me out, since she'd interrupted…" she paused a moment and put the cup down on the ledge behind her "…our earlier conversation." She stepped closer to narrow the short distance between us.

Okay, so this game was a little different than I thought it would be. I wasn't expecting this more, well, forward sort of behavior. And okay though, maybe that was my fault: I'd been the one to start changing the rules, anyway. Her hand reached out and I stepped back a little nervously, smacking back against my soundboard.

Oh yeah, the soundboard. I was working—or supposed to be, anyway. "Okay yeah, sure," I agreed and smiled. "We can talk. I, um, I've got to set my tunes," and I gave my attention to the board.

We were so close to one another my hip brushed against hers as I turned.

Did I mention this wasn't a very big space to begin with?

I slipped my headphones back on and checked the play status on the disc.

Everything was going smoothly and exactly where I wanted it to go. I ran nimble fingers across the dials then grabbed the next two discs, setting them up in succession—they would fade beautifully into one another. I closed my eyes as I tested the mix, listening, sinking into the music's mood, my fingertips resting lightly on the knobs as I adjusted the program, tweaking a bit here and there to get it just right. Oh yeah, there it was. This was going to be nice, very nice. I swayed along with the beat and set a few automatic times, still tweaking the sound and moments until they were perfect.

A soft fingertip slid slowly down my bare back and it took a lot to control the light shiver it caused. Hands strayed to my hips and Blue danced with me. I could feel the heat of her body on my back as I locked the mix on the board, and as we swayed in time together, I realized she was slightly taller than me.

She was subtle as she pressed up against me, and I felt the light touch of her lips on my neck as I caught the rhythm with her and swayed to the beat. She nibbled her way up to my ear.

God, I *love* that…

Well, if I hadn't been stirred before—which I was—this situation had just jumped me up a little higher, but it was time, more than time, to take it in hand.

Maintaining body contact, I twisted around, and, glancing up at her eyes for a moment, grasped her hips, bringing us closer. We moved together for a few moments, then I brushed my lips up along the line of her neck, then to just under and behind her ear. She inhaled sharply and I couldn't help but smile at that.

I *love* it when things work the way they should.

"I have to check the board," I whispered, lightly kissing the skin right below.

"How are you going to do that if I don't let you go?" she murmured into my hair, readjusting the grip she had and holding me firmly.

I brushed my lower lip against her ear lobe, then looked up into her eyes. "Just like this." I grinned and neatly sliding my leg between hers, I pulled her in closer and pivoted, using our combined weight for leverage.

I controlled her descent by holding her hips and her back landed neatly and with the slightest heaviness to the left of the board. Now I could face the room, if I wanted, and the controls.

But God damn, though, that system had good shocks: the sound never skipped through the room.

"This work for you?" I asked her with a smile, releasing her hips so I could bring up my headphones. As I leaned over and across her to reach for the console and the microphone so I could introduce the next song, my lower body pressed into hers.

She hooked a leg around my hip and reached up, pressing her breasts against me and burrowing her lips into my neck. "This works just fine for me," she breathed out.

"Good," I whispered, enjoying the pattern she was weaving on my throat.

What can I say? I guess I'm just a sensualist at heart. "Shhh," I cautioned, indicating the microphone as I brought it up.

She paused a moment and nodded against me. I set my headphones in place, I keyed the mic.

"Brothers and sisters, boyz and grrls, lovers and leavers, this is the Dominion," I informed the dancers as my eyes scanned the now-crowded floor.

Oh wow!

A lot of people had come in to the back room since I'd started, drawn by the music. Hey, all was cool, it meant they liked it and that I was doing my job well.

Blue slipped her leg up between mine and pressed it firmly where it meant business, and there was not a doubt in my mind about what kind of business she meant.

The throb that flew threw my body mixed in with the music and the buzz I already had, and a low and throaty "Mmph" escaped from my lips and into the room as I set the sound flying and returned the pressure Blue was sending my way.

We spent a few more moments like that, moving with one another to a beat that was sensual to begin with and heated further by our contact, so when she set herself along the small available space on the board and arched her neck back, quicker than it takes to tell, she dropped the leg that was pressed against me and I was between hers.

Still dancing, just a slight movement of hips and shoulders, I dipped my head to the line that ran the length of her throat and traced it very softly with my lips until I reached hers. I gently nipped at her lower lip requesting access, and received it.

Her lips tasted like cherry-flavored balm and her tongue had that sweet beer taste. Blue was definitely good at kissing, and as my hands made their way along her ribs, I felt a hand run up and down my back and sides, and one snaked into the space where our bodies met.

Tempting, very tempting, but not where I wanted to go: not in this place, not on these terms. She wanted to play and this was now my game. Carefully, I took her hand away from me and my lips from hers.

I gazed into her eyes and whispered, "No, baby," as I brought her hand to my shoulder and held it there. "This is all about you."

I reached for her mouth with mine, and I brought my hands around her hips, massaging her gorgeously firm ass.

She moaned into my mouth and gripped my ribs with her knees. Gently, almost lazily, I encircled her waist, and drew a soft line along her thigh with my free hand until it was under what was left of her skirt. She'd already pushed it up and mostly out of the way.

Skirts are great sometimes, ya know? I like 'em—lots.

My fingertip grazed the spot where the thigh meets the body, and I stopped kissing her for a moment and stilled my hands to consider—what exactly, I'm not sure—but this was going a bit further than I'd originally intended.

Raising my head, I scanned the room once again. Everyone was grooving, the mood was working, both in the room and definitely in the sky box. A hand waved in the air and caught my eye—Trace, trying to get my attention. I nodded and gave her a small smile.

"I dare you!" she mouthed at me.

I smiled back at her and shook my head. "Fuck you!" I mouthed back with a grin and a roll of my eyes.

"I'm not the one you're fucking!" Trace yelled back as she laughed.

She spun Van around until they were both out from my line of sight.

Blue merely waited for me, gently stroking my ribs as I removed my hands, and I took advantage of the moment to make some last small adjustments to the board: I had a ten-minute song followed again by an eleven-and-a-half minute one. The music would be good to go for a decent length of time without my direct attention.

Blue's legs relaxed a bit and rested on my hips.

I reached for the last set of knobs that would lock my current settings when suddenly, Trace was at the request window. I raised my eyes to look at her. "What?" I asked silently with an interested arch of a brow.

"You're such a baby, just so really fucking adorable, you know that?" she yelled up at me with an evil smile, then danced away.

Goddam, how did she manage to always fuckin' do that to me? I reached blindly over for my cup of water and drank unthinkingly, forgetting—again—that it wasn't water but what was left of the tequila pop. The drink was like acid in the back of my throat and I let it burn all the way down.

Fuck it, I thought as I finished it and tossed the cup into the pail under the board. I stood there a moment staring at nothing, letting everything run through me, burning like the tequila—the frustration with Trace, the arousal from Blue, and the normal restlessness that rides everyone's blood on a summer night. Okay, maybe that's just hormones, but you know what I mean.

Maybe the moon was full, or I'd had more to drink than I thought. Could be I was still a little annoyed, maybe even a little raw about the "cute" comment. I don't know why I had such a need to have Trace see me differently (okay, maybe I do know now, but let's just move on) but I was scanning the dance floor, finding Trace's cold grey eyes and holding them with my own.

Blue's arms reached and twined her arms around my neck and I tangled my hands into her hair, drawing her head back. My lips were almost on her throat, just a breath away, before I broke that eye contact with Trace, and this time, it was definitely on my terms.

Cute this, I thought as I brought my teeth to bare along the column of Blue's throat and my hands were in the mix, too. I had both of them by the twin junctions of her thighs, and was alternately gently scraping along their length with my nails (yes, I keep them short, but not bitten) and massaging the firm muscle.

Blue was busy, too. Gratifyingly responsive to my kisses and caresses, she hungrily and skillfully licked and sucked on my neck, her hands tracing the contours of my face, her knees now firm against my ribs.

I lifted my head away from the assault, then dipped it, questing for her mouth. My hands rested lightly on her parted thighs and as I slid my tongue between her welcoming lips, I softly brushed my thumbs along the narrow strip of material that held her secrets. She gasped into my mouth and her body surged forward. I pressed my thumbs harder against her and could feel the valley she wanted to welcome me into under the damp material.

"Are you sure?" I whispered into her ear, interrupting our meeting of the mouths, and she bit my neck in response.

Burying my lips into Blue's neck, I lifted the flimsy material away with my right hand and stroked over the fine damp hairs that lined her cleft with my left. Her clit was hard and wanted my attention, and I complied, sliding my thumbs around its base, stroking it.

She was soft and slick, swollen with want and wide open to me. Turning my left hand palm-up, I poised my index and middle fingers right at her wet and welcoming entrance.

She moaned softly and leaned back upon her elbows, her head hanging back between her shoulders.

I leaned forward over her and once again slid my free arm around her waist. She brought her head up to mine and I kissed her softly. "Are you sure?" I murmured into her lips. "We can stop if you want."

She grabbed my wrist. "Please Nina," she asked, and kissed me deeply. "Fuck me," she whispered into my ear, and as she leaned back again, she pulled me with her, but still I stayed my hand, at her entrance, but not in it. "Just fuck me."

Hey, you never deny a lady a direct request, right?

Right.

I kissed her again, slowly, was gentle as I explored the lovely rich wetness between her lips. With small and steady movements, relishing the feel of her, I entered by slow degrees, getting to know her, making sure she was more than ready. When the very tips of my fingers were inside her, I felt more than heard her anticipatory groan. That, and the complete opening of body—you know what I mean, that sudden, total, there're-just-no-barriers-here-I'm-wide-open-to-you welcome that tells you *"Now, right now!"* were the cue I wanted, had been waiting for. It's always, in all ways, all about timing.

I pulled her closer to me and in one swift, almost savage movement, slid my tongue all the way into her mouth, pressed my thumb hard against her clit and my fingers almost as far as they could go into her pussy.

She gasped and shuddered, gripping the edge of the bench with both hands and bringing one knee straight back, she stretched the length of her leg over my shoulder. I slid even deeper inside that slick, tight, space, and the rhythm I set was fast and furious, the time for formality and shyness way over.

I felt her pussy tighten around my fingers and instead of sliding in and out, I stayed deep within her, moving easily through her wetness, fucking her with short thrusts as her hips pushed back against me.

"That's it, baby…" I whispered. "That's it."

Encouraged, she groaned, grabbing the edge of the board with one hand, a leg now pinning my arm, a heel dug into my ass, and she groped around for something else to hold onto. She grabbed the microphone.

"Oh yeah baby…*fuck* me like that…just…like…that," she groaned out, chest heaving, her body a glorious wave.

Using my hips, I pressed further into her, the weight of my body against hers adding intensity to the pressure on her clit and the fingers inside.

Her pussy tightened again, a hot suck on my fingers as she undulated against and beneath me. My clit, already throbbing, jumped with intensity. I love, I mean, really *love*, the feeling of a woman getting ready to come.

"You're so tight," I whispered throatily. "Go ahead, squeeze me baby, hold me in you." She was gonna come and I was making sure she was would, but *good*.

Fucking *hard*, and fucking *good*.

I increased the pace.

Blue let out a small high-pitched gasp and grit her teeth a moment. I painted stripes along her neck with my tongue, then found a spot to focus on. Nibbling and sucking, I stayed there, and realized she was speaking, chanting something, over and over.

"So *good*, so fuckin' *good...*" she ground out repeatedly through her teeth. The sound of her fuck-heavy voice seemed to surround me, and for whatever reason, I looked up a moment.

Suddenly I realized there I was, stretched across this girl, buried deep in her cunt, the knee on my shoulder pressed almost all the way back to hers, her head and shoulders thrown back against the Plexiglass and the microphone keyed in her clenched hand.

Her pussy kept rocking, sucking my fingers, then started to spasm, squeezing and releasing. "Oh yeah, yeah," she gasped out, and as her voice husked over the rhythm that played in the room I thrust in her hard, fast and steady.

I found Trace's eyes upon me as she stood still upon the dance floor, the only one not dancing, really, and Van had seemingly departed to parts unknown. He'd probably gone for another drink or to the bathroom, I briefly figured. Trace crossed her arms over her chest and there was definite anger on her face as she watched me.

But fuck her—this moment wasn't about her.

Blue cried out, a beautifully sensual breathy sound that floated out and over the dancers, mixing perfectly with the beat in the room and with a final surge of motion, her body rose up, sealing her chest against mine, her legs coming down tightly around my waist. She released her grip on the bench and tossed the mic to parts unknown, then put both hands on my face, bringing our mouths together.

She sent that gorgeous primal cry down my throat as I felt the waves go through her. I wrapped my arm even tighter around her, supporting her, holding her close and my fingers still while her pussy softened and relaxed, while Blue buried her lips into my neck, whimpering softly.

"Shhh," I soothed and I rocked her gently against me for a few moments, murmuring nonsense into her hair, hearing her breathing ease. Her arms wrapped loosely around my shoulders and I very carefully withdrew my fingers from within her.

"Boy!" she exclaimed airily as we came apart.

I cocked my head and arched an eyebrow at her. "Not hardly," I grinned.

She caught the grin and smiled back and after a moment, we both laughed.

"For which I'm thankful," she responded, laughing some more.

She hopped off the bench and straightened out her skirt. The scent of sex, her sex, hung in the box as I dug under the bench for the baby-wipes. Now I knew why Darrel always made sure we had plenty.

I grabbed a few out and turned. "Here," I reached up and gently wiped the light sheen that glowed on her skin from her face and neck. "How's that?"

Blue took my hand and kissed the palm. "Very nice, thank you," she smiled.

"It certainly was." I smiled in return. "Thank *you*."

I took my hand back and in moments, both of them were lemony-fresh again. I gave the board a quick glance to make sure all was good in the world, and Blue turned to make her way to the door.

"Hey, where you going?" I asked her, slightly confused. Hadn't she originally said she wanted to talk?

"I guess...I should...um, let you work, right?" She smiled at me, but the smile didn't seem all the way right, and her eyes questioned me.

Oh no, this was going to turn into drama very soon if I wasn't careful. "Hang out a sec? It's okay," I reassured her with a smile to the mute question I could read in her eyes.

I decided to scan the room—I wanted to catch the waitress's eye—and when I finally did, I waved her over. She deftly picked her way through the crowd to the request window.

"Hey Andra. I need a plain cran and orange juice and—" I looked over my shoulder "—what are you drinking?" I asked Blue.

She had to at least be thirsty, right?

Besides, she *was* a guest in my booth.

"Corona." She smiled at me, and this time her smile seemed genuine, or at the very least, relieved.

"A Corona," and I glanced back over my shoulder with a grin, "with lime," I finished.

Just in case you don't already know, Corona is a beer, and that's the way you drink it. Why? I don't really know, because I don't really like beer—I'm more of a mixed drinks or wine type of girl. But I'm told that it's good, and that's the way everyone seems to like it best. Try it if you haven't already, but drink responsibly: make sure you have someone around to stop you from puking on your own shoes.

"I'll be right back with that." Andra smiled up and batted her heavily-lashed eyes at me. "Anything else? Are you sure you're um..." she raised her eyebrows "...satisfied?"

Huh. What do you know—I'd always suspected Andra might have been flirting with me, now I knew for sure.

Cool.

"Hey, I'm just getting started." I grinned back with a quirk of my lips "But thanks—I'm totally fine."

"So we hear," she shot back, now smiling widely. She turned to go, then turned back a moment. "I like your mix tonight, you've really got the um, mood..." I watched her mouth as she ran her tongue along her teeth "...going." She favored me with a smoky look, then slid back into the writhing throng.

"Thanks," I called out to her retreating form.

I glanced at my meters and turned back to Blue, who had made herself comfortable along the back bench.

"Listen, I've got about forty-five seconds to set my next mix. Just hang back here a moment, go through the discs, see if there's some tunes you'd like to hear. I'll see if I can fit them in, okay?" I asked her with a smile.

I didn't want to her to think that I'd fucked her and wanted to forget her (not my style, and I wasn't Darrel, after all), but I really did have to spend some attention to my job—I *was* supposed to be working and all that.

I focused on the board and reset my headphones. *Andra's right*, I mused, swaying to the beat. *This is a seriously good groove.* I checked the next tune and set my fades and timers for the next insert. I hadn't spoken to the room for a bit, so it was time to be a little more interactive—with the whole room, I mean.

I reached for the microphone.

Fuck.

Where was my microphone?

Finally, I sighted the wire trailing across the board, where it had been tossed over the dividing screen. I grinned to myself. Well hell, if it had gotten wrecked, at least it had been for a good cause, I figured.

Slowly reeling it back, I placed it carefully down where I needed it, checked my volumes again, and listened for my entrance. Okay, there it was. I eased the fade in, the end of one song lowing into the beginning of the next. I'd already brought the mood down as far as I wanted it to go. The one that was about to end had started the climb back up, and this next one would cement that move.

I reached for the microphone and keyed it. "Fellow freaks and frenzied followers." I brought the mix up slightly and the volume down a bit "You are in the Dominion with Nina," I reminded them.

Whoops, hollers, and applause broke out across the room, and I stared out at the crowd as the dancers all paused to cheer me in the skybox. Usually, when I announced songs or just uttered some encouraging enthusiastic phrase, I got some enthusiastic hollers, but this—this was a standing ovation.

I was honestly and momentarily stunned.

"Do it, Nina!" someone yelled out over the music.

I was shocked out of my daze, and my ears burned with embarrassment because I was pretty sure that was not a reference to my DJing, although it could have been. Most people looked at the floor and each other when they danced, and they couldn't really see anything behind the partition except for heads. Anything they'd heard they probably thought was just part of the mix, add-ins by the DJ to enhance the music and the mood. It seemed to have worked, intentionally or not.

"Experience Dominion!" another person yelled, and the crowd picked up the cry until it became a chant that reoccurred over the closing strains of music and beat that flowed through the room.

"Dominion! Dominion!" The sound from the eager dancers seemed to swell and grow.

I placed my hands on the board and looked out at the crowd a moment longer: their attention firmly on the sky box, and not on the music apparently. Hoo boy. I'd started something I'd had no intentions of even beginning, and I wasn't sure of how to go on or what they were asking for.

Scratch that.

I knew.

Fuck it.

This wasn't something I'd normally play with, but I was feeling reckless anyway, and the burning in my ears was nothing compared to the burning in my skin or the rising flood threatening to overwhelm me that being with Blue had done nothing to stem.

I set my headphones firmly, set a hand on a fader and keyed the mic. I brought the level up as I spoke. "Is that what you want?" I asked the room in a low and throaty voice.

Cheers broke out.

"Are you sure?" I pressed them in the same low voice, bringing the fader up a bit more. The mix was still in the background, but now discernable through the other song.

More cheers and applause answered me.

I checked my timing, and went with the rhythm. "Fine then," I purred out.

Careful now, timing, that's what it's all about, I reminded myself, listening for the entrance.

"Have it."

I brought the faders up on full and the mix was complete. The room was off and grooving and I grooved along with them to the music. I pulled out the next few selections and set the tune that would follow on the board, checking my levels for time and volume.

Andra had come back with our drinks and set them in the request window. Done with my board for the moment, I picked them up: a cup of cran and orange for me, a bottle of Corona for Blue and, wait—there was a third?

Yes, another cup of what looked like cranberry juice and orange.

"Thanks," I told Andra, who had waited to make sure I saw the drinks. "Who's this for?" I asked, pointing to the second cup I had left on the ledge.

"For you," Andra grinned, "in case you're too busy...um...*grooving,* to remember to get another."

"That was very cool of you, thanks," I smiled back. It was true; that was both cool and nice of her to do.

"You're very welcome," she answered. "Oh, and by the way?" She stuffed a piece of paper into the hand that held the cran and orange cup. "You can start with me, anytime." She gave me an appraisingly smoky look, then walked away.

Stunned, I blushed then managed to collect myself. "I'll keep that in mind," I called to her back and grinned. Andra turned around, gave me a saucy smile, then wove her way through the dancers back to the main bar.

I shook my head.

Yep, definitely flirting, I thought, bemused.

I turned, drinks in hand and found Blue still sitting along the back bench, and she favored me with a smile as I handed her the beer.

"Thanks for your patience," I said and grinned at her, holding my cup up in toast.

"No worries," she grinned back at me. "You'll want to keep that," she pointed with her beer.

"Keep what?" I asked, confused.

"That..." she reached over and plucked the paper I'd forgotten out from between my hand and my drink. She folded it neatly and tucked it into my sleeve, stroking my wrist as she did so. "You'll want to keep it," she grinned at me. "She's very pretty."

I wasn't sure of what exactly to say so I thought it wise to say nothing and merely gave her a little smile of my own. Sometimes, it's the only thing you can do.

Blue merely smiled wider, then clinked the top of her bottle against my cup. I gratefully lifted the cup to my mouth and drank, the juice nice and cool, soothing even, as it made its way down my throat.

Surprisingly, I was thirstier than I thought and drank rather quickly, so it was only somewhere between the second and third swallows that I realized there was more than juice in my cup. *Ah well,* I shook my head mentally, *there went stopping for the rest of the night.*

I finally settled myself back along the ledge next to Blue so we could actually chat a moment; while the mix I had on wasn't terribly long, at least not as long as the ones I'd had on before, it was long enough that I could actually take a break if I wanted.

"So...do I detect a bit of an accent?" I turned to her and asked, remarking on the slight lilt she had in her voice. I'd noticed it much earlier actually, but this was the first chance I'd had to ask about it. We had been rather...um...distracted.

"Um, yes." She glanced down. "Most don't hear it," she said finally, looking at me with what I suspected were pink cheeks and a faint grin.

"Ah, well, most don't spend all their time listening for inflections in sound." I smiled at her. "I tend to hear things others don't. It's charming, by the way," I added with honest admiration. "It adds this lovely little roll to your voice. It's really quite musical.'

This time she was definitely blushing. "No one's ever told me that before. What a nice thing to say," she finally said, and she studied me seriously.

I let her inspect me for a moment, not sure why she was so somber. And it was true, about her voice, I mean. The lilt underneath her words made everything she said lyrical, so why shouldn't I mention it? It was lovely, even a bit sexy.

The silence grew a moment longer. "Something wrong?" I cocked a brow and asked lightly. The mood was getting way too serious, and I wasn't comfortable. I also wouldn't let it continue if could help it.

Blue seemed to give an inward shake and collected herself. She shook her head. "No nothing." She nodded, then took a sip of her beer. "It's just, you're not just trying to charm me, are you?" she stated more than asked.

I focused my gaze on her with greater intent because that confused me. Charm? For what? I didn't get it—what the fuck was that all about? All I'd said was that her voice was lovely. Oh, she meant...Well, wouldn't I have done that before we, um, I, uh, well, you know, before I let someone use my microphone for distance tossing? and I said as much.

Blue sighed, almost grinning in relief. "You've a point there, don't you?" she commented, and rubbed my thigh.

I felt the strength of her fingers run up and down the muscle, then lightly took her hand in mine, and twisted a bit on the bench to face her. The flood that had risen through me before was starting to ebb, and I think I was finally starting to feel a little normal again—whatever that was.

I took a small sip of my drink and considered, then took another. Nope, it really wasn't just juice. Funny how you couldn't tell right away.

Finally, I put the drink down on the bench behind me, then faced Blue again. "So," I began with a smile and her hand delicate and warm in mine. I lightly touched my fingertips of my freehand to hers. "You still haven't told me where you're from."

Blue laughed, a sensual and somehow sophisticated sound. "I'm from the UK." The curve of her lip was undeniably attractive as she spoke. "I'm spending the summer holiday here on the advice of a friend, well, an ex, um, sort of." She grinned, but seemed slightly embarrassed.

I can't tell you why, but I found that attractive, too.

"You know how these things can be," she added.

I nodded in polite agreement. In reality, I didn't—know, that is. I dated, I occasionally fooled around, but my first girlfriend I hadn't spoken to in quite a while, though I'd seen her at the club from time to time, and besides, I never dated anyone long enough to become anything other than friends, and didn't want to, either. People, once you trusted them? Fucked you over, and I'd been fucked enough, thanks.

Besides, I had too much to do to have time for that sort of stuff.

"She's an American. From here, I mean, New York, actually," Blue added.

"Don't ask me if I know her," I cautioned her and laughed. "New York's a very big place." That was something everyone from everywhere did, and as far as I can tell, still does, you know, the "Hey, I'm from X," followed by "Oh yeah? I know Y in X—do you know him/her/it?" I think it's funny and sort of cute, even heartwarming in its own way, how we all want to reach for these connections, bridge the gaps of time and space/place.

"How big is Staten Island?" she asked me with a small twist of her lips and appraisal in her eyes. "Because that's where she's from."

"Not nearly as big," I said and laughed again. "Sooner or later, you find that everyone is someone's cousin or sibling or something like that."

"Well, that explains it then," Blue smiled, "you must be a cousin." She put her bottle down beside her.

That was weird, and I gave her a puzzled look. "What do you mean?" As far as I knew, all the cousins I had in this state, and there were only two of them, were in grammar school, and in fact, they lived with their mom in my parents' house.

"You look so very much like her, and there could hardly be two of you, could there. I mean, she never mentioned a twin of any sort, especially not with the same name."

My head started to tingle and I could feel the skin on the back of my neck tighten. *This is more than the alcohol, this is a sign,* a part of my brain said. *Have another drink and don't be a moron,* the other part told me. Since that was the part that I thought made sense, I listened to it and took yet another sip of my this-is-NOT-juice juice.

But...still...

"What's your friends name?" I asked, my curiosity more than piqued. It could be possible, I mean, maybe I did have a cousin I hadn't known of before. Lord knows, history—hell, the world—is full of stories like that. Some of them even true, or something like that. *Okay, that's the alcohol thinking for you,* said the part of my brain that had just told me to have some more.

"Oh no, not my Ann, but a girl she once knew a few years back," Blue corrected. "She has pictures, from secondary—I'm sorry—high school yearbooks, and you look very much like her friend. But," and as she paused, the expression in her eyes softened, "sadly enough, Annie's friend passed away quite some time ago and you," she ran a finger along my cheek, "you're quite alive." Blue smiled sensually and showed me her teeth as she gently stroked my chin with her thumb. Her eyes lingered appreciatively on my lips.

My cheeks grew hot as I blushed, but still I considered what she'd said. It was possible she was talking about my high school and year book, I mean, I'd been in pictures all over it for each of the four years I attended, but I didn't remember anyone named Ann, or not at least that I'd hung out with, and I couldn't remember anyone that had died, at least not recently.

I mean, there had been one girl who'd been a freshman when I was in my sophomore year, a lovely girl named Susan who'd been born with an incomplete heart wall—a blue baby.

Sadly enough, for whatever reason, that poor heart finally stopped one day, and the entire student body mourned the loss of the beautiful soul that she was and the person she could have become.

But still, even with the sad death of Susan, I couldn't think of who it could be. Besides, she and I had looked nothing alike, unless you subscribe to the general sentiment that all *Homo Sapiens* look alike. She'd been a light ash-blonde to my auburn-infused brunette, and due to her condition, Susan had been very slightly built. On the other hand, while I wasn't terribly tall, I had definitely been more robust.

Well, I'd *had* to be. I'd been on the swim team, after all.

It must have been simply that the DJ booth was dark and clearly, Blue and I had both been drinking. Ergo, she must have made a mistake. Just because I didn't know or remember an Ann at school with me didn't mean there wasn't one in some other school. After all, there were at least two other all-girl ones, not to mention the almost dozen other co-ed and public ones, on Staten Island.

"No," I slowly shook my head. "I've never gone to school with an Ann," I told Blue. "Do you know what school she went to?" I asked, thinking that if I didn't know her, there was a good chance that I already knew someone who did.

"Oh no. Annie, Ann," she smiled broadly and reached out to touch my shoulder, "that's her nickname. Her name is really—" but she never got to finish the sentence.

The door to the booth slammed open, and as Trace flounced up the three little steps, the force of her push allowed the door to bounce back shut again. She looked upset.

I jumped off from my seat in alarm and Blue followed suit. I stepped towards Trace. "What's wrong?" I asked with concern as Trace's eyes burned.

Correction: Definitely upset, very upset, and possibly angry.

"What the fuck do you think you're playing at?" she spat out venomously. "Just what the fuck do you think you're doing?"

My concern vanished; I knew what was going to happen. Trace was just about to pull one her famous jealousy scenes. I'd witnessed a few in the past, all them unleashed on her current boy toy, but this time, for whatever her reasons…she'd decided to focus on me.

I quickly checked over my shoulder, ensuring Blue was safely behind me—there was absolutely no need for her to be in the line of fire, after all—stepped closer to Trace.

"My job and *nothing* that you wouldn't do," I ripped back at her, and pointedly studied her a bit.

Who the fuck was she to question me, anyway? She'd set me up in the box with Blue in the first place. Fuck her if I called her bluff, and fuck her and her jealousy. She had no right to it.

"Don't be a fuckin' smartass, Nina," Trace warned. "I mean—" she gestured at Blue, but continued to glare at me "—her."

"I was just showing…" I paused a moment.

Fuck.

My fingers still knew what it felt like to be inside her and I didn't even know her name.

Christ.

In my head, she was Blue, but I was sure she had a name other people used, like the one she'd been born with, perhaps? I glanced at her and luckily for me, she picked up on my thoughts.

"Candace," she whispered to me.

"Thanks," I staged whispered with a quick and what I hope was a reassuring smile before I turned to face Trace again. "I was showing Candace the booth, and letting her pick out a few tracks. She's keeping me company," I added blandly.

Well, what else was I supposed to say?

Blue—I mean Candace—slipped beside me and made her way next to Trace by the steps.

"I can see you and your girlfriend have some things to discuss so I'll just say goodbye now," she said by the top of the steps.

"She's not my girlfriend," I affirmed to Candace.

"I'm not her girlfriend," Trace ground out from the corner of her mouth.

I watched as Candace studied Trace and I realized for the first time that she was more than a bit older than me, maybe mid to late twenties. Not that I cared, that's not a big deal or anything, it's just that I hadn't noticed before.

"No, you're not that," she said with a thoughtful expression as she made her own discovery of Trace, "and not quite a friend either, I see."

Blue, um, Candace took a step back towards me while Trace mulled that over. I tucked that into the back of my head to think about later, because at this moment, I agreed with Candace. I suspected she may have spoken truer than she knew.

Candace leaned towards me. "Watch out, love," she whispered into my ear. "That one has fangs." She kissed my cheek briefly but warmly, and I returned it as we gave each other a quick embrace. She went back down the steps to the door.

"Lovely meeting you," she told Trace politely, here hand on the latch. "Nina?" her voice lifted and she smiled at me.

"Yes?" I couldn't help but smile back at her in inquiry—I really liked the sound of her voice.

"You're simply lovely. I'll see you soon, love," and with that, she went down the steps and out the door, closing it behind her.

I downed what little remained of the—not juice I'd already started, then tossed the empty cup into the waste pail. Grabbing the one Andra had fortuitously left for me, I sipped it as I ignored Trace, who simply stood there glaring at me with her arms folded, and went back to my board.

I'd lost all feeling for the night.

No flood, no rush, no buzz—just an emptiness that was heavier under my skin than the restlessness from before.

But it didn't matter whether or not if I'd lost the feeling, I still had a job to do. Plenty of people out there and counting on me to provide their good time, and I was going to do that.

Donning my headphones once more, I checked the meter and set my fades, timing for the next cue, sliding it into the mix. Scratch what I said before.

I wasn't numb, I was drained.

I could never figure her out—Trace, I mean. She was ready to fuckin' chew me a new asshole, and I didn't even really know why.

She'd sent Candace to the booth in the first place, what in the world was she so mad about?

I finished my drink and looked back up and over the dance floor. I spotted Andra and when she finally saw me, I signaled for another round. She nodded and disappeared.

Funny, I mused as I pushed the headset off my ears and around my neck, then looked blindly through the discs I'd pulled out earlier to lay them out in their upcoming order, *once you pass the second or third sip, you really don't taste the alcohol anymore.*

A gentle hand touched the bare skin of my back and I stiffened slightly. "I'm sorry, Nina," Trace whispered into my hair and kissed the soft skin behind my ear.

I worked on in silence as she etched light patterns onto my skin.

That...was just typical Trace.

In like a flash flood, out like a gentle spring rain. Okay, more like a hormonal spring flood. But me, well, she just left me confused at best.

If I was angry, I couldn't stay that way, and if I was happy, I couldn't stay that way. No matter what I did, it wasn't the right thing to do, and whatever I was, it apparently wasn't the right thing to be.

And now she was sorry.

What an ugly joke—I should have just kicked her out of the booth—but her apology softened my anger and she began massaging my neck and shoulders, adding light, sensual kisses to the back of my neck between pressure points.

This proves one thing, I told myself. *It proves I am a complete idiot.*

As I added the finishing touches to the mix, affection for Trace rose and blended with the frustration, and the sensual stirring that Trace created wherever she went.

I let myself lean back into her a moment, then caught myself and stopped. Trace wrapped an arm across my shoulders and one around my waist, anchoring a hand on my hip.

"Come on, Nina, you know how I am," she cajoled softly, following it up with little kisses.

"Yeah," I answered shortly.

Andra had already come back and dropped off another beverage without a word. I grabbed the new one and downed it.

Trace was driving me crazy, and she knew it. She was manipulating me, and *I* knew it. I didn't respect myself for responding, even if I didn't let on how effective she was. In fact, I was angry: with Trace for trying to play me, and with myself for being so damn easy to play.

I found more knobs on the board to adjust.

Trace pulled me tightly into her arms. "Nina, you know how I feel about you," her voice persuaded in her honeyed-whiskey tones and she let the very tip of her tongue played across that sensitive spot right behind and under my ear.

I set my mix and with a shrug of the shoulder, I turned within that tight embrace so we were face to face. I looked up at her, and caught her eyes with mine.

What the hell was that supposed to mean? What the fuck was she trying to say? Why didn't anyone ever just come right out and say what they meant?

Also, what had she done to Van? Was he sitting, brain melted and blood drained, in a corner somewhere? She done with him, too?

My skin felt like it was on fire and my throat burned. The constant sexual tension and half toned seduction, the all too confusing words—I couldn't, I just *couldn't* any more—my chest felt like it would explode with pressure.

"No, Trace—I don't," the words tore from my lips, harsh and jagged, "because you've never told me." I looked up into her eyes and even in this dim light, they flashed silver. "You..." I started softly as I reached for her face "...play games."

Before I fully realized what I was about to do, I kissed her, hard and full, on those baby soft lips that answered mine with a surprisingly slick sensuality.

A moment passed, then another. Putting my hands on her shoulders I pushed her away, breaking the contact.

Trace stared at me, her expression undefinable and unknowable.

"You kiss me, you pet me, then you go fuck whoever and when they lie, when they hurt you, *I'm* the one..." I placed my hand over my chest, heat running so high within me I could feel my ears burn. "Me, *I'm* the one to heal you and hold you through it, until you feel better, until it's time for the *next* one."

Trace waved a hand in confusion and reached for my shoulder. "Nina, I—"

"No, Trace," I brushed her hand away in impatient frustration. "You tell me we're friends, that what we are together is beautiful."

I raised my fingertips to her cheek, and traced it lightly. My thumb brushed gently against her lips. "Oh Trace," I sighed as she kissed my thumb softly. "I'd fuckin' die for you if it would make you happy, but I think you'd just laugh."

I watched her face for a reaction, any reaction, as I tried to control the short, hard bursts that forced themselves through my throat and passed for breath.

A part of my mind—probably the part that had called me a moron—marveled inwardly. I'd never spoken to anyone and especially not Trace, like this before. I was always the understanding friend, the supportive, comforting presence. In the past, I had been hurt, I had been confused, but never before had I been furious and let it show. I might not have understood it, but I was definitely just going with it. Well hell, I'd already been doing that all night.

With surprising speed and motion, Trace grabbed my wrists and held them to my side, then, using the height she had on me to her advantage, she backed me into the board, pinning me with her hips. My back thudded against the ledge, though I barely felt it.

This time, the sound *did* skip.

My headphones slid off my neck and down my back. They landed with a felt smack onto the board.

"Nina, that's not true, you *know* how I feel—" she leaned her forehead against mine"—about you."

I swore I could hear the beginning of a laugh bubbling in the back of her voice.

Alarmed by her speed, by her force, by the position I was in, I tried to free myself from her grip to at least rescue my headphones, but I could barely move my arms.

Man, what the hell's wrong with me? I asked myself in a near-panic. I couldn't move, and believe me, I tried. My muscles just wouldn't obey the commands my brain was sending.

God, I was drunker than I thought, and I was *scared*, scared because I couldn't move, and *really* scared for the first time, of Trace, the intensity of her words, and the raw power of her body against mine.

I'd forgotten, or maybe just ignored, how for all her delicate looks, Trace was also incredibly strong. And it had never occurred to me, for even a single second, that things could or would *ever* go in this kind of physical direction.

"What do you want from me?" she hissed into my ear, then scraped along its edge with her teeth.

With a quick twist of her hips, Trace pressed between my thighs and with a strong sweep, she spread my legs so wide I would have fallen over, if she hadn't had me pinned to the board. How the hell did she *do* that?

Her arms pressed mine even more firmly than before, locked down by my hips and yet she was still able to reach all the way around and grab my ass, the very tips of her fingers on my inner thighs, up against the sides of my pussy.

Whatever this was, wherever this was going, I didn't like it, and I wanted it to end. "Trace, stop!" I ordered with as much strength as I could muster.

Wherever this was going, I didn't want it between us.

Heartbreakingly beautiful, Trace was a striking combination of slender lines and strength, a vulnerable fortress.

How many nights since I'd moved into the building that we shared had we spent together, in her apartment or mine, my arms around her while she cried, because of old wounds that still ached, new ones that still bled, or just because there were things in the world that simply touched her that deeply?

How many mornings had she woken me with kisses and caresses, made me breakfast and made sure I took my vitamins? And then there was time we spent together, just cuddled up, talking of nothing, everything, listening to music, just wrapped up against each other, listening to one another breathe...

But in all that time and all that closeness, even with all the flirting and sleeping skin to skin, we had never, and I mean *never*, gone to that next step.

Slept together, yes, but it was *sleep*, and not sex. Hell, this was the first time we'd ever really kissed, I mean, without an audience that is.

I'd never wanted to push for anything, I'd just wanted to let them go the way they naturally would, whatever that was.

But maybe Trace was tired of waiting, because she ignored my request. "You want me to tell you how I love you, that I honestly want you..." Her lips slid along the sensitive column of my neck. Teeth replaced her lips with such strength that I knew she'd drawn blood. But then, when didn't she, one way or another?

"You want me to tell you how I feel...how *you* make me feel..." Her hands, her fingers, they held and pushed so hard into my skin, pressed into the muscle.

"Because you hold me and...Nina...I feel peaceful, and my dreams are filled with *you*, you holding me, me loving you..." and she slid a fingertip along the slight depression that marked my lips "…and if I let you, your love makes me feel whole." She pressed harder, massaging me with her finger tips through my stockings.

"Trace, you don't want to do this," I said as steadily as I could.

My heart pounded, my head swam, and the skin along my arms felt tight, cold, numb, grabbed and slammed down in the vice that was Trace. I couldn't explain then how I felt, but I can say it now:

I loved her.

I pitied her.

I wanted her…wanted to help, to hold, to *heal* her, somehow.

She scared the *shit* out of me.

I was caught between horror and desire. Yes, I wanted her, but I wanted something between us to be real, not real scary. This just felt so wrong, so very wrong. *I hope I wake up soon. Real soon,* I wished.

"But I do," she answered, ripping at my lower lip with her teeth.

I could feel her fumbling for the seam, and I felt her fingers gain purchase and pull, her hands hard against me.

"You want me to…" she whispered into my ear.

Jesus Christ, she wasn't going to *stop*.

Her mouth continued working on my neck, weaving exquisite patterns on my throat while her fingertips continued to trace my outlines. I could feel the groan that she tasted as her lips nipped a particularly sensitive spot and as I arched my neck and offered her my throat, I began to think, *okay, maybe she needs this to be able to let go to just be…be real. If I surrender—completely—then maybe, so can she.*

The part of my mind that wasn't drunk surged forward. *What am I, fucking crazy? More likely—she'll suck my soul dry.*

Summoning strength from I don't know where, maybe it was just that Trace's grip slipped, or that my brain and spine had decided to communicate with each other again, together my brain, spine, and I remembered an old move from the judo I had been forced to study in high school. My legs set as they were, I couldn't move up, so I managed to bend my knees a bit and slid down. Rotating my arms outwards and applying pressure from my elbows to hers, I was able to break her hold and bring my arms up, while removing Trace's hands from my body.

Emphasis on *mine*.

Don't get me wrong, I'd been aroused earlier, and this situation wasn't doing anything to lessen that, but it was my body that responded, not my mind, not my heart. I didn't want this, not this way, and I discovered something: there was a limit to just how much I could give.

Nightmare over.

I was wide awake now.

"Goddammit, Trace," I spat out as I wiggled free, "fuckin' enough. Just stop." I pushed up against her chest and she fell back a step.

But still, her words were spinning through my head, confusing me, twisting me. I managed to bring my legs together and stand somewhat upright.

My chest felt like it had two jack hammers playing off-rhythm to one another and my head was starting to feel like someone had sped the merry-go-round up a bit too fast, but still, through the hammering and the dizziness, all I could think was, *she's right, though—that's what I want. Everything.*

My eyes burned as I turned back to my board. Where were my fucking headphones? Oh, there. I grabbed them and set them firmly around my neck.

I ignored Trace completely as I reoriented myself to the board and my world, and a drop of water fell onto the soundboard. What the fuck?

Oh, it was me. I hate tears, especially mine. What the fuck was I crying for, anyway? The leak stopped.

I could feel Trace as she approached my back. Her hand was gentle again as she touched my shoulder. I reached for the microphone.

"Nina, I'm sorry," she began softly, her mouth inches from my ear, but I held up a hand forestall her.

I needed quiet at the moment. I was, after all, still on the job. I watched my fingers tremble, betraying how the body and mind felt as I took a deep, shaky breath, and keyed the microphone.

"Boyz and grrlz, the freaks are out tonight." My voice came out steadily and with the right tone as the audience clapped and howled in agreement. I waited a few beats for my next statement. "Tonight the moon is on the rise…better watch out 'cuz no one knows in who a monster hides," I finished, bringing the mix back up on full.

I shut the mic and squared my shoulders and set my face. A burning cold hardness that I had felt only once before, once when I'd had to defend myself from the people who were supposed to love me, filled me, and I turned around to look at Trace directly. There must have really been something in my face, because as her eyes met mine, she stepped back.

We watched each other a moment, her eyes confused, evaluating, mine hard. She reached out for my face. "Nina, truly, I didn't mean..."

I'd had it for the night, maybe forever, who knew. But either way, my expression stopped her cold, mid-word and mid-motion. I stared at her hand, suspended between us until she dropped it.

I crossed my arms over my chest and settled back against the board, languidly stretching one leg over the other. My guts shook, my head hurt, and the spot I was leaning on ached in the way only an incipient bruise can, but I'd be damned, twice damned, if I let her see any of that. I was back in some semblance of control, and real or no, mask or no, I was going to hold on to it for dear life if I had to.

And with Trace, I had the deep certainty that I had to.

I took a slow, deep breath and let it out silently. *Focus,* I reminded myself as I breathed. Center, and focus. That's what I needed, and that's what I was after. "Trace?" I inquired quietly, arching an eyebrow at her.

An eerie, hyper-real calmness filled me, and I was as steady and strong as a rock.

"Yeah?" she answered softly, her eyes wide, shocked, as she studied me.

"If you want something, you have to ask," I stated quietly, letting my words hang in the air.

I observed her face, took in the gentle quirk of her lips and sharp jaw line, the hint of pain and confusion in her now-darkened eyes as they studied me in return.

Trace took a step closer to me. "I'm sorry, I don't know what—"

"Stop," I interrupted. My voice was low and hard. "Trace?" I asked again softly.

She nodded at me.

"Get out."

Unused to these tones from me, Trace was bewildered. She held her hands slightly away from her body, as if she didn't know what to do with them and she stared at me, more in shock I suspect, than anything else.

No one, as far as I'd ever known, had ever told Trace what to do—ever. "Now," I said, unfolding an arm and pointing towards the door.

It became a contest of wills as we stared each other down. My gaze was steady and unflinching, and my hand never moved from the direction it pointed in.

Trace's expression changed from shock to sadness as she dropped her eyes from mine, and her heels scuffed along the carpet as she walked to the steps, gazing floorward. I re-crossed my arms, just watching her. As she reached for the door, she looked back up at me.

She both sad and frightened. "We need to," she began. "I mean, I want..." she trailed off, gazing at me with an uncharacteristic uncertainty.

By now though, I had no patience left. This had to end before I softened again, gave in and just let her kidnap my soul. "We'll talk," I promised, knowing full well what she wanted.

But at the moment, all I wanted to be was alone. I was angry with Trace, yes, but much more than that, I was furious—disgusted—with myself, with what she'd forced me to see.

Trace searched my face a moment, then finally nodded and stepped out, closing the door behind her. I stared at the closed door, as if almost expecting yet another person to burst in.

Finally, I stood up straight.

I stretched my back a bit.

It hurt.

Ah well, I thought cynically, another day, another bruise. Besides, there'll be plenty of time for self-loathing and analyzing later. I still have to get through the night.

I took my headphones off and walked down the little steps to the door. This time I locked it.

SHE SELLS SANCTUARY
ONE DAY I WAS INTRODUCED TO POWER
SHE HARDLY SPOKE—SHE NEVER SAID HER NAME
I WAS PREYING IN MY DARKEST HOUR
AND SHE WHISPERED TO ME, "BLOOD CANNOT BE TAMED."

"I Fall"—JD Glass

THAT NIGHT, AFTER I COLLECTED my pay, I was so tired I practically crawled home and made straight for the shower, since no one else was around. Trace, I knew, wasn't there yet, or if she was, she hadn't come upstairs, and my roommates were still out and about—working, drinking, doing whatever it was they did.

Once in the bathroom, I set the water running in the shower, kicked off my boots, and stripped quickly. I balled the dress up and tossed it on the hamper, then inspected the stockings.

Yep, ruined. Absolutely wrecked.

There were several holes along the seam. For a moment, I could feel the bruising strength of Trace's hands pressing against me, but I shook it off.

I tossed the nylons into the garbage pail.

I checked my back in the mirror briefly. The promised bruise had materialized on my back, and I knew it would be tender for a few days. And… Yes, there, I found a few scrapes along my neck that stung when I touched them. Ah well, what was life without a few bruises? *Probably nice and painless,* I wryly answered myself.

I wondered if my buddy—you know, my pal, my girl, my best friend, my favorite body part—would end up with a couple of bruises. Trace's hands had been pretty rough, especially when she was ripping through the nylons…

What a fucking event that *had been,* I mused as I stepped into the shower.

I got soaked as quickly as possible, and went through the routine of bathing. Finally, when the soap was clear, I stood under the shower itself, and simply let the water pour over me.

Trace's words pounded over and over through my head, so hard my head ached.

It was definitely time to get out of the shower. I reached for and shut the taps half-blinded, then reached for a towel.

My hair wrapped, I grabbed one of my robes from behind the closed door (I have three of them: tiger stripes, leopard spots and black) wrapped myself in the black one, and began to rub my aching head through the terry cloth.

Suddenly, it occurred to me that perhaps my head hurt because I may have actually been a little hung over, and the follow-up thought to that was maybe, just maybe, Trace had been a little drunk as well, because I could think of nothing else that would really explain her behavior.

But that made things more confusing, because didn't alcohol lower your inhibitions? Supposedly, it just lowers your guard, your brain is definitely not functioning well enough to come up with new and novel ideas, thanks to the effects of oxygen deprivation. So what did that mean? I mean, I'd wanted more between Trace and me, but I didn't "go" for it, and Trace had pretty much literally attacked me, which was still just unbelievable.

And I'd frozen. What the fuck was up with that? I'd been fine, or at least, I'd thought I was, just a little while before she appeared. Was it the really the tequila pop? Or was it something else? There had been a moment there, when I'd actually considered just letting things happen—if I'd just, well, given over, that it would have been what Trace needed, it would help her to be whole, somehow.

Why fight it or her anyway, I mean, it's not like I didn't know that it didn't matter who Trace was with, she always wanted to be with me in the end. Except maybe now, after this, this thing, she wouldn't. I admit that something inside me was afraid, and I wasn't sure what I was more afraid of: that we'd continue the way we'd been, or that it was maybe, just maybe, finally over and I was free.

Free.

That was a strange thought, and I shied away from it.

Free from *what*, really?

But something in my mind insisted that I'd done the right thing, that this whole thing wasn't just about whether or not we ever fucked—I mean, look at me and Blue, um, Candace. What happened between us was pretty damn intimate, can't really get much closer, physically. But, I felt no tie, no connection to her, other than a warm friendliness and an honest lust. The only game between us had really boiled down to this: she was interested, was I?

And there was no deceit about it. Yes, I was. Okay, maybe it had gone a little further than I normally would have let it, and for Christ's sake, in the skybox of all places, but really, no harm, no foul. She wanted, I wanted, it was very happily mutual.

Too much, it was too much to think about, the words, the feelings, and this strange sense of...shame, somehow, all floating together.

That was weird, the shame, I mean.

I didn't feel any about Candace—it was from what had happened, after, with Trace. I felt like my whole body was as raw as my neck, as if I'd lived out that nightmare everyone has sooner or later, you know, the one when you go to school and you suddenly realize you're naked.

I brushed my teeth (I'm a Crest baby), and somewhere during the rinse and spit cycle, I realized that my hands were shaking.

Maybe my blood sugar is too low, it's been quite some time since I've had anything solid to eat, I rationalized. Besides, that made sense, in a purely biological sort of way.

Wrapped in my robe and stepping out of the bathroom finally, I made my way to the kitchen and served myself some orange juice. That would take care of the sugar. I left the light on over the stove, since it would shine nice and dimly in the living room, then went to the bedroom that I shared with my roommate, Jackie.

Oh yeah, roommates. I had two. Captain, otherwise known as Cap, who was a police officer and had a room of his own, and Jackie, a truly good friend who'd invited me to move in when life had become unlivable at my parents, since they'd given me the boot and all that, but that's another story.

In fact, actually, it's a whole other book, maybe even a graphic novel or something...

Huh, I laughed to myself as I thought about it. Maybe I'd call it *Punk Like Me*, or something like that.

Maybe. Someday. But for now, I was tired.

Since the room, located right off the living room, was really small, Jackie and I shared a bed. This wasn't quite the hardship that it would seem, given that I spent half my time downstairs in Trace's.

But when Jackie came home, and she would soon, since she worked at another local bar and was probably doing the after-hours hang-out—that's basically a "members only" not-a-real-bar-but-we're-gonna-make-our-own-anyway sort of location—she'd want to talk at the very least, and I was in no mood to chat, or to listen, or even to sleep next to anyone, at all.

I took a pillow from the bed and a blanket from the closet in the back of the room, then made myself a nest on the sofa. Why is it that a pullout sofa feels terrible when you actually pull it out, but leave it closed, and it's great to sleep on?

I was glad I'd left that light on by the stove because I hated sleeping in the pitch-black dark, and Jackie always shut off the small lamp I'd leave lit on the dresser in our room. Jackie didn't like a lot of things, come to think of it...

But I was too tired to think about that at the moment, and satisfied with my bed engineering, I lay down on my side.

Definite mistake.

The moment my knees touched, my favorite body part twinged. My poor buddy, all pain and no gain. I didn't have another pillow, and since I hate to let my head droop to the side and I didn't feel like sleeping on my back, I scrunched up the blankets between my knees.

That was better—not much—but better.

I don't know when I fell asleep but I thought I was dreaming when I heard Jackie come in, talking with Trace. I guessed they must have gone to the after-hours together. That wasn't too surprising. Jackie and Trace had been best friends since high school, (in fact, I'd met Trace through Jackie) and were twenty three and twenty four, respectively, to my twenty.

No doubt, they were very *definitely* a lot more used to partying than I was, on every level.

"Hey, she's sleeping," Jackie's voice was pitched low.

"Yeah, well, it's been a full night," Trace's voice whispered back. "She hooked up with this girl and…" the rest trailed off into a quieter whisper that I couldn't make out, and I didn't care. I snuggled tighter under the blanket, trying to force myself back into a deeper sleep.

In that mostly unconscious state, I thought I heard Trace say that she needed to talk with me, I heard Jackie say goodnight and go to bed.

I drifted further into darkness, everything silent, and I was warm, just oh-so-toasty warm. A body pressed against my back, and arms wrapped around and held me firmly, but with love. I could feel it so clearly.

I dreamed of the beach, and eyes that shined at me, and for the first time in ages, held warmly in that embrace, I dreamt that I was surrounded by friends, that I was loved. One of them smiled at me in the setting sun.

"If you're ever lonely, come to me, I know what it's like to be lonely. If people hurt you, because you're not like them, come to me, I know what it's like to be different. When you hurt, when you ache, let me take that from you…I ache, too," I heard, a fervent low whisper in my ear. A soft hand caressed my cheek, and the sun, surf and my friends, all of them, disappeared.

I had truly been dreaming, after all.

My muscles cramped with longing for that warmth, for that connect, a hard ache that ran through my bones the way it does when you've spent the night sleeping cold. A chill chased after it as I realized it was Trace's voice I heard. But this time, I really couldn't move at all; I was just too damned tired.

Trace had somehow wrapped herself behind me on the sofa. It was her body pressed against mine, her arms holding me, her words sinking into my brain and every single one of them…

Broke.

My.

Heart.

"Let me take care of you, you will never feel lonely, or hurt, or sad again," her soft words insisted. "Just come to me. Give yourself over to me, make me your world and I swear you will be mine."

The arm beneath my shoulder pulled me in closer and the warmth, the feeling of genuine affection that poured from her was wonderful. "I will love you and I will protect you." She punctuated each promise with a soft kiss and a caress. "You will never, ever, need anything again—I promise you, Nina," she swore and kissed my cheek gently.

The warmth, the words, the emotions were tempting, and I wanted to believe them, all of them, I wanted to believe *her*. I almost gave in, I was going to turn, and snuggle deeper into her, throw my arms around Trace and nuzzle against her neck as I'd never done before, but as I shifted my legs, the bruise at their apex throbbed and instead of turning inward, toward her, I turned further away, almost onto my stomach, the blanket clutched firmly around me.

"No," I whispered, still only half awake, and safely tucked away, I fell back into a deep sleep.

Trace was gone when I finally woke up, on my stomach and half off the sofa. I blinked a few times and rolled onto my back.

Ouch!

That...had been a bad idea. I'd forgotten about the bruise there and the other one that nestled up in my crotch. Both reminded me of their reality, and I remembered how I'd gotten them.

Geez.

What the fuck was I going to do?

No way that I would tell Jackie or Captain about it, I mean, Jackie and Cap were both friends with Trace first. I wasn't sure they'd believe me, and even if they did, somehow, I was sort of sure that it was my fault, anyway, which meant that I'd been dumb.

Besides, what was I going to say?

It was no secret that I felt so strongly for Trace; Cap would probably tell me I was an idiot for not "going for it," and Jackie? She'd never, ever, believe it. She'd tell me I misunderstood, that I didn't understand Trace, that I was just too young, too immature.

I could just imagine Captain, his dark skin, high and tight military style buzz-cut and wide, bright grin. "Two, in one night? And one of them Trace? Not bad, kid, not bad," and he'd slap my shoulder and laugh.

And I could see Jackie's face as well, auburn hair and porcelain skin broken only by the firm line of her mouth. She probably wouldn't say a word, at all. Hell, she probably wouldn't talk to me for a few days, then at the end of that time, walk in one night after work and start yelling about the spoon in the sink or something. Then we'd have a big talk, or rather, she would talk, and I would listen, while she told me how and why exactly I was wrong.

I sat up and swung my legs off the sofa, the blanket half covering me, and bracing my hands on my knees, I stared at the floor. It was starting to occur to me that maybe, just maybe, I didn't have the best friends in the world; at least, not to live with anyway.

I stood up and stretched, letting the blanket fall to the floor. Everything was a little sore, but that was no big deal. Glancing down, I realized I'd slept in my bathrobe, and I had terry-cloth textured skin. I tied the ends together and quietly made my way to the shared bedroom.

Opening the door slowly, I stuck my head in. Jackie was out like the light she always shut on the dresser, and I was surprised to see she had her arm thrown over Trace, who was asleep on top of the blankets in a t-shirt, facing the wall.

I didn't want to wake either of them, so I slipped very quietly to the closet where our clothes were.

I grabbed a t-shirt, a pair of shorts, some pants, socks, underwear—you know, the usual. It didn't matter what it looked like, most of what I wore was black, anyway.

As I sneaked to the door, Trace shifted.

"Nina," she called quietly.

I froze in place. I certainly wasn't ready to talk with her yet. Trace moved again, and resettled on her side.

Good. She was just sleeping.

A part of me hoped she had nightmares, then quickly felt guilty. I knew better than most that she did.

Back in the living room, I dumped my stuff on the sofa, and neatly folded the blanket, putting it neatly on top of the pillow.

If you sat on the couch, the bedroom was behind you, TV in front, windows to the left, kitchen to the right, and the door to Cap's bedroom just a bit past. Since his door was firmly shut, which it hadn't been when I'd gotten in last night, it was a safe bet he was home and sleeping, too.

Good. I didn't want to deal with anyone, anyway.

I dressed and began a set of floor stretches. The thigh stretches were a little more painful than usual, but otherwise, everything was in good working order.

Warmed up, I was ready to go for a run. I didn't do that all the time, but today seemed like a good day to do it. There's a very interesting serenity to running, and it's similar to swimming in that your mind goes blank sort of, but not really.

Somehow, while you're focusing on the very basic steps of breathing and moving simultaneously, your brain figures all sorts of things out. Besides, exercise, especially strenuous exercise, was and is good for breaking down all the stuff your body creates when it's stressed, and I was for sure feeling stressed.

The table was right by the door, and all of us roomies put our shoes under it when we came in, to avoid tracking crap across the floor, literally or figuratively, so I sat for a moment at that 1950s off-white Formica and glitter-topped table a moment, focusing very clearly on tying those knots just right.

And yeah, I do "bunny ears." I know, I know, it's supposed to be "rabbit in the hole," but hey, my laces never come loose. It's my thing.

Sneakers set, I grabbed my keys, tucked them into a back pocket and was out the door.

I glanced up.

The sun was shining brilliantly and still climbing; it was going to be a warm day.

I stretched again, then started running, down the block to Bay Street, past the park, up the hill (yes, we have hills on Staten Island and it reminds many people of San Francisco. Wait, did I say hills? When you're running up them, they're damn hills). I then went back down Broad Street, which was the street I lived on, past the projects and the fire house, past my apartment, then did the circuit again.

I'd gotten into a nice rhythm by the second go-round, and well into the third set, I was deep in the flow. Cars, trees, cement, burnt lots and lost auto parts, all part of the whole—step, breathe, step, breathe, the air was a continuous flow in and through my body, the sun shining and warming my skin.

Bits of glass winked up at me from the asphalt as I glided past.

I didn't know what exactly I was going to do when I got back to the apartment, besides the obvious of showering and dressing, but I was certain on one score: I needed to find something new, maybe completely different. I wasn't sure what, really, but *something*.

My feet kept hitting the ground, flying past the scenery as facts and thoughts flew by in my head.

I had enough money for the rent for at least another month tucked away, and if I watched my expenses, I could pick up that guitar today. I had my eye on a beautiful double-cut Ibanez Artist, and it had a sound so sweet, I couldn't wait until it was mine, all mine, to have and to hold, to play until my fingers bled.

I was about two, maybe three blocks away from the apartment, and coming up to the fire house, when it hit me—not only had I worked the night before, I'd gotten paid time and a half for it!

I hadn't even counted the money Rich had put into my hand, but I calculated that working from about midnight, which would be a little after Darrel had left, to four a.m, I should have something over two hundred dollars.

Since I only owed about another hundred on the guitar, I'd be able to pay it off, put half away, and maybe actually have a little fun with the other half.

Hey, cool! I smiled to myself in happy anticipation. I'd go get my guitar today, let the rest work itself out somewhere in the back of my mind.

I trusted my subconscious to come up with solutions and then share them with me when the time was right. I frowned a little bit at that. Hope it came up with something soon, though. As clueless as I could be sometimes, I had the nagging feeling that I may have been in more trouble than I actually knew.

As I approached the fire house, I managed a last burst of speed for my end sprint, and I was cooking by the time I flew past the steps that led up to the three-story brownstone I lived in.

Someone was sitting on the top of the steps, and as I finished my sprint, down to the corner, then the next one that bordered Bay Street, I recognized my brother, Nicky, waiting for me.

No, Nico, I mentally corrected, *everyone calls him Nico now,* I reminded myself with an inward grin. I stopped myself before I crossed the street and took a few deep breaths, then jogged back to my door, waving to Nico.

With a genuine smile, he jumped down the steps as I approached. "Hey, Nina!" he greeted, and he opened his arms for a hug.

With the same smile on my own face, because I love him so much and I was, then and now, always happy to see him, I moved into his arms with a hug of my own.

"Nico!" I greeted him enthusiastically, drawing out the "oh" sound in a way I knew he enjoyed hearing.

We gave each other a kiss on the cheek, but I didn't hug him as tightly as I normally would.

"Hey, I want a real hug," he protested, squeezing me.

"I don't want to get you wet," I explained, a bit breathless still from the end sprint.

"Wet, shmet, I don't care," Nico replied, increasing the pressure, and I hugged him tighter, resting my head on his shoulder. "It's just a little water and salt."

He leaned back, picking my feet up off the floor, bouncing me a little. "I want a real hug."

For all that he was my younger brother, he had finally beat me in the height department. Oh, we were still smaller than most people our ages, we had (and have) that slower metabolism thing going, (which our baby sister, Nanny didn't—she was bigger than both of us) so we'd both still grow over the next few years, but he had an inch or so on me.

Since I'd been bigger for so many years, say approximately our whole lives up until then, he loved to tease me about it. By picking me up and bouncing me.

I held on to him as if I'd fall of the planet if I didn't, and not just because of the bouncing. Despite the natural endorphin goodness of the run, I'd been feeling pretty darn alone in the world, and now, I wasn't. I had Nico, and I'd be fine, or at least, better.

A few more moments of Nico's testing the strength of my rib cage, then he put me down, but I continued to hold on to him.

"Nina, are you crying?" he asked, and I could hear and feel his concern.

I guess, maybe, a little, I realized, picking my face up and noting the little wet spot I'd left on his shoulder.

"Naw, Nico," I grinned at him lightly, because I just didn't want to go there yet. "It's just a little water and salt."

His eyes, the same shade of blue-grey as mine, except that his had a thin butter-gold ring in the center that you could only see when he was really mellow, searched my face.

"You'll tell me later?" he asked, brow furrowed, and not put off or fooled by my joke.

I glanced up at the door to the building then back at him. "Yeah," I promised quietly. "I'll tell you later."

I meant it, I would talk with him later, but for now, the sun was shining, the birds were singing, well, somewhere anyway, and it was a beautiful summer day.

"Come on up," I invited with a bright smile, and started up the stairs. "Hang out while I shower, then let's blow this popsicle stand." I pulled my keys out and opened the door. "You eat breakfast yet?" I turned and asked, staring pointedly at his stomach.

One thing for sure. Neither one of us would really eat often, but when we did, watch out, especially if we were together. Whole gallons of milk, entire loaves of bread and full cartons of eggs were known to be transformed into French toast and disappear around us.

"Yeah, I grabbed something, but…" he grinned at me "…I'm not fully fueled yet."

I was pretty hungry, too. Usually, I made myself something, and if Nicky—I mean Nico—and I were together, we'd cook together, splitting up prep work and clean up, a tradition we'd started years ago when our parents would work overtime on Saturdays and we were home alone with Nanny. But I honestly wasn't sure what was in the refrigerator upstairs, and I really didn't want to hang out in the apartment longer than I had to.

For whatever reason, the thought made me queasy.

"I worked last night and got paid," I told him as we rounded the first landing, "you want to go to Jerry's? My treat," I offered.

Jerry's Pancake House looks like a little dive from the outside, oh hell, the whole neighborhood was divey, but Jerry—there really *was* a Jerry—made the best pancakes around, with all sorts of variations of fruit, chocolate, ice cream, whatever, and the portions were huge, enough to make even me and Nico happy, for a very reasonable price.

If you ever find yourself on Bay Street, stop in there, you'll be glad you did.

"Oh, cool, yeah," Nico answered enthusiastically as we came to the top landing, "I'm getting strawberries and bananas, then."

I smiled to myself at that. Nico ate so many bananas, he was living proof that humans are related to apes, and in fact, our dad used to call us monkeys (in a nice way) when we were small and being silly. Of course, we were monsters if we were bad, but that's another thing altogether.

I keyed the lock and we made our way in. Nico dropped himself casually into a chair by the table, and I made my way back to the sofa, to gather my real clothes for the day.

Captain's door popped open and he stood in the doorway, yawning and stretching.

"Hey, Nina," he greeted through a yawn, scratching his chest, his eyes still slit from tiredness.

I should probably mention, he was stark naked.

"Morning," I greeted back. I nodded my head in Nico's direction. "Nico's here."

Captain's eyes popped open with embarrassment. "Oh geez, hey Nico," and he took a step back into his room, shutting the door.

It opened again a moment later and he stepped out, wearing a pair of boxer shorts.

"Hey, man, sorry about that," he grinned at Nico, and clapped him on the shoulder.

"No problem, man," Nico answered noncommitally.

But I noticed the tips of his ears were a little pink as he bent over to fiddle with his shoe laces. Captain grabbed another seat at the table.

What is it with some guys?

They don't care of you see them naked, but another guy, oh, then they're all modesty, unless it's a locker room. Then they're all punching and smacking each other with towels and stuff.

Or maybe it's just me. I mean, I'm not much interested in the package so, it doesn't matter whether I see it or not, and not just because of the male-female thing—if it were a girl, I wouldn't have had a problem being completely neutral either.

Well, that could have been from too many years in locker rooms, myself.

Okay, maybe there had been one exception, a long time ago, but let's not go there—it's not what you're thinking, anyway.

Maybe it depends on the context, I mused to myself as I made my way over to the kitchen sink, about five feet directly in front of the table, to get a glass of water.

Captain yawned and stretched his arms over his head. "You hanging for the day?" he asked Nico mid-yawn. "You guys want to watch stuff with me?"

He brought his arms down and looked from Nico to me, "I got a few new videos," he wheedled in his most tempting tone. "Lots of babes in action."

Nico and I looked at each other a moment. We knew what Captain meant, and it wasn't movies; at least, not big screen ones with ratings for the general public, and leading ladies rescuing people and things, no dialogue, but enough explosions to keep the keenest pyro happy.

No, it was more like things that could only be filmed in certain places (I hear tell there's a few spots in California that "specialize" but that ain't necessarily true) so the cops wouldn't arrest the crew, half of which would be naked, and all the explosions would be of a more, um, specialized, biological, sort.

Not that Nico or I were particularly averse to pornography, I mean, we'd seen every video our dad had ever hidden in his workshop, and discovered that they were really funny if you played them in fast forward or reverse (and the faster you play it, the funnier it gets).

Besides, they were in their own way a valuable educational tool, I mean, when a person gets to that part of their learning, no one ever talks about technique, just anatomy and ducts, and really, once you understood the mechanics of fertility, pregnancy, venereal disease, and AIDS, no one ever taught anything else—like how to enjoy it.

I mean, really.

Everyone wants to tell you how your genitals work, and all the things you should be paranoid about for them (and for good reason, too) but not how to use them, so we'd gotten a lot out of those flicks.

But still, sitting and watching one with Captain didn't sound like a good idea. I was sure it wouldn't be a popcorn throwing, smart-ass commenting, technique dissecting session. In fact, from the look in Nico's eye, the suggestion was making him just as uncomfortable as it made me, and I was pretty sure he was hoping I'd handle it, and handle it to the negative.

I didn't disappoint.

I finished my water.

"Thanks, but we got stuff to do today," I answered, not missing the quick, grateful grin Nico threw my way. "We're going to pick up my guitar."

Both guys turned to look at me, eyes wide.

"Oh, wow, you're gonna get it, today?" Nico asked, smiling, "That, Nina, is so cool."

"Hey, nice, very nice, congratulations." Captain nodded, obviously impressed. "How'd you manage to pull that one off so soon?"

"I worked last night, so I got paid a bit extra," I smiled with real joy, "and now, I'm going to shower, so we can run out there."

"Well, hey, don't let me keep you," Captain said, "but if you get bored, you know where I'll be."

"Yeah, I do," I answered as I made my way to the bathroom.

And I did know.

He'd be on the sofa, eyes glued to the screen, with one hand on the remote, watching blow job scenes and "money shots" over and over, the other hand, well, you know where it would be—and not motionless, either.

Not that I cared, I mean, masturbating is a healthy thing, it was just, well, no thanks—didn't want to see that.

The shower I took set record time for speed, as did the doing of my hair. Dressing was just as quick. Required undergarments, a black "Love and Rockets" T-shirt with Hopey, my favorite character playing with her band, on it, button-fly black jeans and a pair of engineer's boots.

Black, of course.

Did I mention that I wore a lot of black?

One last check in the mirror, and I was good to go. Let's see, my hair was up, my clothes were on and I was ready to rock and roll.

I stepped out of the bathroom and headed for the door, stopping only to grab an old army bag that held my wallet (complete with last night's pay), sunglasses, cigarettes, lighter; you know, stuff, all the stuff that you need during the day.

"Hey, Nina," a female voice creaked out my way as Nico stood to join me. I turned to toward the sound.

Jackie stood in an extra-long sleep shirt leaning against the sofa back, a cup of tea cradled in her hands. Her hair was disheveled and her face still swollen with sleep. Add in the knee socks she was wearing, and she looked all of about twelve or thirteen years old, except her eyes: they were slit, and glaring out at me over her mug as she sipped.

"Morning, Jackie," I returned with cheerful wariness.

It was hard to tell if the glare was her usual morning grumpiness, because Jackie could be an absolute horror show before she finished her morning caffeine ritual, or if it was something else. I was *definitely* erring on the side of caution, either way.

She drank deeply of her mug, then lowered it to her chin, looking at me across its rim. "We need to talk when you get back," she said finally. "I have a few questions for you."

Oh, great, just great, I inwardly rolled my eyes.

Over by the sink, Cap's shoulders shook with suppressed laughter. "Someone's in trouble," he sing-songed to me with a smile.

I returned it with a sickly approximation of a smile, then glanced at Jackie again.

"I'd prefer," she sipped again, "to talk now, though."

She finished her cup, looked in it to double check then back at me.

"Hello, Nicholas," she greeted my brother, without a smile, not looking at him.

Her eyes were fixed on me and her face was grave as Nico muttered a low greeting in response behind me.

"Well, I think I'll just scoot along," Captain interrupted, a mug and a bowl in his hands—coffee and "Cheerios" drowning in milk from the looks of it. "If you'll excuse me," he bowed slightly towards me and Nico.

He turned back to face Jackie, square on. "I hate to get in the way of these sensitive chats," he told the room in general, his voice as flat as his expression.

Captain turned back to me and shrugged his shoulders.

Well, he was right. What could you do?

"You didn't do anything, kid," he muttered to me from the corner of his mouth, "bear with it, then ignore it. Later!" He grinned brightly and briefly to me and Nico and with that, he turned on his heel and walked the few steps to his room, opening the door with his foot.

It closed behind him with a sharp slam, and Nico and I stood there for a moment as the air settled from the sound.

Apparently more than one conversation went on while I was sleeping, I concluded very quickly.

"I, um, I'll go bring the van around," Nico said into the awkward silence that had descended into the room, and nimbly slipped out the door.

Jackie silently walked over to the sink and washed her mug in silence before turning on me. "What the fuck do you think you're doing?" she launched at me. "What the hell did you do to Trace?"

Her eyes blazed and her voice ripped at me with anger. She folded her arms across her chest, waiting for an answer.

I stood there silently, attempting to take Jackie's anger in and understand it. How was I supposed to answer that? What did I do, anyway?

Okay, maybe there was a reasonable way to work this. Jackie was generally speaking a rational person, and she'd been a good friend for a while. If I explained, I was sure she'd be able to help me find the middle road that I absolutely knew had to exist somewhere between responsibility and blame and if there was a burden to be laid upon me, bring it on—I wasn't, then and now, afraid to face myself or my faults.

But first things first.

"Where's Trace?" I asked.

I don't know why I cared, but I did. If we were going to work something out and still be friends, I wanted to know if she was okay.

Despite the bruises that I had, the memory of her curled up on her side sleeping, of the gentle vulnerability she let show when we were alone, touched me, softened me. I couldn't really be too angry; I loved her.

Of course, a little voice in the back of my head warned me, too, *if Jackie and Trace gang up on you, kid, you're done for.* I was trying to ignore that voice, but it was insistent, and it told me that I'd been calumnized, if not at the very least, misrepresented.

Oh, shut up voice, I thought, *suspicion isn't very honorable.* I'd hear this out before I came to any conclusions.

"She left before you came back," Jackie said softly, anger diminished for the moment. "She said she couldn't bear to talk with you yet."

Jackie shifted and leaned back against the sink. "So, I'm asking you again, what did you do? I've already heard about your—" her mouth tightened for a moment "—escapades. Did you drink too much? I can understand that," she told me quietly. "And I can understand that things may be coming to some sort of head for the two of you."

Jackie paused, and glanced down a moment, studying the floor as she considered her next words. Seconds stretched into hours before she finally she looked up, the lines of her face hard and set.

Well, she certainly doesn't look sleepy anymore, my mind noted.

"What I can't understand, though, is how, is why," she shook her head and held her hands up as if they'd help her ask and understand, "why you…" and her eyes now held both anger and tears "…you of all people, would want to fuck with someone's head like that? Haven't we all been your friends? Didn't I take you in when you had no place to go?" Jackie's voice rose. "You're here because of me!" she yelled.

"She pays more rent and more often than you do," Captain called out from in his room.

I glanced at the door, then back at Jackie. *Thank you,* I thought to him silently. *At least I'm not completely alone in this.*

Jackie gathered herself again, folding her arms and leaning back on the sink. She took a breath, a bit calmer than before. "Be that as it may," she stated calmly, "you share my home, my bed for Christ's sake, how could you do that? How could you go and fucking treat a friend, *my* friend, like that?"

Told you so, the little voice in my head said, a bit smugly too, I might add.

Well, okay, I'd heard her out. I could even understand how she felt, I mean, I'd feel the same way if someone I'd trusted had, or I thought had, hurt a friend of mine. But, that's not what happened, at least, not as I saw it. I'd just have to explain my side of it, or at least, most of it.

I was going to leave some stuff out, like where and how I was bruised, I just couldn't really bring myself to talk about it, not here, not now, especially not at this moment, although I knew the information might turn those tables so fast we'd all see double. But that didn't seem right to me, it seemed sort of like, I don't know, hunting for butterflies with atom bombs or something.

Besides, somehow, I can't really explain why, it felt like this was my fault, anyway.

"What exactly is it that you think I did?" I asked in an even tone. If I was going to attempt to be a rational adult, it wouldn't do me any good to attack in return.

Right?

Yeah, I thought so, too.

Jackie straightened up from her position and took a step toward me. "Don't," she hissed, "don't you dare use that prep-school cool on me."

She waved a finger in my face. "Right now, you're fucking nowhere and no one, and I'll kick you out of here faster than you can, you can…you can just go fuck yourself if that's how you're going to be."

I took a step back. Not only do I have absolutely no love for anyone getting into my personal space without an invitation, and especially when they're angry and waving their hands (and God help the person who actually makes a move to my head or face) but that icy heat was starting to burn into my face. Right now I still had control of my mouth and my body, but if she got louder, if she fuckin' so much as touched me in anger, I couldn't guarantee that I could maintain that.

At that moment, Captain's door opened and we both turned our heads to look as he stepped out, wearing t-shirt and jeans on this time.

"Okay, if anyone has anything to say about who lives here, it's me, and right now, all three of us live here," he said firmly as he approached us.

Outside, I could hear a car horn blow and I could tell from the way they cocked their heads, Jackie and Captain heard it, too. Nico must have brought the van around and was waiting for me.

We stood in that little area in the kitchen, facing each other in a triangle. "Nina, go, have a good time with your brother, I've thought of a great space for you to put your guitar in," Captain told me very calmly, motioning me towards the door. "Jackie," he turned to her and continued, "lay off. Nina's one of your best friends, you don't know what really happened, and you know that Trace, well…she's Trace"

What else was there to say about her, anyway? Liar was too strong, because I didn't know what she'd really said, and drama queen wasn't exactly right, either. Crazy wouldn't have been hard to prove. But this wouldn't have been the right time to find the right adjectives, anyway.

Jackie and I glared at each other a moment longer. Finally, I turned on my heel, walked the few steps towards the door and opened it. "I'll see you guys later," I tossed back to them as I slung my bag over my shoulder and stepped out.

Running down the stairs, because I didn't want to keep Nico waiting, I reviewed the "discussion" in my head, and thought about different ways I could have handled it. The French have a phrase for it: "espirit d'escalier," or roughly, "spirit of the stairway," which is what happens when you run down the stairs thinking of different ways you could have done or said something, now that you had a moment to think about it. *That's what I've got—stairway spirit,* I concluded as I passed the landing that held Trace's door.

Not that I could think of anything else to have said or done, really. I guess I could have just interrupted Jackie and, using sheer volume, explained my side of the story, but that just wasn't my style.

I could still hear Captain and Jackie upstairs. "You never stop to think, Jackie," I could hear Captain's deep growl. "You forget, I know Trace better than you do."

Jackie's reply faded to my ears as I got to the bottom and made my way out the front door.

Nico's face peered anxiously out the passenger side window of the hulking grey behemoth that was his pride and joy, a gun-metal grey conversion van—converted from utility to mini rec room, complete with pullout sofa-like thing in the back (and a box of assorted toys: footballs, Frisbees, baseball gloves, swim fins, stuff like that, as well as towels and t-shirts), a little porta potty in its own privacy cupboard, and sink with assorted car-type parts and tools that might one day prove useful beneath it.

"You okay?" he asked as I made my way over to the door and slid in to the seat.

"Oh, yeah, I'm fine," I breathed out as I buckled myself in. I rooted around in my bag for my pack of cigarettes, found one, then lit it, the first one for the day.

Nico nodded his head in understanding and pulled away from the curb as I blew smoke out the window. I let my thoughts drift away with it as we drove in silence.

Nico respected my need for head space and soon I was able to recapture my 'good morning' mood. There would be time to let the back of my mind work towards solutions. Besides, my stomach rumbled, reminding me that I needed food, and really, who can think if they're hungry?

"So, we still going to Jerry's? 'Cause if we are, you're going the wrong way," I informed him as we went in the opposite direction.

"Oh yeah," Nico grinned at me, "we can still do that." He sought down the street for a likely block to turn on and set a signal.

As we drove down the street, sunlight flashing on the sidewalk through the trees, it occurred to me, it was July after all, and though the summer felt endless, there wouldn't be all that many sunny and free days left. Soon enough it would be time to wait in line for Registration, buy books, and juggle classes and work schedules for me, and off with his trunk packed with new undershorts and linens for Nico, on his way to his own schooling.

Fuck it.

I don't like to waste rare beautiful days, we could go to Jerry's some other time, when it was raining.

Now was now.

Even if I didn't swim, I could still roll my jeans up, and chances were very good that Nico had a couple of spare shorts in the back of the vehicle—somewhere. And they were probably mine.

Besides, I could pick up my guitar after the sun went down, and maybe, just maybe, if I got lucky, I'd find a little time to squeeze in some drawing, or better yet, some painting, before either everyone got home or I had to go anywhere.

But for now, for *right now...*

"You know, we could just grab some bagels and chocolate milk and go to the beach," I suggested, putting my thoughts into words. "Whaddya say?" I grinned at him.

"Shit, yeah, the beach," he responded enthusiastically, his eyes shining brightly at me for a moment before he had to return his attention to the road.

"Sun and sand, here we come," I sang out, visions of the surf crashing against the shore filling my head and the taste of an egg bagel with a little mustard and Muenster cheese followed by a Nestlé Quick chocolate milk to wash it down filling my mouth.

I was there already.

SEXY EIFFEL TOWERS

LET ME TELL YOU SOMETHING DARLING,
YOU'RE DOING FINE...
NOW YOU'VE SHOWN ME ALL OF YOURS I'LL LET YOU INTO MINE
BUT ME, I LIKE A PRETTY BOY, I LOVE A HARD-EDGED GIRL

"For The Love of Boyz 'n ' Grrlz"—JD Glass

TRACE AND I DIDN'T SPEAK for to each other for days, but it wasn't as if the opportunity was readily available. Between my roommates, Cappie and Jackie and their respective schedules, combined with mine as well as Trace's, it was a wonder if any of us ever got to see each other at all.

And I honestly, wasn't trying too hard.

I did see Candace, though: the next week, in fact.

Totally sober and with the door safely locked, I was at work, grooving in the booth, eyes closed and feeling fine, swaying along with this phenom beat I'd discovered a few days ago, when a voice with the loveliest hint of a British accent floated up to me.

"Hey lovely DJ, do you take requests?"

I opened my eyes, slipped my headphones down around my neck and looked down into Candace's smiling face.

"Maybe. It depends on what you have in mind," I informed her with a saucy grin and an arched brow.

"I'm thinking...French," Candace replied, her even, white teeth sparkling up at me.

"Ah, too bad," I shook my head with mock regret, pretending I didn't know what she meant, "I can't read minds in French."

"Colonist!" Candace laughed back at me. "Can you even speak anything other than that fractured language you borrowed from us?" she asked with a wide smirk.

"Hey, I take offense at that." I scowled good naturedly. "My grandparents are from South America and I happen to be fluent in Spanish," I told her, which happens to be true, "and, don't forget, this is Staten Island. I can speak and read a little Italian as well." Which was also true—and in that part of New York? Occasionally necessary.

"Well, that explains quite a bit then," Candace smiled at me, and gave me an appraising look.

"How about you—imperialist?" I asked her, half joking, half challenging.

I mean, yes, as Americans, of course many of us have natural ties to Europe, with its grand culture and history, not to mention a couple o' wars, but on the other hand, we were the ones who invented the steam engine, the car, the internet, and rock and roll, not to mention a few other things.

Besides, we had other countries and continents that had lent us their best people too, and though I liked Candace, I wasn't going to deal with any "my country is better than your country" bullshit.

Even if there were different times in history, past and future, where that might have been true.

"I give, I give!" Candace held her hands up in mock surrender. "Now forgive me and let me take you to dinner," she cajoled and smiled charmingly.

I raised my eyebrows and cocked my head in interest.

Seeing that, Candace continued. "It's a little place I've discovered in the East Village—it's called Port Marseille—I'm so sure you'll love it!" she enthused.

I couldn't.

I had to work, I had guitar practice, and I certainly didn't want to get involved past, further, or more than what had already happened, and I hadn't even really intended for that, well at least not in that way, either.

Friends.

I wanted to be friends and that meant no dates.

What Candace suggested sounded more than vaguely like the latter as opposed to the former, but as I tried to form an answer that wouldn't sound offensive or hurtful, Candace's face wore an expression of such obvious sincere affection, that it made it difficult for me to think.

"My schedule's really tight," I replied instead, "when where you thinking of—"

Candace must have noticed some of my internal struggle. She interrupted me with a wave of the hand and reached through the request window. "No pressure, Nina." She smiled and patted my hand. "Whenever you'd like."

Cool. Okay then. "Okay." I nodded slowly. "I'll let you know." I gave her a small grin.

"Hmph," she answered inscrutably and took her hand back, then smiled at me. "I'll see you later." With that, she made her way back into the crowd.

I watched as she left and noticed that tonight, she wasn't wearing her usual blue—the body skimming one piece Candace had on this night was black.

I went back to my board and slipped my headphones back up on my ears. Hmm…

I set my faders for the next mix and grabbed the microphone, waiting for my moment. "Oh yeah," I encouraged the crowd, "it's time to set the night on fire!"

I began to bring up the next tune into the current one, a heavier beat mixing well with the tail of the one still playing.

"Scorched earth mix," I announced and brought the song in fully as I faded the other out completely, sending the custom compilation flying through the room where the people cheered in anticipation.

I set the lights to pattern reds through yellows, with occasional flashes of blue thrown in for dramatic relief.

I dance along for a bit, then went through my selections for the night. My set was in good order and as long as there were no changes, the music would cycle through moods, from earthy hip to fiery house and on to airy techno, finally ending with liquid trance.

Hmmm…

I dug under the shelf for a pen and piece of paper, then leaned over by the small worklight to write down the settings for the light shows per segment. Done, I reviewed it again. It was solid, a nice piece of musical experience, even if I did say so myself.

I reached for the microphone.

"Duh-Darrel, come to the sky, Duh-Duh-Darrel, come to the sky." I sing-songed to and through the beat, looking for Darrel's bobbing Mohawk among the dancers.

Of course he'd be around—don't ask me why, but for whatever reason, when you work in a club, you tend to hang out there on your time off. Of course, we used to say that the Redspot wasn't just a place, but a way of life.

You know what?

It really was.

"Duh-Duh-Darrel, come to the sky, Duh-Duh-Darrel, come to the sky," echoed the crowd, thinking it was a part of the performance.

And in a way, it was.

I finally spotted him all the way on the other side of the room, leaning against the wall and chatting with one of the many pretty young women who frequented the place.

He looked up towards the booth and nodded at me in acknowledgement so I waved him over.

"What's up?" he asked when he reached the request window.

"Come in," I answered instead, and went to the door, unlocking it.

"Hey! What's up?" he repeated, this time a bit more seriously as he mounted the steps.

I got right to the point.

"I need you to take over for me," I explained as I returned to the mixing board.

I visually checked the faders and knobs, just ensuring everything was where it had to be, then grabbed the list I'd made off the board and handed it to him.

"Here, everything's already set and in order" —I pointed to the stack of discs— "and here are all the lighting switches and their cues," I explained, indicating where I'd noted them.

Darrel studied the paper a moment. "Nice, Nina. Nice music, nice setup." He pursed his lips and nodded with what I could swear might have been honest admiration. It was definitely approval at the very least.

I allowed myself a small smile. Fuck nice, it was good, really fucking good, and I knew it. And it was good to have someone else, that did the same work too, I mean, think so too.

"So, why you leavin'? You alright?"

"I'm okay." I smiled widely because I knew why I was okay, and why I was leaving, and he didn't. "Just something I really gotta do."

I searched through the Plexi window among the throng. Where was she? Not this corner, not that one. My eyes continued to roam. Ah, there. She was harder to pick out among the crowd now that she wasn't wearing her trademark blue.

"Oh," Darrel drawled out, "I got it, you mean someone."

I turned back to look at him. "Huh?" I asked, brow furrowed in confusion.

Darrel gave me a knowing smirk. "It's not something you have to do," he explained, "it's someone." He snorted.

"Shut the fuck up." I backhanded him none too gently on his well-defined ribs, though I grinned while I hit him.

If I didn't mention it before, let me say it now: Darrel was quite the hottie and everyone knew it. From his blue Mohawk and silver-blue eyes, to his sharply-drawn cheeks and delicate mouth, down his wide shoulders and well defined upper body—which no one could miss, since he usually wore either very loose or very tight tank tops—Darrel was beautiful.

And…he knew it.

"Abuse! Abuse! The DJ's trying to kill me!" Darrel joked, clutching his side as if he'd been dealt a mortal wound.

I rolled my eyes at his antics, but I couldn't help smiling. For a Mr. Stud Muffin, he could be such a goof, and he reminded me in a good way of Nico.

"C'mon man, will you do it?" I asked him again, once his agonies had abated.

He looked back over the crowd, to see for himself again who it was.

"Nina," he asked slowly, an incredulous twist to his mouth, "is that Blue?"

"Candace," I corrected without thinking.

"Candace? Candace? As in, I-want-a-piece-of-that-candy-ass Candace?" his voice rose as his eyebrows climbed higher.

I thought they might disappear into his Mohawk.

With surprising speed Darrel whirled and grabbed my shoulders firmly. "Nina," he began solemnly, "you must go. For the honor of the order of hot

DJs everywhere, of which we are but a humble two…" and I snorted with self-derision as he gave me a little grin "…you must go."

"So, you'll cover for me?" I asked again, torn between impatience and amusement. I brought up a wrist lightly to knock his hand off my shoulder and he removed the other without assistance.

"She's fucking hot—ah!" he enthused, clapping his hands to his face.

"Great. Thanks," I told him and grabbed my jacket from the bench.

Black, of course, and leather, too. Highway patrol style. It was late summer after all and as scorching as the days were, the nights were starting to get a bit cool after midnight.

I slid it over my shoulders and made my way to the door.

"Thanks again, Darrel," I called back to him. "Thanks for covering for me—see you tomorrow."

"Hey, Nina?" Darrel called.

"Yeah?" I asked, turning my head as I reached for the latch.

"Here," he tossed something small at me and I automatically reached up to snatch it out of the air.

At first, I thought it was a wet-nap, you know, those little napkins filled with soap, but my fingers felt a ridge and closer inspection revealed something else.

"Um thanks?" I hazarded, waving it at him. What in the hell was I going to do with a condom?

"It's not for luck," he smiled, probably misunderstanding what I meant, and he came over to the steps. He squeezed down next to me by the door. "It's for safety." He gently took my hand and folded my fingers over the rubber, squeezing lightly for emphasis.

"This…" and he carefully lifted my eyes to his, fingertips soft under my chin, "is for luck."

Just as softly, just as carefully, and as gently as he'd handle a disc, he kissed me.

I was so shocked by his actions and by the feel of his lips on mine that I did nothing for a few seconds—I think I even forgot to breathe. But, as soon as the initial shock wore off, I pulled away.

"Darrel?" I asked, letting the surprise I felt reign in my voice.

He wouldn't look at me, staring instead at the ground. Even in the dim light of the booth I could tell he was blushing; a deep pink suffused his ears that his Mohawk couldn't hide.

"You know I don't...I mean, I like you but not like that, you know I..." I trailed off. I mean, really!

Hello, Darrel? Gay girl, remember?

"I... I know," he mumbled, still not able to look at me. "I just, um, it's just..." He gave a heavy breath then finally raised his eyes to mine for a heartbeat, then dropped his gaze again. "You are so..."

"So, so what?" I asked a bit angrily and wanting some clarification. "Nice? Cute? *Gay?*" My voice rose with some of that anger on that last one, and he dropped his eyes to the floor again.

Jesus H. Christ. And a couple of saints, too.

I'd known Darrel, for some time now. He was extremely good looking, he was an outrageous flirt, and I knew he almost always got at least one blow job in the booth on every night he DJ'd, if not two or more—and usually not the same girl. He was the original "fuck 'em and forget 'em" poster child and I was getting really pissed off that he thought he could pull that shit with me—especially knowing that I was absolutely not interested.

"Thanks for covering for me," I finally told him flatly. I grabbed the door again, then swung it open. "I'll see you tomorrow."

I stepped through and turned to close the door behind me, but Darrel stepped up and grabbed the edge of it before I could shut it completely.

"You're so beautiful, Nina," he said quietly, finally looking at me directly.

I stared at him for a long moment, then shook my head in negation and rolled my eyes as I turned away. I heard the door finally shut behind me.

What the fuck, Darrel likes me? I thought confusedly as I made my way to where I'd seen Candace last. Maybe I shouldn't have been so surprised though, because with the exception of the five o'clock shadow that graced his cheeks and of course, his Mohawk, he looked almost exactly like his sister. His lips even felt similar, well, except for the stubble, I thought wryly, remembering of her grey eyes.

Well whatever, because that was enough of that, though, I was on a mission and I probably said hello to everyone in the club and on the dance floor before I finally found Candace in the ladies room, checking her hair in the mirror.

"Hey there!" I greeted with a grin into her reflection as I slid into the spot next to her and put an arm lightly around her waist. "Let's go."

She dropped her hands from her hair and turned to face me. I kept my hand on her waist.

"Now?" she asked, while the shine of her eyes and the delicious curve that grew along her lips told me I'd made the right decision. "You mean, right now?"

Mm. Her tones and accent were so alluring that as her hands fluttered up to play with my collar, I felt a desperate need to just forget about everything—dinner, whatever—and take her home, if we made it that far. Darrel was absolutely right—she was so fucking hot—but I didn't really need him to tell me that.

From her smile to the surge in my blood, I already knew it.

I didn't give into that feeling, that pull on my blood, completely, though. Instead, I let it show in my voice as I leaned in close to whisper in her ear. "Well," I drawled, blowing softly behind her ear, "I do recall you were thinking in French." I nuzzled her neck a bit, gently pulling at the skin with my lips.

"That's nice." Candace exhaled and arched her throat towards me. "I thought you couldn't read minds," she reminded me as she twined her arms around my neck.

I placed light kisses along that center column, until she shifted slightly to lay butterfly kisses in the hollow above my collarbone.

"Only in French," I reminded her as my eyes closed and I enjoyed the sensations she was giving me. Oh... My brain groaned at me. Just forget going home, the car is closer. "I can't read minds in French."

I twisted my head away and sought her mouth with mine and tonight's kiss tasted like cherries and bubble-gum. As that kiss deepened, Candace's fingertips moved from behind my neck to place a light patter of touches from my neck to my chest. We really had to leave...

I brought my hands up to her face and as I did, Darrel's little parting gift fell from my hand where I had held it all this time, and it slid down Candace's shoulder. That did distract her.

"What was that?" she asked, breaking our kiss.

"Nothing, nothing of importance," I assured her, brushing my lips right behind her jaw. I straightened my shoulders and looked around.

The bathroom had started to get a bit crowded—whether it was because our little make-out session had drawn a crowd or because it was merely that communal time—whatever we were going to do, it couldn't continue here. Most of the women either acted bored or impatient as they waited, and as I caught the eye of one or two, they blushed and looked away.

I didn't care though, because unless this was their first visit to the club, I was definitely not the only woman who had kissed another in that bathroom or any other place in the club. For some of the patrons, that was part of the attraction, and definitely part of the club's reputation.

Fuck the occasional total straights that came in there, though. They either came for the show, or they left soon enough. I did mention earlier that this was one of the coolest places to see and be seen—and that meant a lot try-sexual activity. There, in the corner by the sink, was proof. Two girls I'd observed on the dance floor with what I was pretty sure had been their boyfriends, were leaning together face-to-face, stroking each other's hair, laying occasional kisses on each other's cheek, trying to get up the courage to take it to that next step.

I know what that's like, I thought to myself with a smile.

I glanced back at Candace, who had noticed what I had. "Do you want to get going?" I grinned at her, and indicated the girls in the corner with my chin.

She glanced their way, then looked at me again. "I thought we already had," Candace murmured with a small grin and caught my hand with hers. "Yeah, let's go."

I led the way through the press to the door and as we passed the girls by the sink, a sudden inspiration made me pause.

"Hey there." I greeted each of them with a smile. The first was a very pretty girl with a deep tan, and red and gold streaks in her dark hair, whose back was against the counter. The other was an equally stunning almond-eyed brunette, who looked slightly familiar to me; from somewhere other than the club, I mean.

Well, Staten Island really was a small place in many ways, after all. Maybe I'd seen her on the bus on the way to school or something over the years. "How you doing?" I asked.

To their credit, while they may have both blushed, they neither stopped holding hands nor changed positions. Why is that to their credit? Because it meant that they weren't ashamed or embarrassed. Good for them. Maybe I'd have to reevaluate my estimation of their male companions' status as boyfriends.

"Okay," answered the girl with the tan noncommittally, with a slight shrug. Her head bent closer to her companion's shoulder.

"Fine, thanks," answered the other. "You spin great tunes by the way, really love these Experience Nights." She beamed shyly.

"Thank you," I told her, eyes wide and honestly taken aback.

I hadn't thought I'd be recognized. Perhaps that was foolish. I mean, it's not as if I was completely invisible up at the booth and let's face it, neither my hair nor my attire were non-descript, especially when I was working. And quite frankly, as long as I was still in the club, I was still on the job, especially since this was supposed to be one of "my" nights.

"Oh, you're DJ Nina!" exclaimed the girl with the tan in dawning realization. I smiled as I noticed her arm steal around her companion's waist. "You really play great music!" she said and smiled at me with obvious enthusiasm.

"Thanks, thanks a lot, really," I said sincerely as I blushed a bit myself. "It's very nice of you to say that."

From the corner of my eye, I could see Candace pull her phone out of the bag slung from her shoulder.

The brunette stuck a hand out at me. "Oh, I'm Gina by the way," she introduced and I shook her hand "and this is—"

"Mary," the tan girl interrupted, putting out her free hand. "I'm Mary."

"Nice to meet both of you," I answered with a grin, "and right now, it's just Nina, Nina Boyd." I shook her hand as well. "And this is…" and I turned to find her staring at me as she spoke into the phone. "Candace."

She shook her head a moment and instantly her expression changed. "Hullo, girls." She waved then directed her attention back to her phone. "Yes, on Bay Street, wonderful." She closed her phone with a snap.

"We'll have a car in ten minutes," she announced with satisfaction. "So let's go have a drink in the front while we wait?" she asked, offering me her arm.

"Oh, okay," I answered, slipping my arm through hers.

I turned back to Gina and Mary. "Nice meeting you guys." I smiled. "You have a great night."

"You too," and "Nice to meet you too, Nina," they answered severally as we left.

"Oh, by the way?" I turned back and asked.

They now had their arms around each other and looked up in inquiry.

"Don't do anything I wouldn't do," I said and winked at them.

They laughed as Candace and I left.

"Barbarian!" she jokingly scolded, lightly slapping my bicep.

"That's 'colonist' to you," I smiled and licked my teeth as we made our way to the front bar. "You called a car?" I asked. "So we're going to, what was it, Port Mar See?" I exaggerated my bad pronunciation to see if I could get a rise out of her.

"Port Marseille," she corrected, obviously amused. "You aren't going to let the 'colonist' thing go, are you?" she asked, her hand rubbing my bicep she had just slapped as we walked through the hall arm in arm.

"Hmm…" I considered playfully. "You know what? 'Colonist' is such a novel thing to be called," I answered, smiling to take any possible sting out of that. "I mean, I've been called many things, but still…"

Stopping as we reached the front of the Cadillac bar a few feet from the door. I freed my arm from hers, put my hands on my hips and faced her. "I think it's going to take some time for me to recover," I told her in mock seriousness.

"Well, then," she said and smiled coyly at me. She brought her fingertips to the edge of my neckline while she played with my collar. "Let me buy you a drink and we can let the reparations begin."

I traced gentle lines down her cheeks with my fingertips and her skin was so very smooth. "Oh, so now you're trying to seduce me with your decadent European sophistication?" I asked with a small smile of my own. "Besides, you can't."

"Can't what?" she asked in a throaty whisper, kissing my ear. "Seduce you?"

I closed my eyes and let her continue. "You can't buy me a drink," I murmured as she licked the hollow in my throat. "I work here—it's one of the perks. So, what would you like?"

"You…" she said, nipping lightly on my neck "…on silk."

That sounded really good to me too and as her lips reached the hollow of my throat, a light growl escaped me. As I turned my head, I opened my eyes and realized—the club. We were still in the club. We were supposed to be leaving and I was supposed to be doing something.

Oh yeah!

Drinks!

I was getting those. "I meant…what would you like to drink?" I finally sputtered. "Since you're getting dinner, let me get you a drink."

Candace trailed her fingertips up and down the column of neck as she straightened. "You know," she said thoughtfully and smiled, "that's not a bad idea. Do you recommend anything specifically?"

"I do recommend you stay away from doing pitchers of Red Death," I told her, ruefully twisting my lips as I remembered my recent occasion of over indulgence.

Oh, but I did have an idea. "Would you mind if I surprise you?"

"Hmmm, surprise away then," she said. "I'm sure you've got good taste, if your looks and your musical choice are any indication, obviously." She waved at me with her hand.

"Great, I'll be right back." I excused myself and walked to the end of the bar. "Hi, Dee Dee!" I called to the bartender, yet another stunning example of women the powers-that-be have placed on this earth.

A statuesque "five foot twelve" as she called it, Dee Dee had light brown skin, very curly blonde hair and startlingly hazel eyes that shaded from golden amber to an incredible light green, depending on her mood. Honestly, I couldn't tell you what I found most attractive about her—her eyes, her personality, or her drop-dead gorgeous accent.

She was just purely sexy all around.

Born in Bonn, Germany, of a Japanese-American father who'd been stationed there while in the army and the wife he'd brought there from Port-Au-Prince, Dee Dee (the living example of how beautiful human beings would be if we all just got along) had come to the United States to finish her education and went to the local private college where she was getting a master's degree in chemistry—which was probably why she was such a great bartender in the first place, sort of an extension of natural talent, I guess.

Why she lived and worked on Staten Island was beyond me, but I knew that I for one, was glad she was there.

"Hallo, Nina!" She glanced up at me from a cocktail she'd been mixing. "You're well tonight?" she asked, tossing a little flurry of ice flakes on the concoction she'd just finished and passing it to the waiting customer.

"I am...*wunderbar*!" I answered, using the only German word—wonderful—that I knew as she came over to me.

Well, there were a few others, like *hamburger*, *achtung* and *mach schnell*, but I don't think any one of those would have been appropriate, especially since I'd learned them watching movies.

"*Wunderbar*, eh?" she asked, raising her eyebrows, and widening her eyes at me. "And is that the reason?" She pointed with her chin towards Candace, who was watching from a window for the awaited car.

I looked with her then glanced down at the bar to hide the rising red in my cheeks. "Maybe," I said and smiled, because I couldn't help it. "Can't it just be a beautiful summer night?"

Dee Dee pursed her lips in what I recognized as amusement and picked up a glass. "Right. A beautiful night. Yet another for you, then?" she asked with a little smirk as she focused on polishing the glass.

"I don't know what you're talking about," I told her with as straight a face as I could muster. "Most summer nights are beautiful, don't you think?" I cocked my head inquisitively at her.

"Hmph," Dee Dee snorted, putting the glass down and wiping the bar. "What I think," she told me with a raised eyebrow, "is that you are going to get lai—"

"Lady-like?" I jumped in, interrupting before she could finish the word. "Lazy? How about literal or better yet, literary?" I smiled even wider. "Shall we discuss our favorite authors?"

I don't know why I wouldn't let her say "laid." It's not like I didn't know what it meant. It's just, well, it didn't seem right or polite somehow, as if it would be disrespectful, both to me and to Candace. That's it—it would have been disrespectful, and I didn't want that.

"Hah!" Dee Dee laughed, and threw the rag down under the counter. "Good for you, Nina." Her cheeks dimpled slightly as she looked me up and down with unmistakable approval. "Good for you. So," she continued, "what do you want at my bar?" She spread both hands on the counter to lean on her elbows and talk with me.

"We're going out for a late dinner, French, so what do you recommend?" If anyone knew what went with what, it was the bartender, and Dee Dee was one of the best.

"Hmm. " She pursed her lips and considered. "Start with a merlot? Or, what about a white?" She moved to another part of the counter and searched under the bar.

"Here—" she presented me with two glasses "—start with white for now—" and she filled the glasses about halfway "—for a fresh palate and—" she moved to a shelf and came back with a dark bottle "—finish with a good Bordeaux!" She put the bottle on the counter in front of me.

I stared at the bottle. "You're not seriously giving this to me?" I asked, stunned. Even with drinks on the house, that was a pretty pricey gesture.

"Why not?" Dee Dee shrugged. "You never really get anything from the bar. Most of the time, that is." Her lip curled slyly. Besides," she continued, "this way you will impress her and you can get, um, literary." That sly curve twitched when I raised an eyebrow at her.

But still, I was rather doubtful, I mean, I would have rather paid for it and said so.

"Nina, you make the club lots and lots of money, think of it as bonus!" she insisted. "Now, go!" Dee Dee ordered. "Go give her the glass, and I will put this in a bag for you." She waved her hands at me, shooing me along. "Well, what are you waiting for?" she demanded, a hand on her shapely hip when I didn't move fast enough.

"I'm going, I'm going." I raised my hands in mock alarm and jumped away from the bar, taking the wine glasses with me.

"Don't forget the Bordeaux!" Dee Dee called to my back.

"I won't!" I assured over my shoulder and I carefully returned to Candace, trying not to spill anything anywhere. I didn't want Dee Dee's rag to make a sudden and snappy appearance near me or even worse, on me.

I had a very visceral memory of the sponge: you know, the you've-got-some-dirt-on-your-face, come-here-and-let-me-clean-it-for-you stinky sponge that every household in creation has. Not that Dee Dee's rag was like that, she was a bleach fanatic. It's just, well, that's what it made me think of. I shuddered, remembering the nasty, wet smell of that sponge, but controlled my hands quickly—I didn't want to spill the wine!

"Try this," I offered a glass to Candace as I neared, relieved to not have to balance it anymore.

"Thank you," she said as she lifted the stem from my fingers. "White wine for a fresh palate?" She swirled the wine, then held it up. "To a beautiful summer night?"

I stared a moment, surprised to hear the words I'd said moments ago to Dee Dee, but I recovered quickly enough. "To a beautiful summer night," I agreed.

Candace lightly tapped her glass to mine, then took a sip. I did the same—not bad, not too dry, not too sweet. Knowing Dee Dee, it was probably a German Rhein.

"Very nice," Candace commented contemplatively. "Wonderful in fact." She sipped again, finishing the glass.

I nodded in agreement and did the same.

"So, ready to go?" she asked, looking at me from her glass. "Because I think…" and she peered out the window "…yes, our car is here."

"Oh yeah, would you just, um, " I glanced over at the bar, "give me a moment?" I took her empty glass.

I wasn't going to forget Dee Dee's gift since she was so politely insistent, and I figured it certainly wouldn't hurt my karma if I made the waitresses' job a bit easier and brought the empty glasses back to the bar.

"Certainly," Candace shrugged good naturedly and touched my shoulder. "I'll meet you in the car then?"

"Great. I'll be right there." Back to the bar I went.

Dee Dee hurried over, package in hand, as I approached.

"Here," she announced, placing medium-sized baby-blue gift bag on the counter as I set the glasses to one side. "If you don't get to discuss your books, it will not be the fault of the wine!"

She laughed as I peered into the bag. She had wrapped the bottle in black tissue paper and placed a little silver ribbon around the top. As I reached into the bag for it, Dee Dee stopped me.

"No, that is for later, after the books!" Dee Dee grinned with almost-secret mirth, "Promise?"

"Fine, I promise," I agreed, still wondering what it was.

Impulsively, I leaned over the counter and kissed her on the cheek. "Thank you," I told her warmly. "That was just so very nice of you," I explained as I leaned back on my side of the bar.

Dee Dee stood up straight, put her hands on her hips and nodded her head from side to side, just looking and smiling a wide smile at me, so I just smiled back in sincere appreciation.

"So, go!" she shooed finally, picking up her rag to wave it at me. "What are you waiting for?"

"Have a great night, Dee Dee," I wished her as I lifted the bag from the bar and made my way to the door.

"French—hah!" I heard her call to my back, "You let me know when you want *real* food, *liebchen*!"

I laughed as I walked out the door, visions of sausage and sauerkraut with large mugs of beer in my head, although maybe I was wrong. I'd have to investigate, I thought, just to make sure—and maybe bring some Southern Champagne, otherwise known as Coca-Cola with me, just in case it was truly well, whatever. Coke would make it all better.

I was still thinking about Coke as I walked to the car, owned by one of the many local companies that exist on the Island. For whatever reason, there are no yellow cabs or gypsy cabs on Staten Island; the county doesn't allow them. If you want a car, you have to call and reserve one. That's just the way it is.

Most of them seem exactly like regular cars and don't have any identifying marks except the phone number on the door. But I could tell which one I was going to because the door was still open for me.

"There you are!" Candace exclaimed as I slid in and closed the door.

"Where we going again, ma'am?" the driver asked as I settled the bag by my feet. I didn't know, of course, so Candace gave him directions.

"By the way, earlier, did you say your surname is Boyd?" Candace asked with studied nonchalance as she settled into her seat.

I could tell it was an act, though, because her eyes were way-wide and she pursed her lips too tightly.

"Yes, why? What's yours?" I asked her with a grin, trying to set her at ease. You know, for a moment there, she'd looked as if she'd seen a ghost.

Candace blinked and recovered herself, "Oh it's...I didn't hear you clearly, that's all. Mine is Neills, by the way, Candace Lindsay Neills, actually."

"Well," I grinned, "it's nice to officially meet you, by the by." I held out my hand.

Actually, I was surprised at myself that I hadn't told her before—I usually always tell people because there was one thing that really, really, bugged me, to the point where I had promised myself I wasn't going to do it. What is it with lesbians and no last names? That just so pisses me off...

Sorry.

Had to share.

Back to the cab now.

Candace stared at, then finally shook my hand. "The pleasure is all mine," she grinned back. "So then, what's in the bag?" she asked, reaching over me for it.

I caught her shoulders as she lunged across my lap.

"Hey, that's for later," I smiled as she looked up at me and I released her. "It's supposed to be a surprise."

Candace twisted her body so that she faced me, and she reached her arm across my legs to lean on her hand. "Confident, aren't you?" she commented and smirked at me. Her free hand reached around my head and pulled me towards her.

"Now, now," I admonished as my mouth closed in on hers and I wrapped my arms around her waist. "That's colonist to you." I lightly flicked my tongue between her lips, then slid it in.

Oh, but she could kiss, and when she sucked on my tongue, squeezing it with her mouth, the sensation sent a chill down my throat, through my chest and shooting through my stomach. I could actually feel my lower abs tingle with want, not to mention everything else. *Great technique,* I observed as I enjoyed. *I'll have to try it sometime.* And I did, the very next second I could.

We made out the whole way to Manhattan and by the time we got to the restaurant, I was stretched out along the back seat with my back against the little side window and Candace on top of me.

Somehow, the driver got paid and we stumbled out of the car, bag in one hand and the rest of me busy with Candace. I don't know how we got through dinner, but I do remember that the maître d' gave us a private table. In between feeding each other with our fingertips, sharing glasses of wine and trading little kisses all throughout, I don't even know what we ate, never mind how we left the place or came to the conclusion that we would go to hers. It made sense though—it was definitely closer and positively more private than mine.

Finally, somehow, maybe the Bordeaux we'd opened as we walked had teleported us, we were in her apartment—somewhere on 6th and Avenue A, I think—and in her bedroom, the Bordeaux half gone as I sat on the edge of the bed and poured out another pair of glasses on her night table.

Candace lay on her side propped on an elbow, watching me through hooded eyes and wearing nothing but her boots. "I love the way that looks on you," she purred, an appreciative look in her eyes.

I glanced at myself then back at her. "Glad you like it, since you requested it," I reminded, and smiled wryly at her.

It had been an unspoken yet understood thing between us tonight—despite the fact that I doubt there had been any question in either of our minds that this was exactly where we'd end up—we weren't rushing, perhaps to compensate for the last time. No matter what the reason may have been, we teased, we tortured, we tantalized each other to that promise of sex and while we mauled each other on the way through her apartment to her bedroom, we slowed as we got to through that door and Candace fumbled for, then found, the light switch.

We blinked at each other for a moment in the half-light then kissed each other languidly. She removed the bottle and the bag from my hands and led me to the bed. I slowly rolled her dress up and off her and she rolled mine down. I have to say, that as sexy and revealing as Lycra combined with whatever other material can be, it's actually not that easy to remove; it's for looking, not for touching, that's for sure, and we giggled a bit as we fumbled with the stretchy fabrics.

We stopped kissing and caressing a moment when Candace grabbed my jacket from where it had landed.

"Would you wear this?" she asked me with a gorgeously sensual twist to her so-pretty lips.

Wordlessly, I put it on and Candace slipped her arms beneath it, pressing her skin to mine.

Wine.

I had to have some wine before I just fucked her again and again.

"Wine," I muttered hoarsely, gasping for air. "I need a drink."

Which was how we ended up as we were at the moment, as I handed her a glass.

Candace accepted it with a smile and held her glass up to me in a silent toast and I matched the gesture. Candace sat up to twine her arm around mine and switch drinks so that I'd have hers and she'd have mine. We each took a sip and then, it was time, and more than. I placed my glass on the night stand and leaned into her, kissing her neck, gently leaning her back onto the pillows.

Our mouths met again as I slowly lowered my body over hers and as I shifted more fully onto the bed, she reached a leg over mine and urged me between her thighs. "Are you okay?" I murmured softly in genuine concern, propping myself up on my hands so I could see her expression for myself and know for sure.

Candace looked up at me, raised her arms over head a moment, then placed them on my ass, running soft trails with her fingertips up and down my spine under the jacket. "Fabulous," she smirked into my eyes, then brought her glance to my chest. "Magnificent, your breasts are magnificent," and she brought her hands away from my back to touch them, tracing their contours, filling her hands with them.

I arched my back, pressing my lower body into her and my nipples into her palms. My eyes closed when her thighs came up to embrace my hips and she tilted hers in such a way that that lovely cunt of hers met mine. I opened my eyes again when her hand reached between us to spread those luscious lips—hers and mine—and I don't know which one of us sighed as my aching hard clit moved against hers, sliding and grinding in warm wetness.

I spread my thighs and pressed them against her, increasing the contact and the pressure, moving slowly, building the sensation.

"Oh, this is wonderful," Candace moaned, and I admired her expression, open-mouthed and head back below me.

When her eyes finally met mine, she smiled, then reached for the wine. She took a sip, then passed it to me.

I took it from her, riding her pussy in a smooth, languid wave as I straightened my spine and tossed my head back to drink. "Mmph, it is," I agreed, handing her back the glass.

She set it on the table and reached to shut of the lamp.

"Don't," I requested rather breathily, and Candace's eyes questioned me.

"Don't shut off the light. I like to watch," I explained, a sensual smile gracing my lips as I rolled my hips and slid against her in such a way that she arched her neck, and pressed even harder against me.

"Kinky," she breathed out as she undulated under me, the muscles in her stomach rippling and her breasts heaving. "I like it."

"You're the one who insisted I keep the jacket on," I reminded her.

I picked up the pace, my movements a little sharper, harder, just more deliberate and Candace her spread her legs further as her cunt licked mine. Occasionally my clit would slide right into her and we'd both gasp.

"Oh, yeah," I breathed when her hands grabbed my ass, squeezing and massaging the muscles, pulling me closer to her.

Legs spread wide, her ass moved with the rhythm I now set and I tossed off the jacket so I could feel free. I grabbed each of her ankles in turn and pulled her boots off—and tossed them wherever.

"Yes, yes," she hissed, her clit thumping solidly against mine as we drove for that final push, unable to tell whether she was moving me or I was moving her.

Her fingers scraped up my spine and down my shoulders to my ass and I arched into the added sensation, tossing my head back and lifting my upper body, power building as I felt heat rush up from my happily-moving cunt, a flush that rose steadily up my stomach.

"Oh God, you are beautiful," Candace gasped as we fucked in desperate earnestness, that hot slide a pussy-pounding glorious sensation. "Fucking magnificent," she breathed again and her hands came off my ass to trail across my shoulders and my breasts and when I felt a drop of sweat slide down my neck and I opened my eyes to look at Candace, really see her, she wiped it away with a finger, then just so sensuously slid that finger in her mouth.

"Ooh," I groaned as I watched her, the erotic thrill adding to the roll of my hips, "Fuck...yes. "

I wanted so much to feel more while the sensual haze I'd been caught in slipped away. She scratched a sharp trail down my rigid biceps, then squeezed my ribs before moving back down to my hips.

"Fuck, yes," Candace echoed, "fuck, yeah, oh, yeah, yeah!" She groaned, her hands clenching and unclenching my ass.

Her face revealed an almost unearthly beauty as her head tossed back and her cunt strained in mine. "You're pussy is just so goddamn *hot*, " I told her. "You…are *so*…fucking…hot!"

When that crimson flush began to crawl up her body, painting her breasts with a rosy glow, she arched her back and pulled me into her as hard as she could. "Oh fuck," she groaned and I could actually feel her clit throb against mine as her hips bucked, her thighs squeezing my waist.

"That's it, baby," I encouraged, firmly holding her hips so that no matter how she moved, the pressure would stay where she needed it most.

For myself, honestly, I felt nothing.

Nada.

Zippo.

I don't know why that happened, but it did. One moment, I'd be riding the wave and getting to the top and another, well, I might as well be playing in the bathtub for whatever that was worth.

But if only one of us was going to come, I was glad it would be her.

I would make sure of it.

"Oh yeah, that's it, that's it!" Candace ground out from her clenched jaw, her body tensed under me, the tendons evident in her neck and shoulders as her hands dug into me, and I felt a pleasant rush shoot from my chest to my head.

"God, Nina…" she purred as her legs relaxed and she rolled her head from side to side a bit as she lightly stroked my lower back. "What did you just do to me?"

I rest my head on her chest a moment and I stroked her arms lightly as I caught my breath. I could hear the deep and steady pounding of her heart.

"Hmmm…" I exhaled. "What felt right, I guess," I answered honestly. "Did you like that? I mean, did you…" I leaned up on an elbow to see her face.

Candace stretched under me, bringing her arms over her head. "Come?" she filled in for me and smiled. "Can't you tell?" she teased and brought a hand to my shoulder and the other skimmed my nose, while I played with the tendrils of hair near her temple. "But you didn't though," she stated softly, the corners of her luminous eyes crinkling with observation.

I smiled gently. "It's okay," I reassured her, then nuzzled her neck. "I like making you come," I whispered as I slid my body down hers and painted circles on her breast with my tongue.

"Oh..." she groaned softly as her nipple hardened between my lips "...but Nina... "

I switched my attention from one breast to the other and I twirled the one wet from my mouth between my fingertips as hers dug lovely trails up my neck. "Shhh..." I gentled her and kissed the center of her chest. "Let me..." I trailed off and licked a path to her navel, scratching lightly down her ribs.

Her hips jumped beneath me a moment and I could feel the hair from her pussy rub against my sternum.

"Fine then," she sighed as I fit my shoulders between her legs and lightly bit and licked at her thigh. "So," she breathed, "what do you think of French?" she asked in an attempt at conversation.

"Well..." I paused a moment, glancing up at her. Her eyes were closed and her head tilted back, exposing the long length of her throat and opening up her breasts to my view. "*Je comprends le Français un peu,*" I told her in mock seriousness, then sucked on the tendon that ran from her thigh to the light brown hair of her pussy. That brought me another rewarding, somewhat anticipatory groan, and Candace shifted her hips. "*Eh, je parle un peu,*" I told her as I brought my hands up to her hips, and my thumbs massaged along the edges of her lips. "*Mais, pas très bien,*" I finished, grinning at her.

Candace leaned up on her elbows too look at me. "You understand a little French and, you speak a little?" she asked, shaking her head incredulously.

I blew softly on the curls before me before answering. "*Mais, pas très bien,*" I reminded her.

"But not very well," she translated, then smiled at me in appreciation of the joke. "Is there anything else about you I should know, you wicked, clever girl?"

I drew my lower lip up against the length of her lips before answering. "Yes," I breathed against her, "I'm an American, not an idiot—they're not synonymous, so no more assumptions." I lightly parted her lips with my thumbs. I glanced at her a moment, my eyes glinting with humor.

"And you were right," I whispered. "I am a colonist." I flicked the tip of my tongue against her clit then drew it into my lips.

CHANGE YOUR PRETTY MIND
SEND A PERFECT HERO FOR ONE DAY
RIDE RIGHT IN—TAKE ALL THE PAIN AWAY
THE HERO HALO'S BROKEN—ANOTHER LIE IS SPOKEN
AND I'VE A BROKEN HEART WHEN THE IMAGE FALLS APART

"Lead Me On"—JD Glass

IT'S FUNNY.

After I picked up my guitar, I locked myself in the only private place in the apartment—the bathroom—and played for three hours, enjoying its full and glorious voice: well, as full as it could be without an amplifier, anyway. When I finally came up for air and realized I had to go to work that night, I gently lay my guitar into its hardshell case and for the first time, I really could see just how beautiful the instrument actually appeared: a beautiful amber-honey burst.

The sound and feel of it had so entranced me since the first moment I'd played it in the shop, I didn't even know what color it was until that moment. It wouldn't have mattered if it was avocado green with pink stripes. It played with delicious ease and sounded so incredibly fine.

Okay, maybe avocado green and pink stripes might have mattered, but still, it wasn't an eyesore, it was both functionally and visually beautiful.

Funny thing. Despite the fact that Cap, Jackie, and Trace had all gone to high school together, I always got the feeling that, somehow, Cap was older, though he wasn't—not at all.

I'd mentally thanked him and added a note to the end of his:

You, dude, are awesome. Thank you. Nina.

I played every day (still do, in fact), getting used to the different feel of an electric guitar as opposed to an acoustic in my hands in those first few weeks of having it, and that night, like the first, I reluctantly slid the case into the walk-in closet in Cap's room and went to work.

I was still actively avoiding my roommates: Cap was always working anyway, Jackie still had no kind words for me, and Trace, well, the whole thing just confused me.

Since I didn't know what to do with my feelings, I decided I'd better get my head clear before we spoke again rather than be so off-balance when I saw her. Given the mutual work-shift craziness and my penchant for traveling into Manhattan and staying over at Candace's on occasion (well, not staying exactly—I never really slept there—I went back to Staten Island—"the Rock"—around sunup), it was pretty easy not to see anyone.

I was coming home kinda late. I'd stopped at a local studio so I could finally plug in my guitar and play it at its full honey-throated throttle. I had a bona fide, honest-to-goodness possible new band audition/meeting the next day, and I wanted to be more than ready for it. After I'd played till my time was up, I'd stepped out to pay for it and ended up speaking with the owner, and then some guys came in, and the next thing you know, we were back in the studio just jamming out some tunes for fun.

Needless to say, this had put me in a really great mood, so when I rounded the landing on the second floor and came running right into Trace, it didn't throw me as far off-track as it could have.

"Hey Trace," I greeted her with my usual smile. Ah what the hell, right? I was feeling way too good, the rhythm and the melodies running through me head and as I shifted my gig bag on my shoulder, my fingers twitched with playing memory.

"Hey yourself," she drawled back, the beginning of a smile edging her lips.

"Off to work?" I asked. It wouldn't be unusual for her to pick up a night shift.

She hesitated a moment before she answered. "No, just, you know, hanging out. You?"

I smiled widely, I was too happy to contain it. "Actually, just getting back—from the studio," I told her. "I have an audition tomorrow."

Trace nodded and smiled and when she did, her eyes grew wide and deep. "That's really cool, Nina, really cool. You're gonna do great," she said with the warmth she usually had for me in private.

"Yeah, well, we'll see how it goes, you know?" I answered. "I'm a little nervous," I admitted.

"Well, you know the cure for that, right?" she asked with a grin.

I kinda sorta thought I did—preparation and focus—but maybe she had a better idea. "What?"

"A good run—gets the nerves right out."

I smiled again despite myself—that was pretty much my daily habit anyway. "I was kinda sorta gonna do that anyway." I grinned at her.

"Ah," she grinned back, "but it's always better with company. Want some?"

That startled me. It had been so long since we'd really spoken and even longer since we'd run together, especially after what had happened between us.

Well…I thought about it. Oh hell, why not, right? Maybe we'd be able to communicate, maybe there was some way we could work things out.

"Yeah sure, that'd be really cool," I agreed.

"Set then," Trace returned, clapping her hands together briskly. "Come get me in the morning?"

"Sure. Cool."

"Yeah, cool."

We said our good-byes and I continued up the stairs to my apartment. I took loving care of my guitar, checking out the strings, wiping off the fingerprints, and then giving it a good polish before I carefully put it away. I took a few moments to pick out what I'd wear the next day, took a shower, then hit the bed after I snapped my little light on and I made sure I left enough room for Jackie when she got home.

So, bright and early, I carefully wiggled out from the bed, holding my breath so I wouldn't wake Jackie and I was dressed and ready in moments. I hurried quietly down the stairs to Trace's apartment in the early morning silence.

I knocked, but no answer. *Probably still asleep,* I figured, so I let myself in like I'd done a thousand times before and made my way to her bedroom. I opened the closed door, expecting to find Trace in bed.

I did.

She leaned over the mattress, forearms braced against it as Van pumped her furiously from behind. She must have heard me open the door because her expression turned from a curious, somewhat inward concentration, to concern.

"Nina—wait," she called out to me as she straightened up, trying to shake Van off her.

He snaked an arm around her waist and she slapped it.

The sound snapped me out of my shock and I shook my head as I closed the door.

"Get the fuck off me," I heard her tell him as I walked to the exit and I heard the sound of hurried feet as I made my way down the hallway.

I got to the front door and opened it.

"Nina!" Trace called from the hallway above.

"Later, Trace!" I called, waving my hand behind me.

I didn't look back once as I shut the door. I went for my run, hating my stupidity and the look on Van's face when he finally opened his eyes and saw me. That fucking smirk—like Trace was a toy we were fighting over.

Bastard.

Like he even really cared about her.

I ran for miles—I don't know how far.

Dumb...dumb...

Dumb.

That word beat itself into my head with every other breath I took. In between, all I could think of was how everybody kept saying I was cute, how they treated me like I was just some stupid kid with a cool haircut.

I couldn't talk to anyone: Nico wasn't around, he had his own stuff to do for school, Jackie would ignore me at best, try to tell me how I'd misunderstood because I was so uninformed at the next level, or tell me how I'd brought it on myself or it was my fault anyway, at worst.

I didn't know what Cap would say, but as much as I liked him, I wasn't as close to him as I had been to either Trace or Jackie; and I didn't think watching porno was the answer to all issues.

Forget talking about anything with my parents—we were only first being civilized to one another. Anything that reminded them that I was gay wouldn't be helpful.

God, I missed them, though.

No. I needed my own space. The large walk in closet in Cappie's bedroom where I kept my guitar was about eight feet by five feet wide and by design quirk, it not only had a door in his room (which locked from the inside), but also an egress in the back—if you walked to the end of the wall, you'd discover an opening about two feet wide. Go through it and you were in the front closet by the entrance, and it had its own door.

Jackie could, as a "senior" roomie, close the door to "our" room whenever she wanted, especially if she had company. When that happened, I'd have to wait or get comfortable on the sofa, or Trace's.

Hmmm…maybe that's why I had previously spent so much time down at her place. But I didn't want to do that anymore—the sofa, or Trace's. And I was tired of always having to go to someone else's place if I wanted to spend time with them, too. So what if I had to walk through the closet? At least I'd have my own door. Besides, the closet thing was funny if you thought about it, and I've never been one to ignore an inherent irony.

The way I saw it, I really did pay more rent than Jackie, and Captain wasn't using that closet for anything except my guitar. Besides, it also had its own window, with a southeastern exposure. I love the light in the morning, and Jackie insisted that the room we share be blacked out, all the time.

I was tired of being in a small, dark, cramped space. I wanted to be able to read at night if I wanted, roll onto my back and smile back at the clouds in the morning, and not worry about jamming my elbows into anyone or being jammed in return.

I wanted to be able to draw on something other than my knees, or paint cramped up against the kitchen table, scrambling to put everything away when everyone came in, so my stuff or my work wouldn't get wrecked or worse. For whatever reason, having any of my stuff out like that tended to piss Jackie off, even if I kept it neat and contained.

But whatever.

And I really wanted my privacy.

Not that I had anything to hide or something like that, it's just that if I wanted to be alone with my thoughts, or my paints, or my guitar, or even just to read anything at all, I wanted to *really* be alone.

After what I'd seen this morning, I wanted, no, I *needed* to be alone.

I approached Captain about it that day, after I'd come back, showered and dressed from my morning run, and he'd finally come out of his room.

I sat at the kitchen table, which had been shoved up against the wall, two feet in from the entrance. Well, it wasn't the world's biggest apartment.

I had turned my chair so that I could rest my arm on the table, but I looked out onto the rest of the room, my back against the wall, drinking a cup of tea (Earl Grey, with milk and sugar, thanks), reading the hardcover graphic novel "Camelot 3000" for the who knows whatever time, and smoking a cigarette, my first of the day.

I figured I'd let my subconscious compose the words I'd need in my head, and entertain the forefront of my brain with futuristic sci-fi, King Arthur, his Round Table of knights, including a Tristaine who had been reincarnated as a woman. Besides, it got me away from my thoughts, which were beyond confusing at the moment.

I was just getting to the part where Tristan runs into and remembers her true love Isolde, when Captain stepped out of his bedroom door, dressed in the usual: the skin he was in.

"Coffee's made," I told him as he grunted a feeble hello and made his way to the counter.

"Thanks," he answered in tired surprise and I exhaled smoke calmly as I waited for him to join me at the table, cup in hand.

"No problem," I answered with a slight smile when he pulled out a chair.

I slid my cigarette pack and lighter across the table towards him and with another grateful nod, he took one and lit it, inhaling deeply.

"How ya doin', kid?" he asked me finally.

"I'm alright," I answered, and closed my book with one last look at the four-color panels, sliding it over by the wall, "How about you?"

"I'm good," he nodded, "just hunky-dory." He took a deep breath, then downed his coffee as I watched his face change from sleepy softness to a more alert tension. Not a negative thing, mind you. Captain was always pretty cheerful in the morning, it's just that I could see his brain was starting to engage.

I waited until he put his cup down with a small exhalation of satisfaction.

"That hit the spot," he smiled contentedly, and dragged on his cigarette. We sat for a few moments in companionable silence and I carefully gathered my words.

"Hey, Cap? I'd like to ask you something."

Something in my tone must have worried him, because his expression instantly cleared to concern. "You can ask me anything, you know that.

Everything okay?" he asked me with a furrowed brow. "Is Trace giving you shit? Do you need to—"

"No, no, nothing like that," I raised a hand and interrupted. Besides, I wasn't ready to talk about anything other than what I had in mind yet. "It's about the living arrangements. I'd like to propose a change." I launched into my request and explanation while Cap sat silently the whole time, his eyes focused on mine. "So," I concluded, "what do you think? I'm pretty quiet anyway, you know that, and I've never been disrespectful of your things."

The silence dragged on, so long that I thought he'd say "No," until I saw the tiniest bit of a grin tugging at the corner of his lips. "Well you know, I have to think about it," he started, but the effort not to smile was too much and he burst out laughing.

"You bastard." I laughed as I wadded up a napkin and threw it at him. "You had me going for a moment there."

"I gotcha good!" he chortled, batting away at the second and third missiles I sent his way. "But..." and his face went somber, "there's one thing. I have to move something out of there, and I want you to know where it is. I also want you to know how to use it."

I stared a moment, puzzled as I tried to figure out what he meant. Oh, I got it! An "oh" of understanding formed itself on my lips.

Of course...he had a large footlocker in there, and he was a cop. He could only mean one thing: his gun.

"Oh," I said. What else was there to say?

"In fact," Cap continued, "are you free this afternoon?" He watched me expectantly.

"Um, yeah, I don't even have to work tonight, I was just going to catch up on some stuff," I answered. "What do you have in mind?"

Twenty minutes later, I was in the passenger seat of Cap's jeep and pulling into the lot of the local firing range, a huge one-story brick building with no windows. Well, I guess those just wouldn't be necessary, right?

I found myself in a little cubby staring down a lane at a tiny target that seemed to be at least a hundred yards away, with others separated by a distance of several feet on either side.

"Put these on—" he handed me a yellowish tinged pair of shooting glasses "—and these—" he handed me a pair of headphones "—but wait until after you fire your first shot."

I put the glasses on and curled the ends around my ears. I carefully placed the headphones on the rug-covered ledge that was slightly higher than waist high before me.

"Okay now," Cap began and I turned to face him.

He held a matte charcoal pistol in his hands, barrel pointed up, its profile facing me. It looked just like something out of a movie, any movie with a bad guy. In fact, it looked like a bad guy sort of weapon, not like the revolvers that officers seem to have either in their holsters on the street or even on screen.

First of all, it was metal, all metal, and second of all, there was no round chamber section—you know, like the ones you see cowboys twirl and—never mind.

"This is not my service revolver," Cap explained.

Well, yah, I figured that. But I said nothing—my mind was amazingly blank, all I could focus on was the fact that there was a real live gun in front of my eyes.

"This…" and he paused a moment, "is a Glock 9 millimeter. This…" and he clicked something and a cartridge fell out of the pistol grip and into his other hand "…is your ammo." He slid a finger into the cavity, and finding nothing, he slid the top forward and back. "In case there's a round in there—that'll pop it out. You never know," he cautioned me. "Okay, you load it like this—" he demonstrated, pointing the weapon towards the floor and sliding the cartridge home.

It made an audible snick sound. "Then set your safety." He turned the gun so I could watch him thumb it. "You try it." He handed it to me.

I was very conscious of its cold weight in my hands as I somehow managed to slip the release, the clip sliding out easily into my free hand. I examined it; it seemed full to me. Bullets practically bristled at the very top.

I turned back to the range so I wouldn't accidentally point the gun at someone. I admit it—I was afraid, and I didn't know if there just might somehow be a stray bullet in the chamber. "This a full clip?" I asked in as casual a tone I could muster as I sighted down the barrel of the hopefully empty gun. I handed it to him.

"Yeah, it should be," he answered, examining it carefully, "but you're doing the right thing, pointing it away from yourself or others—never look down the barrel, there could always be an unfired round in the chamber."

He put a very gentle hand on my shoulder; I guess he could tell I was scared. "Here," he handed me the clip, "now before you put this in, check and see if there's anything in there."

I checked as I had seen Cap do it, and slid a finger in. I felt nothing other than the contours inside.

"Okay, now clear it and double check."

It took a moment to figure out, but I did it and safely checked the chamber. Nothing fell out so that had to be a good sign, right?

Man, I hoped so.

I glanced over my shoulder. Now what?

Cap answered my unvoiced question. "Load it, Nina. Load it...and shoot." He had put on his shooter's glasses.

I took the clip and slid it in. When it didn't click, I let it slide out about halfway. This time, I slapped it in with my palm and was rewarded with a solid "snick." I set the safety.

I looked at the target and carefully wrapped my right hand around the handle and my left cradled it for stability. Both thumbs were pointed at the target.

"Nice, Nina," Cap said softly behind me, "that's the way. Alright now, release the safety."

I eased my thumb over the safety and carefully curled a forefinger around the trigger.

"Whenever you're ready," Cap whispered behind me.

I swallowed and nodded nervously. Straightening a bit, I squared my shoulders and sighted as best I could to the target: a humanoid figure with a gun.

"You okay?" Cap asked behind me.

"Yeah, I'm fine... just trying to aim," I responded through dry lips.

In truth?

I was stalling—I didn't think I could do it: aim, shoot, hit the target. I was caught between scared and incompetent, and neither of those felt very good.

"If you're too scared, you could just watch me if you want," Cap offered, voicing my feelings. While his voice sounded friendly, I was sure I heard something else, not mockery or derision, exactly; more like a hint of disappointment, like he'd expected something different from me.

Great, now I'm not tough enough either, I thought.

This was just the end, the absolute living end. Not old enough, not smart enough, not enough of whatever it was Trace wanted, too cute, too intense, too stupid, too much me and just not right.

"I'm fine," came curtly out of my mouth.

I breathed out softly and in that same moment, I found my target line, then promised myself I wouldn't blink.

I pulled the trigger.

The blast was louder than I'd expected and seemed to echo in the concrete chamber as I looked around the range. I could feel the kickback from the shot in my hands; it felt like catching a baseball barehanded and my palms stung lightly.

My knuckles were white as I brought my hands down and rested the pistol on the ledge.

"Nice shooting!!" Cap enthused and clapped my shoulder, "let's take a look at it." He edged in next to me and pressed a button I hadn't noticed before. A chain creaked its way on a pulley, bringing the target back with it.

The paper fluttered and grew larger as it came closer and I could see the results for myself: a neat hole with slight scorch marks around the edges went through what had been the drawn shirt pocket of the figure.

"Man oh man, straight for the heart—great shot! You're a natural, Nina," Cap said excitedly. "Let's try that again." He pressed the button and as the chain wound its way back, another target appeared at the end.

I could smell something in the air, I didn't know what, and my ears still rung. Oh my God, I had a loaded gun in my hands and I was afraid to let go, to drop it, to move in any direction and accidentally hurt someone.

That kept repeating itself in my head, that I could decide at any second to turn that gun on Cap, on myself, at anyone and that would be that. I could kill someone, including myself, thanks to this thing in my hands.

How could someone not be overwhelmed by that? There was, there is, no other purpose for a gun—I couldn't use it to dig, or to plant, or to build. All it did was what it was made to do: to make holes in things, and maim or even kill living ones.

I couldn't find anything redeeming in that, and I couldn't put it down because I couldn't think or see any place that would be safe.

"Put the earphones on this time," Cap reminded me.

I cocked the safety with my thumb and pointed the gun to the floor and looked at him. "Um, which hand should I use?" I asked him, the nerves adding a touch more acid to my words than I'd meant. "The one that steadies it or the one that pulls the trigger?"

"Give me that," he laughed, "and put those on." He indicated with his chin towards the ledge where my 'phones sat.

I let my left hand relax off the grip, but still careful to point it down, I handed him the gun. I looked up and could see he had both a pair of green tinted shooting glasses and bright orange earphones on.

My rental ones were blue and they felt heavy as I slid them on, not at all like my DJ headphones.

"I'm gonna take a shot, okay?" Cap asked, his voice muffled and distant through the protective gear as he squeezed beside me to look out at the range.

"Yeah sure, go ahead," I answered as loudly as I could so he could hear me and nodding as well, just in case he didn't.

I backed out of his way as he leaned his elbows on the ledge and took aim.

"You so do not shoot like a girl," he chortled, thumbing the safety and taking position at the ledge.

I watched over his shoulder as the sound of a distant firecracker went off and light flared for a moment from the end of the pistol.

I tapped him on the shoulder and he turned his head in inquiry. "What's that supposed to mean?" I asked him with real curiosity and a touch of annoyance.

"I'll show you." He grinned and turning, he quickly set himself up and popped off another two rounds.

He pushed the recall button and as the target swung its way back to us, I could see three new holes: one next to mine, another in the belly and the third dead center of the pants zipper.

"You see," he explained, pointing, "girls tend to go for the gut and the groin, even when they're not looking at the target."

He pressed another button that would set up a new target, then glanced at me with a sidewise look.

"Always remember that, Nina. Girls will always go for the gut or the groin."

"Hey!" I protested, "that's not fair—I'm a girl, that's not what I—"

"You're a woman, Nina," he interrupted me, waving a hand, the other one holding the gun securely on the ledge and pointed towards the range. "A young one, but still, a woman—and one with an edge, at that. Even more, you're an adult, something rare." He leveled a serious gaze on me.

I arched an eyebrow in return. I didn't feel very adult or womanly— edgy, maybe, but I figured that was due to hormones. I mean, I didn't feel like I knew what I was doing, or had some sort of internal sense of, I don't know, something, something I assumed that adults felt, but I didn't.

Cap must have understood the look. "Keep shooting straight for the heart, Nina, and you'll be fine," he told me softly.

We were silent for a moment, Cap letting his words sink in, and I quietly absorbing them, then Cap grinned at me. "Come on, it's your turn. Let's work on your technique and make sure you know what you're doing."

We spent a whole lot more time getting me comfortable with a gun, and between that and the whole morning thing, I had a lot to think of on the drive back to the apartment.

I so wished I didn't feel like I was always trying to catch up to everything and everyone around me, I thought as I watched the streets fly by from the window.

"Trace," Cap said quietly as he drove, "she's not it for you, right?"

Great. Awesome. Straight to the one thing I didn't want to talk about. Forget shooting for the heart—this went straight for the gut.

Pain bubbled up in my chest, so big, so hard, it squeezed me airless, and even worse, it *hurt*, throbbing in time with my heartbeat, because deep down, I *knew* what, I knew the sort of person it was for me and it was *never* going to happen.

Cap swung the jeep over to the curb so quickly we almost tipped. He set the car in park and twisted in his seat toward me. "Nina, what happened?" he asked me, his voice full of concern. "Is it Trace? She get a little too, ah… nuts…with you?"

I faced the window, took a breath and then another as I got swamped between waves of memory: this morning and Van's eyes, and the very visceral memory of my family that I was estranged from, my friends I didn't see.

But it wasn't just that or them. I'd known such wonderful people, had such great friends. Like Samantha, with whom I'd been so close during high school, and then just disappeared. Or Fran, Francesca, whom we'd called "Kitt" on the swim team and her perfect smile: a really good friend, someone I'd even liked and spent a lot of time with outside of school. And there was Laura and her flaming red hair; so determined, so *fierce*.

Even my first girlfriend, Kerry, who'd been my best friend for a time. You'd think she'd have shown up at the Red Spot every now and again; after all, she'd introduced me to it.

But I saw no one—except Nico when he was around, and very occasionally our parents and little sister Nanny since I'd moved/been kicked out/ran away—that perspective depended upon who you asked. But still, even with the buffering presence of my aunt and cousins, that was strained at best. Everyone else was new to me in one way or another, and I always felt like I was struggling to catch up or something, because I just wasn't where they were at.

And all at the same time, I had this ideal in my head, this guiding thought that there was a certain way people were supposed to be, a way *I* was supposed to be, things I looked for and expected in myself, in others, qualities I'd seen and wanted to be and thought everyone should have, did have, but honestly?

They didn't.

Not really, not much.

So why was I so...so...*different?*

That knowing, how so very unique I was...it filled me, made my blood flay me from within as it flowed and all my brain was able to form was Trace's image and Van's expression, and they were twisting together over and over and making me nauseous.

God...it *sucked.*

After some unknown time, I was finally able to breathe through it, the nausea, the weird coldness that sucked at my skin and left my chest hollow. I tore my gaze from the window to answer him.

"It's not Trace, I mean, not right now, anyway," I said finally as I faced him.

Yeah, that was lame, but that was all I had—I couldn't tell him about this morning, I mean, what the fuck, Trace went out and got laid, big deal, right?

She had every right to, didn't she? I should've either just played it off or stopped down later.

Dammit, though.

Why should it have bothered me? How did I explain that? How could I explain it? Silence settled between us like the heavy humid air.

"Why don't you tell me about whoever it is, then?" Cap asked, his words cutting through the silence. "I can see that someone still means a lot to you and…Trace will never be it, and she knows it, too."

Floored, I stared at him wordlessly.

Trace made me hurt, in ways I didn't know I could, and I'd been through quite a bit already, but the ache Trace left in me was a ghost, a ghost of the yawning chasm between what she was and what she could be.

I could see that potential, could feel it, had experienced it in special small doses, that were crazy-good.

But it never lasted, not for long, not for more than that moment.

Cap was right—it would never be Trace, but it would never be anyone I actually knew, either. Because the last time I'd known anyone who could be that constantly, consistently wonderful…it had been years. And even had I wanted to connect with anyone I'd known, I had no way of even knowing where to start looking for Sam, or Fran, or even Laura—anyone else, for that matter.

Who knew? Cap had taken me out to teach me how to handle a gun, and he'd given me the key I needed to break free. That…was the past, not the present. And not the future either, my brain told me mournfully, but I told that part, *Stop. It's way past time, so just get over it.*

I took a deep breath and considered my words before I answered. "Cap, Trace could've been it. We could've really had something, something really good, if she just didn't—"

"Attempt to seduce every living being in front of you?" he finished and gave me a wry look. "You know she's just playing the 'I Dare You' game, don't you?"

"Huh?" I arched an eyebrow at him.

Did he know what had happened this morning? I wasn't going to tell him if he didn't—it was just so damned, I don't know… I just felt like shit about it.

I fished my cigarettes and lighter out of my back pocket. If this conversation was going to continue in the direction that I thought it was, I was going to need nicotine.

"Nina, come on. You show me yours, I'll show you mine, that game?" he hinted.

I gave him a look that said I thought he'd left his mind behind in the shooting range. Besides, it wasn't as if Trace and I hadn't seen each other naked before. We'd taken showers together for Christ's sake, and slept skin to skin half the time, well, before now—I realized that was *never* going to happen again—I just couldn't, y'know?

"Um Cap? I've seen Trace naked." I blushed as I said it, thinking of just how naked I'd seen her this morning.

But otherwise, it wasn't as if he didn't know; everyone in that building felt free to barge in on each other and there were plenty of times he'd bounced into the bedroom and onto the bed, waking us both up and forcing one or both of us to cover ourselves or each other. Actually that kind of—no, wait—it *did* piss me off.

But now wasn't the time to discuss it.

Cap gave a small snort. "Yeah, I don't mean that." He smirked at me. "I'm talking about feelings—show yours first, then she'll show hers."

I exhaled slowly, and let the smoke drift away. I'd been on the right track then, it really was about mutual surrender, and one on mine would have meant one on hers. But I wasn't comfortable with that, why did it have to be this whole dramatic submission thing? I voiced that part to Cap.

He grabbed a cigarette of his own and lit it. "Why did you turn her down, kid?" he exhaled. "You had no problem with that chickie you'd just met—the one up in the DJ booth."

What was this about? Did he and Jackie and Trace get together to discuss this, or had the story just made the rounds? Or was it just that I was currently their only topic of conversation? Either way, I wasn't happy about it.

"Hey, look," I began, defensively. I mean, none of this seemed fair, you know? "First off, Trace sent her in there in the first place. Second of all, it's nobody's fuckin' business, and you know what? She didn't play any fuckin' games with me—she was honest about what she wanted and I was feeling loose enough to go with it!" I finished sharply.

What the fuck was up with these people? What, everyone's allowed to screw around but me? Oh hell, they probably all got together when I wasn't around to laugh about me.

Cap narrowed his eyes at me. "I'll bet you didn't let her touch you though, did you?"

My cigarette burned unheeded as I stared at him in shock. What the hell did he just say? "What the hell did you just say?" I finally blurted out.

Slowly and methodically, Cap ground out the end of his cigarette into the ashtray until the unburned tobacco fell out in shreds. "I said..." he began very slowly and evenly, "you don't let anyone touch you."

I shook my head from side to side in disbelief. "I can't..." I waved my hands before me in negation. "This is just..." I didn't know what to say.

I flicked that dead cigarette far out into the street then ran my hands through my hair, making it stand up higher.

That was it.

Enough was enough.

I'd absolutely had it and this conversation was *over*.

I unsnapped my seatbelt and got out of the jeep. "I'll meet you back at the apartment. Thanks for the lesson," I told Cap as I closed the door.

I started walking. Oh hell, it was only about a mile back to the apartment—I ran more than that, so this was not really a big deal.

I stared blindly at the sidewalk as I mechanically moved my feet step by step. God, how un-fucking-believable, though. What made him even think of saying that? True or not, that was beside the point—what gave him or anyone else the right to discuss whether or not I allowed anyone to touch me?

My body.

Period. End.

There should be no discussion, at least, that's how I see it.

Cap and his jeep pulled up alongside me. "Get in the jeep, Nina, this is a bad neighborhood. You don't want to walk through here," he coaxed.

"Yeah well, I know how to handle a gun now, I'll be fine," I shot back at him with a glare.

I stopped and quickly lit a cigarette, then kept going.

Cap paced me with his jeep.

We traveled that way for a few moments, me walking, him trailing me with the jeep, until finally I stopped and faced him. Cap cut the motor.

"Why do you care?" I asked him across the space between us. "What does it matter, anyway? It's my body, and I decide, not you, not anyone else, what I want and don't want on it, in it or around it." I placed a hand on a hip and waited for his answer while Cap stared down into the passenger seat. No answer came. "Exactly," I muttered.

I was disgusted with the whole thing and incredibly angry, too. I turned on my heel and continued my walk.

I could hear the roar of jeep as Cap started it up again and seconds later, Cap caught up with me. "Nina," he called, "come on, you have to trust somebody, sometime. Please, just get in."

I walked a few more steps and considered. Maybe he had a point, maybe I had to change something. I already knew that I needed something different, maybe this could be the start.

"Okay," I said finally, and turned towards the jeep. I put my hand on the latch. "But," I cautioned, "I won't discuss that with you—it's none of anyone's business, except mine, and it wasn't necessary for you to say that, either."

Cap listened to what I said, then nodded. "Fair enough, I should have put that differently, and I won't ask for details, except for when I need some pointers."

I let go of the door and was about to step back when Cap threw a hand up quickly. "I'm just joking, just joking, come on, let's go home."

I finally opened the door and climbed in. Once I settled in my seat and snapped on the seat belt, Cap pulled forward.

"Nina, I'm just trying to let you know that you're not the only one hurting. Trace hurts over it, too. I mean, she kind of put herself out there for you and you turned her down—and it's not like you don't want her or anything."

I rolled my eyes and shook my head. "You know what, Cap? She didn't offer, she tried to…" Trace's hands bruising against me flashed through my mind and over my skin. I had no idea of how to even begin to describe that, nor even what to call it. "Never mind," I sighed. "Just fucking forget it."

"Look…" I tried again as the scenery rolled by. "Do you really want to give your heart to someone who's fucking everyone in sight? Ever think for a second that that's what everyone else does? Fuck her, then forget her?" I paused a moment, then continued. "Yeah, so she comes on to all of them—and of course they respond—who wouldn't? I don't want to be one of those, I don't want to hurt her, and…"

I took a breath.

"I'm not going to be another fuckin' notch for her, either."

We rounded the corner of our block and Cap pulled into a space across the street. He unsnapped his safety belt and lit a new cigarette. "Take one," he offered.

"I've got one, thanks," I answered. I took one of my own out, but didn't light it. It was just something to hold onto for the moment. Cap smoked quietly, and I sat there with him while we both considered what we'd been talking about.

"Don't you think if someone was really into you that they wouldn't go after anyone else, especially in front of you, want you to watch, wouldn't play with you like that?" I cut through the silence.

"Nina, what about you? You did that girl, you didn't seem to have a problem with that. And if it's just sex, then why don't you just go for it?" Cap look genuinely puzzled as he spoke. "Besides, what the hell is it going to hurt—I mean, it's not like you have to worry about getting pregnant or anything." He smirked the last part at me.

"You just don't get it, do you?" I countered, exasperated. "It's not just about sex. Okay, yeah, with Candace at that time, it was sex, but for Christ's sake I was fucking drunk, give me a break. And it was honest at least, I didn't have to lie to her or pretend shit or try to, to break her will or anything. Dammit, leave me alone already! If I pull out the phone book, you guys have fucked half of it."

I lit the cigarette and took a deep drag. "Just because I don't have to worry about getting fucking pregnant doesn't mean there aren't any fucking rules," I told him. "At least for me. Yeah, I fucked Candace okay? I fucked her because she was there, and she wanted me to and Trace dared me to, and you know what? I never do that, never just pick someone up, I actually go out on dates first. So what, I enjoyed it, enjoyed her, so sometimes if we get a chance we hang out and actually talk or something, because I actually like her—she was totally upfront, she hasn't stopped being that way and I *like* honesty—that's the way to get me, okay?"

"Whoa, girl." Cap held up his hands to mollify me. "You're preaching to the choir about just enjoying it, and that's what I'm saying. You should just stop being so damned guarded all the time, let someone in, ya know?" He took a drag on his butt. "Once you and Trace...you know..." and he exhaled "...things'll probably calm right down." His tone was reassuring, but his words proved he didn't get it. Maybe I wasn't saying it right. I thought I was.

I blew out a frustrated breath. "No," I told him flatly. "It's never going to happen, don't you get it? I want it for *real*, I actually really, truly love, um, care about her, understand? As long as I'm not involved with anyone, I'm a free agent, but believe me—and it has nothing to do with my own past—if I had an honest-to-goodness real clue that she could even partially be what I need, I wouldn't ever, ever, fuck around, not with anyone."

I took a drag on my butt and blew it out. "Candace would never have happened," I continued, "but I'm not gonna fucking waste my time—do you get it yet? Someone, someday, is going to be there for me, and I wish, I would love it to be Trace, but if it's not, well, why I should I pretend? Why should I let her pretend to me? Oh...hell..." I threw my hands up in confusion and frustration then undid my seatbelt. "Just fucking forget it already, man, I'm going inside."

I didn't even know what it was I was trying to say anymore, and I was tired of trying to understand myself. "I've got to practice, I've got a rehearsal-audition today," I told him as I opened the door and slid out of the car.

Cap undid his belt and got out, double checking to make sure the alarm was set. "Hey, you've got your own room now, have fun." He smiled at me as he made his way to the steps.

We climbed up together in silence and I tried to clear my mind.

I really did have to get it together. I was going to meet with some people I'd met at the bar a couple of nights before: Stephie and Jeremy. They'd liked my style, they'd liked the tunes I'd spun, and they'd liked me. We'd see what would happen, if we clicked musically. There was no drummer yet, but we'd work that out, if the first couple of rehearsals gelled in the way I had the feeling they would.

"Nina, you really are a virgin, aren't you?" Cap broke into my thoughts as we approached our door.

I rolled my eyes. "Can we just leave that alone?" I asked, exasperated. I keyed the lock and let us both in. I made my way to my closet to get my guitar.

"Yup, thought so," he said mostly to himself. "Not that there's anything wrong with that," he added hastily, "just that it sorta makes sense of everything else."

I turned back and faced him, hands on my hips. "You know, just because I don't let anyone who wants to *fuck* me doesn't mean I don't know what sex is about or feels like," I informed him. I'd had it with this heavy conversation, it was time, more than time, to add a little levity somewhere. "Besides," I added with a grin, "have you ever had anyone do it better than you do it yourself?"

Cap stared at me for a second, then started laughing. "No, actually, I've never experienced that."

"Well, there you go then," I told him with a smile. "Maybe you're a virgin, too."

He guffawed. "That'd be the best line. Nina, I think I'm gonna use it. That's just too good."

His laughter was infectious, and it was such a relief to not feel like I was on the defensive, I started laughing with him.

"Feel free," I offered, still grinning, "I figure I'll probably marry the person who can make it feel that good." I clapped a friendly hand on his shoulder then turned back to get my guitar.

"Nina, " Cap's tone was serious, so I turned to face him again.

Damn, though—I *really* needed to practice.

"I never thought of it like that before. You know, if you can trust someone that much," he said, his face considering the thought, "you should."

I answered him with the seriousness he deserved. "I already figured that. I'm shooting straight for the heart," I told him somberly and with that, I went into my room to play guitar.

COLDER

I HAVE HEARD THE STORY OF THE GARDEN
THE SERPENT CAME AND TOOK IT ALL AWAY
I AM ALWAYS SORRY IN THE MORNING
BUT RIGHT NOW? LET ME SLIDE IN—LET ME STAY

"I Fall"—JD Glass

THE REHEARSAL- AUDITION WENT WELL—BETTER than expected in fact, because we'd left it with three brand-new songs and the beginnings of two more.

I liked Stephie and Jeremy. Stephie, who was a little taller than me and had this lovely angular look, was smart and tough and carried a very artistic picture she'd taken of her boyfriend; she'd designed his Mohawk and she'd done a nice job. She'd done her own hair, too. It shaded from blonde at the top to red to black and it looked like a match tip and the ends curled under her ears.

Jeremy was the same height as Dee Dee and maybe a little darker, but that's where the similarities ended. He was shaped like a large bear, albeit a large, bass playing monster rhythm bear and he kept his hair clipped as closely to the skin as possible and said he only took his army flak jacket off to sleep—or when his mother wrestled it off him to wash it—whatever came first.

Most importantly though, we had fun, we had chemistry, and we knew we could make music. We planned to get together again in another few days and start making schedules from there.

I pulled my guitar out of the case, played a few licks, then put it back. I was restless and edgy. A lot had changed between the day before and now.

I moved a few things into my new space. Tried my guitar out in different areas.

I couldn't get the image from the morning out of my head. Trace and Van. Did she like it? Did she really like him? Why him, if he was going to be so smug about it? Did it matter? Did she care?

Maybe, just maybe, it was me. Maybe it all meant nothing. Maybe I should just go ahead and "do my own thing" before someone did their own thing to me. I was so tired of being cute...

I called the club to speak with one of the owners. "Hey Mickey, it's Nina. Who's got the back room tonight?" I asked him when he answered.

Hell, if someone else was DJing, I'd go in and back the bar. Hey, at least I'd make some money and in between I could check out the new disc spinner, dance, see if they were any good.

"It's Darrel, but I think he's gonna blow it soon," Mickey told me. "He's been doin' whatever at the booth again."

Silence.

"You guys set up the rear lounge yet?" I asked.

They'd recently bought the adjacent building and were setting it up with both a booth and a stage, with a capacity for five hundred.

"You're wired for sound, why?" Mickey asked me.

"Let me run a session in the back room?" I asked. "Test the wiring, bin placements, all that sort of thing, so that way you guys don't have to bring me in for a day session."

I swore could hear the wheels in his head turning. If he let me in tonight and it went badly, he'd gotten the room tested for free. If it went well, more people could fit in the club. The bar staff might be a little shorthanded, but there'd be more money all around, so no one would complain too terribly.

"If you get people, you can stay back there. If no one walks in, just give me a run down on any bugs you find—if any—and, you wanna barback tonight?"

"Yeah, sure," I agreed enthusiastically, "I'll be there in twenty minutes."

I hung up and got dressed to kill. I grabbed a stack of my favorite tunes and quickly stopped into the bathroom—had to check my hair.

Cap was right, I thought as I made sure everything was how I wanted it to be. I'd had no problem with Candace. Thinking of her made me smile.

She was sharp, sexy, direct.

She knew what she wanted—and wasn't afraid of it. I could deal with that. *Hell, I should probably learn from that,* I thought.

Everyone was doing whatever they wanted but me. It really seemed I was stupid enough to think that caring meant anything when pretty obviously the only thing that had meaning was the fuck.

No wonder everyone treated me like such a baby—I *was* one.

Not tonight.

Not anymore.

My hair was perfect and I looked pretty damn good if I did say so myself.

Okay, I thought as I contemplated myself in the mirror, *I've got a room to check and if it's up to me—and it is—I'm gonna have that room full and rockin' way before it's time to close.*

Fuck barbacking tonight. And maybe, just maybe, if the music was good—and it *would* be—and the mood was right—it definitely *should* be—I'd invite someone up to the booth to party with me.

Fuck Trace, fuck Van, fuck Cap and Jackie.

Fuck everyone who kept treating me like I was some precocious little idiot.

Fuck 'em all.

SAVE A PRAYER
NOW I'M PRETTY—DO YOU LIKE ME?
NOW I'M SMARTER—DO YOU LIKE ME?
NOW I'M ANGRY—DO YOU WANT ME?
DO YOU WANT TO LEAD ME ON?

"Lead Me On"—JD Glass

"Oh God, Nina, what do you want?" she groaned as we pressed into each other, kissing desperately and hard as we lay entwined together on her bed—shirts off, pants and shoes gone somewhere with the shirts.

Don't even ask about the socks, I still don't know.

I slid my tongue deep between her lips and was met by hers. "You know what I want." I broke off and caught a breath before I traced a line from her collar bone to her jaw. "I want you."

I gently bit her throat then scraped it with my teeth before sucking on it gently. "I want you...I want all of you." I kissed her lips again and the sensual fullness of her response, the sincerity of it, made me feel faint with rising desire.

"This," she whispered and thrust her body up to mine as she kissed my throat, "this is all I have to give. Nina...please..."

Her finger nails ran sharp across my shoulders and somehow she flipped me onto my back. She ground herself into me and my body responded, my hands on her hips and aching need returning her pressure.

Her luminous grey eyes drove into mine; begging, pleading for understanding. "This... This is all I have," she whispered. Her mouth was soft and achingly sweet on mine.

I splayed my hands and ran my fingers down her back, sensuously massaging along the way as one of my legs wrapped over her hip. One of her hands ran down lightly along the curve of my breast, down my ribs and past my stomach to my waist then grabbed my hip, bringing our bodies harder together. The other repeatedly ran across my face and through my hair until finally, I lifted my chin and broke that soul-searing kiss.

She raised her head and leaned up for a moment on an elbow to look at me and I looked straight into her beautiful grey eyes. "Okay Trace, you win," I told her throatily. "We'll just give each other what we can."

"You don't know how much I…I *want* you," she said softly, tracing my face with her fingertips.

Slowly, softly, she leaned into kiss me again, and I closed my eyes to the feel of her lips pressing blatantly carnal kisses down my chest and stomach towards my—

No, this wasn't a dream, this wasn't even a stroke-fantasy, although it seems like it might have been a good one.

This was really, truly happening.

By late August, Candace had returned to Merry Olde England and after a goodbye that was harder than I really let myself feel, I'd thrown myself into my work and my music. The band was going great guns and although we'd been through two drummers already and searching for a third—I swear, I'll just never know what it is with drummers (and no offense if you are one—but y'all are a strange breed, you know), we'd started to write a couple of songs and were really getting to know each other, bond, and have fun.

"All right, I've got to split in a few, I've got dinner plans," I announced to Jeremy and Stephie as the last notes of our latest tune died down in the air around us.

A *crunch* sounded through the room as Jeremy unplugged his bass, along with the soft thud of Stephie putting the microphone back on its stand.

I shut down my amp and unplugged my guitar, carefully setting it in a stand, then began to disassemble my wires and pedal effects. I put the pedals in my bag and stood to coil my patch chord.

Jeremy came over, bass slung in its bag over his back. "Gonna ravish some poor innocent?" he asked me with a sly grin.

"Yeah, right," Stephie interjected and came over, punching my arm lightly. "Like Nina ever has to work for it."

"Hey, hey, hey!" I turned and faced them both, placing the now-coiled chord in with my effects, "I take offense to that!" I joked and picked up my guitar to place it in the gig bag. "I work my ass off in here!" I gave a little wiggle to emphasize my point.

"Yeah, like that's not part of the attraction," Jeremy answered, staring pointedly.

All right, maybe I shouldn't have done that. I rolled my eyes in annoyance. "Cut it out, man," I told him.

"You're such a jerk sometimes," Stephie reprimanded, and smacked the back of his head.

"Ow! Hey! Ya didn't have to go and do that!" Jeremy protested, rubbing his scalp vigorously.

"And you know, it's not like any of them are innocent anyway," Stephie informed him, pointing to the small window in the studio door.

Jeremy and I both looked and saw there were some people out there, trying to see in.

"That's the next band, hoping we're done," I hazarded, shrugging my shoulders.

"Yeah, that's the next band," Jeremy agreed.

Stephie rolled her eyes at our collective denseness, and I grinned and shook my head in response, then returned my attention to my equipment.

I slung my bags with their effects, cables and guitar strap over one shoulder, hoisted my guitar over the other, and we all reached for the door.

"Right," Stephie finally said sarcastically, "that's why they don't have any instruments." She opened the door and made a sweeping gesture out into the hall.

Once out of the studio, it was pretty obvious that Stephie had a point. It was three, no, four girls, um, young women, and she was right—not an instrument in sight.

"Oh hey, you girls a singing group?" Jeremy stopped to ask one of them amiably, flexing his shoulders.

Stephie and I shared a look and kept walking towards the store at the end of the hallway where the exit was, nodding polite 'hellos' as we passed.

"Yeah, we're working on a single," one of the girls answered, laughing, and another giggled with her.

Stephie and I made our way through the exit and down the stairs that led to the store front.

"Think he forgot to tie a shoelace or something?" Stephie asked in the companionable silence as we descended.

I snorted a laugh. "No, but how much do you want to bet he ends up catching one?" I countered as I carefully made my way down. "Those lines of his are pretty awful," I commented as I waited for her at the bottom of the steps.

Stephie rolled her eyes again. "God, he can be such a jerk!"

I smiled but said nothing as we walked through the repair shop and picked our way through the various disconnected and disassembled instruments that littered the area. What was there to say? That pretty much described everyone, anyway.

A bell tinkled as we walked through the rear entrance of the store and headed to the register.

"Hi, Stephie. Hi, Nina," the long haired young man behind the counter greeted us. He gave us each a big smile, but his eyes rested on Stephie.

"Hi John." I smiled back, watching his eyes on Stephie. I dug into my pocket for my money.

"Hi," Stephie flushed as she looked down and made a big production out of digging into her bag for her wallet.

I grinned at her but quickly hid it. I knew she liked him, and I was pretty sure he liked her, too.

John waited patiently as I found my money and put it on the counter. "Stephie, we want the same time next week?" I turned to her and asked as she found her wallet.

"Yeah, let's do that—Adam's Rib, same time, same day," she said to John, then quickly turned her head to me. "Hey, do you have the jerk's money?" she asked with a smile.

"I don't have jerk money," I smiled back, almost laughing.

The bell tinkled again as Jeremy stumbled into the store. "Can you believe it?" he asked loudly. "They're—" and he pointed with his thumb over his shoulder "—doing a single for DJ Nina to play on 'Dominion' nights. That's just un-fucking-believable."

It was my turn to blush. "Got your share?" I asked him, and I looked down at the money under my hands.

Since I'd done the sound check in the new back room at the club, well, believe me when I tell you I blew it out—it was now mine.

So, Darrel and I both worked DJing Saturday nights, only now he was in the same room, and I had the new room.

And yeah, Saturday was Dominion night in my room—that was what everyone who attended called them, anyway, in tribute to that night with Candace. The assumption was that in honor of that, I occasionally entertained company in the booth.

Everything has a consequence, right?

"Oh yeah, here you go," Jeremy answered quickly, handing his money over to John. "Are we booked for next week?"

"We're done, we're good," Stephie answered him quickly and rushed to step out of the store and into the street.

"Oh yeah, yeah, we're all set," I smiled. "See you next week, John." I readjusted the strap of my guitar and stepped to the door.

"Cool beans, dude," John answered. "And tell Stephie I said 'bye' for me," he called to my back, the jerk, um Jeremy, behind me.

"Yup," Jeremy answered, and we were out the door and on the sidewalk, the still-warm air smacking our skin in the early twilight.

Stephie waited for us on the sidewalk, smoking a cigarette and enjoying what she could of light and the weather.

"That was a pretty good rehearsal, guys. What did you think?" I asked, looking at each of them in turn and lighting a cigarette of my own.

Stephie blew a few smoke rings just to prove she could, then grinned back at me. "We're doing fine, we're getting stuff down!" she answered enthusiastically.

Jeremy shrugged a shoulder under his gig bag. "We're really starting to groove, but...if we could just find a drummer..." He trailed off, frowning.

Steph and I shook our heads in chagrined agreement. Where the hell were we going to find one, anyway? Ah well, I had the next few days to ponder that and discuss it with the two of them as ideas came and went.

For now though, I had plans, and none of them included a drummer.

Despite the fact that Candace had left a few weeks ago, I still rarely spent time at the apartment. Honestly, I just could no longer deal with anybody except for my brother and the band—especially after the last time I'd spoken with Trace.

So I either made sure I was home at a time when everyone was out, or staying somewhere else, either visiting my family or jamming all night at Steph's with Jeremy, composing, rehearsing, and making ourselves sick on ice cream.

Yeah, we were musicians who didn't do drugs—sue me.

But maybe it was because of my rather obvious absence that Cap decided we needed a "roommate party:" He'd very assiduously combed through all of our schedules and picked the one night everyone happened to be off, then asked us all to meet him at "Dock Street," another popular bar on Bay Street.

He'd made the invite an open one: bring anyone, siblings, friends, significant others and outside of rehearsal, well, that was all I had to do that night. I'd already invited my brother Nicky, I mean, Nico. He would meet me there later.

I was suddenly inspired. "Hey, do you guys want to come with me? I mean, to Dock Street? It's my roommates and their friends and you guys haven't met my brother yet—he'll be there—and what do you say? Wanna go?" I asked in a rush, "I mean, if you guys don't have stuff to do."

This would be the first time we all hung out together; outside of rehearsal, I mean.

"Sounds good to me," Jeremy smiled. "You up for it, Stephie?" he turned to her and asked.

Stephie pursed her lips and considered. "Trace gonna be there?" she asked me in an undertone.

As Stephie and I had become better friends, we'd discussed a lot of things, and of course, we'd discussed the weird mess that was our lives. I had confided in her about the strange relationship that Trace and I had and that I was trying to avoid, and yeah, actually, Trace *would* be there, and I hadn't really seen her in a while.

"Yeah, actually," I answered. "I'm a little nervous about that."

Stephie nodded as she considered. "I'm there then," she decided seriously. "You need back-up." She grinned at me.

"Thanks." I grinned back in relief.

"Hey, no worries, that's what friends do, right?" She smiled and punched my shoulder lightly.

"Yeah, we're your back-up," Jeremy confirmed, and punched the other arm, quite a bit harder than Stephie had.

"Oww, " I groaned out, rubbing the spot out—that really had hurt. "Jerk!" I scowled at him, "I'm a girl, not your bass." I elbowed him in the ribs, 'cause that was all I could reach; he was darn tall, after all.

"I am so sorry." He shook his head in self-recrimination. "I'm really sorry, I didn't mean—Oh! Hey!"

Stephie had whapped the back of his head again. "From now on, you are the 'Jerkster,' Jerkster," she told him, then whapped him again for good measure.

Jeremy, um, I mean, the Jerkster, kept rubbing his head. "Fine, fine, just stop hitting me," he agreed, scowling as he tried to heal himself with his fingertips. "We should make you the drummer, you like to hit so much."

She and I both laughed at that and the three of us walked to Dock Street together.

Cap had managed to get three tables pulled together and we all sat around laughing, eating and drinking, and for the first time in ages, I was having fun with my roommates. Jackie was being hysterically funny and even Trace, who'd shown up with Van, was actually being nice for once.

I sat with Nico, Stephie, and the newly christened Jerkster, joking around, sort of having our own party within the party until the larger conversation caught up with us.

"That's it for me, I've had it for the night," Nico announced, pushing away from the table and rubbing his stomach.

I dug into my pockets and pulled out my keys. "Here you go, Nico…" I tossed them at him. "You know where my room is."

He was staying at my place tonight since we were drinking and I didn't want him to drive. Since I lived only two blocks away, this was not a problem.

"Yeah, I didn't wear my drinking clothes," he joked with me, referring to those parties all that time ago and the guy who always wore a plastic garbage bag just in case he puked.

I laughed with him.

Somebody said something, I don't remember what, and I quipped back to the table at large.

"Shut up, Nina!" Trace called jokingly down the table.

"Why don't you make me?" I joked back and turned back to my conversation. Come on now, I had every right to say stuff, too.

In what seemed like half a second, Trace came over and yanked my chair out. Momentarily off balance, I raised my arms trying to get my bearings and in a flash, Trace slipped around, threw a leg over mine and stood before me, straddling my legs.

I looked up into her eyes, unreadable in the dim light and I kept my face expressionless.

"I think you should shut up," she warned me, her voice deadly quiet.

The bar went still and silent around us, and I could feel everyone's eyes on us in the ringing emptiness.

"Yeah?" I asked insolently, tilting my head in challenge, "I think you should make me."

There was no way I was going to let Trace try to intimidate me, especially not in front of my brother or my band.

We watched each other a moment, no quarter on either side, then suddenly her hands were on my shoulders, her lips were on mine and her tongue slid deeply into my mouth and while my brain was stunned, I gave back as good as I got. This was war.

We battled in that sensuous way for however long until we mutually declared temporary détente. Trace lifted her head from mine, her hands still on my shoulders.

"Got anything else to say?" she asked, a triumphant laugh in her voice.

"Yeah actually," I curled my lip at her. "That the best you got?"

Good. Now she was shocked, and I grabbed her hips, bringing her down firmly onto my lap. Don't ever dismiss the notion of Dutch courage, because that must have been what was fueling me now. Well, that and the fact that I absolutely refused to lose face in front of my band, my brother, my friends, and even the bar at large.

Releasing one side, I touched her face and gently brought it to mine. I looked into her eyes and whispered, "I don't think you can handle me," then kissed her softly, my lips and tongue an easy glide against hers.

Her fingers slipped from my shoulders to run through my hair as she responded to me, her stomach pressing into my ribs.

"Hey—get a room!" someone called out, probably Cap I thought, and various other catcalls followed as well.

Again, Trace lifted her mouth from mine and she carefully stood up directly in front of me, sliding her body not half an inch from my nose. It would only have taken the slightest movement for me to catch her between my teeth.

"Do you wanna take this outside?" she asked me, her voice all throaty challenge.

An ironic smile graced her lips but the silent grey of her eyes had deepened and they searched mine with an intensity that I knew was no joke. But still…that smile…and the message everyone got…I knew how to play this.

"Nico, take my guitar home?" I asked him.

I didn't even glance his way when he agreed.

When I stood I deliberately gripped her hips for leverage and let my breasts skim lightly against her on the way up. The sharp hiss of her breath as I did it made me smile. Finally, we were eye to eye, and I dropped my hands. "Fine, then."

She neatly stepped out from our almost-embrace and made way for me, and I strode to the door, stopping only when I got there. I faced her, mutely waiting. This was the last chance to back out and down, and the perfect opportunity for either one of us to crush the other in front of everyone.

Forget points, we're talking burning score cards here.

I don't think there was anyone in that room that didn't know this could only go one of two ways: we could either punch the fuck out of each other or fuck.

If the room had been quiet before, it was now absolutely tomb silent. You'd think that it shouldn't have mattered so much to anyone else, but it seemed like every eye was upon us as Trace sauntered her way over, all liquid curves and predatory grace.

I held out my hand for the last few steps and when she grasped it, she reached up with her free one and drew me in for a searing and bite-my-lips-bloody kiss.

This time, the room erupted with cheers and when we broke off that kiss, I glanced around to see everyone on their feet, even Nico, Stephie and Jeremy. Nico's expression was inscrutable, Stephie gave me a small grin, and Jerkster, well, he held his beer up in a congratulatory toast.

The sharp sound of glass being struck rang out across the crowd and we all looked over to see Cap, putting down the cutlery he had just used to ring his glass with.

"Nina, Trace," he began, his tone somber, but his eyes twinkling, "go. Go and either discover that it's destiny or..." and he paused dramatically, then grinned at the rest of the room before looking at us again "...get it over with, so the rest of us can get some peace!"

Everyone laughed and somewhere, almost under the table, I heard Van's muffled, "Here, here!"

Trace rolled her eyes ready and turned away, ready to leave, but I couldn't just let it go yet. "Fuck you!" I mouthed to him with a slight grin, then followed Trace to the door.

"Uh uh!" I heard Cap call out to our backs as we made our way outside. "That's not who you're fucking!"

Not even half a step past the door and Trace pounced.

It was all tongues and hands, aching grinding need and nipples hard enough to hurt—and that was just the walk on the way back home. My next conscious moment, I found myself in Trace's bed and as her lips and tongue tortured me on their way to the waist-band of my button fly jeans, I groaned as she reached the top one.

"God, I want you, Nina," she stopped a moment to tell me, and her hand splayed out against my belly. She ripped the first button open with her teeth. "I want you so *fucking* bad," she whispered into that first opening, then one by one, she released the rest of the brass buttons, her lips, teeth and tongue sending waves of sensation that crashed through me.

The last button opened and Trace discovered that I wore no underwear as she planted heated kisses at the V where the fly ended. I squirmed lightly under her and as she reached to pull the jeans off, I sat up and blindly reached for her face, pulling her up for another deep kiss. We lay back down together and while her hands continued to push my jeans off, my hands reached for her waist to help her remove her own.

Between the pushing and the pulling we somehow finally managed to get everything removed and as I lay between her legs, my fingertips gently stroked the high sharp planes of her cheeks, the luxurious length of her neck and the sharp cut of her shoulders. She was so achingly beautiful, I wanted to cry from the pain of it, because I was touching her skin and I wanted to touch her heart.

Some of this must have translated through from my fingertips to her, because that's when she asked me what I wanted and as I closed my eyes and enjoyed the trail of fire that Trace blazed down me, an image of sunset over the desert formed behind my eyes.

Her lips came softly to the top junction between my leg and my desire and I exhaled a long, low breath as she pressed her lips first to one side, then the other.

My whole body ached with a deep, wrenching need and I wanted this, I wanted *Trace*, and here she was and I was, together, in this intimate space, and I certainly thought that I was ready when she pressed her lips against that desperate ache. I groaned and arched my back a bit as her tongue slipped between my folds and teased my clit lightly.

With a slight tilt of her jaw, Trace's lower lip stroked me from right below my opening to the base of my clit, and she pulled her head back a moment before bring it back down, sucking my clit between her lips, hard.

That felt really nice, truly, but somehow not as intense as the anticipation had been. Maybe it was positional, so I sat up on my elbows and flexed my legs, raising my knees. That did help somewhat, and Trace wrapped her arms around my thighs, using her hands to spread me as her hair draped over my legs. I had a flash of memory—of the last time I'd been in that room, of the last time I'd seen her over the edge of that bed.

Van.

Fucking Van.

Mother.

Fucking.

Van.

I shoved that thought down as hard as I could.

Oh, but this wasn't working and as much as I knew that I should just relax and enjoy this, and I really, really wanted, no, I *needed* to get off, I was slipping out of that desire-induced haze and I was feeling less and less physically, and more and more acutely conscious of the sheets curled under me and how quiet the room was, of the light coming through the window to tell me the sun was coming up, and of the fact that I was naked with a beautiful woman's head between my thighs, lips riding my pussy, and I was feeling absolutely nothing, not physically, not emotionally—just a heavy leaden weight that seemed to spread through my chest.

I knew two things right then and there: I was the desert and the desert was cold.

Finally, I reached down and gently lifted Trace's face away from me. "Trace…" I spoke into the silence that filled the early morning air.

Her grey eyes filled with concern as they met mine. "Are you okay? Something wrong? I really want to… " she trailed off as I shook my head negatively.

Yeah, something is wrong, probably with me and my retarded hopeless body, I thought wryly to myself, but I was careful to keep both my expression and my voice gentle, because her expression was so vulnerable, so childlike. I didn't want to hurt her. "No, I'm fine," I assured her and smiled. "Just… come here," I invited, indicating that she lie either on top of or next to me.

Trace slid up my body and came to rest next me, one leg still between mine. I put my arms around her and cradled her head to my shoulder, then leaned back against the pillows. We snuggled for a moment, and I kissed her forehead.

All I could think of was Van fucking her.

She raised her eyes to mine a moment, then shifted her hips so that she lay between my legs again. Trace wrapped her arms around ribs and kissed my chest, over my heart. "I really want to make you come," she murmured, pressing her lips against me again.

I ran my fingers through her hair and lovingly stroked her shoulder. "It's okay, don't worry about it," I responded.

She slid a hand down and cupped my pussy. "Well, what if we…" she asked me with a sexy grin as she began to press her palm against me.

I put my hand over hers to still. "It's not, it's just…" I pulled her in for a kiss, hoping to distract her or something, I'm not sure what. We broke it for a moment. "I think I drank too much," I lied. "Just…stay with me."

I thought of all the girls I'd had and the way they made me feel. I'd really, really want to, and then whammo!

Nothing.

But I always made sure they came.

Maybe, just maybe, the difference here was that Trace was drunk. I'd wanted this so much, but I'd wanted it clear and memorable, not accompanied by a headache and a hangover. But right now, it wasn't Trace's fault, no matter what.

For the record, I have to say that from the moment Trace had grabbed my chair, I was stone cold sober.

"C'mere." I smiled at her and pulled her up over me so that her legs tangled with mine. "Now let's…" I licked her neck and flipped her over "…just not worry about this…" and I lightly nipped and licked a path down her chest as our hips ground against each other.

Frankly, Trace actually *was* way too drunk and while it turned into an incredibly sensual make-out session (and I think I still have scars from it on my back—somewhere) bit by bit, every caress became slower and her eyes stayed shut a bit longer.

Eventually, she snuggled under me and fell asleep, but not before turning one last time. She nuzzled the space between my breasts.

"You've got perfect breasts," she breathed with sleep warmth against my nipple before she pulled it lightly between her lips, teasing the peak with her tongue.

"Thank you," I whispered and kissed her ear. "Shush now…sleep." I stroked her shoulders and gently removing myself from her kiss.

Her lips gently touched my breast once more then with a little sigh, she rolled over, tucking her body into mine.

We lay like that for a while and I listened to her breathe, the cadence of her breath soft and easy as it always was when she slept in my arms. I slowed my own breath and tried to sleep but I was now over-tired, over-wired and overwrought.

Finally, when I knew that Trace was fully asleep, I left my arm under her neck as I rolled onto my back, tucking my side against her so she wouldn't get cold.

This wasn't the first time I'd wanted, really wanted, sex, but somewhere, somehow, I'd lost the desire. It was very frustrating, this touching and not being able to be touched and although I usually was able to avoid the awkwardness, there were times, like tonight, where if Trace had been more sober, it would have just gotten stressful.

I mean, what person except for the occasional callous asshole, isn't going to have their feelings hurt if the person who just made them come can't? I know it would bother me if I was on the other end of it.

But, I couldn't fake it, either, so I just avoided it all together when I could and made it up to myself later.

But it didn't make sense. I mean it couldn't be biological, because, hell, on occasion things did work—okay, not as well as they worked when I was by myself, but still, both those things proved that it had to be something other than physical. Not that technique doesn't count, of course…

I sighed quietly.

Candace was gone and even though we'd promised to keep in touch, we weren't anything more than friends. Trace was right here and even though it could have been so much more, it was never going to be.

Dammit.

Had we both been sober, this could have potentially been something amazingly beautiful. And no matter who it was with, if I wasn't doing it for myself, I wasn't getting off. Not that I didn't enjoy and get really turned on, because I did, but it was like no matter what anyone did, they just couldn't touch me.

And if it wasn't them—and I didn't think it was—then it was definitely me. And if it wasn't biological, then maybe it was something else. Maybe Trace couldn't deal with being gay; maybe she needed to get drunk and needed to play all these games just to get to a place where she didn't feel so afraid.

Oh hell, maybe I just had to get my head together, maybe I was just coming (no pun intended) from a different place. If it hadn't been for the band, I wouldn't have done anything even remotely beneficial for myself in the last several weeks. I'd been drinking too much, I'd been fucking around too much and nothing felt good. I was disgusted with myself.

Okay then.

I had made a decision.

I sighed and quietly slipped my arm out from under Trace and got out of bed, careful to tuck the blankets around her. She might be disappointed, but she wouldn't be terribly surprised if I wasn't there when she woke—there were plenty of times I'd left her place early to go for a run before she opened her eyes. Usually, she'd meet me later upstairs and we'd eat together. *But not this morning,* I thought with slight regret as I re-dressed in the early morning light.

Maybe it was all in my head, and maybe it was my environment. Maybe there was nothing wrong at all, and this was just not the right place for me. *Well, it wouldn't be the first time for that,* I thought wryly and smiled to myself grimly.

I watched Trace sleep for a long moment, her lips a perfect bruise in her pale face, soft and peaceful in the morning sun.

Moving carefully so as not to disturb her, I leaned over and kissed them. Trace stirred. "Love you, Nina," she mumbled sleepily and kissed me in return, then settled back into sleep.

Stunned, I merely stood and stared a moment. "Love you too, Trace," I finally whispered back and noticed that my voice sounded thick and harsh.

Dammit.

I was crying.

About Trace.

Again.

I let the tears fall as I walked to the door and as I stood in the frame, I looked back at her sleeping form.

"Bye," I whispered in that same choked voice and I walked out, quietly closing the door behind me and careful not to make any noise as I made my way out of her apartment.

There were two conclusions I had come to and they were:

I had to leave, I really had to leave. I just really couldn't take it anymore: not Trace, not Jackie, not even Cap, even though he was well meaning— when he wasn't horny. I had to get away from all of these places and these people, find out who I was, because I didn't like the person I was being.

And the other thing? I wasn't going to even so much as kiss another human being unless the words right before it were "I love you."

That was it.

No heavy making out, no crazy lines and wild sex with what amounted to friendly strangers.

Dates.

I was going to go on dates, like a normal person, and if I liked them, there'd be another and if there wasn't, well, hopefully I would have spent time with someone interesting. *I'll know the right one when I meet them*, I figured as I walked the corridor.

Instead of climbing the stairs to my apartment, I let my feet lead me down.

I meant it: I was going to Jerry's Pancake Place to pick up the newspaper and check out the adverts for, well, if not an apartment, then at least a room.

I fumbled in a pocket and found my cigarettes then lit one as I walked through the door, closing it behind me.

What if there isn't anyone for you? my brain asked me. *What if you end up alone?*

I pondered that as I walked down the block I usually ran down.

The answer was honestly very simple.

There was a difference between lonely and alone, and if I never met "my match," well, I liked my own company well enough—and with all the music and art I had to constantly work on, because I just couldn't (and still can't) help myself—I'd never have time to be lonely.

Okay, my brain countered, *what about sex?*

What about it? I asked back. I mean, it's not as if I enjoyed it too much.

Okay, I loved the thrill of the chase and there wasn't anything I enjoyed better than reveling in the ability to create all those delicious gasps and moans, feeling when a woman was so ready to—okay.

Stop there.

Yes, I enjoyed that when it was happening, but still, it left me empty. Besides, I told my brain as we entered Jerry's Pancake Place, it's not as if I didn't still have my favorite sexual partner—and I had never let myself down.

No, we, meaning my brain and I, were going to get out of there, focus on art and music and the things that were important. It would be fuckin' nice if I took some time somewhere and actually went to my favorite comic book store, Universe, and picked up the *Love and Rockets* that I had fallen so far behind in.

It's definitely time to get some clarity, I reflected.

Fuck it.

I was hungry and after paying for the paper, I sat down and ordered breakfast—cream of wheat with a soft boiled egg on the side.

If I was never going to feel something, that special pull, then I wasn't going to settle for something else, either, I determined as I spread the classifieds before me. I wasn't going to waste my life pining for things that wouldn't happen, and I was going to take some responsibility for who I wanted to be: someone honest and real. If I wasn't going to settle for less in myself, I wouldn't settle for less in someone else, either.

I circled a couple of likely candidates as my food arrived and as I ate in silence, I looked at the want ads, too.

Oh hell, maybe I'd just change everything while I was at it—why not, right?

I looked and found a few things that seemed likely. As soon as I was done with eating, I was going to go to my apartment, shower, dress, and wake Nico. Maybe he'd go with me to look at a few of these places. I thought, in fact, maybe we could do that, then go back with him and visit our parents and baby sister for a little while. Heck, now that we were all talking to one another again, it might even be nice.

I smiled as I got myself together and went to the counter to pay. I counted my change and, paper clutched under my arm. I took a moment to just feel the air around me when I stepped back outside. *Yep*, I agreed as I smiled back to the brightly shining sun, *today's a brand new day.*

JUST ADD WATER
SOMEBODY TELL ME WHERE TO FIND THE THINGS I HAD BEFORE
I NEVER ASKED FOR NOTHING MUCH BUT NOW I'M NEEDING MORE
THAN A SLAP ON THE BACK OR A KICK IN THE TEETH
AND A LOOK THAT SAYS THAT I SHOULD GO
NOW I'M DRESSING IN BLACK AND I'M DRAGGING MY FEET
AND I FEEL LIKE I'VE GOT NOTHING TO SHOW

"Just Add Water"—JD Glass

NICO DID COME ALONG WITH me to look at a couple of places, though he didn't say much. He would look around and nod judiciously.

I agreed.

Nothing knocked me out, either, until I got a tip from Gun, a bud at the Redspot who was a barback and did set up with me, before the place opened.

"Hey, you still lookin' for a place?" Gun asked me one afternoon right before sunset as we prepped the back room.

"Yeah, actually—everything I'm looking at is either too much for too little, or too far from everything, y'know?" I said to him as we raced with the mops across the empty floor. That spot would be packed with people later…

"Well, if you don't mind doing a house sort of thing, my uncle's looking to rent a room in the house—it's pretty large, you've got your own door and everything, and yeah, well, you'd have to share the bathroom and the kitchen, but it's just me and my uncle and I can give you a ride sometimes to work if you want—whaddaya think?"

I'd paused when he'd started to look at him as he spoke, and as I watched him, Gun and his softly spiked brown-blond hair and amber-brown eyes, watching me with an expression that seemed to me a combination of both shy and hopeful.

"Wow," I began, "I don't even—"

"And it's got great light and he doesn't want a lot—so you could save money, be in a good neighborhood, and have plenty of room and stuff for your music and your art," he added quickly.

Well, Gun *had* dated my roommate, Jackie, for several months (emphasis on "had"—and it wasn't a pretty ending, so we didn't talk about it or her much) so it wasn't as if he didn't know the living situation.

In fact, there had been many nights that Gun had stayed over which had led to my thinking of the sofa as my bed…

I nodded at him as I thought about it. "You know what?" I said finally, "I think I will check it out—where is it?"

"Awesome, I mean, cool, cool," Gun answered. "It's right near High Rock Park, and…"

I took the address from him, put it in my pocket, and promised I'd stop by the next day with my brother to check it out.

It was everything and more that Gun had said: it was a huge, huge, one room studio, and it wasn't far from High Rock Park, the nature preserve in the middle of Staten Island. Mind you, it wasn't right off the park, but it was only a few blocks away—which was absolutely perfect for my morning runs, while the yard in the back had a plenty of room for me to work out in; it was time to revisit my martial arts training.

The room was seriously bright and large—*especially* compared to the closet I'd lived in.

Y'know, I considered, *if I use the space right, there's room enough both for me and to create an art studio, instead of having to draw and paint while balancing something on my knees.*

Man, that would be nice, or to live without the constant shoving of everything I was working on—music *or* art—away and out of sight, totally disrupting flow, and worrying about pissing Jackie off—again.

And…the place gave me good vibe. It had a warmth to it that was more than the space and the light that streamed in from two windows, one with a south and the other with a western exposure.

In short, it was perfect and except for the excited sparkle in his eye when he looked at me, Nico and I managed to contain our excitement while I worked out the details of the rent with what was about to be my new landlord, Mr. Rabbitz.

Gun hadn't exaggerated: it actually came out to less than I was paying sharing a space with my roommates.

Mr. Rabbitz, the landlord and Gun's uncle, was an older bachelor gentleman who shared the house with his nephew, and a couple of pleasantly chunky cats. "Just watch for Mr. Chubbles," he said. "He likes to investigate things."

I laughed and promised to be careful, then handed over the money and Mr. Rabbitz gave me the keys.

"Where to now?" Nico asked as we got into the van.

There was lots to do and lots to think about but first—"Let's make a quick stop at the hardware store?" I asked him.

"Done, Chief," Nico smiled at me. "Dude, you've got some beautiful space in there—you've got room for all your art *and* your music stuff! And did you check out that incredible light?" he asked excitedly. "Between that and the space, you can really get some great work in!"

"Oh yeah!" I agreed enthusiastically, equally excited by the possibilities. "I think I'm gonna split the space into a studio…" and we discussed the possibilities on the way to the store.

"This…is for you," I told him as we settled back into the van. "'Cos if my mama is your mama, then mi casa es su casa." I handed him a copy of my new key on a red carabiner key chain.

Nico's eyes went wide with surprise then he grinned at me. "I'm so glad your mama is my mama," he said through his smile. "Sperm to worm?"

"You know it," I agreed, with a smile that matched his. "Womb to tomb, bro, womb to tomb."

I celebrated my twenty-first birthday by taking a single trip with Nico's van to get all of my stuff—clothing, books, supplies, and instruments—and another trip to Jerry's Pancake Place for fuel and where I begged for a bunch of milk crates they'd had lying in the back lot of the property forever that I was going to put to good use.

Sunlight streamed in on two sides of my space most of the day and using crates for book shelves, I had two completely separate areas. One was for my bed, which was the first one I'd ever bought. It might have been cheap, but it was new, it was clean and it was mine, all mine.

I kept my guitar right next to it.

The rest of the space, separated by a book case I'd created out of all those milk crates, housed my equipment and my art supplies, while a nice sized closet contained all of my clothes.

As far as the building itself went, at one point in its past, the house had been a funeral parlor, so the setup was a little strange: two kitchens, living rooms, libraries, one on top of the other, with a small barn in the back that had been converted into a garage with a loft on top.

And when you walked into the garage, there was a little "room" off to the left that had a rectangular space dug into the concrete.

Gun told me that's where the elevator used to be, from where they lowered the bodies. I realize that might have creeped some people out, but it didn't bother me—the dead didn't really hurt anyone, being inert and all, and while sure, yeah, I'd seen ghosts on and off my whole life, I'd never met one that ever wanted to hurt anyone.

Besides, ghosts had better things to do than haunt a funeral prep place, y'know?

Anyhow, while both my "room" and the loft were big enough to have the entire band over with equipment for practice, the loft was almost four times the size and would make a great complete living space. It needed some serious fixing up before it could be really habitable, but as soon as I had the cash, I was going to enquire about maybe renting that part and doing the repairs.

Hey, I'm a lesbian—I know how to use a hammer!

But since Christmas had come and gone a bare month before, my cash supply was a little lower than what I normally liked, so that would be some other day. I'd started working a new job right before the holidays, because I really needed to just get away from Staten Island and the whole gang I constantly ran into.

Yeah, I maintained my DJing status most Friday and Saturday nights at the Redspot, but I was getting sick of the whole scene and was trying to slow it down—but the more coldly polite I got, the more persistent everyone became.

Steph and Jerkster and I also started doing some sound backup for other bands and clubs here and there, so that was good, income-wise, and I got offers to do private parties, including a few great gigs at NYU's legendary

Fiji house, with their very well deserved and many-times-over hard-earned reputation as the all-time best-time party house around.

There's a saying about Fiji parties: when a Fiji party gets louder than it ought, the mayor knocks on the door in a bathrobe.

Stephie and Jerkster came with me to them to help with the sound set-up and so we could throw in a little "unplugged" performance—test the water, so to speak.

After this particular one, we decided to grab a bite and walk around the Village, to enjoy the 24-hour surround sound scene, and talk a bit about the next party we were doing, which was set for the first day of spring, as well as the work we were getting doing back-line sound work here and there for some clubs.

Hey, it was money, and it helped us get better and better prepping for our own live sound.

Work stuff aside though, they were my friends, and buddies that they were, they figured it was time I saw a gay bar that wasn't the depressing dive on Staten Island. Oh hell, maybe what I needed now was to be more heavily involved in gay culture—or more specifically, lesbian culture.

The more I thought about it, the more sense it made.

Maybe part of the problem was that I was inundated with straight messages—on every level. Besides, part of my new rule was "don't mess with straight chicks." Yeah, they seemed to like me, but yeah, they were nuts (um, Trace, remember?).

Anyhow, I'd walked into the bar with the band, had a cranberry and orange drink (I'd already had some alcohol, and I didn't want to get wasted at all) and looked around. Crowded—and way after midnight, too. One bartender in the front. One bar and bartender in the back. One bouncer by the door. No waitress—anywhere.

They needed help in my humble opinion.

Hmm…what the hell, I figured.

The bouncer was a big, and I mean big, woman. She was at least 5'10" and she seemed very intimidating. The arms crossed against her chest, spiky hair cut and the set straight line of her mouth didn't do anything to add warmth to her, and the scowl she wore as I approached wasn't encouraging, but hey, what the hell, right?

"Hi there, I'm Nina." I held out my hand with a smile. "You are?"

Her scowl deepened and her arms flexed a moment before she finally uncrossed them to shake my hand. "Jen," she growled at me finally. "Whaddayawant?"

"Nice to meet you, Jen," I smiled even wider as I shook her hand.

Okay, this wasn't someone who believed in social niceties, I could definitely tell. I took a breath. Straight to the point, then.

"You guys are really busy tonight," I observed and Jen looked around the bar before nodding in agreement. "Looks like you can use some help."

Jen squinted at me, looking me up and down. "Yeah, and...?" she asked helpfully and she crossed her arms over her chest again.

"I can help," I stated simply and shrugged my shoulders nonchalantly.

All right, I'd put it out there, guess I'd see what would happen.

The way I saw it, the worst thing that could happen was nothing, and since nothing happens without anyone's help anyway, I'd be no worse off— unless that deepening furrow between Jens' brows meant she was getting ready to toss me through the window.

I'd deal with that too, if it came to it, but she'd have to catch me first, and I hadn't been caught yet.

But still, I watched her face as I waited for an answer. Man, if those eyebrows came any closer, they were gonna stay that way forever, I thought as I calmly met and withstood Jen's glare. Finally, she nodded, having come to some sort of decision.

"You" —she pointed at me— "wait here." Jen turned her head to shout over the people sitting at the bar. "Hey! Dee! C'mere a sec!" Jen crossed her arms again and favored me with her grim expression. "Let's see what the manager says," she told me.

Steph and Jerkster had stepped away from the bar and I shrugged my shoulders in a "dunno" at them while we waited in silence. When Jen narrowed her beady focus on Jerkster, I could swear I heard him yelp.

"I'm uh, gonna find a bathroom, uh yeah, gotta go," he muttered behind me and made his way through the press.

"Chicken!" Steph hissed at his retreating form, which was rapidly being swallowed by the surrounding press.

I glanced over at Steph and we grinned at each other for a moment before Steph looked suddenly stricken.

"Ah shit!" she exclaimed in an undertone, staring in the direction Jerkster had walked.

"What?" I asked in a stage whisper—the Lady Grim was still staring at us, after all.

Steph leaned over to whisper in my ear. "He's got the bottle!"

"Shit!" I exclaimed in a low tone.

Shit was right.

Drinks were a little pricey there so we'd snuck in a bottle of plum wine (what can I say, it's a guilty pleasure of mine—and it was a gift from the head of Fiji House) and after buying a beer apiece, after drinking the beer, we'd take turns going into the bathroom and filling the beer bottles with wine, well, at least before I'd switched to "just juice."

I'd never done anything like that before, but Steph and Jerkster had, and it seemed like a good idea at the time.

Okay, actually, I'd let Steph drink my beer and have gone straight for the wine—I'm just not a beer fan, well, except for the occasional Guinness.

Besides, I wasn't worried about germs—alcohol killed them.

But still, there were two things wrong with this scenario and first was this: if we got caught, we were out of there. Secondly, Jerkster had the bottle—which meant that if he had it that much longer, it would end up empty, he would end up stupid, and we would end up caught. This would end any chance I had of ever coming here again, forget about getting a job.

Oh, and a drunk Jerkster was very difficult to guide—he was heavy!

"Go get him!" I hissed, hoping that Granite Sides wouldn't hear us over the din of the crowd.

Judging from what I could see of her personality, I figured it was more likely she'd think we were just two stupid kids having an argument.

"I'm on it!" Stephie agreed and off she went through the crowd to find him.

Jen's eyebrows touched as she watched me and I answered her gaze nonchalantly, standing as comfortably as I could.

For a moment, I felt like I was back in high school with all those nuns, and tried to mentally picture Jen in a habit. I shook my head.

Nope, didn't work for me—those muscles would never fit through the sleeves. But still, she didn't scare me—not the way the nuns did, anyway. They'd had a direct connection to God, all Jen had was that scowl.

And her size.

And those arms.

Okay, so she was scary.

Never mind.

Finally through the madding crowd came a figure I thought at first I recognized then two seconds later, I did.

"*Liebchen*!" exclaimed Dee Dee, waving her ever present bar rag before tucking into her waist band so she could scoop me up into an embrace and kissing my cheeks, each in turn. "Where have you been?"

I returned Dee Dee's greeting with a hug and a quick kiss of my own. I was very glad to see her. She'd left the Redspot a little while before I did and it was part of what made the job not so fun anymore: she was not only cool, she was the only other woman who worked there that wasn't a waitress. I attempted to explain over her repeated exclamations.

"Ah Dee, this girl," and the way Jen said it was with such disdain I actually wondered for a second what I'd done to piss her off, "here wants to know if—" Jen continued officiously but Dee Dee waved her off, put an arm around my shoulders and turned to face her.

"No no, Jen, this gorgeous creature is none other than Nina the DJ. *Und* she can have whatever she likes." Dee Dee turned back to me and asked, "What would you like, Nina? I am not just *bierwert*—barkeeper— here, I am the manager!" She beamed.

She seemed so genuinely happy and it made her eyes sparkle. I guess it had been longer than I thought since we'd spoken, because her accent hit my ears freshly, and it made me smile.

Dee Dee had been like that at the Redspot, too. The happier she was, the stronger her accent.

Cool.

"Hey, that's great!" I congratulated her. "That's truly terrific!"

I took a breath. Might as well just get to it.

"I was actually wondering if—" I began but Ham Hands interrupted me.

"The kid wants a job, Dee Dee," she told her in a loud and bored voice.

Turning to me, Jen said, "Hey, are you even old enough to be here? Let me see your ID."

I reached for my jacket pocket, but Dee Dee placed a restraining hand on mine. I had only recently reached legal majority, actually, but no one at the Redspot, or any other place I hung out or worked, had cared—or even noticed.

"Now Jen, that's not necessary," Dee Dee scolded, "I have told you, this is DJ Nina, we worked together. But I'm sorry, Nina," she turned to me and said with true regret, "we don't have a cabaret license, *und* so a DJ is not possible at this time."

She put a warm hand on my shoulder and her voice went from regret to concern.

"But are you okay? Do you need any help, can I give you some money or anything?" she asked me, reaching into her back pocket and pulling out quite a cash stash.

"No, no, I'm fine, I don't need any money," I said, embarrassed, waving her hands away, "but it looks like you could use a waitress—what do you say?"

Dee Dee grinned at me. "You were always a smart girl, Nina. Smart and proud. With that face, you'll make great tips!" she enthused and pinched my cheek. "Done then! *Und* when it's quiet, you'll work with me on the bar, I'll teach you everything I know!" She promptly hugged me again. "Oh Nina, we'll have such fun working together, I know it!" she enthused while she crushed me to her.

I murmured some sort of agreement; I don't know what because I couldn't breathe. Finally she released me and turned to Jen, while I surreptitiously restarted my deflated lungs and fixed my hair. As far as I could tell, my ribs and hair were still functional.

"You'll get the paperwork, Jen, and introduce Nina around. Nina," she said, "come tomorrow at four, and we'll start from there, okay?" She stroked my shoulder and I nodded in agreement.

"That's great, thanks," I answered, and I could feel the smile I wore stretch from ear to ear.

Cool!

A steady job that got me off Staten Island and away from everyone I didn't want to deal with anymore. DJing was great, but I didn't want to rely on it as my only source of income and as much fun as it could be, and doing backlines for sound was also okay, but I was starting to get frustrated, too.

I wanted to focus on *my* music, not someone else's.

"No, no, no thanks for me *liebchen* . You'll be doing me a favor."

Dee Dee smiled. "*Und* now I've got to get back to all those thirsty women!" She pinched my cheek. "Tomorrow, *liebchen*. For now, I leave you in Jen's capable hands, no?" she asked, looking at Jen.

"Of course," Jen answered stonily.

As soon as Dee Dee left, Jen rolled her eyes and shook her head as if she'd just been asked to scrub a prison bathroom with her toothbrush—again. "C'mon kid," she said in that same you're-buggin'-me tone, "let me take you 'round." She gestured and I followed.

She walked me through the bar rather quickly, since her size made a nice sized path for me to follow "And don't think your friends can drink for free," she warned me as we passed Jerkster and Stephie and they waved at me.

I smiled back at them despite the walking bad mood in front of me, and gave them the thumbs-up from behind the Iron Giant's back.

"Oh, uh, yeah, of course not," I answered as she turned around to darkly glare at me again. Apparently I hadn't answered quickly enough.

Mollified, she turned back and continued the tour which included the basement where all the kegs for the bar taps were. It was a crawl space you had to access from outside the building and while I had to walk bent over, Jen was bent almost double.

I tried very hard not to laugh—I didn't want to have to deal with that glare again—and I was pretty certain it wouldn't be too long before I saw it again.

I have to admit, this was one of those many times I wasn't wrong.

After the tour, Jen asked me to show up the next afternoon at two so we could do all the paperwork, and with no "good-bye," not even a "see ya," she steadfastly ignored me the rest of the night. I made sure to find and thank Dee Dee before we left, though, and also made sure to get phone numbers: the bar, her home, and her cell.

Hey, you never know when something might happen, right? I wanted to be prepared just in case it ever did.

Jerkster fell asleep as Stephie and I made plans on the ferry ride back to the rock we called home.

"Oh hey, want to come back to my place or we going to yours?" she asked. "We still going over that stuff?"

She was referring to our upcoming gig. Our upcoming first gig as a full band—ever. But man! It had been hard to book even a crappy night with a crappier time slot. It was two weeks of phone calls just to find out there was a twelve week wait for an available slot, then another two weeks of trying to get in touch with an actual person in charge to get scheduled into the twelve week wait.

The good, no, the best thing about it?

We were in.

But that was also the scary part, too, so we needed to use our time wisely. The plan had been to just hang out tonight then go back to one of our places and work out the rest of our set and rehearsal schedule and the three of us were supposed to be there—the drummer we were working with had already promised to work with whatever schedule we came up with.

But even if Jerkster was there physically—and that looked doubtful, given that we couldn't budge him—he was too drunk to be any good. But still, we had work to do.

Stephie and I could work it out. Besides, we usually handled all the scheduling, anyway.

"Uh, your place, it's closer," I decided.

"Cool then. I've got fudgicles," Steph enthused.

"Awesome," I smiled, "and I know an all-night pizza joint—my treat," I offered in return.

We walked off the boat together, leaving Jerkster to sleep it off. He'd show up at Stephie's house later, that's where he always went.

After a meal of pizza and frozen chocolate flavored chemicals, Stephie and I worked out all the details for our next few rehearsals, the songs for the show and how we'd meet up to get there.

This was CBGB's and it was a big deal for us. The fact that the place was so famous made it intimidating, but the fact that we were the last act on a Sunday let us know what our place was in the pecking order: nowhere.

FAITH
I NEVER THOUGHT IT'D BE SO HARD NOW JUST TO CRAWL
BUT IT'S THE THING THAT KEEPS ME FROM THE FIRE
AND I CAN'T STOP NOW BECAUSE I KNOW HOW FAR I'LL FALL
I'M HAND-OVER-HAND ON A THIN RED WIRE

"Sensation"—JD Glass

IN BETWEEN REHEARSALS AND SLEEP, I worked.

And worked.

Jen constantly picked on me when Dee Dee wasn't there.

"Hey kid, go across the street to the White Horse Tavern and get ice—here's your bucket," and she'd hand me a five gallon bucket and smirk at me, or "Hey, bar's backed up—grab two cases of beer from storage," referring to the crawl-space under the bar.

What she didn't know was that I used to barback for extra money at the Redspot, and the buckets I'd handled were 10 gallon ones, while the boys and I used to race unpacking the beer—and we'd carry four cases at a time, so it was my time to smirk to myself when I saw her or Grace, the other bartender, sweating and straining while they carried two.

Hell, compared to the labor I'd performed at the Redspot, this was a vacation. Well, except for Jen.

What. A. Bitch.

And what was with the "kid" thing, anyway?

"Kid, there's a couple waiting in the corner," she'd order. Like, duh, I was already getting their drinks. Or, "Hey kid, grab a broom, will ya?" Uh, just finished with that.

It was constant and if it wasn't about work it was about something else. "Kid like you should be going crazy—playing the field like tomorrow won't ever come," she told me seriously one day when she caught me pocketing a phone number with a tip someone had given me without a second glance.

"Not my thing," I smiled over my shoulder as I walked my tray to the bar.

I worked the rest of the night, like I did the others: fetching drinks, cleaning, making chitchat and correct change. When we'd closed for the night and the lights had come on for the clean-up, Jen approached me again after we were done.

"Is it cuz you're small town, or is it cuz you're a virgin?" Jen asked me as I sat at the now emptied and shiny clean bar, sipping at a coke and waiting for Grace to come up front with our pay for the night.

The few patrons that remained—all half dozen or so of them—were regulars and well known to the rest of the staff. They were either waiting to meet someone, hooking up with someone from the staff, or just keeping us company and the last of their drink company, I guess.

I suspected one or two of them had romantic inclinations towards a particular bartender, Grace.

"What?" I asked casually, not rising to the bait.

I'd gotten the idea in my head that as long as I kept perfectly calm and didn't react to anything Jen said, maybe she'd eventually back off.

So far it hadn't really worked, but it was better than losing my temper, or at least that's how I saw.

I beat the shit out of the trees in the yard when I got home.

But still... She was the boss when Dee Dee wasn't around—and that was a lot. Seems that managing a bar has a lot more to do with schedules and paperwork than it does with bartending.

"Your attitude," Jen answered, skipping snideness for directness this time. "Are you just really that provincial?"

I sipped my soda quietly as I wondered what the hell she was talking about and considered how to answer her. What attitude, anyway?

I put the glass down carefully. "First—what are you talking about? What attitude? And secondly, how do you know I'm not racking 'em up on the side?" I stared straight into those dark eyes.

Jen's lip curled into a sneer. "Kid, I had to rip them off of you tonight and you didn't even respond—and it's not the first time that happened, either. You get numbers shoved at you left and right and you don't even glance at them. You just smile thanks and stick 'em in your pocket—what's wrong with you?" She finally got to her burning question. "Are you deformed or something?"

Well, it wasn't snide, but it was still rude. I raised an unamused eyebrow at her at that last bit.

Jen did have a point, though. Women stuck money in my bra, their numbers written on the bills. When I brought them their drinks, they'd ask if I could give them a cherry when I brought them their drinks, then tied cherry stems into knots with their tongues and smiled sweetly as they handed them to me.

They brought me cappuccinos and pizza, one had even made me a sweater and another gave me a leather jacket I still have. One called me edible and another asked what afternoon she could pencil me in for a session of cunning linguistics—and yes, I do know what that means, same as it does for "French."

The night before, some guy (and yes, there were occasional guys that came in sometimes. They were either gay themselves or vouched for by the women they were with) actually offered to pay me if I would take his young friend to the prepaid hotel room and help her celebrate her twenty-first birthday—by "making her a woman."

These women were pretty, smart, charming. They were sexy, bold, creative. Some of them were aggressive and some of them were shy and some of them were sweet, but through it all, I smiled, I thanked them for the cappuccino, I listened politely—and I said no.

Every time.

For those that got a little too aggressive for my taste, there was Jen and in all honesty, it didn't matter how crowded the place got, and sometimes there was barely breathing room. All I had to do was turn my head and lift my chin and in seconds, I'd receive an apology—or there'd be room for one more on the dance floor.

Earlier this particular evening, a group of women were celebrating something, I dunno what—could've been a softball game, could have been a corporate merger, the clientele was so diverse—and I'd had to bring two trays of drinks to the table they'd found in the corner.

While I was holding the trays, about four of them tried to strip me—and I mean, *strip* me. I didn't know what to do, didn't want that attention, didn't want to drop the trays, either, and when I looked around for Jen to call her, before I'd even opened my mouth, all I'd had to do was make eye contact and she was there in less than half a second flat.

Good thing, too, because my shirt had already been opened to the waist and the first button of my jeans had gotten undone.

"I mean, nothing fazes you. You know, one day when you're older, you're gonna look back at this time and wish you'd done something with it." Jen nodded at me solemnly. "They're not always gonna throw it at you like that."

I toyed with the edge of my glass. It's not like she was saying anything I hadn't thought before—it's just that I didn't believe that shit anymore.

Besides, how did you explain to someone that you were already, in your heart of hearts, just sick to death of the whole, empty, ugly thing?

None of it meant anything.

At the Redspot, they wanted me because I was the DJ—no other reason. After the incident with Candace and the way I'd continued, they wanted me because they "knew" I'd make them come.

Hell, women and girls, supposedly "straight" ones—would accost me in the club and try to kiss me. I knew they were straight though: the gay girls wouldn't care where they might try to kiss me, the straight ones tried to steal my kisses in the bathroom.

Me, well, I was no innocent. Sometimes I took someone who kissed me into the booth and make out and dance with them there, sometimes two. There had been more than several nights that I'd actually left the booth and prowled the crowd, so restless, so high on that feeling that rides right under the skin through the blood, that unquenchable thirst, that I took the maximum the booth could—three—back with me.

I didn't care who they were, I didn't care who they were with, it didn't matter. For as long as I wanted, they were mine.

All of them.

Any of them.

All I had to do was walk up, smile, and turn my head towards the booth. They knew what to do; they always did.

Usually a party in the booth meant just that: a party. We'd make out, we'd dance, and the girls drank for free. It was sensual more than sexual and I'd sent more than one back to her boyfriend or girlfriend (but usually a boyfriend—the girlfriend usually came in, too) more than ready for whatever they were going to do next.

Unless we were dancing or kissing though, I let no one touch me.

And yes, I fucked some of them and on at least two occasions I'd fucked one while making out with another. No one ever—*ever*—got invited back a second time. My nights had gotten more and more crowded, the dancers themselves took on a new edge. I no longer wore black most of the time—I wore it all the time.

And I earned it.

Jen's voice broke in over my thoughts. "Really, Nina. One day, you're going to be old and alone and not as pretty, I mean, as young as you are now. You should just get out there and enjoy it, you know? Rack up the points while you can."

Ah…points.

There it was again, the concept that got me into so much trouble in the first place.

I smiled at Jen, trying not to chuckle. Jen was being sincere and I didn't want to hurt her feelings. Besides, this was the first time she'd ever spoken to me without her customary growl or glare and I didn't want to spoil the moment.

But it *was* fucking ironic—I mean, everyone put so much pressure on getting laid.

Why?

There had to be something more to being "young, dumb and full of cum," as Cap described everyone under thirty.

Wasn't there?

Something more, I mean.

And I was surprised, too. I mean, okay, I knew straight guys had to deal with that sort of pressure from their peers all the time; I could see that with Nico and the other guys I knew.

But I was shocked to experience the same sort of pressure from women, I mean, from gay women.

Wasn't that the sort of thing every woman pretty much complained about? How all anyone wanted to do was to fuck 'em? Part of the negative aspects of patriarchal culture or some such stuff? So why repeat the pattern?

And why, why, *why*, of all people, pick on me?

Besides, what in the *hell* did Jen know about me, anyway?

She had no *idea* of who I was or what I had done. I mean, for fuck's sake, one night while I was DJing, during the beginning of a really hot tune, I had descended from the sky box to hunt—that was what it was, essentially. In seconds, I had found the right girl. This night had brought me a blonde with an attitude I liked and as I'd stepped up to her, a familiar voice spoke over my shoulder.

"Trace always said you were really cute," said Van behind me.

What.

A.

Fuck.

But interesting, though, because he and Trace weren't together, but he *was* with the girl I wanted.

The last time I'd seen him had been a few weeks ago, after Candace had left and before my first anonymous guest.

In my mind's eye, I could still see the quirk of his lips.

"Don't talk to me," I told Van and laughed lightly, never taking my eyes from his dance partner, who smiled back a bit nervously. "Go wait by the booth."

I've no idea what possessed me to order him like that, but whatever the reason, I wasn't terribly surprised when he actually did it. I'd tracked him until he settled by the door, then returned my attention to the blonde before me.

She wasn't a girl exactly and she was a bit more than a young woman. Whatever she was, she was definitely beautiful to look at, with lanky legs and like I said before, I liked the way she tossed her head.

It was that simple.

"I'm Nina." I smiled and introduced myself although I knew it wasn't necessary. "Join me for a drink?" It wasn't a question—we both knew the answer.

"Simone," she answered with a coy look and licked her lips. "I'd love to."

Yeah, this is gonna be a great night, I thought to myself as I took her hand and led her back to the sky box. I didn't even look at Van as I entered the sky box and they both followed me in.

"Lock it," I requested casually over my shoulder as I made my way to the request window and signaled for Andra. I glanced down at my meters as I passed; I was good for time.

I turned to Simone. "What would you like to drink?" I asked cordially.

"Corona. Corona with—"

"—with lime," I finished for her with another smile and the one she gave me back packed some serious sensuality.

Van piped in. "Hey, I want—"

I held up a hand to forestall him—I didn't want to hear his voice if I could help it. "Tequila. Beer back, right?" I asked, finally looking at him with an arched brow.

Van seemed impressed that I knew that as I turned away from them and back to the window. Andra had arrived and I gave her their requests. "Oh, and the usual for me," I grinned at her.

She smiled and nodded, then made her way back through the crowd.

"Make yourselves comfortable," I invited both of them. "I've got to set a few mix times and cues."

I turned back to my tables and checked my mix, my mic and my headphones. "Any special requests?" I asked Simone, as I slipped them over my head.

She and Van had made themselves at home along the back bench but at that, she stood up. "Only if you'll dance with me," she asked, her voice throaty and low.

"Of course." I laughed lightly, because that was part of the point, because it was part of the plan, and she was eager to play my game. "What will it be?"

She told me and I programmed my next set. By the time I was done, the drinks had arrived and I tossed mine down—a shot of scotch followed by a shot of blackberry brandy. My thought was, if I was going to poison my liver, I didn't want all the extra calories that a mixed drink would provide. In fact, it was a good thing I didn't like beer—turns out that a serving of that has a full pound of them.

Everything and everyone set, I danced with Simone and Van danced behind her. She was a good dancer, and when the timing was right, I kissed her, a thorough, sensual kiss that made promises I just might keep—tonight. Simone's hands clutched at my waist as mine tickled, traveled, and teased up her spine. With my tongue, I drew delicate lines into the hollow of her throat that I knew, from the deep sound that rumbled beneath and through my lips, she enjoyed.

When Van reached forward to touch me, I slapped his hand away. "Don't touch me," I told him with a deadly smile over Simone's shoulder. "You don't talk to me, and you *don't* fucking touch me."

"Sorry," he muttered and looked away, over at the dancing crowd.

"Now…where were we?" I asked Simone as her hips swayed dangerously close to mine, but I held them tightly, less than an inch away from me, building, playing, delaying the inevitable. "Oh…I remember," I said and smiled. "Right about here…"

I returned my lips to her neck.

By design rather than by accident, we'd ended up with Van on the back bench and Simone between us. When Van groaned, it was all I could do to force myself not to think about the last time I'd seen him.

Van spread his legs and Simone nestled between his thighs, her ass grinding against his denim-covered cock as we continued to dance.

I nibbled on her lip and let my fingertips trail along her thighs until I reached her cunt. *Oh…what a nice surprise*, I thought as she tossed her head and leaned back against Van, clutching his thighs. No underwear and shaved. She spread her legs for me and I slid my fingers between her warm, wet lips, enjoying her silkiness. She groaned and I licked the column of her neck.

"God…" Van groaned, his hips grinding behind her.

"If you're not silent, I'll stop," I warned him as I gently played in Simone's waiting cunt, teasing the emptiness that waited for me to fill it. "And if I hear you come, I swear to heaven, I'll slap you."

I meant it, every word of it but far from upsetting him, that seemed to excite him more, and he visibly shuddered as he tried to control himself.

"Shh, Van," Simone husked out, her knees giving momentarily before she righted herself.

"Good." I smiled sweetly at him. "We have an understanding." I took a moment's pity on him. "Here," I told him, grabbing one of his hands that had clutched the bench. "Hold this."

I took his hand and put it on Simone's skirt, lifting it to her waist. He got the idea and did the same with his other free hand. She was naked from the waist down and I was right: she was shaved with the exception of a small tuft at the top.

Simone caught my eye and I watched her, still teasing, until we both looked down to see what my fingers had found—a small barbell above the base of her clit.

I definitely couldn't let that go. "Look what we have here," I commented as I knelt between her legs.

Her shorn pussy looked vulnerable and even more so with the metal running through it. I glanced up to see Van's fingers had gone almost white with the strength of his hold and control.

I flicked the barbell with my tongue and Simone moaned heartily, tossing her head back onto Van's shoulder. Van leaned back for better balance and pulled her with him, his hard cock now pressed up between her ass cheeks.

I trailed my tongue along her length a few times, from her opening to her clit. She tasted like pineapple, I thought, as I slide my tongue inside her. Her hips jumped and I could swear I could hear her mutter "oh yeah," as she fucked my face.

I brought my hands up again and gently pressed against Van's balls, rubbing lightly with my thumb against the denim as it got damp from Simone's pussy. I brought my other hand up and placed the very edges of two fingers against her opening, slick with invitation and played my tongue rapidly against her clit.

Two things went through my head and not necessarily at the same time: I could have done anything I wanted, anything, to Van. He had given me complete control, and I liked that—a *lot*. Too much, even. The other was God, but she was ready, more than ready, and as I got ready to bring a third finger there, I stood and replaced my tongue with my thumb.

Van had burrowed his face into her neck and with the same hand that had gently stroked his balls, I took his cheek in my palm and pushed his head firmly back against the wall as I leaned in to replace him. My thumb pressed firmly on Simone's beautifully hard clit and I my fingers slid ever so slightly inside her.

Her cunt was *hot*.

Simone turned her face and rubbed her cheek against my neck, then blindly lifted her lips to mine. I kissed her fully, deeply, I let her savor the taste of her wanting cunt in my mouth.

I brought my lips to her ear and raked them lightly with my teeth. "Are you ready?" I asked her softly.

"God...yes," she groaned, her hips moving lightly in time with my thumb.

Are you sure?" I teased gently, but sincerely. There was always time to back out if she wanted, but I was pretty sure of what she wanted.

"Yes," she hissed at me, breathless, and I slowly thrust all three fingers into her waiting hole, then just as slowly eased out again, letting her pussy adjust, feeling the length of it. "Oh..." she sighed as I pushed slowly within her, a smooth back and forth.

Two fingers would have been okay, but three meant she was tight around me—and I wanted her to really enjoy this, and I wanted Van to know just how much. I could feel him grit his teeth under my hand, and his body gave a slight jerk, which served the purpose of shoving her pussy firmly on my fingers.

I finally released Van's head and buried my fingers in Simone's hair, drawing her face again to mine to kiss her once more before I fucked her earnestly, her cunt sucking on my fingers as I moved inside her, her hips adding to the motion. She tucked her face into my neck again and I held her firmly as her pussy drew me into her again and again.

Finally, she tensed and she bit my shoulder as she came, a soft sound issuing from her throat. I let her relax against me as I carefully withdrew and I stroked her head where she rest it on my shoulder.

"I've got you, you're okay," I whispered softly into her ear and she sighed.

I finally looked at Van. His head lay against the wall, his eyes closed. His face seemed soft and vulnerable and I noticed a dark stain on his lips.

He must have bitten them till they'd bled to keep quiet, I realized.

Fuck the points.

I'd completely "sunk his battleship" and burned his board.

"Good boy," I'd smiled at him, but I hadn't mean it.

Why had he done that?

Why give anyone one so much power of you? Nothing could possibly be worth that, could it?

And I'd enjoyed it, all of it, including my own violence, which frankly had left me pretty disgusted with myself. I'd felt like the biggest piece of shit.

"I'm not worried about points," I told Jen as I broke from the memory, because I completely meant it.

I'd done enough of that, had enough of that.

It was probably very high up there on the list of stupidest-things-I-have-done. Jen's brow furrowed—dammit—as she focused on me. "I'm not worried about being alone, either." I smiled at her, picked up my drink and stood.

"There's someone for me, or there's not. Either way," I saluted her with my glass, "I like my own company."

I finished my drink with a little flourish and put the glass back down on the bar. Jen got up too, and we walked over to the locked door, where we could see and hear a woman knocked. *Probably here to meet someone*, I thought, *or a very last minute drink.*

"Besides, between work and the band, I've got a lot on my plate," I added as we walked over. "I really don't have time to get involved in all of that romantic crap."

"Kid, you're wrong," Jen stated flatly as she put her hand on the lock. "All that one-person shit is just that—shit. You're gonna waste your looks, you're gonna waste your energy and you're gonna waste time—time that could be spent having fun, getting laid, whatever—and then, you'll get screwed over. Ya gotta make hay while the sun shines and all that."

A buzz filled me, skittered over my skin. Because she was wrong, I knew she was wrong, and the sense of…something…filled me so strongly…

"C'mon Jen," I said and smiled at her anyway through the feeling and my teeth as her hand twisted on the key. "You've gotta have a little faith."

I stepped in front of her before she opened the door.

That was our custom—I'd greet and speak and if I needed back up, Jen was a breath behind me. The door swung open and I opened my mouth with the usual.

"Sorry—we're closed," I began, not really looking at the woman who stood before me, ignoring, too, the buzz that pressed in on me until my skin felt tight.

"Nina? Nina Boyd?" she asked and now I really looked.

Closely.

"Fran? Francesca DiTomassa?" I asked incredulously as I recognized an old friend, and someone I'd been close with, from high school, while the tight buzz that had held and filled me seconds ago now exploded into a warm fuzz that spilled down over my head, then flowed down my body.

The honey-blonde curls poured over her coat past her shoulders and almond-shaped brown eyes were enough to tell me, but if they weren't, there was her picture-perfect smile, exactly as I remembered it.

"Oh my God!" I burst out in delighted surprise, and ignoring the glare I knew for sure was aimed at my back, I opened the door to let her in.

"God Fran, it's been ages!" I exclaimed as we embraced.

"Nina, I knew it! I just knew it!" she declared in return.

She leaned back to look at me and cupped my face in her hands, shaking her head with obvious joy and disbelief. "I can't believe I'm actually looking at you," Fran said, her warm brown eyes twinkling. "I knew in my heart it wasn't true!"

She gave my cheek a solid smooch for good measure which I returned, and I heartily hugged her back.

"What wasn't true?" I asked, puzzled. That was a pretty strange way to say hello, wasn't it? Yeah, I thought so, too.

She shook her head, unable to answer while she played with my hair and patted my shoulder as if checking to make sure I was solid.

"Friend of yours?" Jen asked drily behind me as she moved to let us both in, then locked the door behind us.

"Oh yeah. Hey Jen, this is Francesca...Fran—" I introduced, then corrected at the raised eyebrow she gave me. "Fran? Jen."

They shook hands as they repeated the polite social formulas.

"Like a drink?" I asked, walking behind the bar. I ignored the glare coming from Jen. I was allowed buy-backs and I hadn't used a single one since I'd started working there. The one whatever it was Fran wanted certainly wasn't going to hurt anyone.

"Sure," Fran agreed, settling into a stool in front of me, "that's what I was stopping in for. Guinness if you've got it."

Jen checked the door again and came over to the bar, then grabbed herself a seat close to Fran.

"Guinness from the gun," I agreed, and got a mug. "Want one?" I asked Jen as she settled in.

"Yeah, why not?" she answered with a tired smile.

Huh.

She could smile.

Well and good, then.

I grabbed two frosted mugs from the stainless steel freezer before me, then opened the tap. As the beer flowed, I watched to make sure it came out right, because there's nothing better than a good head—if you're into that sort of thing.

"Here." I presented the beer with a napkin to each of them. "Enjoy."

Fran smiled at me and hefted the frosted glass, and Jen wrapped her hands around hers. Satisfied that they were well served, I drew myself one, too.

Oh, what the hell—it was only one beer and it was Guinness after all.

"To your health," Fran toasted and smiled, then took a hearty swig.

"Yeah, your health," Jen agreed with a twist to her lips that I assumed was a grin.

"Thanks," I returned, with a sip of my own.

Grace came ambling out of the back room as I put my mug down. She had three nicely thick envelopes; it seemed like we'd had a good night. The tips bulging in my back pocket agreed.

Mutely, I held up a mug and offered her a beer and she grinned and nodded her head. She sat on the other side of Jen and as she handed us our envelopes, I handed her the beer. I didn't even look in mine, I just tucked it into my waistband.

Now that everyone was settled and watered so to speak, I figured I could actually have a conversation with my old friend.

"I just can't believe it, this is totally fucking unreal," Fran said, leaning her head against her hand to stare at me.

Well, unless she knew something I didn't know—and given that she kept shaking her head like she did—she was going to have to share it soon.

It was starting to make me a little anxious.

To avoid more of that uncertain feeling, I lifted my glass and took a hearty first swallow.

Eesh.

I'd forgotten how bitter Guinness was.

Fran took a sip and put her mug down. She reached with the lightest of touches across the bar for my hand. I would have moved it away, but her expression, a combination of wonder and sorrow, stopped me as she traced her fingertips over my knuckles and veins with a touch so light, I would hardly have known she was there if I wasn't looking.

I definitely felt the tear that hit my skin, though.

"Fran... What's the matter?" I asked, instantly concerned.

It's funny, isn't it, how sometimes between people the years and the distance don't matter; once you reconnect, it's as if you'd never parted?

That's how I felt seeing Fran, well, after the initial shock had worn off.

I was back to swimming pools and driving lessons, pre-meet pasta dinners and post-race bullshit, hangouts that were almost-dates between us, and the warmth of our friendship, the shared food and shared lockers, shared clothes and shared friends.

And Samantha. I hadn't heard from her in all this time, either. That made me stop cold—maybe something had happened to her, maybe something terrible.

I rubbed Fran's hand with my own.

"Kitt, what's wrong?" I asked gently, using her old nickname. "Can I do something?"

Fran exhaled and squeezed my hand back, lifting her filled eyes to mine. "You're not going to believe this." She tried to smile, and gave a little laugh through her tears.

I needed to get around to the other side of the bar, I had to sit next to her. I glanced over at Grace and Jen.

Grace gave Fran a sympathetic glance, then reached over the bar and grabbed a tissue, placing it next to our conjoined hands before she excused herself.

Fran took the tissue and although she remained silent, she buried her face in her hand and her shoulders shook as she began to cry in earnest.

I stole a glance over at Jen, who looked back at me with alarm in her eyes, and I mutely asked her with a lift of my chin if I could have a private moment.

Jen, thankfully, instantly understood and nodded in agreement as she hastily got out of her seat. I guess she'd felt awkward about just leaving someone to sit and cry at the bar.

I bent my head closer to Fran's. "Hey, give me a sec, okay?" I asked her softly. "I just want to come around to your side."

Fran squeezed my hand then let go. "'S'all right, I'm okay," she sniffed and bravely grinned at me.

"Okay," I agreed with a small smile of my own to make her feel better, but I moved quickly so she wouldn't feel alone. Once there, I took one of her hands, and as she swiveled to face me, I gently cupped her shoulder.

"What's the matter Fran?" I repeated, genuinely concerned for her as I searched overfull eyes that shone at me. "What's wrong?"

She increased the pressure on my hand and tentatively reached for my face. I let her fingers touch me and she lightly rubbed her thumb along my cheek.

"You're supposed to be dead," she whispered, her expression awestruck.

Did she just say what I'd thought she'd said? I sat up straight and gave her shoulder another reassuring rub before taking it away. I could feel my brow furrow—in fact, my eyebrows were probably doing a great imitation of Jen's. "Did you say…?" I trailed off as she nodded in confirmation.

I leaned back in my seat, shocked. "What…how?"

Fran took my hand back in both hers and leaned in so closely that I could count the tears in her lashes.

"I called you, Nina, I swear I called you," she swore, her eyes wide as they stared into mine, "and your father, he—"

"No, no, it's okay." I held a hand up. I knew exactly what she was going to say before she even said it.

I knew what my father had done: the summer after I "came out" (which also happened to be the year many of my friends had graduated from high school; I'd had another year to go), he told many of my friends not that I no longer lived with my family—but that I no longer lived. As in, at all.

I didn't realize how many people that he had told, how many people would have believed it—and why wouldn't they? He was my *father*, and why would someone say such a terrible thing, right?

Shock and anger warred in me; I suddenly knew exactly what it was like to burn with cold fury. But none of this was Fran's fault, so I forced those feelings down and away somewhere and brought myself back to the present, which was where Fran was. My chest hurt seeing how much pain Fran carried in her eyes and it was horrible to know that she'd felt it because of me.

"I'm so sorry…" I put my arms around her. "I'm just so sorry." I pressed my cheek against her head as her hands wrapped around my ribs.

"Looks like this is a good time for a drink," Jen's voice said nearby.

I jumped a bit, and Fran and I looked up to see Jen standing behind the bar. As Fran and I let each other go, I quirked Jen a quick grin.

Jen flashed the tiniest of smiles back to me and it was such a brief little thing I almost missed it—but I hadn't. She was okay, after all.

"'Nother Guinness for you?" Jen asked Fran, her hands already pulling the mug out from the freezer.

"You know, I think I need a shot," she said thoughtfully. "Walker Black, straight up?"

Great idea, I thought. A shot sounded just about right. Maybe even two.

"Righto," Jen agreed as she pulled the bottle, "and you?"

I grinned as I watched her visibly refrain from adding "kid" to that. "Same," I answered Jen, "with a blackberry brandy chaser."

Jen squinted at me as she poured my shots. "Oh yeah, I forgot you do that," she commented as she poured.

"Want to try it?" I asked Jen.

"Hell, why not, right?" She surprised me by actually smiling fully and for real as she pulled another pair of shot glasses.

"You know, me too," Fran chimed in.

Finally, all the shots were on the bar and I took mine in hand.

Fran eyed hers a moment, then sighed. "Okay," she drawled and picked hers up. "I'm as ready as I'm gonna be." She smiled and I brought my own glass up, ready to swallow.

"Wait!" she exclaimed, "we have to have a toast. We can't just discover you're alive and not celebrate!"

I smiled. "I knew I was alive," I told her, "but I'm happy enough to celebrate seeing you again. What say you we toast to that?" I again held my little shot to the ready.

"Or how about…" Fran mused a moment, "to absent friends reunited?" Her smile practically gleamed, showing off her perfect white teeth.

Jen walked up behind me and clapped me—*hard*—on the shoulder, and her finger tips dug a bit. "Howzabout…to faith?" she suggested, more than a touch of irony in her voice, at least to my ears. "Nina knows all about that one, don'cha kid?"

Fran didn't catch the sarcasm. "Hey yeah!" she enthused, "all things in their own time, all things for their own reasons and..." her face grew serious and her eyes over-bright "...we'll stay in touch from now on?" She grinned at me crookedly.

Touched, because the girl whose nickname was Kitt had been kind but stoic and because the woman before me was willing to let me see she had feelings, I gently clinked my glass against hers.

"Yes," I told her and took a sip. "I absolutely promise."

"Me too," Fran agreed and drank some of her own. "Oh!" she smacked her lips, "that's really sweet—what a great contrast."

"Yeah," I began, "that's why—"

"It's time to go," Jen informed us both, a hand clapped on either of our shoulders.

I gazed around.

Oh yeah.

The bar was empty.

She was right, it *was* time to go. I just had to—

"I'll take care of those," Jen said, taking the now empty shot glasses from our hands, "I'll lock up." She herded us forward with her frame with a light wave of her arms.

"Yeah, I'm sorry," Fran apologized as she walked, "I didn't realize—"

"No need to apologize," Jen said breezily, "just have a nice night. You can wait here in the vestibule—Nina'll be with you shortly." She gazed at me for the last part with an intent that I understood instantly.

"Yep, I'll be done in a sec," I smiled at Fran, but inwardly, I sighed. I should have known that Jen would make sure that it was time to pay the piper.

"What do I owe for the drinks?" I asked her as she closed the door behind Fran.

I walked over to the first window to pull the internal gates, first one, then the other until the lock rings met.

"Naw, nothing kid," she answered as she reached over my head and popped the first of four padlocks we had to take care of. "Not a thing."

Surprised, I arched a brow at her. "Thanks," I said quietly as we made our way to the next window.

"Don't mention it," she dismissed as she stood back to admire our handiwork.

Two more to go. When they were done I went behind the bar and made sure everything that needed to be off was, checked the dishwasher once more and made one last inspection of all the garbage pails to ensure that they were not only empty but ready to go for the next round. Finally, everything was away, locked down and we were just about good to go.

I grabbed my bag (black, messenger style—of course) and my coat out from behind the little cubby behind the bar where I had stashed them when I'd first arrived.

"Ready for the outside gate?" Jen asked me as we stood by the door, the place now lit only by the low security lights that never went out.

"Sure 'nuff," I answered.

I slid on my coat and pulled my scarf out of the sleeve where I'd tucked it for safety, and as I carefully wound it around my neck, Jen unlocked the door for the last time this night.

Fran had waited in the vestibule and stepped over as we walked outside.

"Hey!" She smiled. "You done?

"Just about." I grinned back at her, then turned around to face the vestibule.

While Jen reached into her coat pocket for the last of the padlocks, I jumped and reached for the final gate that would seal and lock the bar completely for the night.

My fingertips grabbed an edge and I let gravity and my body drag it down to just above my head. From there I muscled it down to the ground— Jen couldn't bend because of a back injury—then I held it in place by sheer will so Jen could snap the remaining locks in.

Once I heard the pop that meant we were really and truly done, I straightened out and dusted my hands. "Another one down," I commented to Jen as she bent back from the waist to stretch her spine. "See you in the afternoon?"

It was almost five in the morning after all and we'd both be back there by four-thirty in the afternoon.

"Yeah, definitely," Jen agreed with an equally tired grin.

Hey wait, were we actually having a friendly moment? Did anyone have a camera to record this for the permanent record? Wow, maybe we'd even have friendly conversations and who knew, maybe go crazy and actually—gasp! get along! I was actually pleasantly surprised.

"Hey, have a good one, 'kay?" I waved to her in friendly parting, intending to get to Fran.

"Yeah, you too," Jen agreed with a little wave of her own. "Oh, by the way, Nina?" she called to my back. "You know, there's a word for people like you."

Well, as pleasant as our earlier interchange had been, I guess I couldn't have expected it to continue, could I. Ahh...whatever, dammit. I really thought we'd made some headway.

Frustration rose through my head to meet the ache that had started behind my eyes, but I let none of that show. Instead, I merely arched an eyebrow at her in question.

"Yes?" I drawled out, letting the sound flow low, rich and syrupy.

Not for nothing was I a singer, after all and this was one of those times I actually remembered it (the rest are subconscious, honest). I pursed my lips as I watched her, waiting for whatever was coming next.

For once, Jen seemed to lose all of her cocksureness and even some of her constant anger as she mulled over her answer. She suddenly forced a grin through her grimness and clapped me on the shoulder. "I'll tell ya when I think of it kid," she said heartily, patting my shoulder again. "I'll see ya later."

Um okay, that was strange, but it was better than what I'd been expecting—like something along the line of "dumb" or another related word. Relieved, I tucked this thought into the back of my head: whatever she'd been going to say, she'd obviously changed her mind.

"Yeah, when the sun's out," I agreed and waved good-bye for the final time this night.

Fran had retired a few feet away under the lamp post on the corner and I walked over, happy to be done and happier still to have run into Fran.

Okay, technically, she'd run in to me, but the end result was all the same, right? Now that I'd actually seen her, I didn't want to say goodbye just yet, didn't want to just say "nice seeing you" and exchange numbers and lose 'em in the wash. I didn't know what I wanted, I didn't know what I needed. All I knew was that I really didn't want to see her go.

The warm buzz that filled me and the pulse that sounded low and steady in my ears seemed to agree.

"You up for a bite? My treat," I offered as I reached out to tuck her arm in mine, where I briskly rubbed her sleeve.

Besides being the polite thing, it was cold out here and Fran had been waiting for me outside, even if part of that time had been in the vestibule. We started walking north on Seventh Avenue. Not that we knew where just yet, but I did know several places in that direction that would still be open and served decent food.

Fran smiled her brilliant smile back at me. "Don't you have to get a boat or something?" she asked, lightly tweaking my forearm as we walked.

"Nah, there's always another one. Besides, carpe noctem, right?" I smiled and watched her profile as we walked.

The sky had developed that heavy hush of expectation and the skyline had turned grey and red with clouds.

I couldn't believe that running into Fran like this had me feeling as crazy-happy as a puppy who'd just been given a treat and even with the somewhat strange turn our conversation had taken earlier, it was somehow still almost all I could do to keep from skipping. How weird was that?

But judging from the way her eyes shone and from the wattage in that grin, Fran felt the same way, too.

"Seize the night—what, is that like your motto or something? Are you going to melt in the sun?" she joked.

"Hey, it's just because I work nights..." I said and laughed. "It's the only available time I've got."

"Oh, so that's it," Fran said. She dropped her arm from mine and stopped to look at me directly. "I thought maybe, you know, the black clothes, pale face, disappearing for a couple of years and then reappearing as this gorgeous—"

Okay, that was enough and I stopped her right there. "Okay, okay, enough," I shushed, and placed two gentle fingers on her lips. My breath puffed out in the chill air and her eyes locked into mine.

That's funny, I thought, *I'm taller,* and it was true—the last time I'd seen Fran, she'd been taller than me. Not by much though, true, but now, I was taller. Okay, so it wasn't a huge height difference but still...

The caramel of her eyes seemed to warm, glowing under the street light with a honey clear intensity and I enjoyed the fact that Fran was examining me with seemingly the same emotion in her eyes.

I brought my hands down to rest by my sides as the air seemed to mass and warm around us, and the tiny smile I could feel playing around the edge of my lips was mirrored by the one that bordered the corner of hers.

"You don't know how good it is to see you," Fran spoke softly, "or how unbelievable." She shook her head lightly as if to wave away the disbelief.

I smiled at Fran as the air thickened around us, heavier, softer, warmer, as the night took on a red glow, the one that always means—

"Snow," I said quietly as I carefully wiped a few flakes from her hair. Still she stared at me with that look of wonder.

"Huh?" she asked softly, breath misting in front of what could only be described as perfectly, beautiful, kissable lips.

I sighed softly with a feeling I realized was regret. Of course, it figured that I had made that vow of celibacy to myself including the whole I-love-you-thing before even kissing, because I'd always had a crush on her anyway. We'd even kinda sorta quasi dated in high school, although we'd called it "wanna hang out" with a *lot* of unresolved tension.

But still there was that promise I'd made, because otherwise I would have already—

Well, if you ask her, Fran will plead the fifth—she *is* a lawyer after all—(and she always smiles when she does). I don't know exactly who started it, but I can say for certain that Fran's perfect smile, matching teeth, and gorgeous lips, were just a hint of the promise that her kiss held: soft, warm, and full of sweet affection.

I have to admit there was something infinitely soothing in the press of her lips on mine and just as my hands began to come up of their own accord to bring her even closer, I realized two things: I wasn't supposed to do that, and Fran and Samantha had actually, officially, dated in high school.

The realization was like coming-to after being doused with cold water and perhaps Fran had thought along the same lines, because we broke apart mutually.

I stared at her, dazed, shocked, a little embarrassed. "I…um, I'm…" I tried. I settled for one of my crooked grins as my pulse and my heart hammered within me.

This time, Fran placed shushing fingers against my lips. "I always wanted to do that," she smiled impishly at me.

I could feel my eyes widen in surprise as I thought about that for a second and considered. It took me absolutely no time at all to process them and realize, yeah, me too. "You know what?" I grinned back at her.

"What?" she asked, her eyes shining at me while the snow lay crystals in her hair.

"Me, too."

Fran tossed her head back and laughed, a light pure sound in a world rapidly turning white and I laughed with her.

"So," I asked her as I took off my scarf, "did it fulfill your expectations?" I gave the scarf a good shake and brought it over her head and around her shoulders.

"What're you doing? Fran asked as I brushed her hair lightly with my fingertips under the cloth.

"Keeping you warm, it's snowing," I explained as I quirked a smile at her. I neatly tucked the ends into the *V* of her pea-coat, taking a moment to button an anchor-engraved button. "There. So..." I paused and stepped back to admire my handiwork.

"So...what?" Fran asked me, her gaze frankly evaluating.

"Did it fulfill your expectations?"

Uh oh, I thought as I watched her face, *I need to stop sounding quite so cavalier with my questions,* because I didn't mean it that way, not at all, but I was so hazed by her presence, and the vibe between us, and that amazing *kiss...*

Something in my chest grew with a warm hurt that made me feel like I would burst through my skin as I saw Fran's smile turn slightly shy, and unless it was a shadow from the scarf, I was pretty sure that I saw a faint blush rise in her cheeks.

"Well, let's just say..." she began, as her eyes watched the flakes hit the sidewalk, "that I'm glad it happened."

She gazed up at me as those last few words came out and there was only one way to describe the look in her eyes: smokin'.

"C'mon," she said, brushing the flakes from my head and breaking us from the strange envelope we seemed to be caught up in. "Let's get going."

I ran a quick hand through my hair—hey, snow or no, it's got to look good—and allowed her to take my arm.

"What's your plan?" I asked as we waited at an intersection for the light to change so we could cross.

"Well…" Fran paused a moment for a breath. "We grab a cab back to my place, I'll make something quick, you take a nap and I'll send you back to the island later today in a car, whaddaya say?" she concluded as we reached the next corner.

I considered it.

"How about…" I counter-offered "…we walk and try to catch a cab on the way." I gazed around us at the obviously taxi-empty streets.

Don't ask why, but it's the unwritten Manhattan rule: at the first drop of moisture to hit the ground, all forms of public transportation—especially taxi-cabs—disappear. Come to think of it, that rule applies to the rest of the city, too.

Damn.

"Okay…and?" Fran prompted.

"We pick something up on the way."

"Okay…"

"And I'll leave after that," I concluded.

Fran stopped dead in her tracks and whirled to face me.

"Nina, no way," she told me flatly.

I let my expression ask why.

"It's late, it's snowing like hell and you've got to be exhausted," she explained.

I opened my mouth to protest—I honestly didn't want to impose on her hospitality—and I certainly didn't want to give her the wrong idea after that kiss.

Not that I didn't want to—I mean, not that there wasn't…ah, never mind.

I didn't know what was in her head and I didn't want to find out that Fran was like everyone else: all about the fuck.

It was a kiss—just a kiss, I told myself, and as nice and as warm and as sweet as it was (okay, and sensual too, Fran absolutely knew how to kiss well), it wasn't "I love you." I might have made a misstep, but I wasn't going to make another.

I hoped.

I began to explain about not imposing or some such but Fran waved my words away, sending eddies of snow clouds around her.

"I haven't seen you in four years, thought you were dead, and now that I know you're alive and well, how do you think I'd feel if I let you go on your way to freeze to death or get into some sort of accident during a blizzard?" she cajoled with a smile.

I laughed and looked up, blinking away the flakes that fell into my eyes. She was right, though, and if it wasn't exactly a blizzard yet, it was snowing hard enough to be its younger sibling.

I let my breath out in a huff. "Fair enough." I gave in with a smile of my own. "You win."

Fran slipped her arm into mine. "Well of course I do," she laughed as she rubbed my forearm briskly. "I'm still Kitt."

"Yeah, you are," I agreed, and we continued on our quest for food and shelter.

We found a bodega (that's Spanish for "deli") somewhere on Avenue A and while they didn't have any flowers available (apparently they put them "in the back" at night), we picked up the same stuff everyone buys when it snows: milk, bread, and eggs. I don't know why, I mean, what's everyone doing, making French toast? And some frozen pizza. And some ice cream, just because.

We argued for a brief moment over who was going to pay—and I insisted. I'd said it was my treat after all, right?

Right.

I took the bag in one hand and Fran's hand in the other, so it wouldn't get cold, then Fran took that joined grasp and slipped us into her pocket as we walked.

It was such a beautiful spot of warm in the sparkling cold world and whirl of white, and I felt so...so...

"You know," I said softly, not wanting to interrupt the magic I could see and feel happening, "I always love the way the world transforms when it snows—it takes on this purely magical quality, like anything is possible... it's like..."

I struggled to find the right words, because I felt so good, and I felt so different, and something was trying to wake up within me, while I was walking with Fran's hand in mine, so real and gorgeously warm, and the snow was thick and drifting and covering and the world had become something enchanted…

"It's like…walking in whimsy."

We came to a stop under a streetlamp, and Fran stared straight up into the twinkling lights that fell over us.

And she was absolutely beautiful, with that expression of delight and wonder on her face as the flakes fell on and on and on and the air seemed to gather and warm while her eyes shone.

"Look at the snow as it comes down through the lights," she said in a hush. "It's like being in a storm of stars."

I stopped watching the snow fall over her and glanced up instead.

I felt the contours of her fingers as a smooth glide under my thumb as I stared with her.

She *got* it, she knew what I meant, she absolutely got me—and she was *right*.

"Exactly," I quietly agreed, and we walked on in shared amazement.

As we approached her block, the magic faded as I grew uneasy. I mean, I knew this block, I knew the building we were approaching. *Nah, couldn't be*, I thought, *I mean, what are the odds, right?*

But that funky sense persisted and judging from how cool it suddenly got, I think the blood had drained out of my face and was rapidly descending into my feet.

We stopped by the steps that led to her apartment and I let go of her hand so she could dig for her keys.

"Hey, Fran?" I asked as the snow blew around us. It was really starting to come down hard.

"Yeah?" she responded distractedly. "I can't believe I can't find them!" She was complaining mostly to herself, her focus on searching her pockets.

"You wouldn't, um, happen to have had a neighbor named Candace, would you?" I asked as casually as I could.

"Ah, got you!" she exclaimed triumphantly, holding her keys out so I could see them. "I'm sorry—what did you say?"

I put the bag down to give my hands a break and tried my best to nonchalantly shove them into my coat pockets. "I was just, uh…you have a neighbor named Candace?"

Fran whirled so quickly to face me I only had a moment to see the shock in her eyes before it changed to alarm as she lost her footing in the fresh snow.

Her arms flew up, the keys went wide and I rushed forward to catch her before gravity did.

It got us both, and Fran landed on top of me with a solid, breathless "whump" as her body pushed my ribs one way and the slippery sidewalk shoved them another.

I lay there a moment and took a deep breath, then wiggled my fingers and my toes. Everything was operational, therefore, I was fine. I blinked the snow out of my eyes and opened them to first find Fran's curls sliding over my cheeks and as my gaze rose past her chin, I found her lips, grinning widely.

I smiled back ruefully.

So much for my rescue attempt.

"Thank you," Fran's well-shaped lips said.

"You're welcome."

We studied each other as the snow continued to fall, thick and heavy and Fran wiped some off my face, her thumb lingering against my chin.

I really liked the way that felt…

"Are you okay?" I asked, my brain finally engaging enough to speak.

She had fallen after all and even if we seemed to be sitting rather comfortably, it was still possible that she could have injured something.

"Oh yeah, I'm fine," Fran answered. "In fact I—oh shit!" She sat up with a panicked expression, looking about her wildly.

The movement put her solidly and squarely on my groin, sending a bolt from my buddy to my brain which made me jump in return. I swallowed the sensation down and sat up on my elbows.

"Problem?" I asked as mildly as I could, arching a brow at her.

"My keys! I dropped my keys!"

"I'll help you find them—I think I know where they fell," I offered.

I did have an idea, really. I'd seen them fly and if I wasn't mistaken, they were probably behind the bushes that lined the front of the building.

"Sure, thanks," Fran agreed. All of a sudden, she seemed to realize exactly how we were sitting.

She looked down to see just how we were joined and bit her lip. "Uh, sorry," she said finally, giving me a sheepish look. "Are you okay?"

I glanced down where she had, and let the silence and tension build for a heartbeat, the space I needed to gather myself, then gave her back a slow grin. "Never better," I drawled, as cool as in control as I could be, given that I was being straddled by a woman I had shared a very sensual kiss with just a little while ago. "Do you think you'll need a hand getting up?"

"Oh. Ah no, I'm fine." She scrambled a moment in the snow before she stood, but finally, she regained her feet. "Let me help you," she offered when she was steady, and extended a hand.

I took it.

"Thanks," I said with a smile and got one in return. As soon as I was on my feet, I brushed the snow off. But man, was it cold to do barehanded!

"Let's find your keys," I suggested, and we moved in the direction I indicated. We searched through the dried brush together—Fran got the front, I got the back.

"So...did you say Candace?" Fran asked casually as we looked.

I was so sure I'd seen her keys fly over to this exact spot—between the dead brush and the wall where the snow didn't reach, but neither did the light. I felt my way along carefully; I didn't want to cut myself on a stray piece of glass or get bitten by whatever passed for local fauna and consequently die of rabies.

Yuck.

"Yeah," I answered Fran, who hovered somewhere behind me, "is she a neighbor of yours?"

Just scant inches beyond my fingertips some streetlight broke through the bracken and I thought I saw a gleam. That had to be it!

"British?" Fran asked.

"Huh?" I asked back, not certain of what she'd said as I'd inspected what I'd found. A pull tab from a cab—damn. I discarded it and followed that gleam before me—that just *had* to be it!

"Was she a Brit, you know, from the UK?" she repeated and clarified.

Almost, almost, just another…there. I snagged the loop with my fingertip, hauled back and was rewarded with a jingle that could only mean one thing.

"Got 'em!" I announced triumphantly and passed the keys behind me back to Fran. Still bent double, I tried to carefully back out; I didn't want to rip my coat or my face on a branch.

"Yeah, she's English," I told Fran as I crawled. "I take it you know her?" I was almost out, just a little further now and…

"Know her?" Fran echoed. "She sublet my apartment this summer—she's Sam's girlfriend."

Holy shit!

Shocked, alarmed and otherwise totally taken aback, I stood straight up, slammed my head into the brick window ledge above me, and went straight back down.

I saw stars, I saw God, I think I spoke a foreign language as adrenalin beat up through me and the pain in my head flowed down.

"Ow," I muttered, scowling and rubbing my head.

That fucking *hurt*.

"Are you all right? Are you okay?" Fran scrambled through the branches.

I leaned my back against the building and rubbed my head some more. "I'm fine, I'm fine—I'll live," I told her, still scowling.

"Are you sure you didn't hurt anything?" she asked again, and reached down to help me up.

"My ego," I answered with a self-deprecating smile as I took her hand. "I think I broke it." This time I stood and managed not to injure myself.

"Looks fine from here, Raze," she smiled at me broadly, using my old nickname from swim team—Razor. "And besides," she continued, "you're safe with me."

"I think I knew that," I smiled back genuinely brushed myself off as best I could as I squeezed myself out of the space between the steps and the damn dead twig collection. I stopped a moment to pick up the snow-covered bag and cautiously walked up the steps.

The snow had picked up volume and momentum, coming down hard and fast enough to have already covered the area we'd fallen onto in a fresh coating of white and fill up Fran's original footsteps.

Fran unlocked the door and as it swung open into that very familiar corridor, my brain cleared enough to ask, "Did you say Candace was Samantha's girlfriend?" My mouth was dry as those words came out.

"Well, you know," Fran explained as she went to her mailbox, "it's one of those on-again, off-again sort of things and all that. How do you know Candace?" she asked, giving me a quick and curious look, before she went back to sorting through her envelopes.

My guts froze.

I was going to hell, I knew it, I was absolutely, positively going to hell, because I had committed the worst sin I could possibly think of: I'd slept with my best friend's girlfriend.

Dammit, dammit, double damn.

It didn't matter that we hadn't seen each other in years, didn't matter that I hadn't known because Candace told me her ex was named Annie—and definitely an ex.

The facts remained the facts—did I sleep with her?

Okay, all right, we didn't sleep. So did I have sex with her?

Forget all those who-touches-who equivocations, because I knew how she liked her nipples sucked and how she loved me in leather. I had not only a mental picture, but a *very* visceral one of the taste, the touch, the scent and the gorgeous fit of her pussy and how she loved it best when I fucked her slowly and very deeply until I wanted and she needed to come, so I'd bury myself inside her tightening cunt until she was screaming my name and her pussy flooding my hand, and we'd relax a few moments while her cunt pulsed slowly around my buried fingers—Candace called them thank-you kisses—until I gently withdrew.

And then we'd start again.

How did I know Candace? "Cunt thump surrender", to borrow a phrase, that's how I knew her.

And oh, just to add to my current sense of joy, hadn't Fran and Samantha dated in high school? And hadn't I just kissed Fran, too?

Hell.

I was going to Hell, directly to Hell.

Do not pass Go. Do not collect $200 dollars, like it said in the Monopoly game.

Yeah.

Hell. My own private room and everything...

"Oh uh, we hung out over the summer a bit," I answered Fran instead. It's not that I wanted to lie to her, it's just that well, I'd actually really liked Candace and it's just not my thing to kiss and tell.

Ever.

"The only place Candace really mentioned going to was Staten Island," Fran said conversationally as we walked towards her apartment.

Snow dripped in grey and muddy bunches off the bag and my coat. "She said she wanted to know about Samantha's home town."

I swallowed nervously as Fran keyed the lock.

Oh.

God.

I knew that door quite well and how strong it was—I'd fucked Candace mercilessly against it.

"That's cool," I answered as noncommittally as possible.

Fran swung the door open and flicked the light switch. "Yeah, I guess," Fran responded with a shrug of her shoulders. "The only thing," she said as she reached down to unlace her boots, "is that she met someone..." She placed the first boot on a nearby mat and reached for the next. "And I know she and Sam have an arrangement, their understanding, but..." and she got the other one off "...it made me a uncomfortable, you know?"

"Hmph," I responded blankly. I had the feeling that this had the potential to get mama-don't-know-ya ugly and I didn't have the first clue as to what to do about it.

"Boots here—give me your coat," Fran said with a sweep of her arms.

Wordlessly, I took off my coat and handed it to her, then began to carefully slide off one boot.

"Yeah," Fran continued as I eased my foot out, "she said it was the DJ at the Redspot—you go there?" She moved into the kitchen with our coats.

"I used to work there," I called back as I eased off the other boot.

"Oh hey, then you must know who it is," Fran called back from the kitchen. "Is she as hot and wild as Candace said? You know, her hair up in a sort of half Mohawk and what Candace called her Elvis smile?"

My hair was no longer sopping wet, and though I hadn't worn it like that in a while, I maintained the cut and there was still enough gel left in my hair from earlier to set it that way. Even though it had been some time,

I had done it so often for so long that I set it with one hand as I walked to the kitchen and carried the shopping bag in the other. I could feel that wave settle perfectly into place.

Sigh.

It was time to get this over with, and reveal myself, as it were, and if she still liked me, she still liked me, and if she didn't, well...

But still, Elvis smile.

Huh.

I never knew Candace had thought that, but I was pretty sure I knew which smile she meant.

That was pretty cool—and I'd always have that, at least.

I got to the kitchen and leaned in to put the bag on the counter, then put my hands on either side of the archway that led to the kitchen. I watched as Fran hung up our coats.

I cocked my head and my hips and set that half-pursed smile I knew Candace meant on my lips.

"You mean...like this?" I asked Fran.

Funny how it is that all it takes is the slightest changes in the angle of the head and the way the lips are held to be "on."

When she finally saw me, she was obviously surprised.

Well, we were a long ways away from our high school uniform days, after all. But I had to let Fran know who I was, who I'd been, and who I had become so she could make her own decision as to whether or no she wanted to continue our rediscovered and renewed friendship.

If she did?

Great—that would actually make me pretty darn happy and if not, well, I'd lived without her for four years. She might end up wishing I was still only a pleasant if sad memory.

It never occurred to me that I might ever be on the other side of that.

I tracked her as she came closer and I watched her eyes go from serious surprise to smoky contemplation as they traveled from my head to feet and back again.

Slinging a thumb through a belt loop, I leaned arrogantly. The look in her eye told me that she—or at least, a part of her—liked what she saw. It also told me... Well, I didn't want to think about it. As stupid as it sounds, it would've really bothered me to think of Fran as "easy."

But still, that look she threw?

Smokin'.

With a last lingering glance, she took the milk and eggs out of the bag to put them away in the refrigerator; those were lucky eggs—none of them broke. Fran pulled out a coffee pot and walked over to the sink.

"Don't pretend you don't know where the bathroom is," she said finally, a sly smile edging the corner of her mouth. "Go take a shower—there's fresh towels—and I'll drop some sweats in before you're done."

I dropped back half a step and glanced at her sharply. I'd intended to dry off as best I could, then change into the clothes I'd packed into my bag; they'd be drier than what I had on. She finished setting up the coffee pot and peeped at me.

"It's not as if I've never seen you naked before, you know," she reminded me with a wry grin.

True, it wasn't. We *had* been on swim team together in high school and if we did see each other nude on our way back, forth or in the shower, well, it was a locker room after all and no big deal anyway.

"I wasn't going to mention that." I grinned back at her. "I was going to ask you, what color?"

"What color what?"

"What color sweats?"

I gave her my jauntiest smile and Fran in return gave me a look that almost scorched me from head to toe then back again, complete with a slow, sexy smile.

"For you?" she licked her teeth, those perfect, perfect teeth. "Black, of course."

There was nothing else to say to that, except, "Perfect. Thank you."

We smiled at each other then I gave a little wave and made my way to the promised shower.

Fran was right, of course, I did know the way.

I ran the water a little warmer than usual—a trick I'd learned from Cap. All cold water does is drive your blood further inside and spikes it harder through the part of your anatomy that you're trying to cool off. But, and this is important: a warm one dilates your blood vessels, which spreads your blood out a bit.

So yeah, you're still hard, and you might still be aching, but at least it's not like a bolt through the groin.

Okay, it's still rough, but it's manageable—sort of.

Showered, warmed and dressed in the promised black sweats (and after Fran had done the same—she showered, then dressed in red while I waited at the kitchen table) we sat there together and caught up on everything we could. I told her about school—I wasn't going this semester, DJing—I was taking a break, work—keeping me crazy and the band which was my obsession, while Fran told me all about being in Columbia Law School—she had a scholarship, her summer internship in Los Angeles—in the legal department of a movie studio and her plans after graduation—get sunny and warm or find people that were.

But the neatest thing was learning there was something else we shared besides a history: for fun (and from what I could tell, absolute passion), she painted, and designed stage sets, because Fran had spent some time in Japan—and gotten into both the culture and the theater while there.

That...was seriously cool!

By unspoken mutual agreement, and probably because we were too busy rediscovering and learning each other, neither one of us mentioned Samantha or Candace, until quite a bit later.

DRIVEN
I'M NOT ALWAYS RIGHT, I MAY NOT BE THE ONE
BUT ONE STEP CLOSER TO PARADISE
IS ONE STEP CLOSER TO PARADISE

"Dani's Tears"—JD Glass

EVENTUALLY, AFTER ABOUT HALF A dozen cups of coffee, followed by hot chocolate, the demolition of those boxes of microwave pizza, and a pint of ice cream later, we noticed the sky outside the window lightened to a murky grey. I stood from my seat to stretch, then walked over to the window to peer out. I pressed my fingertips to the frosted glass.

"Holy shit!" I exclaimed.

Holy shit was right—in the time since we'd gotten there, the snow had apparently come down even harder and faster than before, and it showed no sign of stopping. A thick, white blanket covered the ground everywhere, and even the few cars that were parked on the street had been transformed into soft and rounded sculptures.

There was no trace of color left; the world had gone grey.

And that was how I felt, as if I had no color, no warmth, as if I was as cold as the falling snow, and as different and insignificant as each.

Bit.

Of falling…

Ice.

"Holy shit!" Fran whispered from behind me as she came closer to look for herself.

Her hand came up and gently held my shoulder as we looked out upon a blurred and rounded world, and her touch on me, soft and somehow tender, the tingle of it through my shirt, thawed my ice, made my pulse beat, soft and insistent, in my ears.

The scant distance between us gradually shortened until the same hand that had been on my shoulder came to rest lightly across my waist while my arm draped softly behind her neck.

She sighed quietly, staring out into the stillness and for just a moment, one of us—and again, I don't know who—pulled a little closer and I let myself enjoy the warm solid sense of her next to me.

It was just nice, you know?

"Bed," Fran announced suddenly, breaking our reverie.

"Huh?" I asked, momentarily nonplussed.

I mean, I liked Fran and all, but I wasn't, I didn't, well, I couldn't—you know, promises and stuff.

"Bed," repeated Fran succinctly, dropping her arm from my waist. "We've gone from 'it's really, really late' to 'it's really way too early' again and I know I, for one, could use it." She smiled.

She was right—again—and I know I was tired, too. But I certainly didn't want her to think on the one hand that I was just there to get into bed with her or conversely—

No, no conversely.

I didn't want her to think that I was even remotely thinking about the possibility of us having sex.

"Great idea," I agreed, following her out of the kitchen. "Just show me where to grab a blanket." I indicated I'd sleep on the sofa.

Fran narrowed her eyes at me and gave a strange look. "Nina, it's not like I don't know you slept here before—without me," she added, a bit archly to my sensitized ears.

Memories of exactly *how* I didn't sleep in her bed literally flooded across my mind's eye, and my skin grew so warm between the comment and the mental images that I could actually feel my ears burn red . Oh boy, was I glad my hair was down so she couldn't see them.

"Yeah well…," I tried. "I didn't want you to think I just—"

"Want to fuck me?" she completed much more plainly than I would have, and an amused smile played about her lips.

Geez.

What a loaded statement.

I think if it had been anyone but Fran making it, I'd have had a snappy comeback—at least, I like to think so, anyway. I mean, sure, yeah, Fran was attractive, even better looking than she'd been in high school, with that sharp jaw angle and the humorous sparkle in her eyes that she hadn't had back then. There was also that kiss to contend with, too.

Fuck it.

There was no way to figure out if she was trying to read my mind (and if my discomfort was that obvious) or if she was trying to proposition me. There was also nothing to say in response anyway that wouldn't get me into trouble, one way or another.

Boy, did it figure that Fran was going to law school.

I mean, if I said yes, was I agreeing that yes, that's what I'd want, that's what I'd wanted, or thanks for offering, yes?

And if I said no, did it mean I wasn't thinking she might be concerned about that (which was a lie), that I didn't want to (sort of a lie—I didn't want to "fuck" her like that, in the way that most people seemed to mean it, some casual and disposable thing) or, thanks for asking, but no?

Not to mention that I might inadvertently insult her. You know, imply that I found her undesirable or whatever and not only was that certainly untrue, that would also hurt her feelings—I know it would have hurt mine.

I wasn't going to do that to her.

But... I can handle this, I told myself.

I was Nina, after all, and I wasn't going to let a nice kiss and a pretty face rattle my cage, right?

Right.

No matter what the pulse in my ears said.

I took a breath, let it out slowly and smiled. "Does that mean you don't have an extra blanket?"

Fran's eyes widened and I could see that she appreciated my non-response. "You're still a wisenheimer, huh?" She grinned at me. "C'mon, this way." She laughed and led me down the hallway to her room.

I waited in the doorway to this bedroom I'd already visited several times in the past while Fran opened up her closet. She disappeared into it for a moment, then came out again with the disputed blanket. She placed the folded brown square in my hands, then took a moment to touch my arm.

"I don't bite, you know," she told me softly.

I smiled at her and took a step back. "How do you know that I don't?" I asked her and searched her face for her answer.

It was true—I was behaving—but I didn't know how far I could push that, given the circumstances, I mean, an old friend who happened to be beautiful and I suspected more than willing and not only that, but also in a place I already had some very intense sensual history. Then, too, there was that sense, that thing, trying to burst through my chest every time I saw her smile…

Oh, it made me *want,* so much, so, so very much *want…*

Besides, my own promises to myself aside, I sensed danger here, that this would get me even more deeply involved into something I really didn't want, or at the very least didn't think I did: not right now, not when there was so much I had to do, to become, to be a worthwhile person.

I had this instant understanding: sleeping with Fran would mean committing myself to her—and while I knew that even after all this time, we still had tons in common, and even more so now, would get along more than just tolerably well, and would probably actually be perfectly happy together, it wasn't…well, I didn't know what.

And besides, even if it was that thing I just couldn't find the right words for, well, I had nothing to offer her, anyway.

I mean, Fran was in law school for Christ's sake, hooked up with an internship that would probably become her career, while I had not only just stopped going to school, I was working non-standard jobs with non-standard hours and spent every spare minute obsessed with music and art.

The only thing I had to offer besides my dreams and my loyalty was the one thing that everybody wanted anyway: my participation in their orgasm. As far as I was concerned? That wasn't enough.

No, tempting as Fran was, if I slept with her and didn't make some sort of promise to her, I'd hurt her and if I made that promise, I'd let myself down—because, well, just because I needed to do more, to *be* more, before I could be worthy of someone else, someone like her.

But oh, my heart was beating so hard and so fast…

Still…

Holding the blanket in one hand, I put my arms around her. She seemed surprised, but only for a moment and as she pressed my body to her, I allowed myself to remember that she had been a good friend to me back then.

Hell, she'd even let me borrow her car for my driver's license exam. She'd been solid then and she was solid now. A few years might have passed, but the innate person—girl to woman—was the same. I don't know how I knew that, but I did (and have since discovered that to be true for most people, but that's another story).

Bottom line?

Fran was a nice girl—I wasn't.

While I might have previously been in the habit of following a lead, I'd never been in the habit of breaking hearts, and I wasn't going to start now, and *especially* not with Fran.

Because I really, *really*, liked her.

Because we had really, truly, been friends.

Because I cared, I really, truly, cared, even after all this time—because that lapse simply didn't matter, not in this here and now, where we were together, in this space, in this place, with her warm in my arms and my heart beating so hard my chest hurt with it.

"I can't believe I'm really holding you," Fran whispered back, her voice a whisper against my throat. "I'd always thought we'd get a chance to hang out sometime after I graduated, you know? I called you, I swear I did. Nina..." her words seemed to catch in her throat a bit, "I spoke with your father." Her voice rose slightly in pitch. "And he told me...he...he told me you had died." Fran broke into sobs and shook against me. "And then, he asked..." she swallowed "...he asked that I please respect the family's privacy by not calling or sending anything."

I didn't know what to say. The anger that I'd thought long gone at my father threatened to roar through me, but he wasn't in the room. Fran was, though: real, solid, crying like a hurt and lost child in my arms, and at the moment that was more important than anything else.

I did the only thing I could do, I didn't even think—I dropped the blanket so I could hold her tighter and rocked her in my arms.

"It's my fault, you know," Fran cried. "I told Samantha, I told her not to call and she did anyway. She didn't believe me, she couldn't believe me."

"Shh...it's okay...it's okay," I soothed gently. I raised her tear stained face to mine. "I'm so sorry," I told her and kissed her forehead, "I'm so sorry you had to go through that." I meant it, too, really meant it.

You know, I dunno how I hadn't read the obvious earlier—I guess maybe I didn't know Fran had cared so much for me back then. Maybe it was because I had been so caught up in my own thing at the time. Or maybe it was because it wasn't me who got told that a friend I loved had died.

I quickly realized that even though my dad had lied, the pain Fran had felt had been very real and I had better get my head out of my ass pretty darn soon and be a lot more sensitive.

This was definitely, no, *Fran* was definitely not all about the fuck.

"Stay with me," Fran asked me. "I don't want to let you go. I'm afraid you'll disappear." She placed a gentle kiss against my collar bone.

God...if I got into that bed with her... I didn't want to *fuck* her, but I did want to soothe her, to comfort her, to let her know that I really and truly cared, that her pain touched me, oh so very deeply, and that I found her beautiful, that being with her warmed me, filled me with a joy I didn't know I was capable of, hadn't known existed before.

But if I did that—if that happened—well, I just didn't know what else to do, because there was this current humming through and around and over me and her and my pulse was pounding in my neck, in my ears, was trying to tell me—

"Sleep, I promise, just sleep," Fran said, looking up at me again.

I laughed lightly under my breath. Either we were on the same page, Fran was reading my mind, or I had been that readable. Since I prided myself on being rather inscrutable, maybe it was the first option.

"Ah Fran," I said and sighed in acceptance of the fact that the hum and buzz made me want to do anything other than sleep. "I can't promise you that."

Fran arched an eyebrow at me. "Really?" she drawled, her eyes still managing to convey a layer of sensuality even through her tears and something else too—something like genuine affection. "And why's that? You don't like my bed? Too firm? Too soft?"

I shook my head no at each of those and smiled, grateful to have something else to focus on, something to distract me from the pulse and the hum. "No, no, nothing like that." I let my hands slide down her arms.

"Well, what then?" she asked, an amused if slightly exasperated expression crossing her cheeks.

It was time to come clean and just tell her. I mean, any more of this, and Fran might begin to think it was her personally, and I didn't want that.

"Uh well…" I stalled, playing for time.

You know, it was amazing how quickly my cheeks and ears could burn. One second, normal skin, normal temperature and the next, I was an overheated Christmas tree. I think Fran may have noticed.

"I'veneversleptinthatbed," I told her in a rush.

Fran shook her head in disagreement. "Nina, I know you were here before—with Candace. She told me all about you, well except for your name or I might have known it was you. It's totally okay, you know?" She gave me a bemused smile.

"No," I said and took a deep breath. "I've never *slept* in that bed." I widened my eyes a bit, hoping she'd understand.

"Oh." Suddenly, she got it. "Oh! Okay, so you don't know if it's comfortable or not." She laughed and threw her arms around me, and after my eyebrows simmered down a bit, I laughed too.

I bent and picked up the blanket and what was left of my dignity. "So… where's the couch?"

"What, you've never been in the living room?" she teased.

"Nope, not once," I answered succinctly, "I've never even been here while it was this light out."

Fran laughed again and rolled her eyes at me. "What are we gonna do with you?" She grabbed my hand. "This way."

I followed her down the hallway.

It was true: kitchen, bed, bath?

Been there.

Living room?

I knew where it was because I'd passed its entrance on the way in, but I'd never been through that portal, and frankly, the only light Candace ever had on was the light by the bed.

Fran didn't need to flip the light switch because as bad as the weather was, it was still daylight. Murky, gloomy, snowy daylight, but still, somewhere above those clouds, the sun was shining and we were getting what was left.

"Here you go," Fran indicated with a sweep of an arm to indicate her sofa, and damn if it wasn't the required East Village futon with a very cool Chinese symbol printed on its fabric: the "double happiness" one, if I had it right.

I took the blanket from her hands, then bent to pull the futon out into its sleeping position.

"Hey, let me help you with that," Fran offered.

"Sure," I agreed, and it was done in seconds.

She straightened, and we faced each other awkwardly.

"Sleep well," Fran told me softly, and bit her lip.

I half smiled back at her, fiddling with the blanket in my hands, running over a seam with my fingers.

"Yeah, you too."

We stared at each other, the silence growing awkward.

Finally, Fran gave me a little wave and began to ease away, but I couldn't, I just couldn't, after that whole emotional scene not five minutes ago, just let her go like that. Yeah, yeah, I know, I know, I was tough and I was cool, but I couldn't be cold—not to anyone really, and especially not to Fran, not after what we had just shared, never mind the fact that we'd been friends and team mates in the past.

My heart still beat hard, but it wasn't threatening to come out of my rib cage anymore, but the pulse in my head kicked back, *hard*, as I watched her step away, and the tingly buzz from earlier, was now back and running through and over me, while the pulse in my head was strong and full and it all shook me, shook me so solidly it threatened to turn my bones to jelly.

I couldn't take it anymore and I made a quick decision. "Hey Fran?" I called to her retreating back. "Stay out here with me?"

"Yeah?" she asked, sounding uncertain and shy.

"Yeah," I affirmed with a smile and tossed the blanket on the sleeping platform. I sat on the edge and patted the spot next to me. "C'mon over."

Fran gave me one of those amazing smiles and I swear I could feel my heart lift up with it.

I'd really, really missed her. It might have been my father's fault for telling everyone who called that lie, but it was also mine for hiding and not trying to find her—or anyone else. The blame for that lay with me and no one else.

"I get the outside," I told her with a grin.

"No problemo," she agreed, climbing over to the wall side.

We got under the blanket and I turned on my side to face so I could say goodnight, only to find her already watching me.

"I really missed you, you know," Fran said softly, tears threatening to fall from the corner of her eye. She patted my shoulder awkwardly.

I couldn't believe I was lying next to her, Fran, the ultimate scholar-athlete—and so achingly fucking beautiful, who'd argue with Samantha as to who'd give me a ride if I'd needed it; Fran, who'd lent me her car and who'd gone to the movies with me.

Fran who'd been my friend—and I'd let time and distance come between us. I shouldn't have allowed that to happen.

I'd been wrong, very wrong.

I reached out and gently stroked her errant locks back over her forehead. "I missed you, too," I told her sincerely. "I'm so sorry."

Her hand came off my shoulder and her fingers carefully circled my wrist. She kissed my palm and the touch was so sweet, just so goddamn sweet that the beat in my chest continued with the threat of burst, and the pound in my head matched it and I couldn't help myself—I wrapped my arms around her and rubbed my cheek lightly against hers, and the buzz once again became a honey-warm spill that enveloped me.

"It's my fault, you know," Fran whispered into my ear. "All of it."

"What's your fault, huh?" I asked gently. "You didn't do anything wrong."

Fran shifted against me and I could actually hear the tears in her voice. "It's my fault about Samantha," she told me. "*My* fault that she changed her name and stayed in England."

"Now, how could that be possible? I'm sure Sammie Blade's a big girl now, making big girl decisions."

"You don't understand," Fran said, and pulled herself slightly away. "I'm the one who told Sammie—"

"That doesn't make anything your fault," I interrupted her quietly and kissed her forehead.

"But it does," Fran insisted. "She wanted to hear it for herself when, before, she was just going to come back and surprise you. Instead, she made that call and..." She sighed. "She never came home..."

I simply held her and listened as she nestled back into me.

"When we finally spoke?" she continued, "she asked me not to call her Samantha, Sam or Sammie—because the two people she missed most called her that. She said she'd be called Ann or Annie from then on."

Fran's tears soaked my shirt and traveled down my neck.

All I could do was hold her and do my best to soothe her as I took her words in. The part of my mind that just absorbs everything took careful note. Candace hadn't lied; her sometime-girlfriend's name *was* Annie.

Honestly, that made me feel a lot better; I really would have hated to think that Candace had lied to me.

I also knew who the two people were that Samantha—Ann—missed the most. One was me. The other was her father, a fireman who had been killed "in the line of duty" as they say, during her junior year of high school.

"I think...I think she would have found you that summer, if I'd just let her find out on her own, surprise you at work like she'd wanted," Fran said. "She'd have found you, she wouldn't have fallen apart the way she did."

She buried her face into my shoulder and shook. "And now you're here..." she said, her words muffled, "...and I still can't believe it."

Her tears tore through me, breaking me, pushing me against a wall I didn't want to hide behind anymore.

"Oh Fran," I sighed and gathered her into my arms. I kissed the top of her head as she sobbed into my collarbone, then kissed her brow.

"I'm right here," I assured her and brushed the hair out of her eyes, then kissed them too. I was frantic with her pain, the need to erase it.

Fran shifted against me again, sliding her legs against mine and I was half on top of her when she raised tentative hands to my face. Her finger tips stroked my cheeks as I balanced myself on my forearms and gazed into her tear-starred eyes, eyes that wouldn't let me go.

"You're real?" she asked in a tremulous voice. "You're not going away?"

Oh, she was breaking my heart, breaking my mind, and I'd never before felt my whole body ache with the need to prove my words, because the honey-warm became a heat, a want, a need, a craving that was filling me...

"I'm real," I agreed and kissed the tear that threatened to slide down her lovely face. "I'm not going away. I promise."

The need to prove that beyond any shadow of doubt drove every other thought, every promise I'd made to myself, right out of my head in the face of that need, while, the pulse and the buzz and the tingle swept through and overwhelmed me, fully compelled me, made me bring my lips to hers again, as that honey-warm feeling surged through me.

Her kiss sent a line of fiery ice straight to my belly and when her tongue played softly against my lips, the only thing I could do, the only thing I wanted, was to invite and welcome her in. Her beautiful mouth was everything I'd discovered before and more.

Her kiss spoke to me, actually spoke to me of loss and longing, and when I lightly bit her lower lip I tasted something different: not the usual desire and need, though that was there too. I tasted the depth of her pain, I tasted her tears, and I felt driven to soothe her, to prove my intent beyond the force of words. Actions, not words, were what counted.

I had to get under her skin and erase that hurt—hurt that I'd caused—forever.

Fran surged against me, her hips pressing against mine, and the cold fire in my belly lurched then spread to my thighs. I leaned over her just the slightest bit and I took hold of the edge of her sweatshirt, letting the back of my fingers trail against her warm skin as I lifted it off her.

Fran lay for a moment with her arms above her head and her eyes were like molten gold. I trailed the back of my hand between her graceful breasts, down her taut stomach.

"You're very beautiful," I told her honestly, because it was undeniably, incredibly, absolutely gorgeously true.

She smiled at me as I leaned over again to lay a kiss between my spread fingers over her navel.

I reached up again to kiss her, and as her lips pressed, gently insistent against mine, she rose up to sit with me. I couldn't stop running my fingers through her hair and over the high planes of her cheeks, simply in awe of her.

Her fingertips sketched my face, then my neck, and her lips followed—short, sharp little nibbles followed by languorous strokes along my throat. Her hands trailed down to my waist where they grabbed a gentle hold of the sweat shirt she had lent me earlier.

"May I?" she asked, her thumbs sliding softly along my skin.

While I shuddered lightly in response to her touch my heart warmed. No one had ever asked me before.

"Yes," I told her simply and in less than a second, it was done. I shivered in the sudden cold and Fran wrapped herself around me.

"Come here, baby." she murmured into my ear before she nibbled along my earlobe, "…let me keep you warm."

The kisses she gave me were tender as she lay them along my shoulder and throat. The sudden heat and press of her breasts against mine sent a thrill of electric shock right through me, and the feel of the beat of her heart against mine made me want to weep with the sheer beauty of this, of her.

How could I have let her go? I could have called, I could have asked her parents, there was any one of a dozen different things I could have done—and didn't.

"God, I've missed you," I gasped and pulled her even closer, kissing her softly, deeply, my hands first lightly tracing then molding against her.

Arms.

Ribs.

A shoulder blade as defined as an angel's wing.

Fran.

I wanted, I *needed* to show her in a definite way that I had admired and loved her as a girl, that I was so sorry, sorry for the passage of time, for the loss and the pain.

I needed her to know how I wouldn't let that happen again and as I planted soft kisses on her neck, down the hollow of her throat and right over her heart, my fingertips slid beneath her waistband and I looked up into her eyes to see if this was okay, if it was what she wanted.

That was all that mattered.

"Let me help you," she offered.

She sat up slightly, set her hands on mine and together, it was done. I crawled up the bed and lay down next to her and Fran twisted on her side to face me. We simply stared at each other.

She reached with those gentle hands and drew her fingertips from my cheek down my neck, to my chest. Her fingers whispered on the curve of my breast and when she reached my waist, her eyes traveled back to mine. "May I?" they asked and I smiled my answer.

"Yes."

I let her slide them off me, and she kissed my navel and then my thighs as they were bared. I sat up on my heels and shivered in the morning cold and Fran flowed up the bed, bringing the blanket with her and throwing it around us both like a cape. Her skin was soft against me as her hand came to my face and the other to my waist.

The kiss we shared now had a new taste—it still held hints of loss and it spoke of desire; I didn't recognize the other part, but it was something I instantly craved.

She trailed her thumb along the edge of my jaw until it came to my chin again, resting and rubbing lightly in the curve beneath my lip. I had never been so aware of that spot before as her lips kneaded a path to that sensitive place between jaw line and neck.

"Let me love you," Fran asked, her voice a low stirring in my ear.

My heart now hammered in triple time: first with an emotion I couldn't name, the second was pure arousal and the third was confusion as Fran pulled back a moment to look at me.

What did she mean?

Was that just another way of saying fuck?

But there was nothing about her that spoke to anything I'd ever known before. Bemused, I smiled and shrugged.

I didn't know what to say.

Fran's eyes went wide for a moment, then she gave me such a beautiful smile my chest went tight with the joy of it. She took both my hands in hers. "I'm not going to hurt you," she promised as she kissed each hand in turn, then held them both against her heart.

She rose slowly on her knees and leaned into me, touching my face as my hands pressed against her chest where I could feel the flutter of her breath and the solid thump under her ribs.

She kissed my cheeks and my eyes, she stroked my hair and ran gentle hands down my arms and up again before she embraced me and laid me down beneath her.

At that very moment, I grew afraid, desperately afraid—I don't know why. I knew I could stop this, this whatever was going to happen, knew I could change this, flip it; all it would take was a toss of the head and a quick turn. I could ensure that this would be just like any other time, any other person, and I could walk away without having lost a thing.

But… I couldn't.

Not under the tenderness of Fran's touch, not in the face of the pain she'd been through, and definitely not in the light of the love she showed me.

I knew, absolutely *knew*, that as surely as my blood ran red, that's what this was.

We'd been friends before and I also knew with the same certainty born of blood that no matter what happened, we'd be friends after. My pulse sounded in my ears.

That...I could trust.

She didn't want points, she didn't want bragging rights and she didn't want a fuck, not like that.

All she'd asked was if she could love me.

I twined my arms around her neck and buried my face into the creamy-silk warmth of her skin. Her hands trailed along my spine then held my head very gently to her shoulder. I pressed my cheek into her collarbone and laid soft kisses into her throat before she raised my face to her lips again.

"I won't do anything you don't want me to do," she whispered.

Her chest pressed against mine again and I wanted so much to simply just *believe* as her heart pounded just as hard as mine against me...

I reached for her face and kissed her desperately. I ran my hands through her hair and across the span of her shoulders, down the narrow valley of her back and spread my hands across the tight width of her hips as her fingers traced patterns down my ribs.

She slid down my body, licking and nipping along the way, while her fingers alternately splayed then gripped my skin.

"I need to feel you," she murmured into my navel while her fingertips rolled my nipple. She fit her shoulders between my thighs and bit the tendon next to my aching cunt then placed her hands on either side. Fran raised her eyes to mine. "I need to drink you in," she told me and dipped her head to my need, kissing my cunt the way she kissed my mouth.

I sighed with the sensation, and when her tongue slid between the lips of my pussy, she did it with such perfect precision I involuntarily arched my back and cried out. Fran's tongue drew soft circles around my clit and I was floating again, my world coming to pieces as she moved my pussy with her lips.

I didn't know what to do with my hands and as if sensing my confusion, Fran reached up and laced her fingers with mine. I held on for dear life as she brought me higher and higher. When she began to use the flat of her tongue to stroke me, creating a constant pressure on my clit, I felt my body swim along the crest, riding the top, riding her tongue.

Until it reached the edge of entrance.

Suddenly the wave I'd been riding gave way and crushed me under it. Van's smirk and Trace's eyes, the feel of her hands pushing against me in the skybox, the sudden hard cool of the floor smacking my head when my mother tried to beat the gay out of me, Cap's enthusiastic "there's the money shot!" and the sound of every woman I'd ever fucked, all combined with the guilty knowledge of Fran's tears, pulling me, shoving me into a tightening spiral and I.

was going.

to drown.

I sat up almost involuntarily. "Fran—*don't*—" I gasped, fighting to breathe.

She'd stopped before I'd even really asked. Wordlessly, she shifted until she was next to me and while I didn't resist when she wrapped her arms around me, I couldn't look at her—I felt about twenty shades of stupid.

Maybe Jen was right: maybe I *was* just a dumb kid.

Fran wrapped her legs around my waist so that one supported my back and pulled me closer. I leaned my head against her cheek and she played with my hair, brushing it off my neck and shoulder.

"Nina," she said gently, "I would never do anything you didn't want to do—I don't want to take anything you don't want to give."

I smiled despite myself, because deep inside, I knew that. "I know that, Fran," I replied just as softly. "It's that… I'm not the person you think I am."

Fran shifted until she kneeled next to me and I instantly missed her warmth as I gazed out the window. It was so grey out, I couldn't tell if it was still snowing or not.

"Look at me," Fran requested gently.

I glanced over and met her eyes, then dropped mine.

I couldn't.

I was such a *jerk*.

"Nina, please…" Fran asked again, and laid tender fingers on my face, but didn't force my gaze. "Look at me."

It was her touch, matching her tone as it did, that convinced me and I finally turned my face to hers, afraid of what I'd find. I stared at her wordlessly and found nothing but kindness shining out at me.

"I know you," she told me, stroking my face, and her perfect smile beaming at me. "I *know* you."

I shifted restlessly and tossed my head in negation. "No, you don't," I told her sadly, staring at her. My hands wanted to touch her but I stopped myself and put them in my lap. "And I don't think you'd like me."

Fran closed the space between us and cupped my face in her hands. "You're wrong." She smiled at me again, a soft lift of her lips. "I do know you." She stroked my cheek, then placed the flat of her palm against my chest. "I know this—I've seen it."

I was touched but I shook my head again. "No Fran, really. I've changed—a lot. I'm not who you think I am." I met her eyes again and they looked at me with such warmth, I wanted to cry.

I wanted her to understand: that a part of what she had suffered had a reality; the girl she'd known *was* dead, had been dead for a long time. I didn't know who I was, but I wasn't her—not anymore, anyway.

Fran sighed and cupped my face with one hand again and drew soft lines along my shoulder with the other. I leaned into her touch. "You were dead Nina, gone. Everything but my heart told me that—nowhere to be found for years. Don't you think I'd know you'd be different? And—" she kissed my lips softly "—think, Nina. Would you have walked me home, lent me your scarf, God," she said, laughing lightly, "saved me from breaking my ass in the snow?"

Fran had my attention and this time, I didn't look away. Could she be right? Was a part of me—*any* part of me—still the person we both remembered? I shifted self-consciously.

"I've done some pretty callous things," I told her, and I felt my face flush with embarrassment.

"Who hasn't?" she asked me simply.

"But they haven't done the things I've done," I responded. "They haven't—"

Fran hushed me and gripped my shoulder. "Nina, you could have lied to me about Candace from the start," she said staring at me intently, willing me to understand. "You didn't have to say anything—she won't tell Samantha more than she told me, well…" She smiled wryly. "Maybe a little more, but not much. There's a very good chance that no one would have known anything." Her free hand cupped my chin and she again ran her thumb into the hollow she was fond of. "Don't you see?" she asked softly.

"But Fran." I shook my head in confusion. I mean, I thought my reasons for telling her were pretty self-evident, "Why would I lie? I mean, you had to know, this is your home for Christ's sake."

I could feel the heat rise up in my face as I said it, but I said it. I mean, how could I *not* tell her? And even if it hadn't been her home, it was someone she knew, people she knew. She had a right to know who she was dealing with so she could make informed choices, right?

Well, I thought so, anyway.

"You're proving my point for me." She smiled, and pressed her fingertips lightly against my sternum again. "This is the same. All the rest? It's just the outside. You know," she laughed lightly, "you were always so tough. Even as a freshman you had this fierce nobility."

I took her hand in mine. "Fierce, huh?" I chuckled. "In that uniform?"

Fran tossed her head back to laugh again that pure bell note, her hair flying about her like a golden mane. "Are you kidding?" she asked. "You actually made postman blue look hot!"

I laughed back with her—those uniforms were terrible. "I thought you and Sammie Blade had, you know, a thing?" I asked her with a slight grin.

Fran smiled and shook her head, and gave me a wry smile. "We did—until you," she told me.

"What?" I asked, shaking my head a little with confusion.

Fran placed a warm hand on my shoulder. "Nina, we used to fight over you. First, I'd said it was because of detentions, but that wasn't exactly true." She grinned at me, charmingly half embarrassed. "And then, you joined the swim team and it became who was going to give you a ride if you needed one, whose car you'd get to borrow for your driver's test—I got that one on a coin toss and the promise that I wouldn't see you before she got back from Europe, let her get an equal shot, so to speak." She nodded and grinned to herself at the memory. "I'm amazed we didn't try to kill each other, but it was a relatively unspoken rivalry." She laughed, and that sound took me back to a place, a place where we'd all been together, back racing competitively in school.

We'd called her Kitt back then because under the cool, collected, and ever-poised exterior, Fran was fire, a jungle cat in school colors, so fucking hot and so fucking fierce she never left the pool without placing first. Hence "Kitt," because she'd been a tiger in the water ever since she was a cub.

Samantha had just come out of a first-place win in the pool, and I' hurried carefully over. "Hey, nice dice, Blade!" I'd given her a hug.

"Thanks, thanks," she'd said, returning the pressure before we'd awkwardly let each other go.

"Oh hey, refreshing electrolyte drink?" I'd asked her and waved in the general direction of the large orange monstrosity that held water and what we'd generally referred to as powdered urine, colored for misdirection.

"Definitely. Required. Now," she'd answered with a smile as we tried not to slip on the tiles over to the cooler.

I'd grabbed us each a cup, then handed one over.

"Nice. Very nice race," Kitt had said to Samantha over my shoulder.

"Thanks," Samantha had answered shortly, then downed the cherry flavored drink.

I'd glanced over to see a bored expression on her face. Not a good sign.

"Well, we've had the slice, we've had the dice. You guys will have to show us all how it's done in the third heat—after the next event, to give us a break." Kitt's eyes had traveled to the other side of the pool, where the overstocked opponents sat.

Samantha had looked with her. "It's a little rest, better than none," she'd commented flatly.

The silence had dragged out.

"Hey, Sam, where's your towel?" Kitt had asked into the silence.

Sam had shrugged in response. "Probably in the locker room," she'd said blandly. "Don't worry about me."

This time, Sam had stared at her and I'd watched as Kitt's face worked. She'd opened her mouth as if she'd wanted to speak but had thought better of it, then taken her towel off her shoulders and tossed it at me.

"Share it," she'd said curtly. "I'm up for the medley now." She'd stalked off to the starting blocks.

Well, that was certainly bizarre, I'd thought. Maybe it had been me, and I'd walked in a circle of chaos, bringing those around me into confusion and personality morphs. That'd sounded about right. Or maybe everyone had been PMSing.

That would have been more likely.

Whatever.

"And you?" Fran continued, bringing me back to the present. "You were so immune to either of us."

I was more than taken aback—I was shocked, although maybe I shouldn't have been. I mean, I'd had the same crush on Kitt that the rest of the student body'd had. Well, maybe a little more, actually, since we did "hang out," and went on an almost-date or two, and I knew that Samantha and I had had—well, we never got that far.

She, like Fran, had been told I was dead and let's face it—I hadn't made myself easy to find. I had no phone number registered to my name, no utilities, hell, I didn't even have a job on the books, never mind a portable phone. And only the people that I *wanted* to know actually knew where I was—and that was sometimes, since I was so rarely home.

Something, I don't know what, shifted within me, broke, reformed, changed. I owed Fran—for her time, for her feelings, for what she had felt then and for what I was putting her through now. An amazing new thought ran through my head with a brand new resurgence of the pulse in my ears—maybe I owed myself, too.

I gave her a soft smile of my own as I touched her face, framing her cheeks with my fingers. "I'm sorry, Fran," I told her and I meant it—I was sorry for everything. "I didn't know."

That would be the last time either one of us mentioned Samantha or anything about that for some time.

Tears starred the corner of her eyes again and she seized my hand and kissed it. "I don't...I mean...it doesn't matter if we make love or not." She kissed my hand again then folded my fingers over and held my hand to her heart. "I don't care what you've done, I don't care where you've been," she declared. "I just love...that, that you're really here."

How could I not respond to that? Here she was, so loving, so kind, and a part of my mind said, so aroused and cheated; how could I deny that?

My former roommates? Honestly, they sucked.

The women I'd fucked? Didn't care about me, well except maybe for Candace, I think she might have tried.

The women at the bar? Just wanted to score.

Besides, it's not like I hadn't seen what happened to anyone I'd observed: lovers came and went. Declarations of romantic love would spread like confetti one night, only to be followed by heartbroken sobs the next.

I didn't want that.

No. I deserved something more than that, didn't I? Fran had made no demands, had pushed no agenda, was still giving me every opportunity, all the room in the world that I needed or wanted to decide how I to handle this.

I made a decision: what I needed, what I wanted, was her.

If I was going to do this, it would have to be now or forever hold my peace about it because I didn't know if I could do this tomorrow—and I saw that this, this whatever could grow between us, had the potential to beautiful.

I wanted something beautiful, I wanted some*one* beautiful, in the exact way that Fran was: inside as well as out. Maybe that was something I could be too, someday.

The pulse in my ears was steady even as my heart beat even harder, and warm, warm, warm, surrounded me, suffused me, made me feel like I was bathing in honey.

I kissed her cheek softly and took both her hands in mine. "Francesca 'Kitt' DiTomassa," I whispered in her ear, against the creamy warm soft of her skin. "It matters to me." I kissed the corner of her eye where another tear threatened to fall.

"I… I want to make love with you," I said quietly.

I could hear Fran's breath catch and her body absolutely stilled. Her eyes searched mine and mine answered me honestly.

"I want you to love me."

She smiled at me with such fierce joy, then looked at my lips with such a sensual twist to her own that the first part made me like I had stepped into the sun, and the second simply thrilled through me.

I was scared, so scared I could feel myself shake as she lay me down with contained strength and kissed me again. This time, fire lanced through me in tightening strings I could feel running to my wrists as my tongue slipped between her teeth and savored the taste of my cunt on her tongue. Her skin was velvety warm as her legs molded to mine.

My fear ebbed when she ran her fingers down my ribs and I gasped when her fingertips grasped my nipple, teasing one, then the other, to hardened, sensitive peaks.

But it was when her teeth closed on the tendon of my neck as her belly pushed into mine that the fire that had shot through me before came racing back like high tide, taking me with it, settling in my cunt.

I seized Fran and kissed her fiercely, trying to show her with my tongue how she made me feel and when finally, finally, I felt the solid heat of her pussy on mine, I let her slide between my legs.

"Thank you," Fran sighed into my ear before she arched her back away from me, which brought even more pressure to bear on my tightening clit. She began a slow and steady glide against me and as I scratched my fingertips along the lines of her back, I snaked the other hand between us so I could spread our joined lips.

"God…" Fran groaned as our clits met, and I agreed.

Fran slid against me with a purpose now and my hips moved to the same rhythm. Every kiss of her cunt took away another part of the world, each time her clit licked mine my skin grew hotter until I couldn't take it anymore and my hands, which had been alternately stroking her shoulders and grasping her breasts, teasing her nipples, tasting them, flew to her beautifully-toned ass that flexed against me.

I pulled her as hard into me as I could, I so desperately needed to hold her, to be completely *with* her, to get even closer under the skin that I wrapped my body around her, my knees pressing behind her shoulders and my hands guiding her ass firmly on my cunt.

Fran instinctively spread her legs a bit and the increased pussy contact made her gasp with me. The intense sensation made me desperate as those slick wet lips hugged my clit and hers ground into me.

The first time it happened I wasn't sure.

The slip of her cunt on mine felt so amazing that even though I felt something different, it was so brief and this all felt just so good, I didn't care. When it happened again seconds later, I definitely noticed—and so did Fran.

"Oh," she groaned, a low and throaty sound and she buried her face into my neck.

I opened eyes I hadn't realized I'd closed.

It felt exactly like, well, I couldn't tell you then but I can certainly tell you now: the tip of a thumb when it moves just inside you.

Fran's luscious cunt now thrust more than slid and I was so amazed by this new sensation that was actually in me, even the slightest bit, that I actually stilled.

"Hey…" Fran asked softly as her pussy eased against mine. "Are you okay?" She raised her head from the spot it heated to look at me.

I gazed back into her tawny eyes and stroked her magnificent shoulders. Even had we not been on swim team together, even had I not known anything else about her, I would've been able to tell by those shoulders.

I traced the muscles with my fingertips then came back to her face and neck, pushing away the unruly locks that fell across her cheeks.

Her face flushed, skin sweat-shiny, and hair loose, she awed me. I have never seen anyone more beautiful than she was at that moment, beautiful, strong, powerful in the most loving way. She was a lioness above me, and the expression on her face threatened to bring me to tears.

I relaxed my legs, content to twine them around hers and Fran relaxed as well, settling her legs under mine, propping herself on her forearms. Her cunt still pressed against mine, for which I was grateful—I didn't want this to end. Her fingers traced my cheeks and she rubbed her thumb across my chin while she waited for my answer.

"I'm okay," I smiled. I got a sudden attack of shyness. "It's just…I mean, I…" I took a breath and tried again. "It's just…I mean, I never—"

Fran cut me off with a kiss that shot straight to my clit and wrapped me in her arms. She was a phenomenal kisser and as I flicked my tongue against hers, I couldn't help but push my body against hers.

She tore her mouth from mine and scraped her teeth against my neck. "I know, Nina," she whispered hotly into my ear, then kissed my throat. "I know."

She traced strong fingers up my leg and slipped her arm under my neck and just as neatly, she shifted over until she was lying next to me, almost on top of me. I didn't wait for her to lean in to kiss me—I wrapped my arms around her shoulders. I'd found her full breast and stroked along its curve before catching her nipple, tweaking it gently. Her kiss set my skin dancing while her fingers nimbly played with my short pussy hairs.

"Mmm…" she murmured. "You know, I've kept the habit myself."

I chuckled despite the rising heat—I knew she meant the swim team trim. Hey, it is a habit you don't break.

Why?

Someone's got to buy all those trimmers, right?

I replaced my fingertips with my lips and sucked in the honey-sweet taste of her skin. Her nipple felt gratifyingly hard under my tongue and I let my free hand glide down her taut stomach muscles to find out if what she had said was true. I had thought so—it had felt that way when her pussy was against mine—but I wasn't sure. When my fingers found her, I knew.

"I see," I whispered back.

She groaned when I cupped her cunt in the palm of my hand, my fingertips alternately squeezing and massaging her full lips, swollen with such need that they'd parted, her clit was so hard I could feel it throb against my palm. I wanted to so much to be in her that my fingers twitched and my clit jumped with hers. It jumped even more when Fran slipped two fingers around it and slid them slowly up and down my pussy.

"You're so soft," Fran said, wonderstruck. She explored my cunt and stroked back up. "And you're so...hard..." she added, squeezing my clit between her fingers.

I couldn't take it anymore, I *had* to touch her; my pussy hurt knowing she was ready for me, slick and open and hard. I took her clit between my thumb and forefinger and began to gently jerk her off while I let my middle and ring fingers play right around the hot wet entrance to her cunt.

Oh. *Yes.*

That. Felt.

Good.

"God, what are you *doing* to me?" Fran groaned, her hips jumping in time with my strokes and pressing against my clit even harder which made me groan in turn.

"I'm jerking you off," I told her honestly when I could think for a moment. She tossed her head and exposed her neck. It was a target I had to take, and I dragged my lower lip along its length before I bit down lightly. "You are so hard...and so wet," I added, teasing my fingers against her opening.

Fran rolled over me slightly and the hand that had been under my neck cupped my head. My lips met her half way and she pumped my clit harder, faster, her hips timed to her thrust, my body meeting hers.

I hadn't slipped my fingers completely inside her yet, but I was dying to, and though I was surprised when she anticipated me and placed a fingertip by my opening, I was ready.

"God...yes," I told her when I opened my eyes to see her watching me.

"Are you sure?" she asked, searching my face. "Really sure?"

I switched the angle of my hand and brought my thumb against her clit, the very tips of my fingers almost, but not quite inside of her. She was so wet I wanted to come right then.

"I want to feel you come inside of me," I told her.

I wasn't afraid anymore. I needed her to feel everything I was feeling—all those wordless emotions that were all about her, everything I'd ever thought or felt and how much, just how so much I cared.

And I did—the combination of her tears and tenderness, my memory and my crush and all the moments we'd shared then and just now made me love her.

She made me love her.

"Fran...I need to be inside you...please..."

She shifted her leg in response, opening herself up to me. It was such a trusting gesture it nearly undid me.

Her pussy was such welcome relief to my fingers, hot, tight, and soft. God, she was soft and slick and I moved slowly within her, the feel of her loving cunt driving me insane with the twin drives of lust and humility—this was *Fran*, and Fran *loved* me, I knew it, I could feel it.

Her body told me.

"You feel so good," I choked out, overcome by the amazing sensations she was stroking out of my clit and the way her pussy hugged me as I moved within her, each stoke an embrace.

I thrust my hips against her, bellies meeting and still, she wouldn't enter me, she maintained her fingertips at my entrance. I pushed against her, wanting to fully to embrace her in return.

"I don't want to hurt you," she gasped into my ear.

I loved that—that she was thinking of me even as I could feel her cunt begin to pull on me, urging me further within.

I thrust deep inside of her and wrapped my leg over her hip. "You won't," I assured her. "I want you to *know* how alive I am."

"Oh yeah..." she groaned as I ground my thumb against her clit and pressed my fingers up inside her.

Her fingertips moved against me, almost inside of me, making me frantic with need, my cunt aching to hold her.

"You're so open to me..." she murmured, her voice catching as she moved her fingers ever so slowly into that ache. "And you are so beautiful, Nina, so goddamned beautiful."

She paused for one heart-stopping moment, raising her head and shoulders over me, and she stared at me, eyes shining bright and wordless.

Her lips lowered closer to mine.

"I love you," Fran whispered over my lips. "I have *always* loved you."

I felt my heart swell, that sense that had been pushing through my skin now bursting through it and I smiled gently up at her. "I know, Fran. I know."

I kissed that perfect mouth again, and as her tongue slipped between my lips, with careful tenderness, Fran slid her fingers inside of me, filling me.

It hurt—a sweet, aching pierce that went through my cunt to my chest—I gasped into her lips as her tongue tangled with mine. My back arched to make room for her inside me.

She watched mine closely, her eyes full of love and concern. "Did I hurt you?" she asked, stilling her fingers within me.

I breathed around this, this new thing, around the feel of her, the knowledge of her body in mine, the *absoluteness* of it.

"It hurts," I conceded, my voice sounding soft and small to my ears. "But...don't stop...it feels good, too."

She slid deeper within me and I could feel every single little bit of her moving in there. I stared with wonder as the pain receded and the pleasure that had been at the back of it came roaring to the front. I realized I had stopped moving within her myself and I kissed her hungrily as I resumed. God, she felt *good*—inside her pussy, inside of me.

I moved on nothing but pure instinct as I dug the fingers of my free hand into her back and hers pulled at my shoulder, rolling me even closer to her. Sweat-slick, her belly rode against mine, and she buried her head into my neck. There was nothing but the sound of our breath, hard and harsh, and the feel of skin to skin until I heard it—soft and wet, like the most tender of kisses.

Fran's cunt tightened around me and I could feel my own bear down on the incredible feeling of Fran inside me.

"Kiss me?" Fran asked hoarsely and I had a moment's glance at the amazing flush of her skin and the golden flash of her eyes before I did.

Her body jumped as we thrust in and against each other, the agonizing cunt-tension riding, tightening, pulling like a thread of light.

Fran broke and took me with her as I felt the unmistakable lock of her cunt.

"God, yes," I ground out, "please come."

Her forearm pressed over mine with such force it was almost painful, and I didn't care, it didn't matter at all because there was nothing but this, this unrelenting beautiful tension, this barely chained divinity.

I prayed to it.

"Come deep inside of me."

She moaned at those words, a low and desperately sensual sound as she tensed against me. "God...Nina," she cried, her free hand digging into my back, "I love you," and she thrust so deeply within me it I felt it in my heart. "Come with me," she choked out then kissed me—*hard*. "Come with me."

My body exploded at her request. "I am," I gasped out, amazed with the realization that *this* was *it* and it was too much, just too much—the feel of her on me, in me, the pounding wave that ground me down before it. I pressed my head against her chest and the sound her heart beat back at me, and I cried out as the storm rode past.

"Hey easy...easy now. It's okay," she murmured into my hair. "I've got you."

Her pussy softened around me and as reluctant as I was to leave that warmth, I withdrew gently, knowing that pressure would soon become uncomfortable for her.

I lay my hand on Fran's chest next to my face.

And cried.

Fran slid gently out of me, leaving me empty. She crushed me to her.

"It's okay...it's okay," she soothed, kissing my head in between, her hands strong on my back. "Oh Nina..."

She covered me with her body, soothing me with tender kisses and words. I gratefully drank it in. Finally, I blinked up at her to find her gazing at me with the same brightness in her eyes and gently cradled her face with my fingertips. My thumb brushed a tear from her cheek, then remained there, just enjoying the feel of her.

"Are you all right? Did it… Did I hurt you?" she asked me with the same warm concern she'd shown me this entire time.

"I'm fine." I smiled at her "Never better." And honestly, for the first time in a long time, it was true.

"I'm glad," Fran grinned back at me, "that was—"

She stopped abruptly, staring at the hand she'd been about to stroke my forehead with. She sat up and flipped it over to examine it.

I sat up with her and leaned over to look for myself.

"What's the matter?" I asked as I stroked her long curls from her cheek back over her shoulder.

The face she turned to me was stricken—then she showed me her hand. It seemed fine until I took it into my own and looked closely. The back was flecked with dark red, the same red that outlined her nail beds, had settled into the knuckle creases of her fingers.

Paint.

Okay, so?

"I don't understand."

Fran closed her eyes a moment, then opened them. She showed me the other side of her hand.

"Oh…" I gasped softly, understanding what I saw, what it meant.

It was as if she had dipped only the front of her fingers in a red so brilliant it seemed almost unreal, while center of her palm gleamed wetly, a darker color, from where it had pooled.

Blood.

My blood.

Fran closed her hand and pulled it away from me. "Nina…"she began and stopped, looking at me with golden eyes gone dark. "Nina…why…I mean, just—oh!" She pulled me into her arms and began to truly weep, tucking her head into my shoulder.

I wrapped myself around her as her shoulders heaved, rocking her, hopefully calming her.

"Shh…shh…" I murmured, planting kisses into her hair. I took her hand, the one she had curled to her chest and laced my fingers through it. I made her open it up and pressed my palm against hers.

It was appropriate to me—this hand had been the one inside of her. Essence to essence. It seemed right to bring them together.

"Oh Fran," I sighed.

My chest was bursting, my skin was overfull, my pulse was a peaceful note in my ears as I kissed our joined hands, kissed her knuckles, her fingertips. I spread her fingers open and exposed her still-damp palm. I touched my fingertips to it and on impulse, painted a dot on my chest with it.

I did the same to Fran.

That looked *right*, that felt *right* somehow, as if a cycle had been completed, a circle closed, and a—

"Why, Nina?" Fran spoke finally into the heavy warm silence. "Why did you—"

She shrugged helplessly when I put my fingers to her lips.

"Don't you see?" I asked, smiling at her gently. I could feel that smile widen as I remembered the sound that I'd heard, the sound of soft kisses. I knew what it was, now, it was the sound of *us*, the sound of making love, and despite the cool morning air, the realization warmed me through out.

Fran shook her head, not knowing what it was I saw or heard.

The warmth of my heart grew within me, filling me, overflowing until it floated above my skin, and I had to share that feeling, that knowledge, with her. I shifted so that her back leaned against my chest and I still rocked her lightly as I told her what it meant.

"No matter what happens," I whispered, "this is yours." I kissed her head, then moved her hair so I could kiss her neck and shoulder. "If I died tomorrow…"

She shivered violently at those words then twisted around to kiss me fiercely. "Don't say that! You're not allowed to say that," she pleaded as she bowled me over with her strength and her fear and her love.

Her kiss was fueled by adrenaline, and I let her surge against me, reassure herself again that I was solid as her lips crushed mine.

"Whatever happens Fran," I explained softly as we broke apart and she gazed at me, "this…" and I took her hand and closed her fingers over her palm "…this will always be yours." I rolled her gently over to prove it.

I woke up on an unfamiliar world, a gentler and wondrous world, one that held the unbelievable sight of Francesca Kitt DiTomassa wrapped protectively around me, her golden mane spread across my throat, a hand that gently cupped my breast with a thumb that occasionally traced across its curve, and a splendidly shaped leg draped over mine. I lay there, absorbing the experience, and I lifted my head to look out the window. It was still grey out, and from what I could see through the window, the world outside had become soft and white.

It would be three days before the roads were fully cleared and transportation would get back to normal, erasing the new world the snow had wrought.

But for now?

It was magic.

CHEMISTRY
LOVE AND LAUGHTER—IT'S WHAT WE'RE ALL AFTER
SKIN TO SKIN—IT'S ALL CHEMISTRY

"Chemistry"—JD Glass

You would think that the problem in being involved in any way with Fran is that it would force me to think about the past, including our friend Samantha and it did, sometimes.

The realness of her was an occasional haze on my skin, and there were times I turned corners and expected to see her back, or I'd look up and expect to see her eyes. It was those times that I was haunted at work, at home, even when I was with Fran.

There were occasions it could even get confusing, because Fran and I'd be in the middle of making out and I couldn't help but think *she and Samantha did this*, or we'd make love and for a moment I'd think of the two of them together and it kinda flipped me out.

I mean, I didn't know how I felt, if I was jealous, if I thought it was cool, or if maybe I was just stupid for even thinking of it at all, and all of that didn't matter, because in those moments, it drove me absolutely *crazy*—the thought of them together made me so fuckin' hot and crazy-something, I twitched.

I don't think it made me a bad person or anything like that, and mostly I just chalked it up to the fact that it was probably due to being what Cap said: young, dumb, and full of um, hormones, actually.

There were days I was really convinced about the dumb...

But honestly, I shoved those thoughts forcibly aside when it came down to it because Fran (to whom I'd taken once more to calling Kitt when we were alone), was so easy to fall into that I really didn't want my head to be anywhere else.

I really loved being with her: it didn't matter what we were doing, even if we did nothing at all—and that helped me to focus the way I wanted to.

This wasn't something I discussed with Fran, though, because this was the one thing I knew for absolute sure: Fran loved me.

I knew it, saw it, felt it, in everything she said and did—I never doubted that for a moment. She never asked me for anything—not even for my phone number or address—although she did make me (finally) get a "real phone" as well as a cell phone.

After those first few days, when we were snowed in together, she must have thought about some of the same things, because the very next time I went with her to her apartment, she'd changed the cover on the futon, rearranged her bedroom, and managed to mention that she'd bought a new mattress—I took the hint and broke it in with her.

Yes, it was quite comfortable.

My life consisted of work, rehearsals, and Fran, who was amazingly supportive of both my art and my music. I couldn't understand why, because she'd never really seen or heard any of my work. I mean, I brought my guitar over and played a bit, practicing lines over and over, composing new tunes, writing lyrics and rehearsing melodies, but still, she'd never really heard the band, or any true full song.

But whatever she heard me do, she always had something thoughtful to say, something that showed she really listened and really cared.

And because it was something *she* was into, and because I thought it was seriously cool, I hadn't told her about it yet—it was going to be a surprise—but I was teaching myself a bit about Japanese language and culture.

The real funny thing was something in me had changed, and it wasn't just the fact that my pseudo-virginity was now myth. I got a brand new pair of buzzers and trimmed my hair. I dyed it black and, with Stephie's help, placed a blood-red inch wide stripe down the back center.

Oh, the smell of Manic Panic hair dye in the morning: crayons and playdough, who could ask for anything more?

And…my pants felt different, as in really different. Absolutely *nothing* sat right over my hips or thighs (ok well, except Fran, but that kinda goes without saying). Everything all just twisted and made me uncomfortable, so I abandoned anything but button fly and army pants all together. I also started to wear underwear because I was just too damn sensitive, but, in keeping with being myself, I only wore thongs.

Besides, Fran liked them, and I liked that.

Things had seemed to change quite a bit at work, too. Jen stopped calling me "kid" as much and while the women that came to the bar still came on to me with alarming frequency, I didn't need her help quite as much anymore.

Actually, I'd been semi-promoted: I now backed Jen up at the door and occasionally filled in for her, while Dee Dee was showing me how the books worked when it wasn't too busy. In fact, I'd been coming in during the afternoons sometimes when we were closed so I could review the bar order and receive the deliveries with Dee Dee.

"A head for business, that's what you've got, Nina," she'd tell me when I asked her questions. I appreciated that; it meant all that math with Atilla the Nun hadn't been in vain.

The night was quiet. I'd had a rehearsal earlier with the band, and Jerkster had decided to come and hang out for a while, which was fine by me—we had some interesting conversations on our own sometimes.

Jen had called to say she was coming in late so I was "doing the door" until she arrived, which means I was greeting the regulars, checking IDs, and making sure the patrons were "safe" for the environment. But there were only three people in the bar, so Dee Dee sat with me, reviewing the bar order and asking me for my opinions and reasons about why we should order what.

My cell rang with the special tone I'd programmed for Fran.

"Excuse me, Dee Dee." I smiled as I reached into my back pocket.

"'Lo Kitt," I said into the phone, with the lowest, sexiest tone I could muster.

It was funny, while that had been her nickname for many years, no one used it anymore, no one but me and it was somehow something very special between us. I could tell she enjoyed hearing it; her smile would get a little bit brighter and her eyes would sparkle more. And I loved, loved, loved, to see that.

"Hey, baby," she answered. I could hear the smile in her voice. "You working tonight? Rehearsing?"

Honestly, no matter what my confusions were, I could and can truly, *truly*, say I loved Kitt with everything I had to love her with and make no mistake, that's not something that has *ever* gone away.

Not a single bit.

"I had an afternoon rehearsal today and Jerkster's hanging out at the bar with me now," I told her. "I'm just watching the door 'til Jen comes and doing some paperwork with Dee Dee—it's gonna be quiet tonight."

"Well, I'm free tonight and… I'd love to see you," she said, drawing the last part out of that out with a little roll that made me smile at the image it conjured in my head.

I *definitely* wanted to see her, too—I missed her.

"I'd love that, but I have to go back to the Rock at some point. I have a rehearsal tomorrow."

"Lucky for us both then that I'm free until tomorrow afternoon—I'll go back with you."

I returned my attention to the conversation. "You're gonna come by here then?" I asked, more than merely pleasantly surprised.

It's not that Fran had never hung out there while I was working—it was just that she didn't do it very often, I mean, she did have classes to attend. I also suspected that the attention I got on some of the more crowded nights bothered her.

But even though we had never formally defined what we were or called each other "girlfriend" or anything like that (and I really *hate* the term lover—it sounds so, so, just, I don't know—I just don't like it as an overall blanket term) I made sure in every way I could that Fran knew *I* knew whose bed I wanted to be in, was going to be in, and it was absolutely without a doubt with her.

"Yeah, absolutely. I uh…" and she hesitated, something she rarely did. "I really want to see you."

"And I'd really like to be with you," I returned. "I miss you."

God, how I meant it—I hadn't seen her in a few days and although we had spoken during that time, it wasn't the same thing at all.

"Yeah?" she asked, her voice softer, uncertain.

"Absolutely," I affirmed.

"Great!" she answered cheerfully. "I'll see in a little while then. Ciao!"

"Ciao, Francesca," I returned and clicked off.

I returned my attention to the bar only to find Dee Dee smiling at me.

"What?" I asked, grinning. I couldn't help that.

"Sie hat dich gern," Dee Dee smiled at me.

I gave her a puzzled look, not understanding what she'd said. I hadn't gotten really past the basic greetings yet—but I was trying.

"She really likes you," she translated as she read my face, her eyes sparkling.

"Well…" I replied and glanced down at the books before us on the bar because Dee Dee's regard made me feel a little shy. "I certainly hope so."

"Love is a very strange thing, Nina," Dee Dee said solemnly, "and it makes us strange even to ourselves." She paused and considered, then grabbed a few glasses out from under the bar. She poured cream into one, juice into another, vodka into the third, and plain old soda into the last one. "Which ones would you absolutely not mix together?" she asked expectantly.

"Cream and juice," I answered

"And why is that?" she prompted.

"It'll curdle the cream of course," I explained, puzzled.

I knew she knew this; she was a chemistry major.

Dee Dee promptly did just that—mix some of the juice with some of the cream in a separate glass. "And you are right, of course," she said as we watched it transform into cheese.

She held up the glass to show me the results, then deftly flicked it away under the sink with a quick turn of her wrist. "But…" and she held up her index finger to make her point. "Watch this."

She strained some vodka through ice then carefully mixed it with the cream and the juice. And even though I was really watching, I can't tell you exactly how she did it—but a few good shakes later, she poured a thick and creamy mixture that looked exactly like a pale orange shake.

"Try it," she urged, so I did.

Jerkster came bopping over from the corner where he'd been sitting and I offered him a sip, too. It was very nice, actually—smooth and cool, velvety and light, with a summery orange taste. It tasted just like a—

"A Creamsicle!" Jerkster announced and I agreed.

That's exactly what it tasted like, a grown-up Creamsicle with just the lightest of kicks.

"How did you do that?" I asked Dee Dee, smiling. "That was some trick!"

No joke, Dee Dee really was the best.

"Ah, nothing," she said, waving away the compliment. "You like?" she asked Jerkster, raising her eyebrows at him.

He peeped over the straw he joyfully sucked on. "Uh huh," he said from around the plastic. The cup started to make that sucking sound as he got to the bottom and he bopped happily off back to the jukebox.

Dee Dee observed him for a few more moments, then returned her attention to me.

"It's...it's a lot like love, Nina," she said, pointing to the two empty glasses. "In the first example, we have two items—mutually exclusive, so different, and when they mix? One tries to become the other or the other tries to absorb the first to such a degree? They create something useless... and both are ruined. But, in our second example?" She paused and smiled. "There's something else—a catalyst that shares elements of both, yet it is separate, different. When it is used in the proper way, all these pieces give up a part of themselves and yet, here they are, uniquely themselves and together, something uniquely different, each a contributing element."

I got it, I really did. "It's a bit like being in a band." I nodded. "Everyone does their thing, but together..." We both looked over to the jukebox where Jerkster was dancing, badly. "You know what I mean." I grinned at her.

"I know what *you* mean," Dee Dee smiled back, "but do you know what *I* mean?"

I reflected. I thought I did, but on second thought, maybe I'd missed something. I scratched my chin. "You know Dee Dee, I thought I did, but I'm not sure. What do you mean?" I asked, paying her the serious attention her tone deserved.

Dee Dee's smiled softened and she gently pinched my cheek. "You should never, *ever*, give anything to the point you are lost—your life will become *dreck*—useless—and you—" she pinched me again "—have too much to offer to waste it."

Her regard was so genuine it embarrassed me, and the only reason it was too bad that I'd freshly cut my hair was that I knew she could see my ears burn as I dropped my eyes to the bar.

"So," I began smartly as she let go, "does that mean I should be more like vodka than cheese?" I gave her my biggest grin and jumped away just in time from the towel that flew my way.

"Wisenheimer!" She laughed. "Nothing cheesy about you!"

"You missed!" I laughed back.

She arched a perfectly curved eyebrow at me and fixed me with her bright green eyes. "I miss on purpose," she said with a grin, "or you'll spend another hour on your hair."

I clutched my chest like I'd been mortally wounded. "Oh! You're killing me!" I straightened up and put my hands on my hips. "Hey, I *like* my hair!" I told her, half joking but serious.

Dee Dee smiled at me again. "I like your hair, too," she nodded in agreement, "but it's your face that makes you money."

"And all this time, I thought it was my sparkling wit and conversational skills," I countered wryly.

"*Ja*, there's that too," Dee Dee allowed with a smile to herself as she wiped the bar. "But you must know by now how stunning you are, no?"

"Uh, no?" I answered as I walked back to the bar. I sat on a stool and pulled the books she'd left on the counter back to me. "People always say it, but, it's like, just bullshit, you know?" I started to review the numbers. "It's just what people say because they want to fuh—um, have sex," I corrected myself and looked up at her. "Right?"

"There's always that," Dee Dee said, and straightened from her task, "but someone's done you a great disservice." She waved her rag at me.

"What do you mean?" I asked, confused.

I mean, yeah sure, people said I was cute or whatever all the time, while the ones that said I was beautiful were the ones actively trying to get me into bed.

To tell the truth, sometimes it seemed like everyone was always trying to *touch* me, especially recently. It was getting to the point where I was starting to find ways of walking around them without any contact—I couldn't bear it anymore—it made me feel invaded, somehow.

By the time I got see and spend time with Fran, I was sometimes all sorts of jumpy because of that weird touch-sense that lingered all over me, but somehow, with her, it would all go away, that feeling of invasion, I mean.

Her touch was soothing, warming, and *belonged*. It just felt right.

But otherwise, other people, especially strangers…

I figured they reached for me like that because they were, you know, rude, grabby and horny—there was nothing real behind it except for their physical need. And as far as those that said I was cute (and I could swear the breath of cold air that whispered beside me for a moment was the touch of Trace's grey eyes) went, honestly?

I'd never heard cute equated with stunning before—unless it was a cartoon and someone was dropping a brick on someone's head—now *that's* stunning.

I said as much to Dee Dee, well, except for the part about touch avoidance and she frowned at me.

"No Nina, you're wrong, quite wrong," she told me, her voice husky and low in her soberness. "People don't do that to everyone—they do it to *you*, because they want to be near someone with your kind of—ah!" She groped for the right word. "Light, Nina. They want to be near your light."

Now I was really confused—what the hell did that mean?

"What?"

Dee Dee poured herself a soda and mixed some cranberry and orange juice for me. "Here," she said, sliding the glass to me, "listen."

"Thanks," I said as I reached for it. *"Salud!"* I smiled as I lifted and took a sip.

"Prost!" Dee Dee returned. She put the glass down with a bit of force. "Let me see your eyes," she asked abruptly.

I looked straight into hers, letting her search for whatever it was she wanted. I loved Dee Dee's eyes—the startlingly amber-to-green combination that tonight shone a mellow grass color.

Finally she nodded, having found what she was looking for.

"Your heart is always in your eyes, Nina, and that's what they want, the part they want to touch. The part you never share."

I had no idea whatsoever of what she meant; she'd lost me somewhere between heart and touch.

"Even I feel that, but I don't want to *fuck* you." She grinned and pinched my chin this time.

"Okay," I said slowly, "I'll keep that in mind."

Yeah.

Now I was *really* confused.

Dee Dee shook her head and chuckled a bit under her breath as I got out of my seat.

"I'm going to go check the lines," I told her, meaning the vast cylinders in the basement that hooked up to the tap lines up in bar. "We're getting something weird from the soda gun."

"Okay, go check," she agreed, outright laughing now. "Too much for you, huh?"

I grinned back at her as I felt a slow burn rise up my neck. "Something like that," I agreed good-naturedly, still not knowing what I was really agreeing to.

She'd given me a lot to think about but one thing I could see for certain—no matter what anyone said about my heart, I knew Dee Dee had a good one. *I'm really glad Dee Dee's my friend*, I thought as I made my way to the door.

A kink in the soda line was forcing it to send out a less than ideal mixture of syrup and carbonated water. I spent a good ten minutes or so wrestling with the valve-seal so I could unhook it, straighten it out, then hook it up again. *It's a good thing I know my way around a wrench*, I thought as I wiped my hands on a nearby rag.

I locked the storm gates behind me and walked back into the bar proper. I observed through the window as I made my way back to the door. Fran had arrived and that brought a smile to my face, but what I saw happening wiped it right off.

One of our regulars, Yvonne, had probably had a little too much to drink. She wouldn't be the first, or the last, to do that, but I'd be damned and double damned if she thought she could cause a problem in the place I worked—and *especially* not with my Fran.

I didn't know what it was about and I didn't care. Yvonne's arms were flailing and I could see from her expression how she spoke vehemently to Fran, who had taken a step back and squared herself off in a defensive position.

My skin tightened and buzzed as I watched. In two steps, I was there and stepped between them, facing Yvonne.

"Hey, hey, cool it… What's the matter?" I asked Yvonne.

She glared at me, put a hand on her hip and shook her head. She turned her gaze to the floor, silent.

I checked on Fran. "You all right?" I asked.

"Yeah," she assured me and nodded. "It's all—" her eyes widened. "Look out!"

I twisted my head to see what she meant, and as I did, a thousand points of light exploded in my head.

I rocked on my heels a bit as the explosion faded.

Oh… I was fuckin' *stupid*.

I'd just let myself get cold-cocked by a fuckin' amateur.

Deliberately squaring my shoulders and hips, I smiled and faced Yvonne, who took a step back, breathing hard.

Warm moisture fell in a tickling run from my nose and lip—I knew *that* feeling all too well. I wiped my fingers across my face, glanced at the blood that covered them, then considered Yvonne coolly.

"First one's free," I told her, then sucked the blood off my fingers.

I never took my eyes off her, but I glimpsed Jen coming up the walkway as I waited to see what would happen next.

Yvonne was shocked and her eyes flickered with what might have been remorse, but I knew, in the same way I knew I wouldn't want to be in her position, that pride was about to overtake common sense. Her face hardened.

"This one will be worth the price then," she snarled as she swung.

Too easy, she was way too *easy*.

Her swing was wide and I caught it with a simple forearm block, while my palm went straight to her shoulder. I could have easily gone for chin, but it wasn't necessary—that was overkill, while a chest shot would have just pushed her further into the bar. Besides, I already knew I'd win in a fight if it came to that—and I wasn't going to let it come to that. The move I chose used her own motion to spin her around and helped me propel her, one arm locked behind her back, to the door.

"*Apréz vous!*" Jen said sweetly as she held the door wide open.

She gave a slight bow as I shoved Yvonne through it, then she tossed the door shut. I knew Yvonne was not one of her favorite people to begin with and she'd been longing for a reason to ban her from the bar. This must have been a pretty sweet moment for her.

My blood sang in my ears even as it dripped down my face. Jen grinned at me. "Nice one, buddy!" she said admiringly as she clapped me on the shoulder.

"Thanks," I said shortly through the pounding in my head.

Fran rushed over, and Dee Dee tossed her a clean bar rag that I was pretty sure had been soaked in ice water. I guessed right, because I shivered violently when it touched my face as Jen and Fran forced me to sit on the nearest bar stool.

Jerkster came over and started singing, and I burst out laughing when Dee Dee joined him on the chorus of "Berserker."

"Hold still!" Fran admonished because I'd made a bit of a mess when I'd laughed—my nose was still bleeding.

"Hey, glad you're on our side, kid," Jen said, still smiling. She patted me on the shoulder again and this time, the "kid" thing didn't bother me.

She was all right, you know?

"Ow..." I couldn't help but complain when Fran moved the towel.

It was a mess. Dee Dee took it and handed Fran a replacement, which Fran then quickly reapplied to me.

"Are you guys trying to tell me something?" I asked, my voice muffled through the cold wet towel.

"*Ja*, Nina." Dee Dee smiled. "That was—"

"Totally cool!" Jerkster jumped in excitedly. "You were soooo cold—dude! You were *laughing*!"

His eyes were wide and his arms wind milled as he mimed what he'd seen with such enthusiasm that I was afraid someone else was going to get whapped in the face.

"I laughed? No way!" I said, looking at Fran and Dee Dee to either confirm or deny. I didn't remember that at all.

"Stop wiggling!" Fran exhorted as Dee Dee deftly exchanged the less-blood-than-before rag for another one—this one full of ice.

Ugh.

I gently pushed Fran's hands away.

"I'm fine—look—it's stopped." I indicated the towel that was now only faintly spotted with pink.

"C'mon...for me?" Fran wheedled.

I sighed and rolled my eyes. "Fine," I capitulated, but only because you never deny a lady a direct request.

Fran gave me a self-satisfied smile and patted my shoulder.

Great.

Awesome.

Now I was a good dog.

Jerkster kept rehearsing that block and punch (well, technically it was a palm-strike, not a punch) with Jen while Dee Dee stepped away to the other end of the bar. She came right back with two shot glasses.

"Here," she said, sliding them over. "This is good for you."

I eyed the little glass warily. Whatever was in one of them looked a lot like bloody mud with a bit of grass sprinkled on top—and I was pretty sure I'd already had my daily limit of that taste. The other looked like clear glue with little things suspended in it. I glanced up at Dee Dee who had fixed me with that firm look of hers.

"I made it special for you," she warned me.

Dammit.

Another direct request.

"Okay, all right, I'll drink it," I groused.

I gave Fran the rag and returned my attention to Dee Dee, only to find her eyes still frying me. *Damn*, I thought, *Dee Dee would have been ideal as one of the nuns I'd known back in high school.* I picked up her concoction.

"You have to swallow it all in one go, or it's no good," she helpfully advised.

Yeah, that just figured for me. I took a deep breath; I had the feeling I was going to need it. I brought the rim to my lips, and in the split second that the gloop was in the air before it hit the back of my throat and swallowed, I *knew* this was a bad idea.

Oh. My. *GOD!*

Nose? What nose?

I couldn't *feel* my fucking nose because my throat closed, my ears burned and my eyes were on fire. Who the hell cared about anything else? And then there was the hot eel sliding down my chest.

I jumped out of my seat and did an impromptu little dance—it might have looked like I was suffering from chicken pox in my crotch.

"Christ, what the hell is that Dee Dee?" I gasped, choking. "Is that horseradish and cough syrup?"

"Jägermeister," Dee Dee said and nodded, "and whiskey and Tabasco with some little, little herbs for flavor." She made a sprinkling motion with her fingers, rubbing them back and forth.

"Flavor? Flavor?" I coughed again and hoped desperately that I wouldn't spit out a lung or a kidney. "You should serve that with a fire extinguisher!"

Dee Dee laughed long and loud at that. "After that shot you took? Nina, you shouldn't taste anything, but you do—because you are berserker."

She laughed again while Fran seized the opportunity to put the ice back on my face.

"C'mon baby, your face is gonna bruise and you have a show coming up," she reminded me.

She was right and she knew I knew she was right, so I let her freeze my skin.

"I am *not* berserk," I said to Dee Dee with as much dignity as I could muster from under the towel and Fran's firm hold.

"Hey, it's a compliment." Jen said as she walked over, Jerkster following right behind her.

"Yeah, a compliment," Jerkster seconded. "'Cuz like, the berserkers were, like, these German-Scandi-cold weather dudes who went totally nuts when they were in a fight. They were, like, the ultimate warriors and you could tell who they were, because they would laugh the whole time, and then after that, they were okay again."

We all looked at him in amazement. I'd never heard so much information about *anything* come from Jerkster at one time.

"What?" he asked, glancing about at our dropped jaws. "I used to be into heavy metal—there's at least one song on every album all about it."

That was it, that was the living end, and I started laughing so hard my nose started bleeding again.

"Well, that's about right, anyway," Dee Dee said, as impressed as the rest of us. "Now drink this, too." She pushed the other shot glass to me.

"Does this one also require any special equipment or precautions?" I raised a brow and asked her. I hadn't totally recovered yet from the last one and I wanted to keep the few taste buds I had left.

"Funny, funny," Dee Dee mocked lightly. "No, that one was for your blood, strong for strong—this one is for you, for your spirit, that it stays fiery but sweet."

That was about as much reassurance as I was going to get, so I went for it. This time, instead of downing it, I sipped and was rewarded with a pleasant tingle.

"Cinnamon?" I asked as I put it down.

"Cinnamon schnapps," Dee Dee corrected, "with gold flakes. Only the best for the best."

"I like it," I commented as I took a final sip.

No, really.

I liked it.

A lot.

"You would." Dee Dee smiled at me. She collected the glasses from the bar and put them in the sink, then gave the bar a good wipe down.

I watched her for a bit. Ah, Dee Dee and her endless supply of spotlessly white bar rags.

I sat there with the towel on my face while Fran stroked my hair. "You okay?" I asked her again, truly concerned. "What happened?"

Fran sighed. "Nothing, she was just a little drunk and a little disappointed I think," she answered. "And…" she gave me a wry little smile. "It looks like you've cemented her disappointment."

I put the rag down to gaze at her directly. "Did I now?" I asked dryly.

I put my arms around her waist and gazed into her almond eyes then down at her perfect lips that curved into the slightest of smiles.

"Can I kiss you hello?" I asked her, the heat of her body wrapping around me like a warm mist.

"Please do." She grinned and pressed against me. "My hero," she whispered over my lips.

"Whatever it takes," I whispered back.

I was instantly rewarded with the feel of that perfect mouth against mine, followed moments later by the warmth within it.

"Careful, baby…careful," Fran cautioned softly, pulling away. "I can feel your lip is cut, too."

I ran my tongue carefully around. She was right—I could taste the blood. "I don't feel a thing," I told her and pulled her closer to me.

"Good, because your lips are way too far away from mine," she purred, then proved it, with her fingertips tracing strong lines along my neck and shoulders as mine outlined her shoulder blades.

I would have loved to have done the natural thing and reached for her amazing ass but I wouldn't do that in a public place—that wasn't something I felt a need to share with the world.

"Harrumph." Dee Dee coughed none-to-subtly behind us.

Oh yeah.

I was supposed to be working, not making out.

"So I was saying…I think I should send you home tonight."

I whirled to face her. "No, Dee Dee, I'm fine, there's no need—"

Dee Dee held a hand up. "No, you should get some rest and besides, it's quiet tonight. Francesca, you'll take good care of her, no?" she asked, looking at her directly.

Fran took my hand. "Absolutely." She smiled. "She's in good hands."

"I thought so," Dee Dee nodded and smiled, "so here" —she handed me my bag from behind the counter— "and here." She pushed some money at me. "So you can get a car home. You should not be riding around on trains and ferries."

I stared at the money in my hands then tried to give it back to her. "Dee Dee, I usually walk to the boat. Besides, I've got money."

"You got hurt at work, no?" she asked rhetorically. "So, work pays to send you home. Now go!" She shooed me away. "And let Francesca nurse you!"

I watched as her lips quirked just the slightest bit at her last words.

Uh huh.

There was a faint whiff of something in the air and I'm pretty sure it wasn't cinnamon schnapps, either.

But you know what? I didn't want to argue. "All right then, thank you," I told her. "'Night, Jerkster!" I called as Fran dragged me to the door.

"Hey yeah, see you tomorrow!" He looked up from his intense study of the jukebox and waved.

Jen was already outside in the street and hailing us a cab.

"Thanks, thanks a lot." I grinned at her when a yellow car stopped.

"Yeah, you're welcome kid." She grinned back. "Get some rest. And you…" she nodded to Francesca, "don't let her fall asleep too early—she might have a concussion."

"No worries," Fran answered with her gorgeous smile as I opened the door to the car. "I'll take good care of her." She got into the car and slid along the seat.

I gave Jen a sharp glance—she was being way too nice and I noticed her lips give the same slight quirk Dee Dee's had.

Uh huh.

Weird.

I got in the car and stuck my head out the window. "I'll see you tomorrow?" I asked, giving her the this-is-way-too-weird eyebrow raise.

"When the sun's up kid," she promised with a smile, "when the sun's up."

"Cool," I answered and waved goodbye.

I settled into my seat, and after telling the driver where we were going, off we lurched into traffic.

"Come, put your head down," Fran smilingly invited, patting her lap, and I very happily complied. "You know, that's the second time you've shed blood for me."

I shrugged my shoulders in response as I settled against her. What could I say?

She threw her pea coat over me. "Got to keep you warm," she said, then smiled down at me.

God, I loved that smile. I couldn't help but reach and I brought her face to mine. "You do that well enough." I grinned and kissed her softly. "And I promise, the third time will be interesting."

"As long as it doesn't involve your head," and she kissed my forehead, "or this beautiful face," and she kissed my cheeks, "or these lips," and this kiss was delicate and tender and it worked its way into something much more intense.

So much so, that I was deeply into the sensual perfection and enjoyment of it, so when her hand slid down my stomach and into my waist band I thought nothing of it—until the car stopped short.

"Kitt baby, what are you doing?" I whispered to her as her fingers tickled even lower and the car moved on.

But even as I said it, my pulse played in my ears, because I wanted her, wanted her so much, so intensely, so *now*...

Her fingers stroked lightly against my pussy, teasing me, caressing me with promise. "I'm not supposed to let you fall asleep, so," she explained as her fingers slipped between my lips, "I'm taking care of you."

I felt the moan that was trying to make its way out and I reached up for her head to bring her lips to mine. "You are *evil*," I whispered before I let that moan out into her mouth.

Kitt's tongue mimicked her fingers as she slowly stroked the length of my swollen cunt. "God...you are so fuckin' *hard*," she breathed into my mouth.

"Francesca..." I murmured in half-hearted protest. "We're in a cab."

"Then you're going to have to lie still and be quiet," she answered as she rapidly fingered my clit.

Damn, but she felt so good.

Fine.

I'd be quiet.

It wasn't going to be easy.

Her hand stilled on my pussy as she shifted positions. "Did you know..." she whispered throatily "—that I can place one, two, three fingertips—" and she paused as she did it "—along your clit when you're this hard?"

Between the words and the actions she had me ready to explode in my pants, and when I felt her hand move again, the sensation was so fuckin' intense as it bolted through me that I stretched my head back against her.

"God, baby, what are you doing to me?" I groaned.

Fuck the driver—if he didn't know what had been going on before, I was pretty sure he did now, and I didn't fuckin' care.

She nibbled along the line of my neck and I rolled against the added sensation before she answered. "I'm jerking you off." She smiled into my eyes, then kissed me again.

The gorgeousness of our kiss and the steady pull on my clit became that cunt throb that lets you know the edge is getting close, and all I could think of was Fran's pussy descending on mine, swallowing my clit. I wanted to do that so badly, I thrust my cunt against her hands as she pumped me good and fast.

"Yes, baby...just like that," I groaned out. "God...I want it inside you."

I heard her breath catch.

"You're making me so fucking *wet*...God..." Fran growled. "Whatever you want, baby, *whatever* you want—do that when we get back."

She was jerking me off so good, nice and hard and tight around my clit, and that combined with the thought of her wet pussy waiting for me—I couldn't even answer her as I thrust hard and came into her hand, my face pressed into her chest and my fingers rapidly fingering her hard nipple.

I kissed her chest and climbed my way up her neck to her lips, straddling her thigh. "We're not done yet," I told her and slid my tongue between her welcoming lips. I tongued her mouth exactly the way I planned to taste her pussy as soon as we got to my place, but there was no way I wasn't going to have her right then and there because her kiss told me how bad she needed it.

I undid the top button of her jeans and slid my hand down, knowing I'd find her wet and waiting. I wasn't disappointed. Her cunt was an ever-thrilling combination of hard clit and soft open pussy and I tickled through her slick lips for a second before I found her clit with my thumb and thrust two fingers into her hungry cunt.

She gasped and bit my shoulder.

"Sh..." I cautioned with a little smile of my own. "You're gonna have to be quiet."

"I didn't know..." she licked my throat "...you were such a bitch." She bit my neck—God I *loved* that.

And she so, *so* turned.

Me.

On.

"Right now?" I said as I pressed against her solid clit and did her pussy hard, "I'm you're fuckin' hero."

She sucked on my skin in response and spread her legs a bit on the bench. I pressed up, deeper inside her and her hand came down on mine. That move got me, got me so good it made me want to come again and I made no protest when her other hand moved into my pants again then moved around to my ass. When her fingers quietly made their way to my cunt, sliding between the folds and tweaking my clit, my hips jerked in response and she had me where she wanted me.

"Oh...yes, baby..." she hissed as her thumb slid inside me.

"Kitt, are you insane?" I gasped with the rare sensation—rare because it wasn't very often that I had her inside me; not that I didn't usually enjoy it, it was just something I was still getting used to, is all.

Besides at the moment, my mind was still aware that we had company even though my hands and cunt and the pulse pounding in my head were not caring.

"It's been three days," she answered, leaning her head back against the rear dash, exposing her throat to my hungry mouth. "Three...whole... *fucking*...days."

The reality of her words swelled in me as I leaned down to kiss her perfect mouth that sighed as we made up for lost time.

Come to think of it? I don't remember paying for that cab ride. I still don't know how I feel about that.

ENJOY THE SILENCE
WOKE UP IN THE MORNING UNDERNEATH THE SUNLIGHT GLARE
YOU KNOW I'D NEVER ASK YOU BUT I WONDER IF YOU CARE
IT'S SO HARD TO BELIEVE—AND EASY TO DECEIVE
DO YOU WANT ME FOR ME?

"Me for Me"—JD Glass

FRAN LAY NEXT TO ME on the bed, drawing lazy circles on my chest with her fingertips as I held her close and kissed her head.

"I asked Dee Dee if you could leave early," she confessed quietly as we enjoyed our closeness.

"Really? When? Why?" I asked her sleepily.

My beautiful lion was making sure I didn't pass out in the best and most beautiful ways possible—I loved her so much for that, for everything.

"Yes, really. when you were in the basement playing with the taps, and because I needed to spend some time with you," she answered in the order that I'd asked.

The gig was in a few days and after that, I was taking some time off work and I'd planned to spend the time with her. If she really needed something, I'd absolutely make sure I was free and there for her.

There must be something wrong then, right?

"Kitt, love, is everything okay? I mean, why—"

"Shh…" she hushed me and slid her body over mine, then kissed me as sensually as she could.

She touched my face softly, running her thumb into that spot on my chin she loved so much, and I loved her to touch, as I ran my hands up along the smooth muscles of her back, then caressed the span of her shoulders.

"I have to go away…" she sighed and murmured into my throat.

I lightly traced her arms as she snuggled on my shoulder.

"I'm leaving Friday afternoon," she concluded.

"That's tomorrow," I realized aloud. "So soon? Do you have to go for a long time?" I didn't ask her when or where—Fran had never pressed me for anything, I wouldn't do it to her.

She propped her head on her hand to look at me. "Long enough that I won't be here for your gig," she answered sadly, "and I really wanted to go."

I leaned up to kiss her head and she sat up with me. "I'll miss you," I said quietly and I reached to play with her hair as it lay across her shoulder.

I caressed her neck as I pushed the long strands back. I would, too.

I might not have been ready to set up house-holding with anyone yet—and I absolutely hated that oft-rumored lesbian tradition, you know the one, how everyone moves in together on the second date? But I loved Fran and wouldn't dream of doing anything that would harm her or us.

Yeah, it may have seemed like I flirted at work a bit, but I didn't really, I was just being myself, and some people took a smile and a friendly question the wrong way. I was never happy about that (still hate it, in fact), but that went with the job territory.

I might not have liked to face it, but the fact remained: it wasn't just my sparkling wit and conversation that made me my money, it was my face, too—and I was the lead guitarist in a band.

But, in light of the intensity of what Fran and I shared, I highly doubted I would ever sleep with anyone else. In fact, I never even thought about it—because I simply didn't want to.

"I'll miss you every day until you come back," I told her and kissed her cheek softly. I put my arms around her and she nestled into them.

"Will you, really?" she asked, whispering into my breast in a small voice and I tenderly pressed my lips to her head.

"Of course I will, Kitt. You're my golden lion," I assured her in between kisses. "You're the pride of my heart."

My pulse sounded full and rich in my ears, the honey-warm filled and overflowed within me, and *Now,* was the command that ordered through me, *now, Now, NOW.*

"Aishiteru…" I whispered the Japanese phrase I'd added to the smattering I'd learned, a phrase I'd shared with her once before. I held her even closer, until I

could feel the beat of her heart against the steady and forceful thud of mine. *"Aishiteru."*

With that, she looked up at me with such an open and vulnerable expression, a smile of such child-like wonder, that the emotions that rose up in me threatened to make me cry and forced me to wrap myself around her, holding her close, protecting that innocence that she held.

"I didn't know that," she said simply and turned her head to kiss my collarbone.

I rocked her closer, loving her, her body curled in within the embrace of mine. "That's a mistake on my part then," I murmured, "because you should know."

"Aishiteru," she breathed back over my heart, and we tangled within each other, bodies so close and tight, there was no way of knowing where I ended or she began.

We lay that way for a while, skin to skin, while her breath dusted over my breasts where she laid her head above them.

"I got you something," she said finally into our quiet, lifting her head and tossing it to shake her hair free.

"Yeah?" I asked lightly, loosening my hold. "For me?"

"Yeah," Fran answered, the smile in her voice and on her lips as she turned in my arms. She tweaked my chin. "For you."

She straightened and jumped up, onto the floor. "What are you wearing for your show?" she asked, grinning.

Huh? I hadn't even thought about that—and I was especially not thinking about it right now.

"I haven't thought about it really. Why?" I'd figured I'd wear some variation of what I usually wore, maybe pay a little more attention to— what else—my hair.

"C'mon, get up," she exhorted, clapping her hands together briskly, "show me what you've got."

I raised my eyebrows at that. "What, you haven't seen enough already?" I asked her, but I complied, stretching my arms above my head and enjoying the appreciation in her eyes.

"Shame to have to cover that," she sighed.

"Really?" I asked cheekily, then caressed her waist and leaned in to kiss her neck. "I think you cover me quite well."

"Mmm," she responded silkily as my lips caressed the column of her neck, "I agree...but I meant with clothes." She touched my arm and I raised my eyes to hers.

"Does that mean you have something in mind?"

Her eyes widened. "What makes you say that?" she asked with a grin.

"Because," I said, grinning back, "you're always taking my clothes off. Well, that and..." I paused a moment for effect "...the fact that you never bring anything up without a reason."

"I do that?" she asked, laughing.

"Yeah, sometimes."

"Well, you happen to be right." She smiled. "I do have something in mind."

"It wouldn't have anything to do with my present, now would it?" I asked, grinning slyly.

"It might, it might," she affirmed nodding. Walking over to the closet, she pulled out her bag, then opened it to remove a plastic shopping bag that had been folded over.

She came back to me, took my hands and held them gently between us. "Close your eyes."

"Closed," I told her as I did so.

Her hands left mine cold as she rummaged through her bag. Then I felt her warmth near me again.

"Okay, lift," she ordered patting my right leg.

I did and she slid something part of the way up. I could feel it puddle around my foot, a texture, a scent I recognized, that made my nostrils flare.

"Other one," she asked and I helped. When both legs were on, she slid them up me and rested her hands on my waist.

"You did not," I said, stunned by what I felt as I ran my hands down my thighs.

"Did not what?" Fran asked innocently. "Oh, you can open your eyes now, by the way."

I did. And couldn't breathe a moment as I looked down, confirming what my sense told me. "Holy shit!" I exclaimed softly when my breath returned.

Soft black leather pants with a light sheen—and a lace up front. They fit me exactly like what they were—a second skin. "Man oh man!" I said as

I adjusted the laces. "And…" I took a step and grabbed my boots, slipping them on. "Straight cut! I love straight cut pants!" I examined the fit and the perfect drape over my boots.

I did and do love a straight cut—makes my legs look even longer. Hey, just because I don't think I'm good looking doesn't mean I'm not aware that I've got nice legs.

I looked up to see her watching me with the strangest expression. "I don't know how I'm going to keep you…" she said softly as she approached. "Christ, Nina, you *look* like a Razor."

"Thank you, thankyouthankyou!" I enthused, grabbing her in my arms and whirling her around until we were at the foot of the bed where we fell onto it.

"You look *so* fuckin' hot!" she told me as she twined her arms around my neck.

"You shouldn't have, you know," I said as I brought my lips to hers.

"What, and miss this? Not on your life," she said. She cupped my face the way she always did, running her thumb over my chin. Her eyes glowed at me, that melted caramel color that I could drown in. "This way, I'll be with you during your show," she said softly, "before you go off and become the star you're gonna be."

"Fran, that's not—" I began, but stopped as her eyes filled with tears. "Oh baby, no, don't cry," I said, kissing her eyes, kissing the tears. I scooped her up in my arms.

"I'm not going anywhere," I promised. "I'm gonna be wondering when you're getting back so I can pick you up at the airport—and I'm going to take a few days off so we can go and do something."

She laughed softly through her tears. "Baby, don't write checks your reality can't cash," she said quietly and kissed my chin.

"What do you mean?" I asked, confused, "This *is* my reality, I'm not going anywhere." In many ways, I thought that was true. I didn't have that piece of paper so many of my peers had that proved I knew how to at least read; didn't have a "real" job. I didn't have much except for the untouchables: the love I felt for her and the music and art in my body.

She smiled at me and wiped her eyes. "Nina, you're too big for this place, and everybody knows it, everybody knows it but you," she said, and kissed me again.

I kicked my boots off, and Fran wrapped her perfect legs around mine. We simply rested there together, my head under her chin as I lay on top of her.

I don't really know how long we had been resting like that when the phone rang. Since it did that so rarely, I answered it.

"'Lo," I said into the phone.

"Hullo!" cheered out at me. "Francesca?"

"It's for you," I told her, glancing at the phone quickly.

I'd grabbed hers by mistake—but the voice I'd heard sounded so familiar…

Fran took her phone from me and I carefully moved so I wouldn't crush her. I lay at her side and tried to get comfortable, but that feeling, the one that made the skin on my forearms was being squeezed, as if I were being held in place.

"This is Fran," she said into the phone.

From the way her voice bounced back from it, I could tell this would be one of those calls where everyone could hear everything. Man, cell phones can be damned annoying at times. I put a pillow over my head in an attempt to muffle the sound.

"Hullo Francesca!" the phone sang.

God, but I *knew* that voice, *knew* that cheery accent. And my pulse sounded again, along with tightening feeling along the skin of my arms…

"Good morning, Candace," Fran answered formally. Her body stiffened as she sat straight up.

I pulled the pillow from my head and read the rigid lines of her back. I pushed the pillow behind me and sat up, wrapping my legs around her, and pulling her into me, making a cage of my body for her to lean into, to take warmth from. I pulled the blanket up and tucked it around her waist and mine, then leaned back, Fran in my arms.

She twisted onto her side and laid her head against my shoulder. I kissed her head.

I had no idea what the call was about, but I knew everything was about to change, and it wasn't just the call, but things like her trip and my gig. I suddenly got this sense that maybe, just maybe, this gig might be a bigger deal than I thought it would be, than any of us, meaning Jerkster and Stephie and I, thought it would be.

Maybe not, though. Could be that sense was just because it was a first with a date, a time, and an exclamation point, and that alone made it important.

But still, and more importantly really, we wouldn't be together for it, and I wanted to be as close to her for as long as possible before everything went wherever it was going to go.

She glanced up at me with a grateful smile and I kissed her forehead. She sighed and snuggled back into me.

"To what do I owe this wake-up pleasure?" she asked with wry politeness.

I could hear Candace laugh that little laugh I remembered so well.

"You know," she began drolly, "if I didn't know better, I'd say that was my lovely lady Nina who'd answered your cell, Francesca. But you know, I never could actually get her to stay."

Heat radiated from her body as she sat up and when she glanced at me again before turning away, I could see (and I freely admit, this kinda thrilled me) the fire snap in her eyes.

"Perhaps because she wasn't 'yours' to begin with?" Fran answered.

I gave her a hug and a kiss to remind her I was there. She looked over her shoulder at me and threw me another brilliant smile, then settled her back more comfortably against me.

"Well, perhaps you're right," Candace laughed, "but then again, who could tame that? Hold on… Are you saying that's her?"

Fran said nothing but all the tension came flooding back into her muscles as she visually stiffened, then angled forward.

I straightened with a sigh. It seemed like the moment we'd been so carefully avoiding was upon us, like a bucket of water perched on a door frame; it hadn't fallen yet, but we were about to get soaked.

I reached over to an amp that doubled as a night stand and grabbed my cigarettes.

"Oh Annie, come here, this is just too rich," I could hear Candace call in the background. "Francesca has bagged my bird."

Oh…fuck it.

I lit Fran a butt too, as she turned eyes filled with anger and pain at me.

"It's okay," I whispered to her and tried to give her a smile.

Hers was small and tight in return as she took the cigarette I gave her. We both knew I lied.

And then, I heard it, through the miles, through the static and that ridiculous tiny speaker. There was no mistaking that sound, the sound I thought I'd never hear again: Samantha's laugh as she picked up the phone on her end.

"Hey Fran," I heard her greet, still laughing. "Candace has convinced me to go back to the States for a visit, and since I have some things to take care of, it'll be New York specifically. Can I use the keys?"

She looked at me, trying to gauge my reaction and I shook my head at her, not knowing what to say, because the moment I heard that voice, a tingle had spread through my skin until it felt like the top of my head—no my whole *body*—was going to dissolve into an electric spark.

Fran took a slow deep breath. "When were you thinking of coming?" she asked, exhaling softly.

I decided to stare at the wall. I didn't want to hear this conversation, but I couldn't help it. At least I could pretend to not be paying attention.

"Why Fran, is that a no?" Sam, I mean, Annie, chuckled sarcastically.

"Of course not," Fran answered, flustered. She jumped off the bed and began to pace. "It's just that I'm leaving for California in a few days and..."

My head snapped back around at that. "California?" I mouthed at her, shocked.

I don't know why I was so surprised—I mean, that's where she'd done her internship after all, and where she wanted to go after she was done with her studies and I knew that.

But it was *so* far...

Fran nodded at me and continued her conversation. "...and I was just wondering if we'd get a chance to meet on your trip, is all." Fran breathed hard, her entire body was flushed, and as she turned to walk the floor again, she bit her lip nervously.

"Oh," Annie answered. "I thought perhaps you were trying to keep your new girl a secret."

Fran's lips tightened. "Annie, I just thought that—"

"I've an idea!" Annie interrupted. "Let's go to the Redspot and see if we can find Candace's favorite attempt!"

"Ann, don't go there," Fran warned. "That's a hell of way to talk about an old friend—and someone you haven't even—"

Annie blithely ignored her and spoke over her.

"Sounds like she's enough to take us all on—maybe it'll take all of us to keep her, what do you say?" She laughed.

"Watch your fucking mouth, *Blade*." She spoke sharply, fire cracking through her voice.

It hurt to hear those words come through the phone, to know that Candace had considered me more casual than I had thought. I'd considered us, at the very least, anyway, friends.

But it hurt even more to know that after all these months, Samantha, I mean, Ann, Annie, whatever, had not only not tried to get in touch with me but that it seemed I was probably the source of foreplay conversation between her and Candace.

The thinking made me nauseous, crumbled something inside me. I looked up from my introspection to see Fran's eyes focused on me, fiercely concerned, hurt for me. She gestured to ask if I'd take the phone.

There was absolutely no fucking way, I thought, and I shook my head violently. "Candace knew how to get in touch with me. She could have called me months ago," I said in a stage whisper.

For fuck's sake, it wasn't as if I hadn't been at the same place for months, and it wasn't as if Mickey and everyone at the Redspot didn't get in touch with me from time to time. If someone had tried to find me there, Mickey would have passed the information on to me. I knew that for certain because he had.

Fucked up, this was fucked up.

I jumped out of bed and stretched, then crushed the cigarette I hadn't been smoking in the ashtray.

"Blade? Blade? You haven't called me that since..." The phone went silent a moment, and as I focused on crushing the remaining embers, I glanced over at Fran long enough to see the spark flaring in her eyes.

"Since?" she prompted, her perfect lips twisted in an angry curve.

"C'mon, '*Kitt*,'" Ann drawled sarcastically, "don't fuck around. You know very well how I—"

"How you feel about her, *Sam*?" she interrupted. "Yeah, in fact, I do, every day. So watch your fucking mouth."

I couldn't hear any more of this—not that voice, not that tone, and not Fran's responses. There was silence on the other end as I stalked to the closet, grabbed the closest shirt my fingers could find, and yanked it over my head. I glanced down at it as walked to the door. "Love and Rockets, Vida Loca" or "crazy life" in English.

How appropriate, I thought as I turned the door knob.

"Where you going?" Fran asked me in a worried undertone.

I gave her the best smile I could manage. "I'm just getting us some water." With the way my legs shook and threatened to buckle under me while waves rose in my gut and punched my throat, I figured I needed a bottle—and Fran looked like she could use some, too.

I opened the door just in time to hear Sam's voice cut across the planet. "You're fucking with me, aren't you?"

Fran closed her eyes and swallowed before she answered. "You know what? I wish I was."

I closed the door quietly behind me as I made my way to the kitchen. Fuck.

I'd forgotten my smokes. Back to the bedroom for me, then. I entered to see Fran had sat down again on the edge of the bed, smoking one of my cigarettes while she held the phone in her other hand.

"Hey, don't blame me, this isn't my fuckin' fault—I left you messages," she fumed into the mouthpiece. "And Candace should have told you months ago! Isn't that your deal or whatever?" she said as I quickly grabbed my pack and left again.

I could barely hear the reply squawk to that—for which I was grateful—my heartbeat hadn't returned to normal yet.

I waved to catch her attention as I reached the door and blew her a kiss. This might not have been the world's happiest moment, but no matter who liked it or not, Francesca DiTomassa and Nina Boyd had something going. Besides, I loved her and I didn't want her to think I'd forgotten.

She gave me a sweet and sad smile, then blew me a kiss in return. I spent a moment miming that it had landed on my cheek, caught it, and put it down my shirt, rubbing it over my heart. Fran grinned, and I sent her another one before I left.

Once in the kitchen, I forgot all about getting some water. I sat at the table and simply stared out the window where it overlooked the fire escape as I smoked. Finally, I muscled up the frame and sat on the ledge, just staring at the sky, watching my smoke float into it.

The metal from the fire escape was a little too cold on my bare feet, so I tucked them up into the frame where I'd wedged myself—my back against one side, feet on the other.

I thought of absolutely nothing and I don't know how many cigarettes I smoked before Fran came into the room. I'd noticed she'd put on my shirt, the one I'd been going to wear to the show, over a pair of sleep shorts.

"Do you want to talk with her?" she asked me in a low voice.

I took a deep drag then, exhaled. "No," I said and shook my head. "I don't. She could have found me months ago." I took another deep drag and exhaled slowly again before I faced her. "You didn't tell me you were going to California," I said mildly.

Fran eyed me, a bit warily I thought. She didn't have to worry—I wasn't mad, and I wasn't going to bite.

"I was going to tell you, before the phone rang." She walked over and put a hand on my shoulder.

I blew the smoke out the window then put my free arm around her waist, swinging my legs back in and onto the floor. Fran took the cigarette from my hand and took a drag while I put my other arm around her, burying my head against her ribs.

"Don't go," I asked quietly, "stay with me or..." and as it occurred to me, I thought it was a brilliant idea "...delay a few days and I'll go with you."

Fran gave a light little laugh under her breath as her fingers stroked through my hair and rubbed the back of my neck.

"I have to," she answered just as solemnly. "It's the only time I can, where I'm...it has to be now."

"Why?" I asked, kissing her nipple through the shirt. I accidentally tore the button when I reached for the curve of her breast. "Why now?"

Her fingertips strayed from my neck and began to dig into my shoulder as I breathed across her hardening nipple.

"Because..." she sighed as I teased that hardened end with my teeth. "There are some cycles you can't break...just like that..." Her hands pressed my head against hers while I massaged her beautifully firm ass. The other began making the journey where I knew it would please us both most.

I reached the junction of her thigh and slipped beneath the leg of the shorts she was wearing. I smiled when I recognized them, because they had been a gift from me.

"Don't… Don't you want to talk about it?" Fran gasped as I pressed along the tendon then ran my thumb along her shape.

I looked up at her finally, to see her undoubtedly trying to be rational, though her eyes were half hooded.

"No," I told her, my breath ragged with want, the absolute wrenching *need* to touch her, while my pulse pounded so hard within me I half-thought she could hear it. "I just want *you*."

"She didn't know… Candace didn't tell her," Fran told me, trying again.

I heard her words, but they had no meaning for me, although some part of my brain realized that Candace had lied—to all of us—she'd known from the beginning exactly who I was.

But right now, it didn't matter; it didn't matter at all. Fran, my glorious Kitt, was before me and the scent of her desire was burning through my mind. All I wanted to do was make her call my name, her voice a trumpet to the sky when she did.

"I don't care," I told her as my fingers grazed her cleft. God, she was wet and she was mine. "Kiss me," I demanded, and she did, her mouth perfectly sensual, demanding, against mine.

I slid my fingers between her folds and glided along her ache, enjoying the moan that sang from her lips as I focused long strokes on her clit. My other hand had strayed from her delicious ass and slowly but surely my fingers pressed, gently insistent, into her waiting cunt.

Fran gasped and swayed, trapped between my arms and hands. I guided her to me, onto my lap.

"God, baby!" I choked out when her pussy encased my fingers and she threw her arms around me.

She raised herself off me only to shift her hips a bit because when she sat back down, she shoved me deep inside of her. Her face glowed and her eyes were both tender and fierce as she grabbed my shoulders.

"Kitt, baby, baby Kitt…you are so beautiful…just so fucking beautiful," I whispered into her ear because it was true, so true.

I could feel how I burned with the vision of her, my blood pulsed, my heart lived and died with her breathless sighs and I wanted more—more of her.

I teased another finger by her cunt, feeling the other ones fly into her while my other hand lavished attention on her hard, hard, clit.

"God yes, please…just…please…" Fran gasped as I began to slide that third finger inside her.

Ohgodohgodohgod I was going to die I was going to come—her pussy was so hot and tight and she was *so*.

Fucking.

Amazing.

"Is this what you need baby, is this what you want?" I breathed out as she purposefully pushed herself onto me again, and I was so deep inside her I could feel her womb, its hard prominence pressing against the back of my fingers.

Fran rubbed her face against mine.

"Yes…" she hissed in that satisfied my-cunt-is-full voice as she rode me, her body a sensual wave, her pussy gliding off my fingers. "Just…God," she groaned aloud when I was sheathed in her again.

I began to thrust into her, shorter thrusts, deeper thrusts, loving her, wanting her, needing her inside me, under my skin like bones, in my cunt like God.

Because that's what this was, this touch of her on me and me on her, this oh-so-fucking-*beautiful* meld and melt of her and me—together we touched the face of God.

"Just what, baby?" I asked as she buried her head in my shoulder.

"Don't stop," she groaned into my neck. "Don't. Fucking. Stop."

Her words set me free and my body jolted with the feeling. I began to fuck her, really and truly fuck her with everything I had—my heart, my mind, I poured my soul out into her cunt through my fingers.

"I won't," I swore wildly as her pussy gripped me tighter. God, her clit was so hard and so big I wanted it in my mouth, between my lips, under my tongue. I wanted it in me, I wanted *her* in me, as close as we could possibly be.

"I won't stop because you're fuckin' mine," I told her, my words coming out in harsh breaths.

They weren't the right words, but they were the only ones I had. I realized then and there that I'd never had the right ones, never would. How could I say thank you for bringing me back from the scary place I had been? How did I tell her that her love for me made me safe, comfortable, easy in my skin and capable of being more than I had ever dreamed?

Yes, she was leaving, I was gigging, and there was that fucking phone call to deal with, and I knew, the way you know when you've just slammed your knee that in half a second that it is really going to *hurt*, that everything was going to change—everything always does.

But this?

This was ours, our time, our moment and we belonged to it, to each other—and I *knew* it.

I gave myself to it, I gave myself to *her*.

"Mine," I growled, nipping lightly at her breast with my teeth. I'd already ripped the button off the shirt. "Mine..." I whispered again and pressed my lips to her chest, sucking on the skin as her heart beat madly against my mouth.

Fran crushed me to her and I tasted blood as she swayed against me, her pussy so tight I was afraid I'd hurt her. I looked up, my chin pressed against her chest as I drank in the sight of her edges, the artful lines of her neck, her chin, her form—the outline of my glorious lion who cast golden eyes to me, eyes full of love and passion, eyes that looked at me and showed me as beautiful.

"Yours," she gasped, and let go of me only to grab a gentle hold of my face and kiss me desperately, as if she were dying and this was her last chance, her only chance, to let someone know she'd existed.

"Yours..." She breathed again when she tore her mouth from mine and she cradled my face in her hands, her thumb brushing over my chin, into the hollow below my lip.

God, I was deep, so deep inside her pussy as those tight slick walls held me, pulsed around me. Her eyes locked on mine, melting, incandescent, and I witnessed her transformation as she gave me everything she had, the rhythm of her heart beating in my hands.

The aftershocks raced through her and she shuddered with them as I eased my fingers away, first from her now-too-sensitive clit, and then from the welcome warmth of her pussy as she hugged me and rested boneless, wordless, head tucked into my shoulder, cheek pressed against the beating vein in my neck.

I let the tears stream down my face, overwhelmed as I was by the intensity of everything, the magnitude of the gift that was my Kitt, Francesca, Frankie, Fran, and I eased us down from the ledge, sliding down the wall until I sat on the floor with my back against it, with her on top of me. I wrapped my arms around her, holding her, crushing her to my chest, rocking her as she cried with me.

When through her tears she kissed me with hunger, pushing me back, forcing me down against the wall, I answered her need. When her fingers reached for my pants I helped her open them.

Words were cheap. I used the language I knew best as we lay down.

LONDON CALLING

IF YOU DON'T KNOW WHAT PAIN IS—I CAN SHOW YOU
THAT'S THE ONLY WAY YOU LET ME KNOW YOU
THINK IT OVER DRINK IT THROUGH THEN FEEL IT ONCE AGAIN
IS THIS THE ONLY WAY THAT YOU CAN LET ME BE YOUR FRIEND?

...

TAKE YOUR MARK, BUT THINK IT OVER BEFORE YOU SHOOT ME THROUGH
THIS BECOMES THE WAY THAT I WILL ALWAYS THINK OF YOU

"Carry The Stone"—JD Glass

FRAN LEFT WITH THE PROMISE to call me after the gig and as soon as she knew when she'd be back. I didn't press her—I felt it was only fair return on my part for her not asking anything of me. Besides, since her obligation was in California, I assumed it had something to do with her past internship and perhaps she didn't want to jinx it by discussing it.

Neither one of us brought up that phone call.

At all.

In the few days left before the show, the band and I rehearsed, invited everyone we could think of, including my former roommates, and generally made the most out of our nerves. In reality, we would be fine. The music was good, our rehearsals were tight and we'd already done a few "unplugged" type gigs, so this was just the same thing, only pre-announced and a little louder, right?

Yeah, I didn't believe it, either.

Six hours to show time and we had to be there in two.

I showered, put on the pants and decided to fuck the shirt—I'd wear a jacket instead. I spent way too much time, even by my standards, on my hair, and then I got my guitar, I got my stuff, and it was time to load out into the van when Jerkster honked outside. By the time we got to CB's, we were all taking out our nerves in different ways and me, well, I had nothing left in me emotionally but to focus on this—it was all I had.

So when Trace showed up and started coming on to me, I let her. It didn't really matter, because I didn't really care. It was odd—I think I felt bad for her. She needed something so much that she couldn't directly ask for it, couldn't reach out for it without hurting whoever she was reaching to.

Besides, no matter what she said or did, I knew nothing would happen—I had no feelings for her other than that strange sadness, and I was way, way too into my Fran to damage what we had.

And without her there, with the nerves and the excitement of waiting to perform, there was only one part of me that was alive—and it was waiting to hit the stage.

A moment of heart-throbbing fear grabbed me when we finally climbed the stage and I faced the audience after plugging in my guitar.

I swallowed, hard, Steph and I shared a look, and I nodded to her—we were okay, we were going to be okay. Jerkster merely stared down at his bass, waiting for our cue.

The sound guy announced us over the PA, the drummer clicked in the time, and just like that, we were off and into it.

It was amazing, the way we worked together, the sound we created, the trip we brought the audience on with us, and they really were with us, every step of the way.

As the set progressed we wore less and less—it's hot under those lights! The encore demanded still more, and we played the same set again.

By that point, I'd lost the jacket and stripped down to my bra, Stephie had stripped down too, and Jerkster wore nothing but his kilt—and I mean nothing. I don't know if anyone picked up his underwear. We all had the same silky sheen of sweat.

The applause was very sweet when we were finally allowed to stop, and there was much back-slapping and congratulating as we disassembled our equipment and tromped off the stage.

When Ronnie the soundman asked as if we wanted another gig, I said, "Sure," then quietly packed my guitar and equipment on the side of the stage. It made me happy to see Nico when he came rushing over.

After he was done congratulating me and I recovered from the nausea his enthusiastic bouncing hug had created, I extracted his promise to watch my stuff when I excused myself to the bar for some water.

Trace came up to me out of nowhere, grabbed my head, and planted a solid smooch on my lips.

"That was great, baby, just great!" she breathed, and kissed me again.

Oh, those lips were baby soft, but I was tired and fuzzy, and the kiss I returned was sincere, but just as tired. And oh, did I *miss* my Fran, wished it was her I was kissing…

"Thanks, Trace, really. I'm just going to get some water. I'll be back by the stage in a minute, okay?" I asked with a tired grin.

Trace studied my face a moment, then smiled. "No problem, Nina, no problem. Sit here a moment, get your water." She had grabbed my jacket and put it over my shoulders. "You don't want to catch a chill." She smiled. She must have had one of those rare moments of empathy, because she kissed my cheek again and walked away.

By the time the bartender finally brought me my water, my head was blank and muzzy, and I had this sense, the one of I don't know what… something, like the uncomfortable anxiety of expectation, or like waiting for the mail. *Probably a holdover from the pre-show nerves*, I dismissively reflected.

I was annoyed when someone came and sat next to me, invaded my personal space, and I shifted in my seat to ignore their presence, regain some sense of privacy.

A beer slid across the bar, and money hit the worn wood surface. *Dee Dee would flip over that*, I thought, as I rubbed a finger over a spot where the varnish had come off.

I caught the shine of silver as I sipped my water, and as my eyes insisted on focusing there, I realized it wasn't coins at all, it was jewelry, it was a coiled jewelry chain, with a shiny and worn miniature sword attached to it. I remembered that sword—it had been a gift I'd given to a friend a long, long time ago. I stared at it dumbfounded while my head roared with the sound of the surf in storm.

I knew that piece, I knew who it belonged to.

When I reached out to touch it, heat warmed my back.

"I don't like your girlfriend," said a voice I couldn't believe I was hearing.

I closed my hand around that shiny little piece of silver, sat up straight, and carefully pushed my seat back.

"She's not my girlfriend," I answered with a steadiness I didn't feel, because *my* girlfriend was three thousand miles away, and my arms ached with the emptiness of missing her, while the pulse in my head pounded and sounded, making me dizzy.

I put both hands against the edge of the bar to balance myself as I stood up.

I must be losing it, I thought, *this cannot in any way, manner or form, be real*. I never read anywhere that hallucination was a part of the post-performance reaction.

And if this was, normal, I mean?

It was going to be a short career.

I made myself turn around, to face who or what was behind me, and my heart hammered in my chest like it had before the show, now with a buzzy thrum that hadn't been there earlier.

Her hair was long and slightly wavy, parted down the center, and she wore a long black coat but I would have recognized her and those diamond-bright eyes anywhere, no matter what she wore.

I folded her to me with an automatic response as immutable, unstoppable, and unquestionable as gravity. As I held my Samantha in my arms—and I couldn't help but think of her as mine—I could feel my heartbeat strengthen: a long, low, solid thump that rang right through me.

I said the first thing that came to mind. "Welcome home, Samantha," I choked out, eyes tearing. "Welcome home."

As I held Samantha in my arms, I could feel my heart beat strengthen, a long low solid thump that rang right through me.

The phone call just scant days before, Candace, everything, everyone, was forgotten in the complete surprise of her presence. "I can't believe you're here," I whispered into her ear and pulled her even closer.

Samantha squeezed my shoulders then buried her hands in my hair as she burrowed her warm cheek into my neck. I even forgot I was supposed to call her Ann.

"I can't believe you're here, either," she answered, her voice heavy and thick as it slid against my skin. Her breath caught a tremor that ran through her. Samantha was crying.

"O ye of little faith," I chided lightly and kissed the top of her head. "Look harder next time."

Samantha chuckled through her tears and finally raised her eyes, those beautiful luminous eyes, to mine. I loosened my hold and brought my hands down the solid length of her arms.

"You're beautiful." Samantha smiled at me and held my hands. "You're right, and you're beautiful. What am I going to do about that?"

"Well…" I drawled, swinging our joined hands lightly. "I still have some work" —I indicated the stage with a nod of my head— "to do."

"Yes, of course." Samantha dropped my hand and backed up a step. "Don't let me stop you. But after…" she trailed off, her eyes staring at me with something I'd never seen in anyone's before.

I think I can only describe it hunger.

"Yes?" I asked, uncertain before that gaze.

She was here, and I was here and this was just all so very strange—it felt good—but weird, too, because it felt so unreal.

Were we really standing here, together, on the same planet, never mind the same continent? Maybe I'd passed out from stage-fright and this was all some strange hallucination, and in reality, Jerkster and Stephie were throwing water on me and trying to wake me or something.

Samantha reached to touch my face, but didn't. She dropped her hand like she'd been burned.

"I don't want to lose you again," she said softly as her hands clenched and unclenched at her sides and I watched as her eyes grew over bright.

I didn't think about anything at all as I stepped back toward her and held out my hand, because if this was a dream, I was going with it.

"Come home with me," I told her simply.

Oh, it was agonizingly slow, the tentative reach of fingers, the wait for the perfect fit of her hand in mine, and when it finally happened I felt like I could hear the tumblers of some giant lock click exactly into place.

"Really?"

Acting on impulse, which seemed to be all I'd been doing for at least the last few hours, I leaned over and quickly kissed her cheek.

"Truly," I answered her and smiled. That smile grew until it threatened to take my ears with it. "Okay then," I said, maybe a little too brightly. "Let's get this show on the road, shall we?" and without waiting for an answer,

I half-dragged Samantha behind me towards the table where everyone sat before the stage.

It might have only been twenty feet away, but it felt like twenty miles and I was conscious with each and every step I took that the warm pressure in my hand was Samantha's fingers in mine, and while part of me was jumping up and down for joy singing "Sammie, my Sammie! Yay!" the rest of me wondered what in the hell I had just gotten myself into.

I mean, sure, yeah, we'd been great friends in high school, and I'd had feelings for her forever, but still—a lot of time had passed since we'd seen each other last. And the feelings that I had for the girl I had known, from the girl I had been, well, here we were now, all this time later, young women, and despite all that history, complete strangers, especially after what I'd overheard not too long ago.

Hey, for all I knew, she could be a homicidal maniac and I'd just invited her home with me. Okay, not that I really believed that, but still, you could never tell, right? And whether I wanted to be conscious of it or not, there was still the strange arrangement that was our lives hanging in the background.

"Hey guys!" I greeted the group at large as we neared.

Everyone looked up with friendly curiosity except for Nico—his eyes widened in shock and he jumped out of his seat.

"Holy shit!" he exclaimed as his elbow jostled Jerkster's beer, spilling it onto his prized kilt. Jerkster pushed back from the table and shook his head, dismayed.

"Holy shit is right," I grinned at Nico as everyone looked up.

"Everyone?" I asked the table at large, "this is Samantha." They all nodded and said their various hellos.

"Samantha? This," and I waved to include the whole group, "is everyone."

"Hi everyone," she greeted the group in turn, until she reached my brother. "Hello, Nicky." She smiled.

"Nico," he corrected tightly.

"That suits you." She smiled again. "Nico."

He didn't smile back.

"Damn, not another of Nina's girls?" Jerkster asked Nico in a loud undertone from his sodden perch.

"No. Definitely *not* that—not if I can help it," Nico muttered back and hearing that, I glanced over at him.

To my surprise, Nico had crossed his arms across his chest, and his eyes had faded to stone grey as he stared at Samantha.

"Good," Jerkster muttered, "because I look like I peed myself." Someone threw him a bar rag and I chuckled a bit, full of high spirits.

"Get a move on there, dude," I teased unhelpfully, "we've still got work to do. Samantha…" I turned to her. "I leave you in…" I looked around at the group "…interesting company." Good hands was certainly not the description, that was for sure.

Stephie, Jerkster and I regrouped by the stage to give it a last look over to ensure we hadn't forgotten anything. Ronnie came over to us as we started to arrange our shit so we could carry it out. He seemed so enthusiastic he was almost bouncing.

"Hey guys!" he greeted. "You know, I just spoke with Graham, Graham Crack from the Microwaves. Their drummer, Paulie-Boy was here tonight!"

We looked at each other in shock—the Microwaves? Dude, they were the one of the coolest ska bands around. And if you don't know what ska is, you're really missing out.

There's a huge debate as to which came first, ska or reggae (and guess which side says which) but in a nutshell: ska is reggae sped up, with lots of horns and totally fun—whether or not the lyrics are political, satirical or allegorical, and sometimes all three. The dance is called skanking, and the people into it are "Rude boys and Rude girls." Those are the basics—now go out and get some gray creepers, a porkpie hat, and a Toasters CD. Oi!

I quickly hid my surprise and so did Steph and Jerkster—we were cool after all.

"Anyhow, you mind if I spin off a copy of your tape tonight and give it to him? They're looking for a band to take on tour—open for them."

Jerkster looked at Steph, Steph looked at me and I looked back at them both like my mind had fallen to the ground. *What? Yes? No? Really? No way!* passed through all of our minds and faces as we searched one another for answers.

"Uh yeah, hey, why not?" I answered Ronnie finally, swallowing through my dried throat.

I kept looking at the band to see what they had to add, but they just kept nodding at me like I had all the answers, so I went on. "Just uh, we don't have an official drummer as you can see," I pointed to the vacant spot our hired gun had abandoned. He was probably home and sleeping already. "That's something, well, we've got to work on that."

Ronnie laughed. "That's an easy fix—Paulie-boy loved you guys! So, I'll give the tape to Graham?"

"Yeah sure," I said, nodding with a casualness I didn't feel.

"Yeah," Stephie finally chimed in "and uh, let us know what he says."

I looked at her with barely-veiled relief.

"Definitely," Ronnie agreed, and started digging into his pockets, pulling out little bits of paper. "Whose number do I have here?"

"Take Nina's," Stephie said.

Jerkster nodded behind her in agreement. "Yeah, take Nina's," he echoed.

"She lives with that thing on," she grinned at me, jostling my shoulder.

I grinned back at her as I wrote the number down for Ronnie.

"Okay great," Ronnie said, clapping his hands together, "I'll talk to you guys soon. This is gonna be so fuckin' cool..." he enthused as he walked away.

I turned to Steph and Jerkster.

"Man oh man, the Microwaves—can you *believe* it?" Jerkster asked, astounded.

"Nah, it's all bullshit," Stephie answered. "This is fuckin' show business—everyone is bullshit."

I kinda sorta agreed, but still... This was New York, home of the "Hey, you never know."

"Nothing is nothing until it's something," I said to Stephie, "But still... sometimes things happen, right?"

"Yeah, sometimes, things happen," Jerkster agreed.

"Uh huh, and it's usually shit!" Stephie added and we all laughed.

We grabbed our equipment and started hauling it out of there, bringing it to the sidewalk so Jerkster could come around with the van we'd rented and we could take it back to our rock.

"Hey, seriously," I asked Stephie as I hefted an amp. "Would you wanna go?" I walked to the sidewalk, Stephie carrying the bass drum behind me.

"What, you mean on tour with the Microwaves?" she asked. She put the drum down carefully between broken glass and gum on the cracked cement, then straightened. "Shit yeah! That's why Ronnie's got *your* number—I wouldn't believe it and Jerkster still believes in the Tooth Fairy!"

"Hey!" I laughed. "I made some good money from the Tooth Fairy!"

"You know..." Stephie thought for a long second. "Me too." She grinned.

Stephie's words made me feel pretty darn good—as if there wasn't enough of that tonight. I was always a little bit aware that I was the newcomer to the Stephie-Jerkster friendship, even though we had started the band together. It meant they trusted me and that was a good thing.

"But..." I said as we carried the drum hardware. "You'd go?"

Jerkster pulled around and hopped out, quickly opening a door and getting his muscle under that damn rack. "Go where?" Jerkster asked as we slid our all-important shit into the cargo space.

"Tour," I answered succinctly. "Open for the Microwaves."

Jerkster stopped what he was doing. "Oh my God—did they call? When? I need a new bass..."

I took pity on his enthusiastic panic—I could feel for myself how easy it was to rush over that "ya ya ya hoorah!" edge. I patted the arm of his army jacket.

"No, dude, they didn't call. But if they did, would you go?"

Jerkster stared at me for a moment and his face seemed to glow as he thought about it.

"Nina...it would be my whole life," he told me, his tone one of wonder and solemnity, something I'd never thought to hear from him. "You just tell me when and where and I'll be there."

I nodded. I understood.

I felt exactly the same way.

Still do.

Stephie came round to stand by us. "Yeah..." she looked at the ground and spit, then looked up again. "Me, too."

I stared at them both, considering, nodding my head. "Me too," I agreed, "me, too. I'll let you know as soon as I know anything."

I don't remember how we got back to the rock we called home, barely remember the after-party our friends threw for us at the Redspot—an after-hours event just for the band and what seemed to be over a hundred of our friends.

I know we laughed a lot, I know that there was lots of noise and what I thought was premature champagne—but it was great fun just the same—I think.

Samantha's presence was like a constant heat at my back even though we weren't always next to each other. In fact, she seemed quite comfortable on her own—although every now and again, we'd catch one another's eye and smile, while Fran's absence was a constant spot of cold hollow in my chest, a strange empty ache in my arms.

I do know at one point, Trace went to sit with Samantha, and that when I saw her a little while later, she looked extremely pissed. Poor Trace—I think maybe more than one person was immune to her charms.

I was tired and drunk off excitement and more than a little champagne, and I was relieved that Jerkster was taking everything to his place for the night—I'd go pick my stuff up in the morning—so all I had to do was carry my guitar (I never let that go) and call a cab. It picked me up in front of the Redspot and Samantha took the ride, sitting in the back seat with me.

I don't think we spoke at all. I leaned on my side and she on hers and all we did was hold hands and stare at each other and I was so tired…

By the time we got to my place, the night had chilled, threatening to become early morning frost, and it woke me up enough to actually feel how tired I was as the car pulled away. Samantha and I stood outside the door that would lead to my apartment, our breath steaming in the air. The last time I'd stood there, it had been with Fran beside me…

I really wasn't sure what would be the right thing to do, but I really was exhausted, and I didn't want to just dismiss Samantha, either, considering how long it had been since we'd last seen each other, how long her trip had been, that she'd actually taken the whole after-gig trip with me—and I knew she'd been planning on staying at Fran's, so where else would she go? And that was quite a trip from here, especially this late at night-slash-early in the morning…

Oh…

Fuck it.

"Coming?" I asked her with a tired smile.

I shifted my gig bag on my shoulder and held out my free hand in invitation.

"Where else would I go?" she asked me seriously, her eyes glittering in the street light as she took my hand.

I smiled back at her as I dug into my pocket for my keys. I found them and opened the door, leading us through the common area kitchen in the back to my room where I snapped one of the lower lights on; honestly, I can't deal with bright ones when I'm that tired—they hurt my eyes.

I spied small glowing embers on my bed. "Hey, scoot!" I chuckled good naturedly as I put my guitar by my bed and reached with my other hand to pet a fuzzy head—one of Mr. Rabbitz cats had gotten into my room. The furball scampered.

"Good-bye, Mr. Chubbles!" I called to the retreating waddle I recognized.

Samantha chuckled where she stood in the doorway, looking about. "Nice space, it suits you," she said with a smile, indicating my art studio set up at the end of the room.

"Thanks," I smiled back in appreciation.

Her eyes were the same blue I'd remembered, the same blue I'd dreamt about, and they held me in place as they came closer and closer.

When I barked my shin off the edge of my spare amp, I realized I'd been the one walking, which shocked me back to a reality where we stood face-to-face, alone together for the first time in years.

A memory from long ago, the beach, the salt taste of the wind, the warmth of her skin, blew through my mind.

She had the very lightest of lines around her eyes, and her face had gotten thinner, perhaps a bit sharper, but it was the same soul that sparked in those eyes and gave me that half-pursed smile I remembered so well.

"Let me have your coat," I asked her through dry lips, my voice sounding low and raspy to my ears.

I shucked mine as she wordlessly removed hers then handed it to me. It was a relief to turn away from that intense connection. I walked to the closet to hang both up, and as I closed the door, I felt her at my back, heat radiating like a rock left out in the sun to warm. Her arms closed around me, and I leaned back a moment to get warm before I turned to face her. I put my arms around her waist and she buried her head in my neck.

"I thought...I thought you didn't want to see me," I confessed to her quietly, my head pressed into her collar bone.

Samantha's hands tightened around me. "Not that, never that," she spoke hoarsely, her lips against my skin. "I died without you." She sighed and let me go, holding only my hands. "I can't let you go," she said finally, quietly. "I never could. I can't go back to living without you." She took a deep breath and looked down at our hands a moment. Her eyes caught mine again and she breathed out slowly. "I won't." She shook her head vehemently.

I tried to remember to breathe myself as the sheer impossibility of everything rode down on me: the high of the gig, the perfect fit-feeling of Samantha, the ripping ache in my gut over Fran.

The right thing to do was to send Samantha back: back to wherever she came from, back to London and Candace and her arrangements and her life, whatever it was she had created for herself, and for me to go back to the life I'd finally started living—my job and my band and yes, my Fran, my Kitt.

I would, too, I absolutely would, but...not now, not this second. Fran had brought me back to life, but just being with Samantha...made me feel complete, somehow, whole in a way I couldn't explain—as if it took both of them to—

Dammit.

That's not the way things worked. I was simply going to have to face it and somehow, move on.

Oh hell, who was I kidding? "Me neither," I admitted softly. "I can't do it either." I took my hands from hers, and sat on the edge of the bed as I put the phone on my amp. I studied Samantha in the half-light.

"You're with Candace," I reminded her as she sat on the other side.

"No, I'm not, not since I spoke to Fran—it's way over," Samantha told me through tight lips. She reached over and wrapped her arms around me again and I snuggled against her.

"I'm with Kitt—Fran," I corrected and I admit I couldn't help smiling a bit thinking about it.

"I know," Samantha answered, her voice muffled in my shoulder. "I know she loves you."

"Sammie," I spoke quietly, and while I enjoyed the sound of her name in my mouth, she had to know the absolute truth of it, even as the pulse in my head sounded loudly. "I love her too."

Samantha's hands tightened on me convulsively. "I know..." she answered, her voice an anguished whisper. "I really do. I just... I just *had* to see you."

"I'm glad," I answered honestly, unthinkingly, and we held each other even tighter, still and silent in the dim light.

I could feel my heart pound in my chest.

"I won't hurt her," I said finally into that heavy quiet.

It was confusing, because I ached with missing Fran, my skin feeling empty somehow, while at the same time the fit of Samantha's body to mine made me feel, well, almost whole, as if I'd been missing the last piece to my puzzle and if Fran was here, too, it would all be complete.

Which didn't make any sense at all.

But I knew that it didn't matter—I'd made a promise, even if I hadn't made it aloud. I'd made it, sealed it in blood.

"I understand that," Samantha answered. "I don't want to—and I won't, either."

She kissed my neck and I shuddered slightly—not because of the sensuality of it, because it wasn't that, not really, but because this *could not* happen.

"Because I love her, too," she whispered.

The way she said it, even as her lips brushed against my skin, made my heart beat even harder, because it felt as if she kissed Fran through me, somehow.

I curved my head away from those baby-soft lips, but pulled her closer to me anyway. My hands pressed against her shoulder blades and I rubbed small circles into her back as her fingertips drew stripes against my spine.

"Nina..." Samantha sighed. "What...what do you want, what are we going—"

"—to do?" I finished for her.

God, nothing mattered. Time, distance, even the person I'd heard on the phone, what we'd done, become, it made no difference we felt the same: to each other, about each other. The sense of...of fit, of *connect*...was unmistakable, as obvious and palpable as it was between me and Fran. But oh...what an impossible situation—because if Candace had been honest all those months ago... would it have turned out differently?

I didn't know, I couldn't say, because what I did know for certain was this: I would never, ever in any universe have wanted to miss the opportunity to love and to know Francesca—and I didn't want to give that up.

It wasn't fucking funny, though I laughed lightly, sadly, and rocked her the slightest bit in my arms before I let her go. "Nothing," I said finally, looking into her diamond eyes, "we're going to do nothing." I shifted on the bed. "Come here," I smiled tiredly and patted the pillow next to me. "Let's get some sleep. I'm too tired to deal with this right now."

And I knew that was true—too tired, I mean, because a voice somewhere the back of my mind told me it would all be okay, and that there was no need to choose because there was no choice to make and all three of us would be fine.

And since that didn't make any sense, either, it was the tired doing the thinking.

Samantha stretched her legs along the mattress and leaned on an elbow, a small smile playing about the corner of her mouth.

I kicked off my boots and lay myself out on the bed over the blankets and Samantha shifted.

"Are you sure this is okay?" she asked, uncertain, "I could—"

"What, sleep on the floor?" I asked with a smile. "I won't let you do that—that's not necessary. Besides..." I stretched my hands out over my head before tucking them under my head. Fuck it. I was too tired to even get undressed or changed as I shifted and closed my eyes. "It's just sleep." I remembered something she'd said to me a long time ago. "We have the rest of our lives to work this out."

I heard Samantha chuckle a bit under her breath, and I knew it was because she remembered that moment, too. I felt her ease her length along the mattress. "Yeah, we do, don't we?" she answered softly.

"We do," I answered as firmly as I could.

I lay there on my back with my eyes closed for a while, but as much as I tried, I couldn't ignore the burning presence next to me, inches away. I finally opened my eyes and turned my head, only to find Samantha staring at me.

Smiling, I turned on my side to face her. I stretched careful fingers to her face, gently drawing the curve of her cheek, and she returned the favor, tracing the line of my face with her thumb.

"Hey," she said softly and smiled at me. "Do you remember that swim meet at Brooklyn College?"

"Of course I do." I grinned back tiredly. "You kissed me."

Samantha laughed lightly, a soft sound almost under her breath. "Actually, I think you kissed me—that was the best kiss I ever had."

"Nah...can't be," I countered.

It had only been one kiss—and one of those chastely romantic ones, to boot. Okay, so I'd never had one like that since, either, but still...

Her fingers stroked along my cheek. "Yeah, it was," she affirmed. "You know, I'd been going to ask you out that night."

"I kinda figured that out later, actually," I admitted. I ran my fingers down her neck and along her shoulder. "You should have, you know." I smiled at her.

"Nah, I couldn't." She smiled back at me, her hands trailing along my arm. "You had a very possessive girlfriend."

I laughed softly myself. "Kerry wasn't really my girlfriend," I answered. "She was my friend and she was just—"

"Experimenting?" Samantha supplied, quirking her eyebrow at me.

"Something like that. It wasn't, it wasn't anything like..." like Fran, or *you*, I'd been about to say, but stopped myself; that was way too dangerous territory to tread into.

Samantha chuckled softly. "Yeah... I get that. Happens to everyone, I think."

"You too, huh?"

How had we gotten closer? There had been at least a foot between us and now I could see every detail of her lashes, the light freckles that sprinkled across her nose. I breathed in her air, and the hand that had been on her shoulder was now on her hip, while hers curved around to my lower back.

She moved it back to my head, gently stroking the long strands that fell over my cheek behind my ear. "I think you might have gotten further with that than I ever did." She sighed and the sound was wistful.

We were face to face now, staring directly into each other's eyes and the dark fullness of hers threatened to pull me in.

"Kerry or Fran?" I asked softly. There was no mistaking the soft press of her thigh against mine. We were slowly but surely falling into each other.

"Both," Samantha answered succinctly, her lips a whisper away from mine.

Oh. I hadn't known that, about her and Fran, I mean. I tucked that into the back of my mind to think about some other day.

"Oh," I whispered back. Wait a minute, did that mean...? "You two never...?" I asked Samantha as I wrapped my arms around her and let her throw her leg over me when I tucked my head under hers.

Because that didn't make sense to me at all: I could feel them, the closeness of them, it was an underlying layer to Fran's skin, as if I couldn't touch one without somehow touching the other.

"Didn't you and Fran ever talk about this?" she countered quietly.

I sighed.

No.

We never had.

Maybe we should have. "No..." I answered, uncertain how to explain.

"You don't, um...talk...much?" she enquired tentatively.

"You're not answering my question, Sammie." I grinned at her sleepily. I knew what she was asking, and it was okay that she assumed (correctly) that Fran and I had an active intimate life, but just how much so, well, at the moment, that really wasn't any of her business.

"We were...we were not...not like you two," she replied matter of factly, her eyes throwing obsidian sparks at me in the half-light of my room. She waited a beat. "You didn't answer my question."

Oh.

Oh yeah.

"We never really talked about you," I admitted quietly. "After I found out about Candace, well, I figured, you know, you knew how to find me. And I have never wanted Fran to think..." I hesitated.

Jesus Christ. An icy chill bolted through my stomach. I disentangled myself from our embrace and sat up, running my hands through my hair.

Shit.

I had a very bad feeling about this.

Samantha sat up with me. "Think what?" she asked with soft concern and laid a hand on my shoulder.

I took a deep breath and ordered my thoughts. "That I was with her because of you," I said breathlessly, shocked at the realization of that deep and previously unspoken fear, shocked even more that I'd said it aloud in front of the one person I probably shouldn't have said anything about that to.

Too late to take it back, though.

That's when the phone rang, the unexpected sound startling me so much that I jumped.

I reached behind me and grabbed it off my amplifier.

"Nina," I answered.

"Hey, Nina!" Ronnie's voice, sounding way too wide awake, cut through the speaker. "You guys serious about touring?"

"Yeah, sure, we're interested." Even half asleep, I knew it wouldn't do us any good to appear over eager. "Who's sponsoring it?" I asked. Thank God my brain still worked on without me. I didn't remember consciously thinking that.

"Uh, not sure actually," Ronnie answered, "let me get back to you on that."

"Cool, no problem."

"Cool. I'll call you back. Later!" and he clicked off.

I stared at the phone a moment, then put it back in its place so I could lay back down. "Sleep, Sammie," I told her as our bodies settled around one another. "I'm exhausted."

"Okay, love, okay." She kissed my forehead and lay back down, while I closed my eyes surrounded by the honey-warm sense of home.

I was comfortably numb, dreaming about the gig, and I barely heard the calling phone break through the deep warmth of sleep. My arms felt like lead as I automatically reached to answer.

"Nina," I answered in a sleep-thick voice.

"Hey baby, how was it?"

"Hey yourself!" I greeted, glad to hear her voice. I got out of bed and quietly stepped out of the room. I closed the door behind me—I didn't want to keep Samantha up and I really wanted to talk to Fran—I was really missing her.

"So…how'd it go?" she asked, her voice warm and filling me across the wires. "You knock 'em dead?"

"I don't know about that, but," I answered excitedly, "I just got called for a new gig—I'll tell you all about when you get here. Oh and hey—

Samantha showed up after the gig? Crazy, right? She's sleeping. I miss you—when are you coming back?" I asked.

"I…uh…I don't know…" she hesitated as she spoke "…but it seems like you're in good hands."

Wait—what?

"Baby—what are you talking about?"

She didn't answer. "Where are you staying?" she asked instead.

"My place," I answered truthfully. Where was she going with this?

"You took her home with you," she commented mildly. "She probably landed today—and you took her home with you."

Dammit.

I knew what she was implying, but that's not what it was. "Baby. It's not—I mean, she showed up right after the gig at CBs—I couldn't just, you know? I mean, I wasn't—"

"Don't worry about it—it's okay."

But it wasn't. Everything about her tone, everything about the way I felt, from the buzzsaw feeling over my skin, to the hurt ice of her voice, told me so.

I had to get her to understand that nothing had happened, nothing was going to happen—no matter what this thing was, it was her and me, wasn't it? "Baby, there's nothing going on, and nothing will. You and I—"

"You need to figure this one out—I can't help you," she interrupted again. She sounded remarkably calm and even, except for that little shake I could hear at the back of her voice.

She wasn't doing this, she couldn't be doing this. I had to let her know something, anything, to make that sound in her speech stop.

Every thought, every feeling I'd had about Samantha evaporated in the face of the pain I could hear in Fran's voice. I wasn't going to lose my her. I knew, or at least, I thought I knew, that the part of me that reacted to Samantha was just a hero-worshipping, infatuation struck kid, but what I felt for Fran was the result of something different, something that had a solid basis. And hey, if that sounds a little too much like the logic I used with myself the first night Fran and I made love, well hey, I was seriously upset.

And besides, I was way into her before anything even got mentioned about anyone else, at all. "God—you *know* I *love* you…" I told her, desperate to get through to her.

"You've never said that before," she told me.

Ah God, she was crying now and I cursed myself miserably—she was right, but she was wrong, too.

I hadn't, not in English, not in that specific way everyone did, because they were just words and words could be so empty, so meaningless, and she meant so much to me. But I had shown how I felt, hadn't I? Don't actions speak louder than words and hadn't I spoken those words in so many different ways?

I mean, there had been a night, just a few weeks ago, when Fran, my beautiful Kitt had come to spend an evening at the bar with me.

As crowded and busy as it had been, I'd finally had a break, and I was spending it the way I'd wanted to: with her.

"Kitt…are you having a good time?" I'd asked in between one kiss and the next, with my lips against her chin, arms about her waist, and my hips between her thighs, as she'd sat at a stool by the bar.

"The best," she'd answered, then kissed me again to prove it.

For me, I had been more than really liking the switch in height sitting on this stool provided us with as we'd held and kissed one another.

"And now?" I'd asked in a low murmur after a brief and hungering taste of her tongue on mine. I had held her even closer, and my thumb rubbed against her ribs, skirting dangerously close to the outer edge of her beautiful, sensitive curves.

"Even better," she told me in a throaty whisper. "You?"

Her hands moved on me in the same way as mine on her and it made my breath catch, honey-warm all over, and pulse full and steady in my skull.

"It'll be better than best when I'm done for the night," I finally answered, then kissed her again, her thighs firm and beautiful under my hands, love and heat and honey a surge through me, through my lips, to hers, felt back in the taste and touch and tangle of her tongue with mine.

"Jen's gonna be looking for you," she warned me when we took a moment to talk in the more usual fashion.

"It's my break—I'm allowed to take a few and this is my first one," I reminded her. "So fuck her royally."

I was very much into and enjoying making out with my Fran, my Kitt, my Frankie, as she had confided she enjoyed being called. Oh my God, but her kiss, the heat of her hands, heartbeat against mine with the feel of her thighs on my hips...the syrupy warmth held me in it, made me forget where we were, and I knew quite well where we both wanted to go—and that was home, together.

"I'd really rather you didn't," she said against the tender skin of my neck, then gently tugged on it with her lips.

Oh...that...felt...*so*...good...

"Never," I agreed, the words barely a groan as she traced elegant patterns across my bared throat with her lips and her tongue. "You know that, don't you?"

The liquid warmth that filled me now had a full and deep pulse in my head, and the need to reassure her, to tell her and show her that there was no one else *but* her powered through me as I lay my hand on her cheek to gaze into her eyes.

"I know that, baby," she told me solemnly, as she closed her hand over mine, then turned her lips into my palm. She kissed it. "I know."

"Good," I told her, relieved, then pulled her in tight to me, just so I could brush my cheek against her jaw, then nuzzle into her neck.

Her arms around me, her within mine, it felt so...complete, somehow, and the honey and the warmth and the pulse were all growing and filling me and spilling over and—

"I think I'm in love with you."

I didn't know I was going to say it—the words were out, dancing in the air, over her skin, from my lips to her in a voice so low I could barely hear myself, didn't know if she'd heard them at all, but I was so overflowing, just so full of this...this *feeling*...

The buzzer on my watch went off, the tingle in my wrist letting me know that my break was over and I'd better get back to it, before Jen came over and said something stupid, annoying or embarrassing, more embarrassing than what I'd already said.

"Back to work for me," I said quickly, and gave her a smile before I slipped back into the crowd that waited for me.

My heart was *pounding*. I didn't know if she heard me or not, I was scared, so goddamn scared that she had, that she hadn't, that it was the wrong thing to say, the wrong thing to feel, just...what was wrong with me?

The incredible honey warmth that had filled me was now a shake in my chest, a grip from outside and on my arms that made me feel like I was grabbed, held, trapped, and the pounding in my heart was the same pounding in my head that screamed at me to *MOVE—NOW!* even while I calmly smiled at customers, took orders and money, and brought back change.

I was cold, cold, cold, even in the heat of the crowded press and my throat closed in my neck.

No one needed my attention at the moment, and my brain insisted I had to see Fran, see if she was okay, see if she had a few days free and maybe if we could go away, somewhere, anywhere, just get out of here...

I was so relieved to see her sitting in the same place, I barely registered whoever was in front of her—the place *was* crowded. I lightly touched her shoulder with fingers I was certain were freezing as I approached. "Kitt, baby, I was thinking—"

I saw who it was.

Any blood I had left quickly moved to my center, and the transformation from cold to pure ice was complete, the shake in my throat now a chill in my entire body.

And all I could think was that I had to get between her and my Kitt, that she was dangerous, and that no matter what happened, I couldn't let her know just how much Kitt meant to me.

Because she was a *total* fuck.

And I knew there wasn't much she wouldn't do to try to hurt and damage what Kitt and I had.

Oh, but this was a monster, a ghost, something I'd thought I'd left behind me, back on Staten Island, with all the other monsters and ghosts and scary and wrong things...

And as I glanced quickly at Kitt, I made a decision.

I didn't know what was going to happen next, didn't know how this was all going to resolve, but somehow, some way, I had to let her know how I felt—because I might not have meant to say what I'd had, but I knew one thing for sure: I had spoken true.

And in case she hadn't heard me before, she'd hear me, now, before I dealt with this mess before me.

There was only one way to do it: because Fran had such an affection for Japanese culture, I'd been educating myself a bit.

And there was a word, a phrase, I'd learned. I'd been saving it, but now was the moment for it.

Kitt would know what it meant, of that I was certain.

Trace…would not.

I caught Kitt's eyes with mine. *"Aishiteru,"* I whispered over her cheek, then I let the ice take over and turned to face the monster before me.

"Hey, Nina-girl," the ghost said in her whiskey and honey voice, with a smile that showed her teeth. "Good to see you."

I knew that smile, knew what it meant.

I was glad for the ice that filled me because there was nothing I could be but cool, cool, cool, with her. Because this I knew with the same cold certainty: show this monster any warmth, any emotion, any connection at all…and she'd *eat* it. And take me, too.

"Hi, Trace."

The exchange was as brief as I could make it. I don't even remember what we said, only that the whole thing left me shaking and shaken, to the point where I'd felt frantic when Fran and I got back to her place later, frantic with the need to touch her, be touched by her, for that touch to *not* be Trace, that the connection between Fran and I be and become something so. Not. That.

And it was that night, that same night, I had asked Fran to—well, something had changed, deeply, irrevocably, between us, then.

"Then be mine, love, because you want to," she had said so softly into my ear, before she kissed along the line of my neck. Her fingers stroked down my arm, became a gentle feather touch against the sensitive pulse point in my wrist.

"Let me love you…" she asked again, like she had the first night, our first time, my first time, as she eased her leg between mine. "Let me love you without you having to do anything other than just let me…"

And oh, I wanted her to, wanted her more than I'd ever wanted anything, to love and be loved by her, with her, the ice from earlier, the alarm, the shake and the chill all gone now in the honey-warm flow that covered and filled me, made me want to reach out and sink into her, feel her flow within me…

She drew a line with her tongue along my throat, kissed the hollow even as she cupped my cheek in her palm, her thumb a light brush in the spot below my lip she had claimed as her own. "Be mine, because it's your decision…" she kissed my chin "…it's your desire…" she kissed my cheek "…because you love me."

The honey-warmth that flowed between us was in her eyes as she gazed into mine, and when she kissed me, I tasted and returned the aching sweet she filled me with.

"Be mine because I love you," she'd said against my lips, and her fingers had shifted from my wrist to my hip, traced along me until she was outlining my shape, then slipping along me, the hardness she'd created, the wet that had been all because of her.

"Be mine…" she'd said as she had warmed me and lifted me and turned me so fucking on and on and on with want and need and desire for her and only her, always her. "Because I'm so very—" she'd kissed me deeply "—much—" she'd so gently parted me, pressing and pausing at my entrance "—yours."

And I was hers, as much as she was mine, I was hers—that, I had thought, was unmistakable, incontrovertible.

All of that was in my head—in my heart—as I spoke to her now. "Please believe me, Kitt baby, Frankie—I wouldn't—I didn't…" I trailed off.

I had shown how I felt, hadn't I? Don't actions speak louder than words and hadn't I spoken those exact words in so many different ways?

What else was there to say? How many more ways could I say it? "I would never do anything to hurt you," I said finally.

"Ah, Nina, sharp as a damn Razor Nina… I know where this is going to go—the two of you?" she asked through tears I could hear fall. "Come on… You have to know what's going to happen." She took a shaky breath that cut right through me. "I'm glad we had our time, I'm glad I've helped you find each other again."

My heart pounded and I could hardly breathe.

No.

This was *not* going to happen. "Baby…baby, please. Just… just come home… please…" I begged. "This will all be fine—I swear."

Too late, I remembered the adage the nuns had beaten into our heads—it wasn't enough to be good, you had to look good, too. I should have never asked Samantha to come back with me. I hadn't been thinking about anything other than the gig and I'd been so surprised… Maybe I could buy

Samantha a plane ticket back to England or to wherever it was she wanted to go.

"I'm stuck here," Fran said, and for the first time, a slight bitterness crept into her voice, "and by the time I get there—Nina, it's *already* too late."

It was the finality in her voice that broke me—I started to cry. "It's not, it won't be, I swear baby, it's not!" I sobbed. I'd fix this, we could fix this—whatever it took and I meant it: anything, everything.

I could still hear her crying softly. "I'll call you when I get home—we'll talk then."

"Can't I pick you up from the airport?" I needed to see her, to convince her, because I knew she'd *know*, just somehow *know*, if she saw me, if she touched me, if I touched her…

"I need time—and you need to know, once and for all," she told me firmly, resolved despite her tears.

"Baby, you're wrong—I know everything I need to know," I insisted, "and I know who I'm with."

"The sad thing, Nina?" Fran said. "Is that I know you mean that, that you'd give up your chance to finally find out what everyone else has known about the two of you forever—you match, Nina, you fit. God, the look on your face when she was on the phone! Your heart was never mine, Nina."

Maybe she was right, but I knew she couldn't be—my Fran, my Kitt, goddammit, Frankie, she was so deeply a part of me that it made words like "love" and "close" sound so trite when I tried to describe even to myself what we had.

Didn't she know?

Had I said it wrong?

I had given her everything, absolutely everything I had that was in me to give—what else was there? "I'd give you my blood, baby, I'd die for you…"

"I know what you've given me," she said quietly. "I'll always treasure that. But…" and I heard her take a breath "…I'm not the one you'll live for."

This was ridiculous. This was insane, this was just plain-out wrong—there had to be a way through it. In person—if we were face to face, I knew if she saw me we would be okay. "Where are you in California? I'll come to you—I'll fly out as soon as I can get a flight," I swore, mentally reviewing airports and airlines in my head I'd call. "Just tell me where you are."

She sighed, but didn't answer. "Where's Ann?" she asked instead.

"She's sleeping—I'm out in the hallway because I wanted to talk with you. Come on, baby. Baby, where are you? You back in LA?" I hazarded.

Fran exhaled slowly and when she spoke, she didn't answer my question and she no longer spoke with tears. Her voice was angry and resigned. "Trust me, Nina, she's *not* sleeping. In two seconds, she'll step out, put her arms around you and these past months will be a beautiful memory. Then? She'll fuck you, then fuck you over."

She hung up on me.

Stunned, wounded beyond belief, I sat on the floor and dropped the phone, buried my face in my hands and wept. When Samantha came out of the room, crouched down and silently put her arms around me, I cried even harder.

"Okay, let it out, baby, it's okay," she crooned softly, "it'll work out." She kissed the top of my head.

"No, it won't," I told her, gasping, choking through the ragged tear that had split me wide open, "and I think it's my fault."

But a part of my mind didn't agree at all. I'd given Fran everything I had in me to give and then some—and it hadn't mattered at all what I did or didn't feel for Samantha, because I not only loved, I honored what Fran and I shared—hadn't I?

"Francesca?" Samantha asked quietly.

"Yeah…" I nodded, wiping my face. "Yeah."

"She's mad…because I'm here?" Samantha asked slowly.

"She's upset because you're *here*," I corrected, indicating my place.

"But…nothing happened," Samantha said, "I mean—there wasn't— we're not…"

Something in me snapped.

The memory of Trace rose in my mind and I remembered—I remembered *everything* she'd made me feel, everything I'd let her put me through—and I had let her do it, because I hadn't known better.

It left a bitter taste in my mouth while a combined burst of anger and shame coiled through me.

Fuck.

It was icy.

I adored my Fran, my Kitt, my Frankie, but I wouldn't do that to myself again, not for anyone, not *ever* again. Trace had made me feel like nothing—I wasn't going to let Fran do that to me. I wasn't ever going to be that weak again. I picked up my phone from the floor, dried my eyes and wiggled out of Samantha's embrace.

I can't really explain what happened, but it was a different person who stood than had sat there crying.

I.

Felt.

Nothing.

"Doesn't matter," I stated flatly to Samantha.

Suddenly, the ridiculousness of it hit me and I smiled, a twist to my face that hurt.

"She dumped me," I said and laughed humorlessly, even though I didn't know why I was laughing when I felt so damned cold. "She told me you'd fuck me over, and she dumped me."

Even in the gloomy darkness of the hallway, I could see Samantha's astonished response to my news.

"You're kidding!" she breathed in stunned amazement.

"About which? The dumping me or the fucking me over?" I asked as I felt that painful grimace cross my face again.

Samantha waved her hands in the air, confused and upset. "Either... both—she broke up with you? On the phone? Just now?" she asked incredulously.

"Yup," I agreed, my voice sounding way too cheerful to my ears, so bright it actually hurt me to hear, and even my ever-observing brain winced at the tone. "On the phone, just now."

This was crazy, this was insane. This was not how I'd ever imagined I'd end my first gig or—and okay, I admit, this had been a dream for a long time, too—see Samantha again. But honestly, I had never imagined that Fran and I would end, either.

I felt the shakes race up my body, you know, that internal shiver that won't let you go when you're just way too fuckin' tired?

I was done, I'd had it.

"Bed," I said to Samantha and indicated my door with a nod. "I'm really way too tired for this."

I walked in and sat down on the side I had before the world had turned upside down, then turned to see Samantha outlined in the doorway.

"Maybe...I should go," Samantha said. "I can—I'll just call a cab."

Dammit. This wasn't Sam's fault. I was being rude and obnoxious and that wasn't fair of me. Still clutching my phone, I walked back over to her. Her hands came up automatically to enfold me as I approached and I put my arms around her.

"I'm sorry," I whispered. "This isn't your fault at all. I'm just really all fucked up right now."

Her arms tightened around me and I rested my head on her shoulder.

"Don't worry about me," Samantha whispered back. "I just want you to be all right. I'll give her a call tomorrow, see if I can talk some sense into her." She rubbed my shoulder.

That's...not a good idea, I thought.

If we couldn't straighten this out ourselves, Fran and I, then adding anyone else into the mix wouldn't help.

And especially not Samantha, not after that last conversation.

I tossed my head. "No. She has no reason not to trust me and if she finds she can't, well..." I gave Samantha a tight little grin "...then we have nothing, anyway."

"Don't you think that's a little harsh?" she asked me, her voice low and concerned.

I dropped my arms from her shoulders and took her hand, leading her back to the promised land of sleep. "No, I don't," I answered, letting my breath out in a contained rush. "It's all about the bottom line."

I stopped by the foot of the bed and faced Samantha again. "Life's too short, Sammie. You taught me that, years ago. She loves me, or she doesn't. It's bone simple."

She searched my face, then finally nodded. "Yeah. I guess you're right." She nodded, looking at the ground. "But still..."

I placed a hand on her shoulder. "I might feel differently in the morning," I allowed with a small smile. "Sleep now."

We gave each other a quick and fierce hug and as I stepped back to "my side" of the bed, my phone went off. I answered it before the first note had completed itself as I sat back on the mattress, hoping it was Fran calling back.

"Hey," I answered.

"Nina!" Ronnie's voice cheered out brightly. "Do you have a passport?"

Thrown for a moment because it wasn't the voice I was expecting, I had to think. "Uh, yeah. Yeah, I do, at least, I think so. Why?"

"You've got six days to get your band, your paperwork, and your gear in order—Rude Records and Skapunkt Records are jointly sponsoring the Microwaves' tour—with special supporting guest, Adam's Rib."

"Are you serious?" I asked him, totally amazed.

Samantha stirred behind me and I felt her sit by my back.

"Dead-on straight," he said. "Bigger than a heart attack but smaller than an atom bomb."

"Holy shit!" I responded, momentarily losing my cool. "Where we going?" I figured we'd be crossing the continent—East Coast to West Coast with a whole lot of "non-coast" in between.

"London, baby. You're starting in London—expect to be gone about eight to ten weeks. Why do you think I asked about your passport?"

Holy Christ on a cracker. I fumbled behind the amp for the notebook and pen I kept there—for songwriting emergencies.

"We're there," I told him. "Who do I need to talk with, what do I need to know?"

I wrote down all the information he gave me, including Graham Crack's and Paulie-boy's numbers. I promised to call him after I spoke with the band, then hung up.

I sat there, staring at the phone.

"Who was that?" Sam asked, gently stroking my hair away from my shoulder.

"That was Ronnie—the sound guy from CBs," I told her while I still stared away at nothing. I grabbed a cigarette from next to the amp and lit it. I wasn't going to sleep after all.

"Oh," Samantha said. She waited a beat. "What did he want?" she asked.

I twisted around to face her, my mind, my hands numb. "To tell me about the Microwaves—we're going on tour."

ABOUT JD GLASS

Artist-musician JD Glass is the author of American Library Association (Stonewall) and Lambda Literary Award (Literature) finalist *Punk Like Me*, *Punk And Zen*, Lambda Literary Award and Ben Franklin Award finalist *Red Light*, GCLS finalist *American Goth*, and the critically acclaimed *X*; selection editor (and contributor) of GCLS Award winning anthology *Outsiders*, listed on the Advocate's Top 100 for *CORE, Vol.1 Iss.1.*, the well-received *First Blood*, GCLS finalist *Nocturnes*, and the fan-awaited *Glass Lions*. Called by some the voice of a generation and the erotic philosopher by others, JD works in often familiar-seeming worlds, with people we know, people like ourselves, people we'd like to meet, and provides powerful stories that allow the reader to rejoice and wonder, stumble and fall, then rejoice victoriously again at the amazing experience of being human.

CONNECT WITH JD GLASS

Website: www.dresenglass.com
Facebook: facebook.com/jdglass2
Tumblr: jdglassbooks.tumblr.com
Twitter: @jdglass

OTHER BOOKS FROM YLVA PUBLISHING

www.ylva-publishing.com

DRAWN TOGETHER
JD Glass

ISBN: 978-3-95533-789-6

Length: 244 pages (80,000 words)

Zoe Glenn Edwards, graphic novelist, is determinedly single and happily married to her work. Dion Richards, author, is trapped in a hostile sham marriage and only happy when she's working. Both creatives are well-known in their respective fields. When they inevitably collaborate on a new project, what happens when two "unavailables" discover they're unmistakably Drawn Together?

MILES APART
A.L. Brooks

ISBN: 978-3-95533-866-4

Length: 240 pages (85,000 words)

Which mistakes are irredeemable? Would you fight to save a five-year relationship after your lover has had a drunken one-night stand? Alex is torn by this question. Then, on a business trip to Canada, she discovers she's drawn to another woman, shattering everything she thought she knew about herself. A lesbian romance that asks the interesting questions, not the easy ones.

THE LIGHT OF THE WORLD
Ellen Simpson

ISBN: 978-3-95533-507-6
Length: 257 pages (107,000 words)

Confronted with a mystery upon her grandmother's death, Eva delves into the rich and complicated history of a woman who hid far more than a long-lost-love from the world. Darkness is lurking behind every corner, and someone is looking for the key to her grandmother's secrets; the light of the world.

STOWE AWAY
Blythe Rippon

ISBN: 978-3-95533-523-6
Length: 279 pages (97,500 words)

Brilliant, awkward Samantha Latham couldn't wait to leave rural Stowe for an illustrious career in medicine. But when an unexpected call from a hospital forces Sam to move back home to care for her ailing mother, a life of boredom and isolation seems imminent—until a charming restaurant owner named Maria inspires Sam to rethink everything she knows about Stowe, success, and above all, love.

Punk and Zen Part 1: The Remix
© 2018 by JD Glass

ISBN: 978-3-95533-918-0

Also available as e-book.

Published by Ylva Publishing, legal entity of Ylva Verlag, e.Kfr.

Ylva Verlag, e.Kfr.
Owner: Astrid Ohletz
Am Kirschgarten 2
65830 Kriftel
Germany

www.ylva-publishing.com

Third edition: 2018

Credits
Cover Design and Print Layout by Streetlight Graphics